BESIEGED BASTION

EARTHQUAKE WAR

BESIEGED BASTION

PC NOTTINGHAM

4 Horsemen
Publications, Inc.

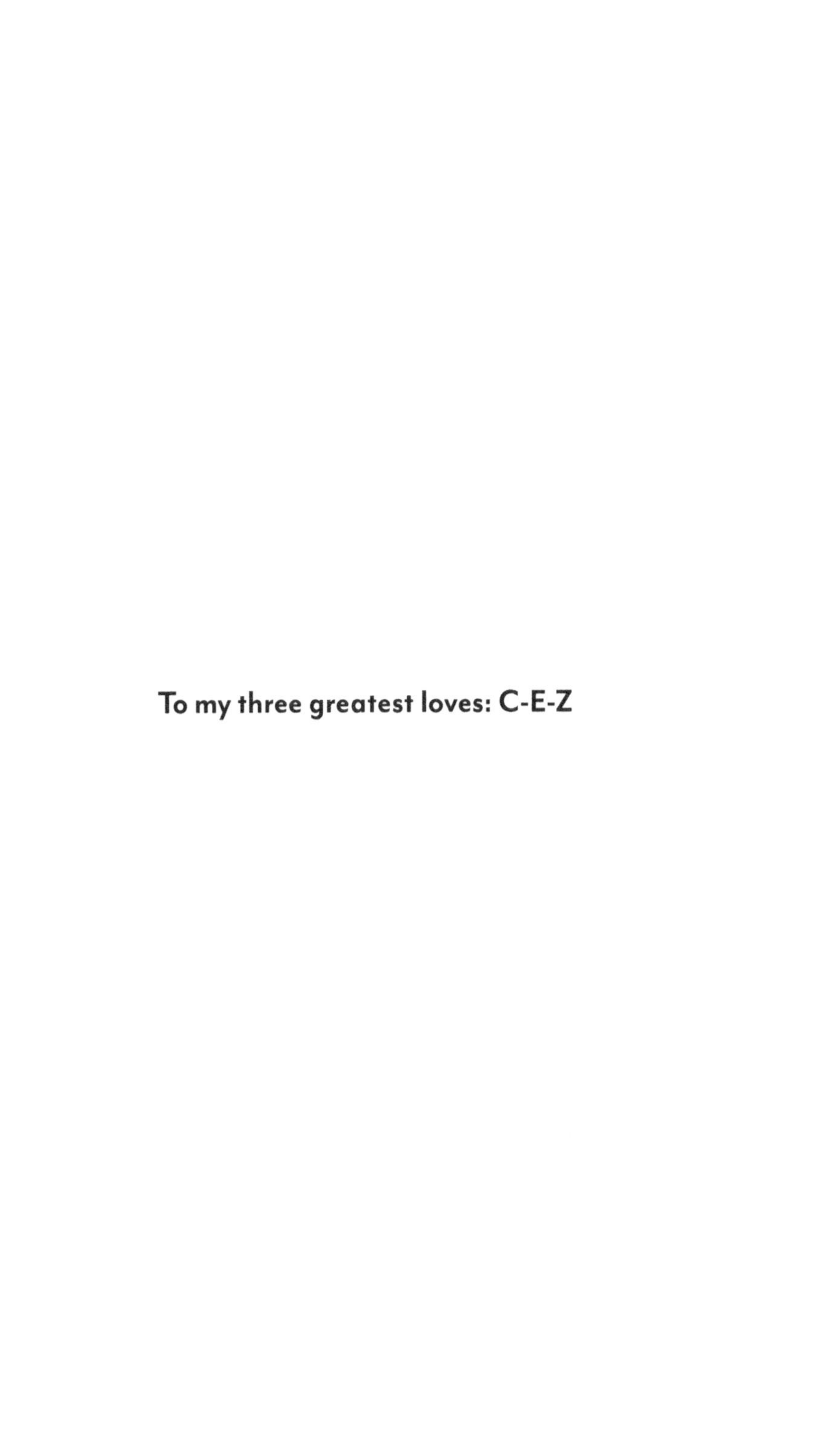

To my three greatest loves: C-E-Z

TABLE OF CONTENTS

ACKNOWLEDGMENTS

THERE ARE SO many people to thank. You, dear reader, for picking up this book in the first place. The amazing team at 4HP for taking a chance on me and guiding me through this process. The phenomenal narrator who brought these characters to life. My poor editor who hates it when characters die.

I was also blessed with some amazing critique partners: N.C. Scrimgeour, Jaci M. Lunera, D. Everett Thomas, Kaela C. Woodruff, Nico Vincenty, Mick Vernant, Cyra King, Jon Gerung, Loren Huxley, Billie Grey, Alex Bree, Morgan Nyx, Maia James, and the whole "Cru" at the Radio Freewrite podcast: WebEater, Krispy, Murph, Spud, and The Lotus. All of you in some way helped get this manuscript better.

They're all amazing creators and worth checking out.

Dear reader, if you're an aspiring writer yourself, look up the Writing Excuses podcast. I never would've gotten published without the advice they give.

x

PROLOGUE

A maximum security prison, hidden in a Collective fortress. On <REDACTED> moon, <REDACTED> star system

ROSANNA MORENO JOINED Earthquake to move the galaxy, and she would make history today.

From the moment of Monsieur Tecton's arrest, Earthquake loyalists concocted a plan to spring their unjustly treated Leader from a prison sentence he didn't deserve; his only crime was loving his people when the traitors Crith and Martinez rolled over on him. Rosanna had her own reasons—Tecton had answers about her brother that nobody else in the galaxy could provide.

Rosanna sauntered through the lunar prison's landing area, cargo hovering in antigrav stasis behind her, the crate big enough to hold three Arkoudae. As she approached the first gate, grizzled rock crunched underneath her boot. The inky azure sky betrayed the moon's thin potassium gas atmosphere. Rosanna's snug spacefaring gear covered her Earthquake haircut and tattoos, disguising her as a meek Human ready to serve her oppressors and shiver in the cold.

She carried a forged shipping manifest: food and hygiene products for the prisoners and guards—no reason to inspect the cargo carefully. The cargo crates floated behind her inconspicuously enough.

The entrance guard stopped her, eyeing her. Staring into his visor revealed an arched eyebrow. "Where's the usual guy?"

Rosanna smiled and met the popsicle's gaze. "He's on vacation. I'm filling in. He told me you and the other guards like *bachar* candies. I brought a double bag for you to split with them." She wiggled her ear, the damned Arkouda equivalent of a wink. "Or not. I brought some peanut butter, too. My grandmother makes it back on Earth." She wondered if he could see her wiggled ear through her space gear, but with an Arkouda's enhanced senses, he probably heard it.

She displayed the jar stowed in her coat, and the Arkouda snatched it up. "My bondmate loves this stuff. Tell the other guy I hope he has a nice vacation. He deserves it."

Rosanna hadn't heard anything like that from an Arkouda's muzzle before. "Thanks. Where's the entrance scanner?"

The guard rose from his seat and tapped the side of the floating cargo crate, either out of an idle habit or a pre-inspection ritual. Rosanna fought the urge to wince. If he tapped too hard, this situation would sour quickly.

"Go forward and take your coat off when you do. You don't have any weapons on you, do you?"

"Not unless you count my teeth and nails." Truth. Her weapons were inside the crate.

The guard snorted. "Hey, I don't believe the stereotypes about Humans being savages."

"Sorry," Rosanna feigned innocent offense with a hand over her chest, "I thought you were the joking type."

"You don't have to disparage your people for my benefit. Go ahead. The scan just takes a second. Got any cybernetic implants?"

"No." Rosanna entered, bypassing the open hangar door with the hovering crate in tow, the guard close behind. Part of her regretted that this guard wouldn't survive what would soon happen.

Scanners and detections sized for Makawe all the way to Arkoudae spanned the middle of the metal-plated room with conveyor belts for items and deep-scanners for sealed crates like hers. Rosanna wondered if the diverse scanners were a sign of lack of trust in the other species since barely anything else in the Collective was diversified.

Not that any of it would matter. Enough research had been done, and they now possessed tech to baffle most Arkouda scanning technology. Smuggling comprised half Earthquake's income.

As Rosanna passed the Human-sized scanner, the guard walked by her side. "Did you bring the good food?"

She wouldn't enjoy watching him die. "Of course not," she replied. "Slop for the prisoners and less sloppy slop for the guards. As it should be. I don't even know why you bother feeding them."

"Eh, there's a chance they're innocent." The guard lazily tapped the first crate. "Families would complain. We'd have fewer riots, though."

The lead crate shifted a half-centimeter, and Rosanna's pulse quickened.

"Hold on a second," the guard muttered. "Did you see it move?"

Rosanna wondered if he could hear the slam of her heart against her ribs as he neared the crate. She had to trust her pheromone-canceling pill would keep her scent in check. "I think the antigrav chip in it is a little glitchy." The guard backed off and turned his head toward her. "It was made in a Human shop, and sometimes we forget to account for the cold."

The guard huffed and adjusted the conveyor's speed. "I bet that is an adjustment—must be rough without fur."

"It is," Rosanna muttered. The back of her neck itched, and she wondered if she should call this all off right now. But she'd come too far to get cold feet now.

The crate scanner chimed, noting the delivery was secure.

Rosanna cleared the Human scanner and decontamination then followed the guard through the winding halls. Metal barrier. Electric barrier. Magnetic barrier—these were negligible dangers to Rosanna but potentially irksome to her cargo.

She envisioned their location on the map she memorized. One more turn and she would be at the spot—just between the kitchens, the commissary, and the block where the Human prisoners were kept.

They rounded the corner, and she slapped the side of the cargo, the *thunk* humming an echo through the cavernous metallic hallway.

The guard glanced at her, opened his muzzle to speak, then the four walls of the crate descended. Rosanna stepped aside, letting the contents spill. Liquid food containers tumbled out.

Rick Crith was pure garbage and needed to die, but Rosanna appreciated his penchant for finding strategy in Earth's history and legends. She'd devised this plan based on prehistoric soldiers hiding inside a false gift. But these weren't true soldiers.

The guard cursed as four shambling bodies lumbered out, stepping over the tumbling food. These were hybrids. Earthquake's casualties—slaughtered Lo-sats—reanimated and spliced with Human DNA and parts, cobbled together with the data from a scientist the bastard Crith killed. They wouldn't last long now that their containment had ended.

With a croaking growl, the hybrids lunged for the Arkouda. Mismatched claws and fingers tore at the guard's armor.

Panicking, the guard tapped an alarm on his armor, then reached for his gun. Rosanna crossed her arms and waited.

The Arkouda started with the handgun. Good. Rosanna could wield it after he died, though it would be a rifle in her arms.

Plasma bullets burst into the hybrids, exiting the other side. Their skin-scale mesh squelched over the holes, lime plasma smoke escaping before the wounds sealed themselves. The hybrids pressed forward.

Rosanna plucked her omni-tablet from her coat and activated the hybrid's neural network.

Alpha: Melt.

Beta: Melt.

Gamma: Melt.

An alarm blared overhead, and their irregular hands glowed crimson.

The stench of singed fur attacked Rosanna's nostrils, accompanied by the sizzling odor of melting Collective armor. The guard's eyes bulged, his last look one of hatred and horror, and the alarm failed to drown out his echoing scream. The invincible armor had become a shrinking oven—saved and damned by Arkouda technology and society, a pain Humans understood on a metaphoric level.

His last seconds must've been torture as the armor melted into his fur and muscle tissue. She wished a more bigoted guard had been on duty today.

With the armor's circuitry fried, it wouldn't be able to transmit a casualty report to the military.

Good.

Rosanna needed a few more minutes, especially if that decay set in.

Stomping boots thudded in the distance. Overhead lights redshifted, and the alarm's blaring quickened. Rosanna input the "follow" command, and the hybrids groaned. They plodded down the hallway.

Time to melt the doors of every dangerous criminal.

They reached the Human cell block, partitioned off by a wrought durasteel gate and a panicking guard.

Before he could stammer an expletive, Rosanna entered the command.

All units: Fire.

The hulking hybrids shifted to face the guard, flanking him as he aimed a pistol. A notification came up that the hybrids' decay rate had increased.

Flames erupted from the hybrids' hands, enveloping the oppressor. Her expression soured as the melting metal odor smacked her nose. The armor probably contained some awful chemicals, so she made a mental note to schedule a toxin and carcinogen examination for herself.

The hybrids turned to the gate and, amid moans, melted the durasteel.

Boots thudded closer.

Inhaling deeply, Rosanna tapped the "split" command. Two hybrids took position behind her and created a flame wall, guarding their flank. The remaining pair advanced, placing their scarlet-burning hands onto the nearest cell door. She'd learned which cell block held Humans but not where she could find their target.

Rosanna's dwindling patience evaporated. These hybrids needed to move faster. It would only take a few more seconds for the automatic sprinklers to activate.

The first two cell doors melted away, revealing useless strangers on either side.

They'd been humiliated by being shaved bald, but their Earthquake tattoos remained, exposed by the paper-thin clothes hanging limp around their emaciated bodies. These were shells of people.

When the first stranger saw Rosanna, his eyes widened. "Y-you're Alejandro Moreno's sister, aren't you?"

The fire extinguishing sprinklers kicked on overhead. One hybrid croak-growled at the sprinkler, and its hand glowed.

Rosanna tapped a new command into her omni-tablet, then glared at the newly freed prisoners. "Guards are coming. If you're strong enough, there's an Arkouda pistol on the floor. Give the hybrids space."

"Thank you!" the first prisoner shouted in a raspy voice. Dried phlegm caked his lower face.

"Cover us," she barked back.

The wall of flame behind her dissipated, and six guards came into view. Another notification pinged that the hybrid's decay rate had increased, though their growing moans suggested as much.

Rosanna squinted through the rising smoke in the cell block. She shook her head and diverted one of the door hybrids to join the attack against the guards. Bullets ripping through the hybrids careened toward Rosanna. She dove out of their path. The *shoom* of the guards' plasma bullets may as well have been from toy guns for how much effect they had on Rosanna's mindless soldiers, but one shot would kill her.

The room's temperature increased, and Rosanna started to sweat. If the flames got too much hotter, she'd fry.

Hissing water from the sprinkler system boiled off the convulsing guards on the floor, muffling their screams. Rosanna coughed against the thickening smoke.

Some part of her wondered how the freed inmates felt fighting alongside her hybrids. As the final guard screamed his last, more thudding signaled a bigger troop approaching. Rosanna input a new command.

Alpha: Heal Beta.

Beta: Heal Gamma.

Gamma: Heal Alpha.

Hopefully that would stave off the decay for a few more minutes.

The three hybrids' hands shifted from white to mauve, then they slapped the sizzling holes where plasma bullets had punctured their skin, which squelched as their malformed skeletons reattached. Grimacing, Rosanna counted another fifteen cell blocks stretching ahead of her. The Collective fleet wasn't that far away, and the healing ring hadn't done much to slow the decay rate.

The next freed prisoner shrieked at the sight of the hybrid and Rosanna shouted at him. "The guard's gatehouse is open. Go smash buttons until you open the whole cell block."

After a shaky nod, the prisoner scrambled forward.

The hybrid shambled toward the subsequent door, and the aghast prisoner, a woman just older than Rosanna, nodded and jogged out, gaping at the abomination that freed her.

Boots thudded closer.

Behind her, the next round of guards arrived, and the hybrids attacked, this time with meager support from the growing inmates.

Two inmates fell. Rosanna looked away—casualties were to be expected.

The guards howled as the mutated monstrosities incinerated them and tripped over the growing pile of charred corpses. Rosanna narrowed her eyes, wondering why none of the guards were running away.

At the risk of increasing the decay rate, she entered a more complicated command to one hybrid:

Beta: End. Create: wall. Material: corpses. Fuse: melt.

The commanded hybrid broke off from fighting and stacked corpses atop each other in a neater pile. It absorbed plasma fire, letting bullet holes bore into its flesh. Each time it stacked two corpses together, Rosanna's omni-tablet signified an increasing decay rate. This hybrid would be a worthless goo pile soon.

It began forming a fence across the hall. Dead Human and Arkoudae joined together, slowly creating a macabre barrier while the other two hybrids soldered more guards.

Gamma: Heal Beta.

The rising corpse partition caused the guards to fire higher, and a few shots seared inside the cell block. The next guards would have combat rifles: bad news.

As the last guard died, Rosanna counted one inmate left holding the line. The inmate inside the gatehouse was smashing buttons uselessly. The hybrid tasked with creating a wall howled its last, collapsing into a heap.

Rosanna input the next command at flaming the sprinkler system, almost more for her own sense of smell than anything else. The steaming burnt cadavers made her want to vomit, especially knowing they might turn into a goopy mass with how much they'd been using their powers.

Rosanna didn't have time for this.

Armored boots thudded again. These were the smarter guards who procured better equipment first. The corpse wall now stood high enough to provide kneeling cover for the one smart prisoner, but it wouldn't last forever, and the hybrids didn't have much longer before the decay became too much.

"Hey!" Rosanna shouted. "If you're strong enough to pull the trigger, aim for their necks. Any other spot will bounce off their armor." The inmate peered back and nodded, balancing the too-big pistol against the desecrated remains of an oppressor.

Rosanna met the next freed inmate to be revealed, and her insides twisted at the sight. Familiarity twinged, and she approached, coughing through the smoke and wincing as the ambient heat scalded her skin.

Jacques Tecton slouched in his cell, arms folded. "Who the hell are you and what took you so long?" Even in wispy-thin prison gear, seated in an empty cell with a shaved head, he presented himself as if he owned it. The gall of this man was as impressive as it was sickening.

"Rosanna Moreno, sir. I'm getting you off this rock." Her eyes narrowed. "In exchange for a promotion and information."

"Hmpf." He rose, grimacing at the hybrid. "I suppose you have an escape plan?"

Rosanna nodded. "We're burning a hole through this place until we get to the transport hangar. We have ships waiting at a safe distance."

Without a command to do otherwise, the hybrid opened the next door, and the other howlers opened literal fire against the oncoming guards.

Tecton observed the unfolding scene. "Are you freeing me or everybody?"

"My plan was to extract you only. If you think the other inmates will be valuable, I can improvise a way to free us all."

"Free them in case I need someone to take a bullet." He observed the hybrid as it melted a new door. "How many freaks do we have now? Did you figure out how to stop the decay?"

"The Bastion is still under construction, but the ground floor factory already produced two dozen. And no. One has decayed already."

"Slow bastards. They should've been done by now and perfected that shit." Behind them, one inmate howled as a plasma bullet ripped through his skull. "That's it?"

"We need a live Lo-sat for the procedure. Kidnapping them is problematic and slow. We need to develop the technology further in order to splice other species. The cloning technique was lost when Crith—"

"Don't say that asshole's name around me."

The hybrid melted another door, and the molten metal fumes stung Rosanna's eyes.

"Understood," Rosanna replied. "The scientist didn't share that technology before his research was destroyed, and he was killed."

Tecton waved dismissively. "Would leaving the freaks here be leaving money behind?"

"Basically."

XXII

"Then they come with us but keep them on the opposite end of the escape ship. They smell like shit. Stop using them until the eggheads perfect the tech."

"Of course, sir." She gripped her omni-tablet tight. She wasn't sure she liked how comfortable she was with the death, but if it would lead to justice for her brother, it was a necessary sacrifice.

ONE

(AMANDA)

Rhea Metropolis, orbiting Saturn

CROWDS GOT LONELY for Amanda Martinez. The last time she'd been around so many Humans, she'd been part of a terrorist organization. Whether she'd seen the light and defected or realized she would get arrested and snitched on her former comrades was still a topic of debate over a year later. Eyes weighed on her, even if she was a person of honor tonight.

Complicating matters was the presence of her bodyguard, one of the few aliens present at the awards ceremony. Even if he wasn't receiving any awards or appearing in any programs, eyes couldn't help but drift to him, which didn't take any heat off Amanda.

The banquet hall's ceiling was transparent, allowing natural light from Saturn to bathe the lunar city through the protection dome. All it would take was a strong hit from an asteroid, and this would all be over.

She knew because she'd been in a meeting that toyed with the idea of attacking this city.

While Amanda had convinced her former employer that this target shouldn't be hit, it didn't exonerate her from being in that meeting in the first place. Anxiety demons whispered that somehow everyone knew. The people around her became like clapping cadavers in her mind, knowing what might've happened.

Her bodyguard nudged her with his elbow. "Look alive. There's going to be a camera on you soon," Bugaro said.

Amanda fidgeted and straightened out her clothes, hoping her bodyguard's size would block any cameras. As an Arkouda, Bugaro stood a meter above most Humans and had enough muscle to rip off an arm. He was near retirement, so it made sense to assign him to a junior member in the government. His kindness provided constant reassurance that Amanda's defection had been the right choice—Earthquake's rhetoric about Arkoudae felt convincing yet was still flawed.

The announcer, a dashing man in traditional Earth clothing, strutted onto the stage, introducing the person receiving an award before Amanda. From her seat, Amanda peeked around Bugaro, trying to see the woman about to receive the award.

"Are you sure it's too late to leave, Bugaro?" Amanda whispered. "We should skip this so you can get ready for Grandparents' Day."

"I don't need to use vacation time today for something next week," Bugaro whispered back, cupping a white paw over his muzzle. "Your people are honoring you."

A woman with a tight haircut at the next table shushed them, and Amanda folded into herself and watched.

Above, the announcer gestured to the front table two spots away from Amanda and Bugaro. "...that invention has allowed Humans to join the Collective Fleet as pilots. Hey," the announcer lifted his gaze to the audience, "who here has a friend or relative who joined the military thanks to Joka Bunear's invention?"

Applause and cheers filled the hall.

Amanda blinked hard, wondering how many of them might have joined Earthquake instead, or if she'd been given a real alternative, she would have made the right choice.

"...and after serving with the Symphora Squad, Joka helped reveal the corruption of Jacques Tecton, getting him out of the government."

The mention of Earthquake's incarcerated leader didn't get as much applause, which made Amanda's skin crawl. Maybe some people here were still loyal or doubtful. Vermin like Tecton were hard to put down.

The announcer finished the introduction, and applause immediately overtook him, Amanda joining in.

Joka Bunear, a woman a few years younger and a few inches shorter than Amanda, took the stage. She wasn't dressed like a scrub, but it was clear to Amanda that this woman had spent most of her life working in the Symphora Squad by the practical outfit. The announcer awkwardly pulled the microphone at the podium down for her.

"Thanks," Joka said. "I know I'm supposed to have something fancy to say, but after that nice introduction, I'm at a loss. Um," she glanced over her shoulder at the announcer and then back to the audience, "it was nice to mention my inventions and the Earthquake surrender, but we know that second bit was mostly Symphora being, well, Symphora." Joka paused, letting out an awkward chuckle. "The most important thing, though, is running my women's shelter out in the Fringe. I asked the awards committee to not give me an award and to use the money they would've spent on a donation to the shelter. There are instructions near the entrances for how to donate and support us there. I'm happy to get this award, but what matters more is that shelter. Um, thank you."

Sputtering applause began.

Even from her table, Amanda saw the look in Joka's eyes. Joka's accent and inflection reflected the kind of person who never had the benefit of a formal education, much like the people she'd spent years with in Earthquake. Lacking resources and options, they didn't have much to offer the galaxy in their eyes. Remembering her own work with the homeless, Amanda found her kindred spirit in Joka. With a deep breath, Amanda decided to participate in a prehistoric Earth thing she'd only read about.

She stood and clapped.

In a room of mostly Humans, this could be seen as a cultural expression or a statement of defiance. But

Amanda just wanted to show honest enthusiasm for a nervous person.

Bugaro cocked an eyebrow at her, but Amanda didn't care.

Joka deserved encouragement.

The other recipients at the next table stood as well, applauding more fervently.

Then the rustling of chairs signaled more people standing behind Amanda, some even whistling as they clapped.

With a grunt, Bugaro stood and joined.

Joka half-smiled, departed the podium, did a half-curtsy, then left the stage.

The announcer strutted back on stage as the applause died. "Wow," he said. "My grandpa told stories about how Collective officials would arrest people for boisterous expressions like that. Look how far we've come! And what a great person to do that for. Joka Bunear, everyone!" The announcer gestured toward Joka, who was already seated and staring into her drink as another wave of clapping shook the air.

"We have two more amazing people to recognize tonight, but I am disappointed to say one of them could not be here. She didn't say why, but we at the committee are sure it's because of her important research. Dr. Alize Oze, the first Human to get a PhD from a Collective university..." The announcer narrated her achievements in archaeology, but the name twisted Amanda's stomach.

Years ago, Amanda worked for the man who tried to kidnap her and kill her: Rick Crith.

Amanda had ordered the operation that led to Alize getting a prosthetic.

That moon had contained some unspeakable horrors. Amanda should've seen Earthquake's red flags on that mission, too, but she stayed in.

As the applause for Dr. Oze died, the announcer turned his attention to Amanda.

He started with running the homeless shelter on New Lodestone and explained how Symphora had jockeyed to get Amanda her spot in the government so she could replace the traitor Jacques Tecton.

Through the applause, Amanda rose to the stage and got behind the podium, where the lights assaulted her eyes. The award itself was a statuette of a nondescript Human holding a ball textured like Earth.

"Thank you," Amanda said, adjusting the microphone. "Thank you. It's really strange to hear a summary of your life to only cover the last five years." An awkward chuckle ran through the room. Amanda knew she should come clean. Apologize here and now for her actions with Earthquake. Everyone loved redemption stories, didn't they?

Amanda placed the statuette on the podium and tried to make eye contact with anyone in the audience, but between the lights and her anxiety, the only eyes she could find belonged to Bugaro. "The reason why I wanted to run a homeless shelter is because I spent my fair share of time in one back when it was just me and my aunt. We didn't have much, but we had each other." She let the cliché hang in the air. "I think that's a good way to speak about Humanity in the Collective. We take care of each other, even though we don't have full rights." Deep inhale. "Yet. We know the person I'm replacing had less than pure motives. My only motive is to make Humans full Citizens in the Collective. This award will be my motivation. Thank you."

Applause came but not the standing ovation, which Amanda didn't mind. She didn't deserve it. She should've said that she joined Earthquake because growing up, everyone had told her that Humans were trash, and nobody was fighting for Humanity except them. She'd followed Rick Crith because he *had* been heroic until his crusade warped him.

The tighter she clutched her Human achievement award, the more she understood herself to be a failure.

TWO

(ALIZE)

In a tattoo parlor on Ka'in'ga, Makawe DMZ

ALIZE ONCE LOST a limb to crushing force, but it hadn't been in a tattoo parlor. Beside her, He'nay squeezed Alize's wrist, wincing through the pain. Alize placed a hand on her friend's black pincer and massaged it gently. "You'll be fine, He'nay. This guy is a pro."

He'nay wiggled an eyestalk at her. "Thanks," she said. "My others didn't hurt so much."

Alize gazed at the Makawe tattoo artist using a chisel to carve a tattoo into He'nay's onyx-tinted shell. While her whole carapace was a tableau of Makawe words and symbols, this new carving stood out among the others because it came from another culture, one Alize and He'nay studied back at their museum, where He'nay worked as Alize's research assistant.

Alize turned her attention to He'nay's mom. "How are you doing, P'oki?"

"Happy that you two visited me here," P'oki trilled, letting the sound echo in her curved beak. "This hurt bad, A'lize. But I worry about your pincer."

Alize smiled, unsure if it would be more polite to correct her and say "arm" or let it go. "He'nay won't crush me, and I'm glad to be supportive."

P'oki tapped her pointed legs against the floor, making a rhythm. "A'lize, you can get tattoo to match us. They can ink a softskin." P'oki swiveled an eyestalk to face the pair of tattoo artists working on mother and daughter. She trilled something in Ma'ak, and Alize caught the words for "also" and "not a threat."

The pair of artists paused, shifted their gaze to Alize, and let out the Makawe equivalent of a scoff.

"I'd rather not get inked," Alize said. She'd been confused for an Earthquake member enough times in her life that getting any ink on her felt repugnant, even if it could be something otherwise beautiful.

P'oki trilled. "I see pain spirits, A'lize. Tattoos make bad memory?"

He'nay released her grip on Alize's wrist. "Sorry," she muttered.

"Not *body* pain spirits, He'nay," P'oki said. "Soul pain spirits. A'lize, is the carve noise a bother? Remind you of time on your moon?"

Alize had named it, but she would never call that sacred place hers. She smiled and shook her head. "It's really beautiful to see a mother-daughter tattoo session. It makes me wonder if my mom would've ever done this with me."

"If your mother was here," He'nay said, "she'd yell at you for not attending that award ceremony." He'nay winced and groaned as the tattoo artists carved a new line in the glyph pattern. "I'm glad you're with us, but you should be getting that award."

Alize shrugged. "With all my years in academia, I can tell you that the only good award is one on your resumé, and now it is. Besides, I need to make sure these artists don't mess up the design. We've studied the Chamayna too long for anything less than perfection."

"Lie," P'oki said. "Dishonesty spirits bubble around you."

Alize stared at her prosthetic leg—a souvenir of getting chased by a cosmic demon, kidnapped by Earthquake, and operated on against her will. Those other awardees were people she had no desire to see. One was Joka Bunear, a fiery but well-intentioned inventor who offered Alize a job in the Symphora Squad. Alize didn't want the awkward situation of seeing someone after refusing a nice job offer from them. The second awardee was Amanda Martinez, the former Earthquake leader who'd been with the team that trailed Alize to the tomb she never should've disturbed. Amanda Martinez was the reason Alize had this prosthetic leg now. Alize had heard about Amanda defecting from Earthquake and joining the Collective government as a reform candidate, but—

"A'lize!" P'oki trilled.

Alize snapped from her reverie. "I'm sorry," she said. "He'nay knows Chamayna glyphs well enough that she could tell if the designs got messed up."

"Lie-truth," P'oki said. "That wasn't the real reason for your other lie. All kinds of dark spirits fluttered around you. Are you fine?"

"I got lost in thought. I'm sorry. The awards ceremony would've dug up bad memories." Like a real archaeologist, Alize wished some things would remain in the past.

"Mom," He'nay moaned, "please don't call her a liar. Can't you see the regret spirits around her?"

The tattoo artist working on He'nay coughed, and Alize felt secondhand awkwardness from him. Maybe she could read "spirits" like her Makawe friend now.

"Can you see the honesty spirits around me when I say that I was flattered to be invited to your homeworld and that this is a nice break from the museum?" Alize asked.

The tattoo artist knocked on P'oki's shell and backed away, and then P'oki scuttled away from the cot. "I do, A'lize." The accusation left her tone, replaced by a motherly one that crossed all language barriers. "I wish you could see mine." P'oki wrapped her pincer around He'nay's and held her tight. "Thank you for giving He'nay job. She loves ancient ones. Nobody give her chance except you."

"Mom," He'nay intoned.

"Be nice to her," Alize teased. "I hope you didn't learn eyerolling from me. I know what it's like to be shut out of academic circles. Without you, I never would've cracked the meaning of those other Chamayna glyphs."

He'nay's tattoo artist tapped her shell and backed away as the other had, and He'nay scuttled forward.

Mother and daughter faced Alize and wrapped her in a hug. When their shells touched, a dim glow radiated from the glyphs, and Alize wondered if she could finally see those spirits Makawe always talked about.

Alize smiled, reading the matching glyphs on their shells, which spelled "Power." The glow faded when they stepped away from each other, which Alize assumed was some trick of the setting sun hitting the lotions the artists had used on their shells.

Even still, this made her eager to return to Hen4 and resume their research. This trip cleared her head, and they would make a breakthrough soon. She just knew it.

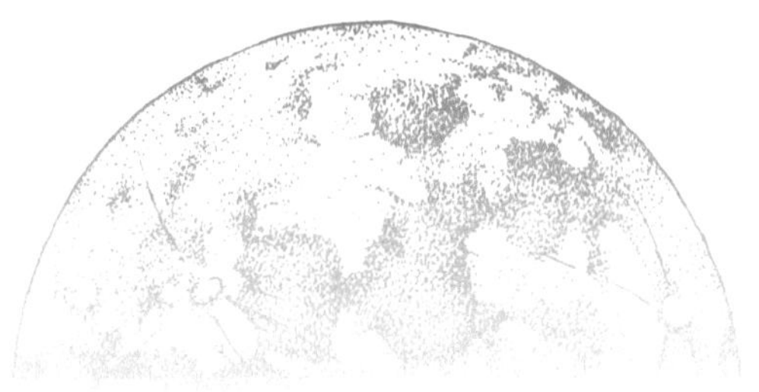

THREE

(MAYNARD)

Bolivar City, New Lodestone, Boudica System

A FIST CRASHED forward, and Maynard deflected it with a left-strike against the attacker's wrist.

"Good hit," Maynard said.

Brother Webster backed off. "The sun was in my eyes."

Maynard gestured toward the dojo walls in a half-shrug. "How?"

"I've just reached that high of a level of mastery." His friend chuckled. "Not even walls can hold my mind."

"That was a good session," Maynard replied, catching his breath. "I almost had you."

Footsteps sounded from behind them, and a third person cleared his throat loudly.

Maynard spun around and forced a smile. "Good of you to join us, Brother Rondo."

Brother Rondo, a large man who made himself small by his posture, nodded back. While the Monks of the Great Mystery were instructed by their doctrine to be joyous, few of the other members in their order could appreciate the joviality of Brothers Maynard and Webster. But there was little anyone could do about it since Maynard was in charge and Webster was the martial arts instructor.

"We have a problem, Senior Brother Maynard," Rondo intoned.

"No need to sound so formal." Maynard grabbed towels for himself and Webster, tossing one to his friend and using the other to dab his forehead. "The titles are nice, but we don't need them. What's the matter?"

Rondo bowed his head, letting his hood cover his face. His scarf, the piece of clothing that broke their uniform, hung down. When Rondo joined their order, he'd told Maynard about a disease that left him cold most of the time and asked to wear a scarf as a concession. Maynard didn't have any issue with it, but Rondo had always seemed to be the picture of health.

"Junior Brother Mweezh."

"Mui-xe," Maynard corrected. "Pause between the syllables."

Rondo stirred, though Maynard couldn't see his expression. "He received a forbidden item."

Maynard cocked an eyebrow and stepped out of the dojo. "Webster, work on not telegraphing your moves. Go over why we teach pacifism alongside self-defense with the little ones today. Rondo, walk with me." The long hallway yawned before them with symbolic artwork lining the walls. Maynard wondered how much they could get if they sold it all off and gave it to the poor, but the other monks would never go for it.

"Tell me what Mui-xe got," Maynard said once they had started walking.

"A letter from a relative," Rondo replied with the same tone one would use for saying that somebody had received a bomb.

Maynard's heart raced. He needed to remain aloof. "And this warranted a complaint directly to me?"

Rondo averted his eyes from Maynard, probably to hide a scowl. "He wouldn't surrender it to me. We're not supposed to have family attachments."

"We're also supposed to practice kindness," Maynard said. "I will speak with him. In the meantime, practice the patience-kindness mantras."

"Senior Brother Maynard—"

"I look forward to hearing about the results of your prayers at dinner. I'm sure it will be an enlightening time in your quarters." Maynard motioned down the hallway where the monks' cells lay.

Rondo didn't hide his scowl this time. "Thank you for the direction, Senior Brother."

Maynard replied with a smile, and they parted.

Some junior monks skipped down the hall toward the dojo, then slowed to a mindful saunter once they spied him. Maynard laughed and called out to them, "Why stop? You'll lose the race!"

The junior monks, orphans left at the monastery between the ages of five and ten, glanced at each other before giggling and jogging forward. "Hurry up,"

Maynard added. "Brother Webster does not tolerate lateness."

There was one junior monk who was not with them, the one who shared their rank but not their age.

Mui-xe.

All of Mui-xe's lessons with Webster were individualized, which Maynard didn't love, but saw no alternative. Mui-xe's biology and anatomy made it dangerous for him to train with the other youngsters. Maynard strode toward the courtyard, wondering how to warn Mui-xe about keeping letters to himself. Mui-xe wasn't exactly like the other orphaned boys since he did have surviving family members who loved him very much. Maynard opened the courtyard door, and there sat Mui-xe, sitting on a bench with his tail draped across his lap, holding paper that looked like it had barely survived space travel.

When Maynard approached, Mui-xe sniffed the air before inclining his head. A soft smile stretched across his elongated face, revealing a protruding fang. "Hi, Uncle Maynard," Mui-xe croaked. His skin was mottled with flesh and scales, and his facial features were the midpoint of Human and Lo-sat, but his resemblance to Maynard's late brother made him pause every time.

Maynard didn't run over but did take longer strides to close the distance. "Remember what we talked about? Just 'Brother Maynard' unless we're alone."

A translucent film of skin wiped across Mui-xe's red marbled eyes, his version of a blink. "We are. I smelled first."

Maynard sighed and chuckled. "Sorry, then. What happened with Rondo?"

"He found my letter from Granny and tried to take it from me. I know it was sloppy of me to let anyone see it." His eyes fell to his hands. "I screwed up."

"Maybe, but that's a lesson for later. You didn't, well, attack him, did you?"

Mui-xe's hairless eyeridge raised. "Did he say I did? I got really mad, but once I felt my hands get hot, I stopped. I used those breathing exercises you taught me. They helped."

"That's good," Maynard replied, taking a seat on the bench beside Mui-xe. While he was a preteen by Human standards, Mui-xe was taller than Maynard and most of the monks in the order. "How is your Granny?"

"She said she still wants to meet me and thinks you hate her because you haven't let her come out yet."

Maynard whistled. "I hate her? That bad, huh?"

"Well, she worded it a bit … stronger than that, but yeah."

A thick cloud passed over the Boudica star in the sky, darkening the courtyard. "This is the only free Human settlement in the galaxy. I don't know how to get anyone offworld to come visit you without drawing the wrong kind of attention."

"Your friend comes all the time," Mui-xe said. "I wouldn't get Granny's letters otherwise."

"True, but he's a professional smuggler. We'll figure out some way for you to see her, I promise. It will be easier once more Human systems gain independence." He really should've said "if" instead of "once," but now wasn't the time for that. "Then there won't be so much heat here. I can't risk the Collective finding you." Maynard didn't need to add the "or else" since

Mui-xe had already experienced it. The monastery would keep him safe.

Mui-xe sighed. "I don't know if I want to live my whole life in these walls."

"Did Granny say anything else?"

"Only prayers and myths. She said if I'm spending so much time learning about your religion then I should learn hers, too."

Maynard smiled, remembering stories about his brother meeting Mui-xe's Granny for the first time.

"I'll find some safe way to let you see her," Maynard said. "I promise. In the meantime, let's figure out a better hiding place for her letters."

FOUR

(RICK)

**Behind a seedy bar on an unnamed
asteroid only scum would visit**

OBNOXIOUS MUSIC PLAYED at a too-loud
volume and stale beer stench tinged the air. A hiveball game played on a crappy TV, not that it was big
enough to be visible or loud enough to hear over the
music. The lights weren't bright enough for anyone to
see their own poor decisions, except for one patron.

Rick Crith sipped his water. Using his image
inducer, it resembled beer to any onlookers, just like
how the sensory hologram covered his missing arm.
That device was a pain to charge, so he only used it for
emergencies like this one. He hoped an extra arm and
letting his hair and stubble grow out would be enough
of a disguise that nobody would recognize his face.

A few meters away, rough guys played angleball with each other, balancing drinks on the table in a way that would make a respectable bartender kick them out. Rick observed the table nearest him. From his periphery, he examined the men there, all wearing hats, which unfortunately complicated things.

But as one spoke, the movements of his neck revealed a tattoo of Earth with a diagonal line through it.

The symbol of Earthquake.

It hadn't received laser treatment like Rick's had.

Under this man's hat, hair poked through on one side, which wasn't a guarantee, but it was an indication that he sported the haircut mandated by Jacques Tecton.

He had one mark.

One of the rough guys at the angleball table also had an Earth tattoo on his arm, but it was amid so many others that Rick wondered if this guy was trying to hide it in plain sight instead of actually removing it.

The sitting man with the neck tattoo stumbled up from his chair, heading toward the bathroom. Rick gulped his water that didn't taste clean enough and trailed the mark.

He slipped between the tables, keeping distance without looking like he was keeping distance. He had no way of knowing if anyone was inside the bathroom, so he needed to be extra cautious. This bar only served Humans, or rather, the only Lo-sats and Arkoudae nearby were the owners of the mining stations in this asteroid clump, and they had their own bars away from the slums. Human-sized bathrooms meant he wouldn't have to deal with a much larger or stronger alien trying to break up his planned interrogation.

The mark opened the bathroom door, using his fist instead of his palm, and the angle of the bathroom that became visible for a second revealed it had several stalls and was not a single occupancy. At this time of night with this crowd, there would almost certainly be someone else inside.

Damn.

The mark took a urinal, and Rick stepped beside him, using the open one on the same side as the mark's tattoo. He'd seen a million grunts like this guy.

Rick grunted. "Moving the galaxy?" Using the motto soured his lips, but he didn't have any other choice. He had to start somewhere.

"Hm?" The mark turned to Rick and scowled for violating the basic rule of bathroom etiquette. Look forward or down and remain silent.

"I spied your tattoo," Rick said. "I got some buddies in the organization."

The mark zipped and faced him. "Rick?"

Rick's blood froze. They made eye contact.

This man used to work for him.

He'd been on the mad scientist's asteroid. He'd seen the abominations unleashed. He'd come within an inch of a vicious death by Rick's command.

His name was Dion, one of the only gunners to survive that excursion. "What the Earth are you doing here? Have you come to kill me?" Dion tensed up, clenching a fist.

"Give me some information, and I'll leave you alone."

"Like hell I will, you son of a Galsan worm. I drink every night to forget what you made me do. I see your face in the bottom of every shot glass. I hear your voice in my nightmares. You ruined my life." His gaze cast down to the hologram around Rick's missing arm. "You got a prosthetic?"

"Not quite." Rick reached for Dion's throat.

Even inebriated, Dion moved fast—it was why he was a good fighter. He ducked his shoulder and charged into Rick, pushing him toward the wall. Rick willed the hologram of his arm to swing for a punch, and as Dion dodged it, Rick uppercut with his true arm.

Dion staggered back, and Rick grabbed him by the shirt and threw him at the open toilet stall, knocking off his hat and revealing his lopsided Earthquake hairstyle.

He didn't have much time before someone else would enter. He was beyond screwed if he didn't move fast. But he'd come so far.

"Who sprung Tecton from prison?"

"Keep his name out of your mouth," Dion slurred.

Rick grabbed a chunk of Dion's hair and jerked his head over the stained toilet bowl. "Wrong answer."

Dion kicked at Rick's ankle, forcing him to release his grip. When Rick stumbled backward, Dion rolled over and used the toilet to help himself stand. He readied a punch, which Rick ducked under, closing the distance and kneeing his groin. No time to fight clean.

"Who sprung Tecton from prison?" Rick demanded.

Wincing, Dion grit his teeth and shook his head. "Eat shit, Rick."

"Good idea." Rick punched his face, spun him around, and thrust his head into the water.

The bathroom door creaked open. Rick grabbed Dion's hair and thrust him into the edge of the toilet bowl.

"Help!" Rick called as he dipped into Dion's pocket, grabbing his omni-tablet. "Help! This guy passed out."

Another patron, one of the angleball players, peeked around the corner. "What happened?"

"Get the bartender and call for help," Rick said. "I'm going to do CPR."

The bathroom door closed again, and Rick stowed the omni-tablet in his coat. As long as Earthquake's internal messenger was still on his omni-tablet, Rick would get that information.

Rick pulled Dion out of the toilet and rolled him onto his side.

Nobody would believe a concussed barfly about an officially dead man surfacing with an extra arm. Rick popped off Dion's credit chit, hoping to make this look like a botched robbery. This wasn't the type of place to have security cameras. He slipped out of the bathroom and shouted, "The guy is breathing but needs medical attention. I'm going to call his girlfriend."

Rick darted out as patrons flooded the bathroom. Once outside, he used the image inducer's full setting to make him resemble another person and slinked toward the asteroid's spaceport.

Maybe old age was making him sloppy. He knew one thing, though. Earthquake was still plotting nasty shit, and innocent people were in danger.

Intercepted message from Hen4 museum:

```
Sender: He'nay KaWhetuMa
Recipient: P'oki KaWhetuMa
Subject: Thanks for the seaweed wraps!
```

Hi Mom,

Yes, they came in time for the holiday. Alize wanted to say she appreciated you getting a vegan version for her. And just like you are pestering me about honoring the spirits, I hope you know Alize is also pestering me about reaching out more often. You can expect my next message in one week, and I promise I won't procrastinate by saying nothing interesting happened. Boring or exciting, you'll hear from me. Even if it's just a hi and I love you.

But I bet I'll have something cool to share next week. Alize and I have some wild new theories about what else the Chamayna chitin can do. She doesn't want me to say too much since she's a bit paranoid about people monitoring us, but let me tell you our tattoo was just the beginning. If my findings get published, I want to celebrate with another one on top of it and below. We have space for more carvings.

Anyway, I know your friends at the scrap yard are going to ask and tell them I'm not dating anyone, just like I wasn't a month ago. I hate to send such a short note, but my break is ending, and there's an alarm going off. Don't panic. It's probably an octopede that got too close to a security barrier around a work of art upstairs, but I need to check it out before Alize notices and scolds me. She's like you that way.

Talk soon. I love you, Mom.
-He'nay

FIVE

(AMANDA)

**In a government office on the
Collective Fringe, Katafugio asteroid**

IN A COLD galaxy, survival came through warmth—both literal and emotional. Getting the former required the flick of a switch or a heat cell, but the latter? Amanda Martinez's inner fire burned hot enough for that, and today she could set the vacuum of space ablaze.

One month after her award for achievement, Amanda strutted through the government offices. Too big hallways, too cold temperature, and too oppressive gravity for a measly Human like her. Amanda's extra layers under her business suit didn't stave off the chill, and her weak gravity harness glitched at least twice a day, but she endured.

Inspired by Joka Bunear, she'd been trading votes and drafting legislation so she could finally introduce hers.

She smiled, wondering how her old self would have laughed at her current employment. Undercover gang manager to homeless shelter operator, to gang defector, to government representative for Humans. Spilling details about her former employer earned both amnesty and the trust required to deserve this job, although they both only stretched so far.

The complex on this asteroid was constructed without Humans in mind. Having an Arkouda bodyguard, a member of the very species oppressing Humans, was its own slice of deliciousness and the first step in dismantling that oppression and indifference. The fuzzy-white soldier with a muzzle strong enough to snap a femur towered over her yet addressed her as Madam Chairperson. Last year, she cringed at the title, and today, she was almost ready to bask in the respect.

Bugaro reached over her head to grab the door handle to the voting chambers. The honeycomb-shaped auditorium sat empty, save for some interns of various species milling about.

Amanda glanced up to her guard, addressing him in his language. "Bugaro, did you hear from your granddaughter?"

"She didn't get the lead in the recital." Bugaro's gruff voice softened. "But you should've seen her land the pirouette."

Amanda resisted the urge to balk at the appropriation of Human culture for Arkoudae kids' dances. "I'm proud of her. I'm sure she'll outshine the whole pod."

"Can I ask you something, Madam Chairperson?" Bugaro asked, edge returning to his voice. "Do you really think you'll get the votes you need?"

"I have to believe it will. Humans deserve full Citizen status after what we've endured."

Bugaro's graying fur and permanent scowl demonstrated his years serving government agents. "You want my opinion?"

"I would. You've been around longer than me," Amanda said. "You also watched," she stopped herself from uttering the forbidden name, "my predecessor suggest laws and get shot down more than once."

"That Tecton guy set your species back. Funding illegal research with pilfered government money? Total trash." Bugaro peered down his snout at her. "You want my civilian's opinion? Or as your bodyguard?"

"They don't have to be different. Just answer honestly."

"Sure." Bugaro reared back. "It'll be rejected. You may have proved yourself, Madam Chairperson, but Humans as a species haven't. When most Citizens—"

Amanda glared at him, and the hallway felt a little bigger and colder in that moment.

"Hey, you said you wanted honest. When Arkoudae and Lo-sats think of Humans, our first thoughts are of the Earthquake terrorists. Sure, there's that one archaeologist and the inventor who worked for Symphora, and you, but that's not enough." He spoke without insinuating Amanda kept ties with

Earthquake: a reprieve from what some of her colleagues gossiped about behind her back.

Amanda somberly nodded, then glanced around the auditorium, wondering which expletive to shout for the best cavernous echo. "Thanks, Bugaro. Please just call me Amanda."

"You're welcome." A grin creased the old codger's muzzle. "And never."

"So my information to get my predecessor incarcerated wasn't enough?"

"Earthquake is still running around." Bugaro's words stung more than they should have. Earthquake's operations were supposed to be the inside secret that Humans abashedly whispered about. "Not to mention your former employers Jacques Tecton *and* Rick Crith escaped prison."

Hearing the name of the worst man she knew made Amanda want to barf, hearing the name of the man she once admired made her want to cry, and the reminder she once worked for them made her want to change her name. "That's not what the official reports say." She flashed a weak smile.

"Yes, ma'am. So what's your bright idea for how you can, you know, *not* get rejected and liberate Humans everywhere?"

"You're acting like it's something simple. Defeat Earthquake. Forever. That's the only way they'll know Humans can be trusted." Amanda exhaled, fighting the propaganda and brainwashing she'd endured under the enemy. "Earthquake isn't just a group. It's an idea: Humans are repressed and ignored by the Collective government and therefore the government is the enemy for Humans. Earthquake will be defeated when their idea is no longer true."

"I'm on your side." Bugaro's tone softened in the same way he'd whisper to his daughter on vid calls. "We don't all think Humans are lesser. I wish none of us did."

She grabbed the tip of his paw and squeezed. "Thank you." Friendships between Humans and other species were possible; she knew from experience. "But you see my predicament, right?"

"Do you know who else *is* on your side?"

Amanda breathed into her hands and rubbed them together. "Just the biggest badass in these halls, present company excluded."

"Don't joke." A cleaning 'bot buzzed around Bugaro's feet, sputtering around while it sucked up dust. The official hearing would start soon.

"Symphora." Amanda let the living legend's name hang on her lips. The warrior who accepted Earthquake's surrender when Amanda defected. Symphora, whose name struck fear into every pimp, slaver, and drug dealer's heart. She'd accepted a job in the Fringe territory government and ensured Amanda's acceptance into the government, despite everyone's reservations. Symphora wanted Human equality, despite being the poster child for the Arkouda race or at least their leadership and tenacity.

That was what Amanda needed to lean into. Symphora wanted Humans to be elevated to Citizen status, so why not go more public? The other representatives feared her while begging for autographs.

Amanda turned on her heel and approached the door, and an Arkouda intern passed them. "If we can get her to put some of her famous pressure on a few other voters who are on the fence, then we will see some real results, I bet."

"Does she want to use her influence to bully others?"

"It's Symphora. Haven't you heard any of the legends about her?"

Bugaro waved a paw. "Those are all jokes. There's no way she bit off a slaver's manhood and sold it to a miniatures collector."

"The one where she force-fed a pedophile the remains of a drug dealer definitely are."

Bugaro sighed. "Well, Madam Chairperson, it's my turn to point out that you avoided the question. Do you think she wants to keep intimidating others at her age?"

"I think we should be more concerned for *your* safety if you suggest she's lost her edge." She couldn't pursue that train of thought, though. If Symphora retired, Amanda's biggest supporter would be gone, and all the people deferring out of respect and fear could turn.

Bugaro pointed to their seats. "I wouldn't dream of saying she's softened. My former roommate did, and he's still in the hospital."

"What'd she do?" Amanda asked as they turned the corner toward Symphora's offices.

"Nothing I'd repeat to my boss—"

A *boom* shook the floor and walls, hard enough to force Amanda onto her hands and knees. Hanging lights from the ceiling swayed, and somebody screamed behind them. Amanda scrambled to her feet as a series of shattering crashes followed, pictures and light fixtures smashing into each other or onto the floor.

When she looked up, she stared into a group of armed Humans who hadn't been there before, fanning out in an attack formation.

She recognized their lopsided haircut, along with matching tattoos of Earth with a diagonal line through it. They sported blue and green painted armor, stolen and then modified from the Collective military.

Earthquake.

Amanda's heart stopped. They had finally come for her, brandishing homemade rifles and armor-piercing harpoon cannons. They'd teleported in. She had seen this happen once, years ago, but not on this scale.

Edging in front of Amanda, Bugaro shouted, "Don't just stand there! Get behind me for Goddess' sake!" He grabbed Amanda with one paw, pulling her beside him. With his other, he tapped a button on his armor, and a static bubble bloomed around them. "How in the Nightmare did they get here?"

The Earthquake ambushers unloaded plasma fire in all directions, gunning down clerks while security scrambled to protect the various representatives and higher-ups.

One Earthquaker, a head taller than the others, pointed at Amanda and Bugaro with his rifle. "I found Amanda Martinez! Kill the traitor!"

Other thugs turned at the call and trained their weapons, unloading fire against Bugaro's shield, hitting so hard and loud Amanda's teeth shook.

The gun-toting brutes fanned out, redirecting their fire. Two teams of three holding Equalizer harpoon cannons adjusted, aiming for where the shield would soon crumple.

Bugaro tapped another plate on his armor, and a compartment opened on the chestplate. He reached in, pulling out a white cube, which unfolded into an assault rifle. "Find somewhere to hide. I'll take down as many as I can."

Amanda steadied herself as he opened fire on her people. Former people but still her blood. "No." Amanda pulled on his elbow. "Run forward."

"Ma'am?"

There was some solace in knowing male pig-headedness crossed species, which evaporated as a gunshot sizzled over Amanda's shoulder. "You heard me with those tiny ears. Run!"

The old soldier clicked his tongue. "Human ingenuity isn't just a myth." A plasma bolt seared toward them, and the shield's blue static quivered. "Keep up, Amanda."

"Actually, I think I do prefer Ms. Martinez."

He strode forward, more of a jog than a full run. Amanda sprinted to keep pace, and the shield buzzed as each plasma shot melted into the static. Confused Humans rolled out of the way as Amanda and Bugaro barreled forward. With Symphora's office in reach, Bugaro grabbed the door with his free paw and shoved Amanda inside.

Static shocks snapped around Amanda's exposed neck as she left the shield bubble, shimmering blue. "What the Earth are you doing? Get in here!"

She stared back at her savior through lime-green plasma bolts that rippled against the failing shield and ignited the room an electric neon.

"You're safer with Symphora." Through a pained smile, Bugaro said, "Ask her to send an autograph to my grandcubs." Gripping his rifle anew, he slammed the door.

The telltale *shoom-shoom* of plasma fire was Amanda's signal to wish him well and find the legend.

A scent of singed fur caught Amanda's nostril.

Catching her breath, a gush of air pushed her forward, accompanied by a *thunk* against the metallic door behind her. Amanda spun and her jaw dropped.

A harpoon tip had punctured the door. White fur and blood dripped off the weapon's point, and the bits of organs that had squeezed through with it squelched to the floor.

"Bugaro," she whispered. Then her training took over. She had seconds to live now, and playing smart would give her hours to mourn later.

She needed Symphora.

Wincing, Amanda passed the empty receptionist desk, the corpse of Symphora's assistant occupying the chair: Dee-vrit, a Lo-sat with a stutter, somebody Symphora saved years ago. Her charred scales turned Amanda's stomach, but she couldn't dwell on it. Symphora had to be there, right?

She'd be fighting.

Amanda smacked the Human-accessible button to unlock the next door, which opened to grunts and growls. A Human was in there, grappling an Arkouda, knocking into the decorations inside her office: skulls of drug dealers and finger-painted drawings from kids strewn about. Symphora's desk lay cracked in half amid a minefield of splinters and screws. Lime-colored plasma smoke obscured Amanda's vision, but a knife heading toward Symphora's stomach was plain as day.

"No!" Amanda shouted. "Stop!"

The squelch of a blade digging into flesh followed, and the living legend roared. The attacker backed off, eyes widening at Amanda. As she fell, Symphora swiped at the assassin's face, ripping off a chunk of her ear and forcing her to drop a pistol.

Purple Arkouda blood splattered on the floor, staining clumps of white hair. The invincible super-hero, savior of the downtrodden, Symphora Ianna, collapsed to the floor. Clutching a paw to her abdomen. Barely breathing.

Before Amanda could rush to her assistance, the Earthquake attacker stood over her, triumphant, holding a blade stained indigo. This stranger's bloodied face tugged at the edge of Amanda's memory. Earthquake haircut and tattoos, scraps of stolen Collective armor. But that wasn't what gave the familiarity. Maybe Amanda had met a relative of hers years ago, but she didn't have time to worry about that.

Amanda's eyes darted to the dropped pistol on the floor, and she snatched it, shakily pointing it at the attacker. This interloper who had come to kill Symphora stared into Amanda's eyes, breathing heavily.

Her dark gaze solidified the connection. Amanda must know who this was. As the stranger's eyes widened, she mouthed "shit," then hurriedly stowed her knife. In a flash, the attacker replaced it with a smooth black rock, which also tugged at Amanda's memory.

The rock glowed.

A *thwip* sound followed, and the stranger disappeared, just like that first group had appeared out of thin air without warning. Amanda's blood chilled—this attacker could potentially resurface anywhere.

On the floor, Symphora coughed. Speaking Arkouda, she wheezed, "What the *skata* happened, Martinez?"

Amanda pulled out her omni-tablet and slapped the emergency button as if the station remained unaware of the ongoing emergency. She threw it aside and jumped to the dying Arkouda. "You didn't have time to get on your armor?"

Symphora winced. "Don't sass me. How bad is it?"

Amanda found the indigo blood geyser on Symphora's abdomen and desperately attempted to cobble a life-saving suture until she could find a medbot. "I'm ripping off your clothes," Amanda barked. "Stay still."

Symphora coughed. "She beat me; definitely nicked some—ow, *skata,* watch it—organs. Woulda killed me if you hadn't showed up." She wheezed. "How'd she blink out of here like that?"

"It's a teleportation technique. I've seen it once before. And sit still."

"I might be about to die," Symphora wheezed, "but I'll kick your ass if you don't fix me up. Where have you seen it?"

Amanda didn't have time to think like a politician and pretty up her answer. "I'm not proud of doing it, but in my time with Earthquake, I aided in kidnapping an archaeologist who'd discovered a lost civilization with means of teleportation—the Chamayna." Amanda increased the pressure on her wound to get the bleeding to stop. "That thing that looked like a rock was a piece of chitin from their exoskeleton. The archaeologist gave us the slip with it. If Earthquake found that archaeologist again and stole her teleportation devices…"

"Then we're in deep *skata*." Symphora coughed again, this time with a clot of blood.

If they timed the assassination of Symphora to Amanda's proposed legislation, then Earthquake had declared war.

With the salvageable bits of Symphora's plasma-tattered tunic, Amanda bandaged the wound and the bleeding slowed, but the clothing was turning purple-black with Symphora's blood.

If Symphora died before a medbot came, her blood was literally on Amanda's hands.

SIX

(ROSANNA)

**Earthquake safehouse: Last place
in the galaxy anyone would look**

ROSANNA MORENO DABBED the bloody remnant of her ear, wincing at the med-gel's searing touch. She hadn't gotten so messed up on her last two recklessly dangerous missions.

The dumbass medic apparently couldn't help himself. "It's so badass to survive against Symphora. Huge reputation points for you, Moreno. Make sure you leave this on for a few hours. Rest here until it heals."

Rosanna shot a glare and he shut up, which promoted him from dumbass to moron.

Scaring the government and ending the legend of Symphora was her mission, not merely surviving. The grunts were supposed to kidnap Amanda Martinez, not let her intervene and distract Rosanna—another reason to kill her, too.

Rosanna stomped out from the medbay, shoving the medic aside despite his mumbled protests. The medic stuttered something about how she needed more rest, but he could shove it. She had another mission, and this one wouldn't come with a bunch of goons to make a mess around her. She counted the remaining shards of Chamayna chitin in her pocket. Five, which was more than enough for a few more teleportations. The moles had at least done their jobs.

She checked her omni-tablet for news about Crith. He was still bouncing around the galaxy, hitting spots Earthquake had targeted. Camera traps kept catching him in odd spots. If Rosanna could get enough of a break between missions, she could nab the bastard. He was making a pattern.

Rosanna fired off a ping to one of the lieutenants at HQ. Earning her status in the organization by freeing the Leader still paid dividends. Ordering around older more experienced assholes brought her a small joy.

[Rosanna: Put out another false message saying we're going to attack the Makawe rebels soon. The same ones Crith tried to recruit a few years ago.]

She wanted to hide out on that planet and wait for the one-armed asshole to arrive. But the Leader had another job for her today. With a heavy sigh, she applied concealer to her Earthquake tattoos decorating her neck, a necessary disgrace for the mission.

Rosanna scratched out the necessary mark in the Chamayna chitin. The ebony exoskeleton glowed black as it absorbed the nearby light. Even though the few meters around her had become so dark she couldn't see her own hands, she closed her eyes.

Thwip. Her insides churned as she traveled millions of lightyears—days of hyperspace travel. In the split second of transportation across the galaxy, she got a vague sense of being monitored. Being judged.

One whisper echoed in her mind: *bringer.*

Thwip.

Rosanna opened her eyes to a maroon sky flecked with wispy brown clouds. That flash must've been a ghost of a bad memory or something, and she shook it off. She was where she needed to be, at least.

The world swirled into focus, and she spat the phlegmy bile which accompanied each teleportation. The archaeologist never warned her about that added bonus. Not that Rosanna was surprised, given how they extracted that information from her.

Beneath her lay cracked chitin pieces—planted by another agent for this mission. They couldn't go on teleporting like this forever since their supply was finite, and the vast trove would be used on a future mission. One shard for the teleporter and another for the destination. But they inched closer to their final solution for the galaxy, and they wouldn't need this advantage much longer.

Wiping the stubborn streak of dried saliva from her chin, Rosanna tiptoed between the razor-straight brickbark trees and stepped onto a gravel path.

Through twisted black branches and yellow foliage, she spotted a stone building constructed in the shape of two Human hands clasped together in prayer. They'd need prayers after what Rosanna prepared to do. She tapped her scabbing ear, letting the pain sharpen her focus. The med-gel had stopped any possible infection, but she didn't need a fancy medical degree to know she'd have a jagged ear for the rest of her life. A little prize for Symphora—a memento to tide her over until Rosanna finished the job.

Forest avians cawed in the canopy above, hammerbeaks or iron warblers based on their clunky chirps. Rosanna nudged beneath them, careful not to disturb their branches and catch their attention and diseases since she wouldn't have the luxury of going through a ship's decontamination. She cleared a spike-bush and stepped onto the dirt road.

According to her intel, most of the monks would be occupied in the city at this time of the day, assisting refugees and performing acts of do-goodery. Most of them, but not her target, the monk who didn't belong here.

The monk whom she'd return to Monsieur Tecton.

The hybrid was codenamed Batch 32, also known as Mui-xe Porandi. An unholy mashup of Human and Lo-sat, and an insult to nature, but also the key to unlocking the next great leap in military technology, something they couldn't let fall into government hands. He was the only hybrid who didn't regress into goop after using his powers.

All her intel warned to proceed with caution. The unnatural science which crafted this hybrid afforded him unnatural abilities.

Her orders were to bring him unconscious. And if he cared for his fellow monks as the intel suggested, she could pluck them off one at a time until he cooperated.

Entering the monastery would be child's play, much less complicated than when she'd broken Jacques Tecton out of prison or kidnapped the archaeologist. With stolen Collective technology, her firearms remained folded into cubes stashed in her rucksack. Her traveler's tunic and overcoat covered the mandatory Earthquake tattoos. With a flick of her neck and the right amount of gel, her hair no longer resembled the lopsided undercut which kept Earthquake members in solidarity.

And they'd said that the double-traitor Rick Crith mastered stealth operations. What a load of boveeshit.

After three knocks on the rubywood door, a hunched-over Human answered, the door creaking as much as his bones. He spoke with the accent of someone who grew up on a space station. "I am too old to bow, but my spirit bows to yours."

Rosanna suppressed an eyeroll and bowed. Some of her squad members practiced Great Mystery and did the greetings, so she'd seen this dozens of times.

"What, may I ask, is the reason for your visit?" the geezer asked.

As Rosanna began her "art student" response, a familiar voice interrupted. "It's alright, Brother. She's received clearance from Brother Maynard and is here to study and document our art for preservation's sake."

The second monk, Earthquake's mole, stepped forward. "Brother" Rondo was the last person to receive an order from Rick Crith and the first person to defy one after hearing of his defection. His youth and vigor made for a stark contrast against the doorman.

Rondo had become a good friend of Rosanna's in the last few years.

He beckoned her inside, and she nodded her thanks toward the old timer before following Rondo deeper into the building.

The monastery reminded Rosanna of the architecture of an Earthquake bunker, not in its form or function, but in its Human proportions. Ceilings that didn't feel like clouds, hallways that didn't feel like canyons, and art that made some type of sense, despite being abstract.

They marched through the stonework gatehouse into the courtyard, passing playful junior monks lobbing ferrous rocks at the walls, trying to knock each other's rocks off.

On a heavily magnetized planet such as this, most rocks stuck to each other, affording them enjoyment. Maybe she would have joined them ten years ago. Maybe even five, before Rick Crith had ruined her life.

As Rosanna passed the children, she wondered how many of those junior monks were abandoned orphans or children of refugees unable to feed them. Wondered if any had been displaced or forced into poverty due to Earthquake's actions. It made her stomach twinge, but she shoved the thought from her mind. Anybody so affected could blame Rick Crith since his defection worsened the situation. He ruined everything he touched. Crith damaged the once-perfect Earthquake—he forced their hand by surrendering to Symphora three years ago. She swallowed hard and focused on the flagstone path bisecting the red-tinted grass.

The junior monks paused their games to observe her, not that she blamed their curiosity. They probably hadn't seen a woman since their mothers abandoned them to this life of prayer so they had one less mouth to feed.

These monks would grow up to hopefully feed the homeless and assist the elderly. Noble, even though it failed to bring Humanity closer to sloughing off the oppressors. They should be stealing food from the oppressors.

Once in the center of the courtyard and far away enough from prying ears, Rondo whispered to her. "Did you kill Symphora?"

She reminded herself an art student wouldn't clench her fists and flexed her fingers instead. "That's not what this mission is about. Where's the hybrid?"

"Sparring with the martial arts instructor."

"Your report didn't say he was a fighter." What else hadn't they told her? Maybe these monks weren't as much into pacifism as they claimed.

"He's hopeless. Mismatched limbs of weird lengths, stubby tail, and I think he's going through his freak version of puberty, so he's even more gangly."

Rosanna nodded, mind racing. HQ said it was a young man, not a teen. But it wasn't Human, so it didn't really matter. "And the Abbot?"

Rondo scowled. "Would you believe he's the hybrid's uncle? That's the rumor floating around. There's a weird resemblance. Not that a tank bred hybrid freak could really have an uncle or parents, but the one scientist who made him used his own DNA—he's the Abbot's brother." And there it was, the technology nobody could truly replicate beyond cheap imitations.

"I know the rumors. Is the Abbot here?"

"No. He's in the city. I think he goes on secret trips—"

The door opened and a rush of junior monks passed them, holding brooms and mops. As they clambered through with the grace of drunk toddlers, Rondo babbled nonsense about their art that she should examine while she feigned interest in a statue. Once the last preteen left the hall, Rosanna stepped closer to him.

"Have you confirmed any of his powers? I'm doubting the quality of my intel."

Rondo scrunched his nose. "I watched him boil some water in the kitchen once to help the cooks save fuel. He grabbed the pot, and it was bubbling in seconds. Sometimes he goes to the infirmary and prays over sick or injured people, and they bounce back, but I haven't seen it. He's jumpy around me."

She knew about the fire and healing from working with Earthquake's attempts at creating hybrids. Too well.

"More to the point," Rondo continued, "if you get the freak alone, are you sure you can extract him without anyone knowing?"

She wasn't sure how she felt about calling the hybrid a "he" instead of an "it." Rosanna instinctively reached for her pouch with the teleportation chitin, then pulled away. "Yes, but that's not for you to worry about. The less you know, the better."

"You can't tell me anything?" Rondo moaned, tugging at the scarf around his neck. The drab thing probably covered his Earthquake tattoo: the planet Earth with a diagonal line through it. Rosanna had just used concealer to hide hers for this mission.

"It's like working with Crith all over again, for Earth's sake," Rondo said. "Do you know how hard I've worked to get some clout among these pricks?"

Despite calling Rondo a friend in their correspondence, Rosanna knew little about him beyond what was necessary for the mission, except that he hated Rick Crith as much as she did. The bastard stationed him here to learn the monks' techniques and then forgot about him, just issuing one order after deciding to betray the entire organization two years ago.

Rosanna flexed her fingers. "I can tell you they will have no clue you were involved." After a breath, she added, "Or either of us, really."

"So you have the jagged knife?"

"It matches the diagram you sent of the hybrid's finger and claw prints. Anyone who sees it will believe it was from the freak."

They approached the end of the courtyard, and Rondo opened the double doors leading inside for them. Junior monks raced about, so the mole picked up the conversation. "You'll see many of our youngsters running around, but the older monks are in the city most of their days." He turned left down a corner. "Which is a sharp change from our previous mission only a few years past. Under the direction of our loyal, admirable, intelligent Abbot, Senior Brother Maynard, we have left our days-long prayers and taken to more direct forms of service. Belief-in-action, he calls it."

The last of the onlookers dissipated upon realizing Rosanna cared more about the statues and mosaics decorating the halls.

Rosanna cracked her knuckles. She'd get this freak, and her leader would reciprocate with some juicy tidbit. Some clue to bring her one step closer to wrapping her hands around Rick Crith's throat.

She paused at a statue to sell the illusion of being an art student. Whatever the carved rock was, it wasn't anything she could recognize. It portrayed some seated figure in meditation, pondering the Great Mystery instead of helping Humanity in a meaningful way. "If the freak can heal, I'll need to kill the other guy, not just incapacitate him." Rosanna eyed him. "You sure you're OK with this? You've been living with these people for years."

"Yeah, this guy is a dick. You're doing me a favor by offing him."

Rosanna narrowed her eyes. Maybe she'd stop referring to Rondo as her friend.

"Come on," Rondo said. "The dojo is on the left."

Rosanna followed him inside. The soapy scent of a hand-scrubbed floor welcomed her. With exercise and hand-to-hand combat training equipment, the inside seemed like the clean and serene version of what she'd grown accustomed to in Earthquake circles. It was almost as if they believed in the scrolls decorating the side of the wall: honor, virtue, aid the weak. Learn martial arts to defend and whatnot. Earthquake's gyms and training centers mostly had slogans like "no mercy, no prisoners, no compromise."

Only two men occupied this room which could have fit thirty. They stood on a spacious padded mat. The older of the two, a stout muscled man, cradled the neck of a gangly youth in a tight headlock. "Use your tail, Mui-xe. Get some leverage."

The gangly youth cleared his throat, the sound resembling an amphibian's croak: hoarse and diseased.

The muscled monk glanced to the door, and seeing Rosanna and Rondo, released the lanky youth, offering a bow. "Brother Rondo, I hadn't expected you." He turned to Rosanna, offering a warm smile and a bow. "And you're the art student?"

She would've preferred weight training to smiling back. "Yes, I'm in my third year studying Great Mystery artwork. I saw the mural of the fighters in ritual sparring. I hoped the two of you could show me some moves."

The master monk gestured to the boy with an open palm. "Certainly. This is Brother Mui-xe, a novice monk here. You may call me Brother Webster."

Rosanna dug her fingernails into her palm to keep the disgust from showing on her face. An unhealthy mesh of scales and skin covered his thin frame—short for a Lo-sat but taller than the three Humans. His marbled red eyes appraised Rosanna, and his nostril slits vibrated.

The youth bowed, lifting his bulbous tail just off the floor, too inflexible for gripping something like a real Lo-sat's tail would. It made her skin crawl.

The master licked his lips and flitted his eyes to Rondo. "Is our guest aware of Mui-xe's circumstances?"

"Yes," Rondo responded with a smile and turned to Rosanna as planned. "We accept all life forms, and this poor child was an abandoned Lo-sat, left to us because of his human colorization and small stature. Among other genetic oddities. I'll leave you all to it." Rondo waved and exited, closing the door behind him.

It was a decent enough lie that would fool most people if the freak wore a hood and long robe all day. "It's a pleasure to meet you. Can the pair of you please spar for my research notes?"

The senior monk cocked an eyebrow. "Do you have a sketchpad or something? Were you planning to record? We'd prefer Mui-xe's identity not be revealed to the greater public."

The youth bowed his too-long neck, avoiding Rosanna's gaze. Good.

Sighing, the monk added, "And truth be told, I was under the impression you were coming later today. Please do not take offense, but I would not have authorized you to come while we were sparring for that same reason."

"I understand," Rosanna replied. "I know not everybody appreciates what the Great Mystery monks do for people society would call outcasts." Rosanna fought against the word "reject" worming into her mouth.

"So your sketches won't display his unique anatomy?"

The gangly teen locked eyes with her, their marble pattern dilating before shrinking back. He was too far away to grab, and the older monk was too far to stab.

She hated waiting for an opening.

"I don't have to sketch him at all. His secret is safe with me." She advanced a half step nearer to the boy, forcing calm on herself in case he could smell pheromones like a Lo-sat. "Don't be nervous. I'm an artist. I'm here to observe and sketch, alright?" She pointed to the hollowed-out sketchbook on her hip that concealed her knife. "Nothing else."

They donned pads around their heads and fists. The master bowed toward Mui-xe, who did likewise. Both lowered into a fighting stance, left leg extended, right leg bowed. His stubby tail curled.

Rosanna appraised their style and movements. Prehistoric Earth boasted a myriad of fighting styles, and researchers were still delving into what they could've been before the collapse and the Eleva War. The style these two fighters employed seemed to be some hybridization, modified for alternative gravitational situations. The way the teacher moved and the student failed to mimic suggested they had no clue how to accommodate for other species.

Which wasn't what Rosanna needed. "Master, can you put him in a headlock like you did when I entered? There was some similarity in your grip to the patterns I saw in your artwork. It would be better if you were fighting for real and not going through motions."

As the master blocked a weak kick from the boy, he nodded to Rosanna. "You have a good eye. That move is named for our symbol of rebirth." With a lateral spin, he reached up to lasso the lanky Mui-xe by the neck, firm like a fighter and gentle like a teacher, bringing the boy down into the same position as before.

"That's not quite right," Rosanna said. "Could you do that pose without all those pads?"

Brother Webster nodded to the hybrid, and they removed their pads and got back into position.

"Can you hold that for a moment? I need to see all angles." Rosanna sidestepped, and once fully behind the pair, she unsheathed her jagged knife from her pack.

Heart pumping, she readied her blade.

A sniff. "Master!" the boy screamed. Damn Lo-sat nose. She'd gotten too excited or nervous for the kill. Two botched missions.

The teacher spun around and kicked Rosanna's hand, forcing her to drop the knife.

Rosanna didn't have time for a taunt or grandstand. She stepped back and withdrew her silenced pistol from the same sack.

As she did, the master lunged at her at an angle. She fired and he dodged; the bullet missed his torso and torched his moving hand, and the stench of plasma-scorched skin permeated.

With her free hand, Rosanna grabbed her dropped knife and slashed, but he dodged.

"Mui-xe, get help!" The master kicked Rosanna's abdomen, but she stepped into the blow, absorbing the force instead of falling.

The lanky kid scrambled for the door. "It's locked!" Mui-xe cried.

Rosanna found her opening and stabbed. Her jagged knife ripped his flesh like a saw through wood. Like a predator through prey.

As he winced and retreated, Rosanna shot him between the eyes.

Plasma-smoke slithered up from the wound, and the hybrid stared, jaw hanging open, displaying mismatched fangs and molars.

Rosanna knelt over the master's body, then slashed at his chest again, creating artificial claw marks. She did the same to the gunshot wounds in his hand and head to cover them. Plasmafire wounds rarely resembled surgical holes, and Rondo could blame the scorching on the hybrid's flames.

As she worked, Mui-xe's expression went from shock to disgust. His hands glowed crimson like his eyes, a foul light that only a twisted scientist could manufacture. Those must be the promised fire hands.

She smirked. *Bring it on.*

Instead of charging her, he turned to the door and grasped the doorknob.

The aberration was going to melt the door and run. This was kidnapping that Makawe girl all over again—Rosanna wanted a fight, not a race.

"No you don't!" She scrambled toward him, stowing her weapons and readying her chitin shard. The room's increased heat smacked her when she got close. This kid could burn her alive.

Nearly reaching him, her fingers brushed against his collar as he pushed through the door and escaped her grasp. The wood around the knob burned away in seconds, and the metal knob congealed into a molten mess, scorching the wood beneath it.

She dove after him as the heat singed her arm hairs.

He scrambled into the hallway, and Rosanna tackled him. Struggling on the floor against the freak boy, she realized Rondo was gone, but a group of junior monks had gathered, gawking.

The junior monks' eyes went wide, and they stuttered questions, but Rosanna didn't have any time. Rosanna palmed the black chitin, scratching a new line with a fingernail, her other arm firmly around Mui-xe's waist. She met each kid's gaze. "Mui-xe killed your master."

He croaked something inaudible as the chitin glowed.

Thwip.

Gone. Clutching the hybrid as they blinked through time and space, the feeling of observation and judgment returned. A distant sound echoed in that stretching half-moment, like a tight drumming, or a wet clacking. Like mandibles from a wrathful insect.

Rosanna pushed the thoughts away. It was probably some weird side effect she hadn't noticed before. Once she'd locked this kid up, she'd need a drink. The eggheads who wanted to exploit his DNA definitely owed her one, and the other higher-ups who wanted him out of Collective hands definitely owed her five.

They rematerialized in a prison block, where he'd remain until they unlocked the secrets hiding in his DNA.

SEVEN

(RICK)

The smoldering ruins of Hen4 city

WITH HIS RUST-BUCKET of a hover-speeder parked under some rubble, Rick Crith shuffled his spacefaring coat over himself, letting the hood conceal his face. The omni-tablet he'd lifted from a former squadmate was still paying dividends. There had definitely been an attack here.

The once-bustling lunar city of Hen4 lay in ruins, victim to a rogue asteroid, according to official reports.

The truth? Earthquake shelled the city from orbit.

A notification buzzed on his personal omni-tablet, breaking news of an attack on the Fringe territory's government offices. That meant three things: Amanda was in danger, Earthquake was distracting from another strike somewhere else, and Rick was too damn late both here and there. Phantom pains shot through his missing arm. Being too late to help had been his lot in life since he left the organization.

Rick had combed the galaxy for a year, desperate to find the clues he needed to take down Earthquake's leader, his former employer, Jacques Tecton. And all Rick had to show for it was disaster tourism and whispers of a building project unlike anything Humanity had ever seen. In the time it took him to stow away on shuttles or book passage under false names, he never got anywhere fast enough. All he had was a long list of places that asshole *wasn't*.

Rick stepped over a burnt street sign pointing to the market district, which likely had collapsed during the fighting. Half a battledart lay over a collapsed house roof; the sleek fighter had probably shot up the whole neighborhood before crashing. Empty streets echoed the loss with each of his heavy steps, and he drew his coat tighter. These homes bore the mark of renovated slums. Economic uplift had happened, only to be obliterated.

Running from this destruction tempted him. He'd seen this before when he was the perpetrator—the innocent people he'd killed with flimsy justification, telling himself that each time he got his hands dirty, he was paving the way for a better future for humanity.

But he'd accepted the truth. Creating a better future with Earthquake was impossible, and he was only enacting his anger issues on the Collective. He cringed, remembering the people he dragged down with him: the archaeologist he threatened, the child he attempted to murder, even the damn thief he enslaved.

And Amanda... the bright spot in his time in Earthquake. He barely dared to imagine the things she could've become if his name hadn't tarnished her reputation: a clean politician with no ties to criminals or a past darkened by Earthquake, running her own business, and never having to worry about a damn target on her back.

He turned down a street corner and froze. On his right, downtown blocks of stores and homes sized for all species were leveled by a crashed warhive, the floating fortress which could level a city with its armaments. When he saw it from orbit, he hoped he was mistaken, but the evidence lay bare in front of him. Earthquake wasn't bothering to steal and repurpose Collective ships anymore. They didn't want a real fleet—Rick's onetime dream. They didn't want a professional military protecting an actual Human government. Chaos and destruction were their only goals now—such unnecessary loss of life. They stole military ships just to throw them at population centers.

And this was his fault. He'd forged the path with his own ambition, never considering how someone with more sinister motives could twist his strategies.

Afraid to approach the ruined district and warhive, he estimated the total casualties of this one scene. A fully staffed warhive would support over one thousand Arkoudae. A downtown block would have thousands more souls. And Hen4 boasted a diverse population, too. Arkoudae, Lo-sats, maybe even the odd Makawe, working-class Humans, and they'd all been slaughtered thoughtlessly.

Wincing, Rick approached the smoldering academic district ruins, knowing that's where the remains of the university and museum would be as well as any clues leading to the whereabouts of his quarry.

Dr. Alize Oze, discoverer of a lost civilization, was a woman with more reason to hate Rick than anyone else. He was glad she'd escaped him all those years ago, but her method of escape had been so bizarre, he wouldn't have believed it without the evidence.

This archaeologist somehow discovered a means for teleportation using the chitin of the long-extinct Chamayna. Hearing the details of Earthquake's attack on the government offices, he knew there must be a connection. How else could Earthquake have managed an attack on a well-defended asteroid? He'd warned about using that teleportation since it involved too many unknowns. But then again, there were a lot of things he'd warned about that nobody listened to.

Approaching the city center, skeletons came into view. He wondered how many people had been instantly vaporized when the warhive crashed or at least instantly suffocated from the resulting debris clouds. Rick scowled, praying these people had painless deaths or at least fast ones—a luxury he denied his victims in his last days with Earthquake.

In the early days, he would've been careful to avoid civilian casualties, believing in the nobility of their cause. But after he chased Dr. Oze all the way to that damn moon, he'd seized an opportunity to turn the tides in Earthquake's favor by stealing invincible Collective military armor and modifying it for Human use, and he stopped caring about who he had to hurt to achieve his objective.

He sidestepped a Lo-sat's skeleton with a child's skeleton clutched in its arms.

Damn.

Rick knelt beside the stiff body. Its claws were still attached. As were the kid's.

Not that it would bring them any comfort or that their surviving family, if they had any, would know, but Rick proceeded to give them a semblance of a Lo-sat funeral.

Skeletal as they were, tendons and muscles burnt off, he removed their claws with little effort, placed them in a neat pile, then stomped thrice with his heavy boot to pulverize them. He dipped his fingers into the chunky powder and rubbed it into his coat. Maybe he'd run into a shaman one day, and they could symbolically complete the ritual, but this was enough for now. If the Lo-sat afterlife were truly a realm of peace, he hoped these two could find some.

Rick surveyed the broken cityscape around him. Crushed apartments, ruined stores, lingering smoke stench.

There must be hundreds more unattended corpses and skeletons. He wouldn't be able to honor them all. Glancing at the scattered powder pile by his foot, he stomped on a solid chunk and ground it by twisting his ankle. That was for all those he couldn't attend to today.

Rick sighed and pressed forward.

A few steps later, a rustling perked his ear—he wasn't alone.

Rick pulled his hood over his face more and tugged on his sleeve to hide his shoulder stump. The device he had to conceal himself completely would lose its charge if he used it now.

Phantom fingers reached for a gun that wasn't there anymore.

An overturned autocab big enough to transport an Arkouda lay on the side of the street, and he darted for it. Ducking underneath, he peered through the shattered window. The rustling increased, sharpening into a series of rhythmic taps.

Straining his ears, he noticed a six-tap cadence. That six-tap formed one of the melodies from his nightmares, reminding him of when Makawe rebels nearly snapped him in half. With their six pointed legs, the sound of their advance was unmistakable.

The interloper scuttled from a pile of debris. Starlight shined on their red-black carapace as they zigzagged around debris piles. Likely an adult—it might've measured up to Rick's knee if standing upright. Its pincer size suggested a female. Earthquake files called their kind "reject Earth crabs from Hell," but he appreciated an elegance in her movements only a sapient could achieve.

One of her four eye stalks swiveled in Rick's direction, and he remembered too late that Makawe could see infrared and heat signatures. She'd spotted him.

He couldn't detect any weapons on the belt that laterally bisected her top shell, but he'd fought enough Makawe in his pre-Earthquake time to know they didn't need guns to be dangerous.

Seeing Rick, she approached the overturned cab. Rick lowered himself behind it—an exercise in futility—as she scuttled forward.

In a thick accent, she called out to him, voice like grating stone, speaking Arkouda, the common language of their oppressors. "Hu'man. Hide not from me."

Rick clenched his teeth. He'd heard that same string of words years ago in the mission which left him between a Makawe rebel's pincers, slowly snapping each rib. This didn't have the same malicious ring, he told himself. She probably wasn't a rebel, and it wasn't like Rick was on the Collective's good side anymore.

With a deep breath, he rose from his crouch and left his cover. He puffed his cheeks to reply to her in Arkouda. "I won't hurt you. I'm searching for … my friend."

She dug her pincers into the cracked road and repositioned herself, squaring with Rick. Her top two eye stalks swiveled in a semicircle, reading Rick. "Spirits say you won't find your friend. Spirits whisper it's not your friend, either."

Rick wondered how his infrared signature must register for her to make those claims. "Let me find this person, then. I'll leave you alone."

"You march to teaching place."

"Did your spirits tell you that?" Years ago, Rick had asked the same question with dripping sarcasm.

"Yes. The teaching—learning place by school. I go, too." A lilt entered her voice. "Search for daughter. Spirits told me to come here, but my ship wasn't fast enough."

He furrowed his brow. *Learning place by the school?* "The museum? You're going to the museum?"

"Moos'yum, yes. My daughter there, spirits whisper. I am P'oki." Hearing a Makawe speak reminded him of the language whispered in his nightmares.

Rick put a finger under his lip and pulled to mimic the Makawe beak shape and struggle through a sentence in her language. "P'oki. Bad man, me." Showing he'd taken the time to learn some Ma'ak might keep him from getting caught in her pincers.

P'oki lowered her eye stalks and responded in Arkouda. "Arkouda I speak and understand." Something in the angle of her eyes suggested she wanted to end that sentence with, "you patronizing asshole." After a huff, she added, "Get pincer out of your beak. You look silly. Spirits tell me your past bad. Present undecided."

He fought the urge to shake his head at her superstitions. "Call me Rick. We can help each other. But understand there are people hunting me."

"Spirits show this, too. If my daughter gone, P'oki has nothing to lose. Rix hunters take me, too." She tilted her eyestalks. "Where is your other pincer?"

Traversing the wreckage to the museum was an exercise in Rick's patience and P'oki's persistence. She peppered him with questions from everything about his childhood to the source of his missing arm to who he was searching for. Rick vacillated between ignoring, politely declining to respond, and one-word answers. Remembering she grieved over a child kept him from shouting at her or abandoning her. Remembering Earthquake wouldn't have had the capacity or confidence to enact this level of destruction without his advancements and strategies shamed him into hiding as much as possible.

P'oki lifted a fallen metal beam blocking the museum entrance. She couldn't get it much over her head. He pushed thoughts of being crushed between her pincers from his mind. She wasn't like that. Those rebels he'd fought so many years ago used scum tactics, even though their grievances against the Collective were understandable: Makawe were Provincials in the Collective, just like Humans, only they lacked the technology and numbers to be as big of a threat as Humans. Rick grabbed the beam, and the pair flung it away, and she scuttled through the collapsed door, Rick ducking to follow.

The museum's dark interior was bereft of power, though a bit of starlight trickled in from the atmospheric shield, snaking around the collapsed roof to illuminate the halls. Rick pulled out a headlamp from his coat and affixed it to his forehead.

Crushed exhibits, crushed dreams. Children would've taken school trips here. Amateur historians would have combed the halls. Avid researchers would have heckled the docents. This used to be a center of learning. Peaceful. No more.

"Do you see infrared signatures from any fallen ships?" Rick asked.

She trilled something in Ma'ak, too fast and quiet to catch. "Spirits say no."

"So no foreign metal or plasma scoring from gun-shots? Something must have collapsed the roof."

"Rix, listen. Spirits say no."

"What are you seeing in the infrared, then?" Summoning the patience to talk to her was more challenging than it should've been.

"Spirits, Rix. There was fighting. Inside."

"Hm." Rick strafed the area with his light. Eleva War artifacts, galactic evolution, Lo-sat stone age hunting gear, extinct animal skeletons—there.

The Chamayna exhibit—Dr. Oze's specialty.

"We need to check there." Rick bade P'oki follow him, approaching the lost civilization's display. Thanks to the archaeologist Rick nearly murdered, this museum boasted the galaxy's largest collection of artifacts from the vanished insectoid race known as the Chamayna.

He found the scratchy art he'd last seen in the tomb, a memory he wished he'd forget.

Mandibles. Dripping and clacking together, so much worse than Makawe pincers and pointed legs.

"Rix?"

Blackness. Eating the light.

"Rix."

Ships plucked from the sky like bushberries.

"Rix!"

The creature of unspeakable evil he narrowly escaped.

Makawe pincers gently grasped Rick's calf, tugging him from his stupor.

Rick breathed deep and forced himself to remember his therapy. *Wavegulls. Gentle shores.*

Mom still alive. He took another breath. *Hours in the library as a boy, surrounded by books about Earth's history.* Rick definitely botched the grounding exercise, but his last therapist sucked.

He exhaled and focused on the objective. "I'm sorry, P'oki—"

"Pain spirits danced around you. Bad memory?"

Rick shuddered. "Their art depicts something horrific. It reminded me of something I saw once. Nothing to worry about." Shaking his head, he hardened his tone. "The glass up here is shattered. Somebody broke these display cases."

He tore away through the debris, scanning for what he wished he didn't have to see. The surviving chitin of the Chamayna species. Their exoskeletons had some biological mechanisms inside them Rick couldn't begin to understand. When the archaeologist discovered their inner workings, Alize had a degree of control over that damned abomination—she'd gotten that thing to ignore her and attack Rick. She could even blink out of existence and pop up halfway across the moon or even the galaxy.

It was how she'd escaped him because he would've tortured her for the secret.

Trudging through the debris made one thing clear: Earthquake had been here and taken every trace of the Chamayna chitin. With Alize's stolen secrets, they'd have the capacity to teleport—a terrorist and coward's ultimate tactic. Perfect for them.

"They stole this Chamayna chitin and planted a bomb and orchestrated a fight outside to cover their intent." Rick seethed. "Typical Earthquake strategy.

Start a fire over there to get away with something over here. Damn." He eyed the Makawe, wondering if she could sense a kidnapping. He winced as the following words left his mouth. "Do you see … kidnapping spirits? Was someone, a Human woman, stolen from here?" His mouth dried. "Or murdered?"

P'oki swiveled an eye stalk at him. "Hu'man woman? Name?"

"Why does that matter?"

She rotated her carapace to face him with her whole body. "Hu'man woman. What name?" A grating edge entered her tone. "Rix. Say."

A name which never belonged on his lips emerged. "Dr. Alize Oze."

"O'ze." P'oki let the name echo in her beak. "Spirits bring us together, Rix. My daughter was her assistant. Friend, too."

"Do you know what they researched specifically?"

"Great power was all I heard. Not smart for ancient things, P'oki is. But we get matching tattoo for celebrate. Look—" P'oki indicated the tapestry of carved tattoos on her carapace. They resembled the mural of Makawe symbols he'd seen variations of, yet one curious shape stood out. Rick had no clue what it meant, but it was a Chamayna glyph. He recognized the style and symbols more from his nightmares than memory.

He couldn't stare. "I'm not good with ancient stuff, either. If your daughter were here, would your spirits tell you?"

"Mother spirits yes. She is gone." After a tremor in her voice, she straightened her six legs. "But not dead."

"If Alize and your daughter were kidnapped together, they've been tortured or worse by Earthquake to extract the secrets of their research. The galaxy is in big trouble if Alize's findings are in their hands."

"You don't have enough polite spirits. But we will find them, Rix. I have ship that can fit you."

As they left, a metallic glint caught Rick's eye. A broken bench, displaying a plaque: *In loving memory of Chet Oze, the museum's unofficial tour guide. A man of unspeakable love and character.*

Rick unsheathed his knife and dug out the plaque from the bench. "If—" he glanced at P'oki, "*when* we find them, I'll give this to Alize. Part of an overdue apology."

"So where we go?"

"To find Earthquake's headquarters." Rick stowed the plaque inside his coat. "And we rip it apart until we find them."

"Spirits guide us."

A buzz at Rick's hip made him pause. A ping came in from someone who swore never to speak to him again.

Amanda Martinez. Maybe she knew where Alize was.

EIGHT

(ALIZE)

Caught by a madwoman

ALIZE SLAMMED HER fist against the lasered wall of her cell, which repulsed her effort. "Let her go, you monster!" This was not why she'd gotten into archaeology.

Her captor, an Earthquake commander named Rosanna, pulled her hand off the shell belonging to Alize's friend and assistant. The commander twirled the titanium pliers she'd been using to remove parts of He'nay's carapace in her hand. "You know what you need to do to get me to stop, Oze."

Her accent along with the tone she used to say her last name gave Alize too-fresh memories of Rick Crith.

And that was why Alize had refused the job offered to her by Symphora's assistant last year. Symphora and Rick Crith weren't too different on paper. Gun-toting outlaws who believed they were in the right. Even though the job was to help Humans in the Collective government, Alize couldn't stomach leaving her museum. If she had, she wouldn't have hired and befriended the Makawe now getting tortured before her eyes.

Maybe if she had trusted that Joka woman who acted on Symphora's behalf and taken that cushy job two years ago, He'nay wouldn't be under a madwoman's boot heel right now. Alize's heart smashed against her ribcage. That was her friend squirming under that armored boot.

Alize and He'nay had spent late nights researching and transcribing Chamayna glyphs together, opening the galaxy to new knowledge. And now they were locked in the basement of a terrorist's corporate headquarters, being tortured by a psychopath.

Rosanna scowled at Alize's lack of response and set the pliers against He'nay's shell.

He'nay wailed, barely able to trill any words through her mangled beak. "D-don't say anything, A'lize. N-not worth—HRRRT!"

Alize swung back her prosthetic leg and kicked hard against her cell's laser partition, the cybernetics boosting her strength but still rattling her stump.

It didn't matter.

Alize focused on the one unique carving among the mural of decorations on He'nay's shell. All were Makawe words and symbols with this one exception. A casual observer wouldn't notice, but Alize recognized the glyph. She'd helped He'nay pick it out as a mother/daughter tattoo idea for Earth's sake. "Power," the glyph said.

Alize meant the original suggestion as something meaningful to them, but noticing the bond between mother and daughter, a theory emerged when she listened to He'nay talk about her mom. The faintest glow came from that tattooed glyph back in that parlor. Maybe the power of the Chamayna wasn't the Chamayna at all.

Perhaps it belonged to something else—something too taboo to even think about directly, lest she put mental words to something unspeakable.

She couldn't let her captor know.

"Promise you won't tell her anything, A'lize," He'nay begged.

Her tormentor smacked He'nay's beak with her pliers, caving in the hollow bone. He'nay's agonized ululating would live in Alize's nightmares.

"That's enough," Alize said.

Expressionless, Rosanna pulled her tool back. "You're ready to talk now?"

"If you don't have the stomach to kill an innocent person, then let us go." Flashes of her best friend's death hit her mind like lightning. "I've lost friends and family members before. You don't need to kill her."

Their captor spit on the fresh hole in He'nay's beak. He'nay writhed beneath her.

"You know this is monstrous," Alize said. "Let us go or put He'nay out of her misery."

Rosanna approached the laser partition of Alize's cell. She tapped on the solid light with the end of her pliers. "Tell me what I want to know and I'll stop."

"You're dealing with a power you can't imagine. The Chamayna didn't even have a word for it because they feared it so much."

"Boveeshit. Tell me how you teleported before I start again."

Alize refused to let her lip tremble as she stared at her friend. "I promise I won't tell her anything, He'nay. We're done cooperating."

He'nay swiveled an eyestalk back to Alize. Her leftmost eyestalk swayed to the right—a gesture of gratitude.

Alize nodded. "I'll bash my head against the wall until my brains spill out of my ears. You won't get what you want." Alize definitely should have taken that job with the Symphora Squad.

Her jailer smirked. "It'll be fun to break you."

The joke was on her. She was already broken.

NINE

(AMANDA)

**In a cramped medbay, fighting
to keep a legend alive**

SO MANY MEDBOTS buzzed around other patients that Amanda couldn't replay the scuffle with the mystery attacker in her mind. Something about the woman seemed familiar, but her mind was too foggy, and she was surrounded by too many injured people to focus.

Instead, Amanda glared at the medbot attending Symphora, as if that would force it to operate faster. She blinked hard. Even the cots made for Arkoudae could barely hold Symphora. This medbay was intended for recuperating hungover clerks and diarrheal interns victimized by bad takeout, not gunshot victims. She wished Bugaro were here.

Earthquake—this piece of her past wouldn't release her, and neither would that *thwip* she wished she hadn't heard. Dr. Alize Oze had used that teleportation technique to escape Rick all those years ago when he awoke the demon which tugged at Amanda's nightmares. From a forgotten moon's depths, that unspeakable creature ravaged a Blekk pirate fleet and solidified Rick's fame.

Amanda cursed herself for missing the warning signs and hated how much she once admired Rick. But he needed to know about this attack. Living off the grid, he could find and slip into Earthquake's headquarters without catching any attention. Someone had access to Alize Oze's research and was using it for terrorism. This attack was probably their opening salvo. Wincing, Amanda found the encrypted address she swore she'd never use and readied her omni-tablet's messenger.

[Amanda: Earthquake has the Chamayna teleportation material. You said Alize Oze had it all. Come out of hiding and take care of it.]

She shut off the messenger, debating the merits of sending a follow up that said "you son of a Galsan worm." Learning about his savagery after serving him so loyally still stung. Maybe any goodness in him died upon beholding the horror on that moon or maybe fighting the hybrid abominations in that scientist's lab. Not that it excused him. Amanda winced—she had been on his side for much of his horrific actions, so she wasn't exactly blameless, either.

Symphora groaned beside her. "Who'd you ping, Martinez?"

"Shh," Amanda said, "don't worry about it."

Hover-gurneys zigzagged across the room, ferrying the dead and dying, running so close to Amanda they rustled her clothes. Senators and staffers filled the cots, some strapped to machines, others mostly shell-shocked.

Many Arkoudae and Lo-sats stared when they thought Amanda wasn't looking—not in a good way. Amanda had her Earthquake tattoos removed and hadn't sported the lopsided haircut in years. But they deserved to be suspicious. Amanda had assisted in terrible things while with Earthquake.

Another Lo-sat staffer marched into the room, and as soon as his eyes landed on her, he stomped over, neck frills extended, sidestepping between hover-gurneys.

Amanda tried to ignore him by studying the vitals monitors attached to Symphora, willing her to pull through.

A round ear twitched. "I'm never gonna get better here," Symphora moaned.

"Need some fresh air?" Amanda asked. The Lo-Sat was quickly advancing, and Amanda would happily take any excuse to escape before he made it across the room. Anyone scowling like that was bound to be bad news, and she was pretty sure she knew what he was going to say.

"There's too much heat here. Call my girl at the women's shelter."

"Joka Bunear?" Amanda asked. "The inventor? Why go there? Does she have medical equipment better than what's here?" While she hadn't heard the name spoken aloud since last year's awards ceremony, it was one Amanda remembered often.

Symphora huffed, readjusting. "What's with Humans and multiple questions at once? She has stuff I need."

"You can't go alone," Amanda said.

"Then take me." Symphora held up her paw, turned her muzzle, and coughed, hoarse and forceful. More eyes drifted over. "It's not like your vote is happening anytime soon."

"I can't. I'm already a suspect. If I leave, it'll look fishy."

The Lo-sat staffer marched over and pointed a long, thin claw at Amanda, scaly green tail coiled behind his back. "Chairwoman Mar-ti-nez, you are required for questioning by the *surviving* ethics board members."

Amanda craned her neck to shoot him the stink eye but remembered she wasn't in a gang anymore. "I'm sorry. Who are you?"

The staffer scrunched his snout and bared a jagged tooth. "I'm the one who's bringing you to the ethics board, and you'll answer for the attack on this station."

Symphora grunted. "You better follow that with a 'Ha, just kidding. I brought Symphora a beer.'"

"I'm afraid not," he replied. His neck frills stayed extended as he stared at Amanda. "Don't make this more damning by resisting arrest."

"Arrest?" Amanda rose with a glare that could've melted metal. "Excuse me?" She closed the distance between them.

The wimp's neck frills retracted.

"This was *my* legislation we were voting on today. Why would I sabotage my own vote?" She leaned in, forcing him to retreat a step. "I am loyal to the Collective. You forget yourself."

The Lo-sat retreated a step. "Chairperson Marti-nez, that is certainly enough."

"Say her name right, punk," Symphora chided. "Now come over here so I can smack you."

The Lo-sat huffed and retreated a step. "With all due respect, this Human is a prime suspect. If she's not directly an informant, someone is tapping her communications."

Symphora snarled, pushing herself into a sitting position, and every head in the room snapped over. "She's clean. Now back off. Run her omni-tablet if you don't believe her."

Amanda glanced at her tablet, which she'd just used to ping Rick. Blood drained from her face, and she hoped it didn't show. "Check my office files. Every last one. I'm a victim of blatant institutionalized racism. I'm being targeted."

A burly Arkouda page lumbered over, pushing aside a nurse 'bot, aligning himself with the Lo-sat. "Tecton said that, too."

"You ganged up on him like this?" Amanda asked. "No wonder he built Earthquake under your noses. Ever regret treating him like dirt? Wondering if maybe events would've turned out differently if you'd treated him well? I'm not saying he isn't scum, but none of you learned from the mistake. I'm not him. I saw he was trash and left."

The Lo-sat folded his arms. "So if you have nothing to hide, hand over your omni-tablet." He snaked his long tail toward her wrist.

Amanda snapped back. "You don't have the right to search my stuff."

"Martinez, come on," Symphora said. "Afraid of them seeing your Block Bash scores?"

"Line Align is my timewaster of choice," Amanda said, stowing her omni-tablet in her suit, still dirty from the afternoon's raid. "You have no idea how many oppressed Humans have reached out to me, begging me to tell their stories to the Collective and liberate my people from this ridiculous Provincial status. They deserve some privacy."

The Arkouda page lunged forward and grabbed Amanda by the shoulders, lifting her from the ground, robbing her of the sense of control she'd fought so hard to earn in her life.

"What are you gonna do to me?" Amanda asked, forcing defiance into her tone. They wouldn't get the satisfaction of rattling her.

Symphora snarled. "Put her the Nightmare down, or I'll—"

"You'll what?" the page asked, whirling on her. "Bleed on me?" The page's eyes widened, and he quickly added, "Um, maybe you should get some rest, ma'am."

Amanda's feet flailed, and her device clattered to the floor. She kicked, but his arms were so long she just grazed his chest.

"Let the record show the gang member attacked us." The Lo-sat cradled her omni-tablet in his tail. "We're taking this to the scanners."

Amanda slackened in the page's grasp, and he put her down, five percent rougher than needed. Symphora offered a weak paw. The pair left, the Lo-sat holding his head up triumphantly and the page still muttering apologies to Symphora.

"Will they have any repercussions for that?" Amanda asked quietly.

"You'll get an apology when they see you're clean. Your kicks need work."

Amanda met Symphora's eyes for a long moment.

The Arkouda wiggled her fuzzy ears. "Well, *skata*."

"I don't think I'll have this job much longer. Symphora, thank you for taking my side. Humanity's side."

"Thank Joka Bunear. She showed me why the Collective needs Human voices."

"Speaking of which, I know she has a certain talent for getting people out of tough situations."

"But uh, you're clean, right Martinez? Just tell me whatever was on your tablet had nothing to do with the attack."

All of Amanda's time with Earthquake flashed before her. Her work at the homeless shelter was the only thing that didn't fuel her self-loathing. "Nothing at all."

Symphora nodded slowly. "I'll ping Bunear. She'll extract you if needed. She could get here in a few hours if she hustles. Her base is close." Lowering her voice, she added, "And thanks for saving my hairy ass back there with that Earthqu—that lady who tried to off me. She really knocked some teeth loose." Symphora massaged her muzzle with an IV-laden paw. "My spleen, too. Good fighter."

"And you didn't recognize her at all?" Amanda leaned against a beeping machine. "Not someone from your gang with a grudge?"

Symphora nursed her new scar. "Nah. Didn't fight like one of mine. The scumsuckers I fought were usually men. The fighting style I taught to my fighting femmes is uh... men specific. We'll leave it at that."

"Right. What should I do before they check my tablet, then?"

"Get your *skata* ready. If there's anything even a tiny bit incriminating, those needledicks will hit you. They need someone to blame; your history makes it easy."

Amanda nodded. "I don't have the luxury of changing my past."

"Nobody does. It's the galaxy's great equalizer."

Amanda shuddered; the word "equalizer" conjured memories of the monstrous harpoon cannons Earthquake used, first designed under Rick's watch and now the instrument of her bodyguard's death. They punctured the seemingly invincible Collective armor like a knife through paper. And she'd been instrumental in funding the research for it.

She wished she could say that she'd only wanted to run the homeless shelter, not get caught in this mess. So much for trying to atone. "If they lock me up forever, will you make sure they find someone else to fill my spot? Another Human who'll fight?"

"Someone who'll fight like Nightmare, Martinez." The aging Arkouda winked as if she were a Human. "I'll get Joka to do it. She doesn't have the same problematic ties to Earthquake."

Amanda thanked her and left. A pair of staffers, both Arkoudae, followed her out. When they trailed her up the stairs and again banked left with her when she shifted toward the representatives' living quarters, Amanda turned on her heel to face them. "Enjoying the view?"

One of them, a first-year representative from a fringe colony, folded his arms over his chest. "No."

The second, another staffer, shook her head. "Do you think you can run away now? We have your omni-tablet. We know you're hiding something."

"I'm hiding my disdain for the system and the society that lets you think you can intimidate a government employee because she's a different species than you."

"Not a different species," the second one said. "That's not the problem. The problem is you're a terrorist."

"And one of the only people not attacked or even hurt during the attack," the first added.

"I saved Symphora's life. Doesn't that count?" She pointed at the younger one. "You probably had an action figure of her as a cub."

The staffer averted his eyes.

"I'll take that as a yes. So back off."

She turned her back to them, expecting them to either give up out of embarrassment or go right on following. What she didn't expect was an outright attack. She hadn't gone two steps before four huge arms trapped her in a vise. She tried to scream but fur filled her mouth and she coughed instead. Then darkness—they'd pulled a bag over her head. Her captor tossed her over his shoulder, wind knocked from her lungs so she could only wheeze for several minutes, though she tried in vain to writhe from his grip. She stopped struggling, letting her training kick in. Her breathing deepened and her heartbeat slowed as she counted turns. Three left. About five minutes apart. Elevator, ninety seconds. Straight ahead, sixty seconds. Right, left, right, stop.

Stupid Arkouda architecture and their hexagons. They could be in about ten different places.

The sack ripped off, revealing an area she hadn't seen before. The architecture of this new spot was even less welcoming to other species than the rest of the government offices. It lacked any climate control to the point where her breath fogged, and the doorknob didn't have any assisting mechanisms for Human operation.

The poorly lit room boasted a long table with a small chair on one end, the only Human-proportioned furniture in the room, and a single lamp. An Arkouda-sized chair sat near the wall, a two-way mirror behind it.

Gasping, Amanda inhaled noxious gas, and the world fuzzed over.

———

Exiting her stupor, minutes or days later, Amanda's tongue could've been sandpaper. Breathing deeply, she willed herself back into consciousness and lucidity.

She shouted into the darkness. "You have a holding cell specifically for Humans? You think your Sleeping Goddess would like this treatment? What happened to equality in the Collective? Want me to list the laws this violates?"

An Arkouda stepped into her periphery. She knew him. This sick bastard was on a committee with her. They'd shared lunch on breaks. He stared down his muzzle, grimacing. "Chairperson Martinez, you were seen shutting the door on your Arkouda bodyguard. Letting him die."

Amanda seethed. "Bugaro was a good man. When you rifled through my omni-tablet illegally, did you see the iceflowers I sent his granddaughter?"

"Hmpf." He folded his arms over his chest, looming over her. "You knew how those weapons would function."

"Of course I did," Amanda hissed. "Vids of Earthquake using those harpoon cannons are everywhere. It's disgusting what they do."

"You have a more intimate knowledge of their construction and engineering, don't you?"

She clenched a fist, only now realizing she was tied to the chair. No wonder they put her in a Human-sized one. "You're holding me illegally." Some of the bubbling anger was at herself. She had provided the cover of a homeless shelter while Rick's team developed that weapon in their basement. She may have been organizing the bread lines, but she knew full well what he'd been doing. Some of this blood was on her hands.

A tinny voice came over an unseen intercom. "Answer the question."

The representative snarled. "You managed the defector Rick Crith's team when he developed that. You funded the research and development."

"I also ran a homeless shelter for Humans who lost their livelihoods due to Collective oppression. You're skipping over important parts of my resumé." She carefully maneuvered her wrists, trying to look like she was stretching, so that she could push against the weak place in the design.

"You also seemed to know Symphora would be attacked."

"I didn't, actually." Amanda timed each scrape and shove against the cuffs to her words. "Earthquake gangsters are glory hounds. Killing Symphora would make someone a legend. It's sick. But I spooked the assassin and saved Symphora's life. Funny how I haven't heard a thank-you yet."

"The assassin was an associate, then?"

"No, but she looked familiar. I might have seen someone in her family." She slanted an eyebrow. "Maybe a family member lost their livelihood due to Collective oppression of Humans and came by my shelter."

The intercom voice chimed again. "We urge you to cooperate, Chairperson Martinez."

"And I urge you to stop breaking your own laws. Thank me for saving Symphora, release me, apologize for my treatment, then get the hell out of my way so I can help. *In that order.*" Amanda angled the cuffs against the chair back at their weak point. The Collective used low-tech confinement for the species they had a low opinion of. Rick had always said the Arkoudae's greatest weakness was underestimating Humans. She waited until her interrogator spoke again before her final push, so he wouldn't hear the *click*.

The representative scoffed. "You think you're in a position to make demands? The scan on your omni-tablet came back. You've been in contact with the defector."

The same defector who taught her how to escape half-assed captors like them.

"Yeah. After we *left* Earthquake, he was arrested and I continued my work with the homeless. Symphora heard about me leaving Tecton and believed in second chances. Rick left me a ping address, and I never believed he stayed in prison or died." Maybe this was too much information, but she needed to be honest about her past. "I learned about some of the atroci-ties he did in the field and grew so disgusted I never wanted to talk to him or see him again. I hated myself for thinking he was heroic once. But like him or hate him, he has the same goal as you. He's ashamed of his affiliation with Earthquake, *just like I am*. He also knows about this teleportation trick they pulled. If you want someone to find and destroy Earthquake once and for all, it's him."

The tinny voice returned. "We're conducting a search of your offices to corroborate your story."

"While government officials die on medical cots? Give me the tools I need, and I can find Earthquake's new base. Rick and I know where their hideouts used to be. I gave you names and locations of all of them, and I know they haven't all been checked. We're the ones you want on your side, not detained and humiliated."

A second click of the cuffs—she was almost ready.

The intercom buzzed, but instead of the tinny voice, an echoing bang came through the speakers, followed by a Human female's voice. "You better step the heck away from that speaker, butt sniffer."

Amanda had heard that voice before.

The Arkouda representative glared at Amanda. "Innocent, huh?" He lunged at her, and Amanda, now free of her cuffs, sidestepped, letting him thud to the floor.

"It was an illegal detention, so I'm not bound to stay put."

He pushed himself up from the floor and snarled. "You'll go away to prison forever." The representative scrambled to his feet and swiped at Amanda, who ducked. This guy wasn't a fighter. Amanda could recognize the type since she wasn't one herself. But she had been trained by one.

As he reared his paw back for another strike, Amanda thumbed her grav harness and increased the setting. Her organs tightened under her increasing mass, and she shot her hands up to catch him by the wrist. Letting her added mass be a fulcrum, she spun him over herself.

"There's a Human saying about how big people fall hard." She fixed her gravity setting and her organs unclenched, sending a stream of acid up her throat, which she spat onto the floor beside him. "Human food is spicy, so have fun smelling that."

The door burst open, and a female Arkouda and Lo-sat rushed inside, sporting the rugged light armor and mohawked helmet of the Symphora Squad. A short Human woman wedged between them, wearing civilian clothes.

Amanda hadn't seen her in person since the awards ceremony. "Joka Bunear. Symphora said she'd ping you."

"And you must be the legendary Amanda Martinez. Pleased as heck to meet you. I really liked your speech last year. Symphora told me you were in deep doo."

"I was about to say the same thing to you." They shook hands in the traditional Human style, earning a nod from the Lo-sat in the room.

The Arkouda flanking Joka wiggled an ear. "Madam Martinez, we came the second we heard about the attack. The military is too far out for a response. We tried tending to Symphora, but she shouted at us to come get you instead."

Joka grinned. "Shouted and made some donations to my swear jar."

They stepped outside and shut the door.

"Thank you," Amanda said. "Earthquake could attack again at any moment. We need to get Symphora off this station because if they kill her, it will be the biggest possible symbolic victory they could have. How many fighting ships are with you?" She didn't want to mention that she couldn't risk losing her biggest supporter, either.

"We have enough ships to kick some tail," the Lo-sat hissed. "Not enough to defend long term."

Joka gestured toward Amanda. "What do you know about Earthquake's plans?"

"Only what I can infer. I have some hunches where Earthquake's base might be. Can the Symphora Squad keep the station safe until I look into it?" She shifted her gaze upward to the other members. "And when I find their headquarters, do you want to take it by storm and undo it at the source?"

"How will you find it?" Joka asked.

"I have some ideas. But look, no matter where you take Symphora, she won't be safe. You need to put her somewhere nobody will expect to find her. She's also proof that Arkoudae can work with Humans, and they don't all hate us. If she's killed by a Human, even a terrorist who doesn't represent all of us, it'll undo all the good we've done for Humanity."

Joka sighed. "She can't go to my shelter, then. Or back with the Squad. If she's in one spot long enough, then someone will figure it out and attack."

Amanda straightened. "Then we don't keep her in one spot. You used a medical ship to get here, yes? You'll fly the ship while Symphora heals, and together, we'll check out the possible Earthquake hideouts."

Joka eyed her. "Symphora vouched for you, but I don't have a good track record with partners." Her gaze drifted to a pouch on her belt. "My last one died."

"And I followed mine down a bad path. I don't want to force you, but we're all running out of time."

After a deep breath, Joka extended her hand again. "I have a swear jar. Every credit funds the women's shelter. No exceptions."

Amanda accepted the handshake. "Understood. If we're traveling with an injured Symphora, you'll be able to buy a new swimming pool." The two Squad members chuckled and bumped claws to paws.

"One more thing," Joka said. She nodded to the Lo-sat, who reached into a compartment on her armor. "We retrieved your omni-tablet."

TEN

(ROSANNA)

**The Bastion. Secure location,
hidden from the weak**

ROSANNA HADN'T STABBED and stolen her way to the top for this kind of treatment.

They weren't supposed to call it a throne room, yet the high-backed chair, the long desk, and wide window yawning onto the dark rocky landscape of the asteroid made Jacques Tecton's office seem like a regal auditorium. Neptune's light washed over him like the praise of his sycophants. He didn't face Rosanna on the other side of his desk, instead standing at the window and meeting her gaze in the reflection.

"I did what you asked, sir." Rosanna tried to keep her tone even in front of the boss. "You said you'd tell me."

"*If* you were successful." His Earther accent raised goosebumps on her arms. That was how Humans were supposed to sound, rounder and softer than her staccato Provincial speech. Uncouth. Backwater. "Symphora is alive. You couldn't kill an old woman."

Rosanna debated reminding him that she was picked for the mission because nobody else wanted to go a round against Symphora. "I was ambushed by Martinez who was supposed to be captured. That wasn't in the parameters."

"You should've put a bullet between her eyes."

Rosanna fought the urge to slump her shoulders. "The objectives were clear. Martinez disappears so she is implicated. I wasn't about to make her a martyr."

A smirk twisted through his jowls. "That's your excuse for letting Symphora beat you?"

For a ghost of a second, she thought she understood why the bastard Crith left Tecton, but she banished the idea. "I kicked her ass. I was inches from killing her."

"A geriatric politician past her prime." He ran a hand through quaffed regulation-violating hair. "You must be so proud."

"I put her in a medbay for the whole galaxy to see—she'll never live down the shame. Now tell me the rest. You promised."

He held up a finger, waving it like a metronome at her reflection. "You get what you want when you get me what I want. You didn't kill Symphora, and you were spotted abducting the freak."

"You didn't tell me the hybrid was so young."

"Even less of an excuse for your fuck up."

Rosanna wondered why he hadn't brought up her breadcrumbs to ensnare Crith. "So what'll it take for you to tell me what happened with my brother?"

"You can teleport with my artifacts, but can you travel through time and un-botch your missions?"

She wanted to do better, let him see how good she was. "*I* led the team that stole those artifacts. I found the stupid archaeologist and her assistant. I pulled the secrets out of them. I'll get more if you let me down to the cell block."

"With your parade of errors recently, I'd rather not." Tecton took his seat but didn't spin to face her. "You want the rest of your story? Bring Crith to me."

So he was paying attention to her other project. "I've figured out his pattern. I'm ready to catch him."

"Oh, I know you *think* you have," Tecton said. A galaxy's worth of implications lay between his words.

Air tightening in her lungs, Rosanna leaned forward onto his desk, gripping the edge. "Do you know how to draw him out?"

"You had the answer right in front of you and you let her go. Find Martinez and threaten her. She and Crith have a history."

Rosanna cocked an eyebrow. "But we need her alive. Once this is blamed on her, people will flock to us. It'll be final proof of the system's failure."

Tecton tapped a button on his desk and faced her. "When you find her, put out a public broadcast that you're waiting for Crith to show up and save her. Stun him from a long distance when he does. Then kill her." He spoke with the same casual indifference one would use to order food. "Or better yet, kill her and broadcast that—you're so desperate for stories about your brother, there you go. He's the one who told me they were close a couple years ago. So yeah, kill Martinez and then Rick will come at you even more angry and will screw up. You're used to that, right? Getting sloppy on what should be an easy mission?"

"I won't get sloppy against him." As if fighting Symphora and kidnapping the hybrid were simple. "Crith killed Alejandro." Rosanna's eye twitched. "I want to watch his face as I make him say his name."

Tecton scoffed. "If you kill him up close, I won't tell you the rest of what happened."

All those years ago when Crith visited their family to inform her parents of her brother's death, he'd said that her brother was killed in action and not much else. The full details of Alejandro Moreno's death were being concealed from her. She would rip open Hell to get the truth and send as many people there as she needed to. Doing so had gotten her very far in the organization, especially with springing Tecton from prison.

Her Leader had it. Rick Crith had it. Maybe Amanda Martinez had some of it. Maybe the archaeologist chained in the basement had some of it, too.

She'd have to cause more havoc to bring the truth out.

"Is this my next mission, then? Lure Crith out of hiding?"

"No. I need you to hit the government offices again first. Then stun or incapacitate Crith from far away and bring him here. Dismissed."

Nostrils flared, Rosanna stormed from the room, glaring at the server 'bot as it closed the door behind her. That luxury proved he'd gone a long way from that prison cell last year since now he lived like a Collective elite on a posh moon of Arko.

Rosanna had one more stop to make before she would prep her team for that mission.

She trudged into the elevator and monitored her reflection in the metal as the lift descended. Even though she trusted her Leader, she wanted to get Crith now.

Rick Crith had murdered her brother and lied to her face. A twitch in his lower eyelid, his words coming too quickly together, and his inability to hold extended eye contact gave him away, not to mention the handful of questions their mom asked which he answered with, "That's classified, ma'am." A military commander would have had practice visiting grieving families.

Their parents believed him because they'd wanted something to latch onto—believing their son died for a worthy cause. Something happened on that uncharted moon that Rick wouldn't say, but she'd rip the truth from his throat if necessary, not in the death-from-afar manner Tecton suggested. Rosanna imagined all the ways she could wring the truth from Crith. Torturing Amanda Martinez in front of him would do it for sure.

But maybe the archaeologist was a better place to start until she got better intel on Martinez. She didn't have to get Martinez in this moment—hell, she may have wised up and abandoned the government offices anyway.

Rosanna punched the special elevator code to arrive at the third sub-basement.

To Dr. Alize Oze's cell block.

Rosanna left the elevator and turned down the labyrinthine hallway, four and a half lefts before a third right to find her prisoner; the confusing layout made for an extra layer of defense against prisoner extraction.

A gentle hum welcomed her as she arrived at the gap in the wall where the thirty-something year old archaeologist sat. Dr. Oze was Alejandro's age. Or at least the age he was supposed to be.

Alize peered at Rosanna through the green particle partition keeping her in place. She sat upright and tucked a lock of frizzy dyed pink hair behind her ear. "Little Rose. Been a long few days without you. Or weeks, it's hard to tell." Her lunar accent made Rosanna want to spit. Bumpkin.

Rosanna patted the holstered pistol at her waist. "Call me that again and see what happens."

Alize waved a finger, displaying the purple scabs over the tip where her fingernail used to be. "Sorry, it gets lonely between our torture sessions. I thought when you pulled my fingernails off to get the teleportation trick out of me, you'd leave me alone."

"You're pretty smug." Rosanna calculated what game Oze might be playing.

"Of course, I figured since that nice Jimmy boy gave me food that you, or at least your boss, hadn't really forgotten about me. He even tightened the screws on my prosthetic." She tapped on her cybernetic leg.

"Jimmy?"

"The guard. You know, I never liked Rick Crith, but he taught me the importance of learning everyone's names." Her eyebrows angled and her tone darkened. "Speaking of which, did you ever learn the name of my research assistant before you executed her? Or was she beneath you because she was a Makawe?"

"What else do you know about Crith?" Rosanna picked at the dirt under her fingernails. She could play this game, too.

"Not going to dignify cold-blooded murder with a response, huh?" Alize folded her arms and scoffed. "Isn't Rick Crith dead? I'd prefer some wine if we're going to talk about him, though. That's why you came, isn't it? It's definitely not to apologize for killing my friend."

That Makawe divulged everything she knew, and Alize offered extra information when Rosanna shattered the Makawe's carapace in front of her. Oze had desperately scrambled for the fragments on the floor. The carapace from a dead Makawe was too brittle, and the piece was too small for Alize to turn it into something dangerous or useful, and it would be something Rosanna could take from her later.

"I'm not here about the Chamayna chitin," Rosanna said. "Unless you have more to say. But there was a member of Rick's crew when he nabbed you on that moon." Rosanna steadied herself. "Alejandro Moreno."

"There are a lot of things that happened on that moon I'd rather not discuss or remember. I regret naming the moon 'I Told You So,' for one." The calm in the archaeologist's voice suggested their game wasn't over.

"Try again."

Alize shook her head. "You broke me before, but I've had time to stick myself back together. I don't even want to know how many deaths are on my hands since we let that out. Go ahead and torture me again, but you're wasting your time." A calm acceptance shone in her eyes. "I would honestly rather die than help you."

Rosanna scowled. "Filenada Kaluteros."

The archaeologist stiffened. "Keep that name out of your mouth." After a slow exhale, she added, "It's not like you have anything to threaten me with. She's gone, as is my only family."

A smirk crept across Rosanna's face, and she didn't bother hiding it this time. "She had family, though. A mother."

"You're bluffing."

"A sister."

Alize pursed her lips. "Most Arkoudae have those."

"And a nephew. His name is Io. I wrote down the name of his school, but I haven't memorized it."

Alize's eyes widened. "You touch a hair on his head and—"

"And you'll cooperate," Rosanna finished. "You tell me everything that happened on that stupid moon. What did you see down there?"

Alize's face sank, cratering like the surface of the asteroid. Alize was studying Rosanna, and she hated it. "You've been using the chitin to teleport, haven't you? It's been observing you, hasn't it?"

"Don't change the subject." This wasn't how the game was supposed to go. Rosanna got flashes of the images from her last teleports. Those unseen eyes evaluating her. "I'm asking the questions."

"That's a yes. The Chamayna weren't using their own power. They were using something else. Something alive. Primal." Alize's face darkened. "You're using its power, Rosanna. Telling it where you are. You're lighting a beacon to it. It's coming for you."

Goosebumps rose on Rosanna's flesh. This wasn't a game anymore. "I'll make sure Io suffers." She'd gone from abducting a teenager to threatening a child in the same day. Rosanna pushed the thought from her mind and focused on Oze.

Alize exhaled and squared her jaw. "You'll think I'm being difficult, but I really can't say it."

"You don't have a name for this vague creature you're trying to scare me with?"

"I don't. But it'll flatten this tower if you keep teleporting. It's what destroyed the Chamayna eons ago." Her eyes widened and each subsequent syllable dripped from her lips like venom. "There just aren't words for it. I *can't* tell you. The full truth is unspeakable."

ELEVEN

(MAYNARD)

Bolivar City, New Lodestone, Boudica System

LIKE A PRAYER angled to heaven, New Lodestone's space elevator pierced the sky, reaching its zenith in low orbit. Only having one elevator marked this planet's poverty and struggle since earning independence. Glimmering dots in the distance, closer than the stars, marked the Collective's ever-watchful eyes on the one free Human settlement.

Construction crews hammered and grunted, retrofitting the concourse to make it more Human-friendly than its original design intended.

Brother Maynard of the Great Mystery Monks rose from his meditation posture in the Bolivar City elevator concourse.

The civilian cargo craft he waited for was docking, and he didn't want to miss his friend. His colleagues at the monastery may have raised their eyebrows at his flimsy story of receiving interplanetary dignitaries as a sign of respect, but no one directly told him that leaving the monastery to visit a friend was breaking their vow of non-attachment. Being in charge had its perks.

A civilian cargo craft disembarked, leaving its passengers to make port. A trickle of other Humans filed out, followed by a lone Lo-sat: Binh Ten-trom. He was walking proof of Mui-xe's miraculous gift of healing. This Lo-sat once suffered from a genetic scales condition yet now sported a healthy verdant sheen.

Upon spying Brother Maynard standing in the concourse, a grin curled up Binh's snout. "Hey, it's the Human with a reasonable haircut. How're you doing?"

Maynard chuckled, rubbing his bald head and making a squeaking sound. "I'm well. Our mutual interest has inquired about you." They embraced; Maynard's head only came halfway up his chest.

"Mutual interest?" his friend scoffed. "So that's what you're calling him now, huh? Didja get me that hot sauce?"

"Of course." They headed toward the elevator proper to return to the surface, and Maynard reached into his cloak, pulling out a tiny bottle. "Imported from Earth. One of the refugees who came last week didn't have any money to offer our begging bowls, so offered this. I saved it for you."

Binh Ten-trom, reformed thief and terrorist, accepted the offering with his tail. He placed it in a pouch affixed to his belt and traded it for a small vial of purple medicine, which he downed. "Planet Magnet Torture, do your worst."

"I wish I could do something about the planet's magnetosphere for you. I hope that helps dull your sensitivity." When the bustle around them in the spaceport grew loud enough to overpower their conversation, Maynard spoke again. "How is his grandmother?"

"Scary and weirdly sexy. She demanded I bring her the kid again. If he's going through puberty like you say, he might need Lo-sat company for awhile." Binh's tone softened. "We can probably sneak him there. They deserve to meet after everything he's been through."

"Do you think it's safe?" Maynard waved Binh to the desk.

"Is anything?" They checked into the descending car for the surface. "Has anything interesting happened at the monastery? More sitting around, I bet."

"We spend most of our time helping the refugees on the surface." Maynard nudged Binh with his elbow. "Others of us are doomed to welcome vagabonds and freeloaders."

"Ooh, I'll need some salve for that burn." Binh stretched his neck but had to snap it back after bonking it against the ceiling.

Maynard smiled wider than usual. "You better not teach Mui-xe any more Lo-sat curses. He is still a growing boy and very impressionable."

"Which is more proof he needs to be with his other people. He's two species, Maynard. He can't just be around you."

"Earthquake might find him. Or the Collective." They wedged between a mass of Humans. A PA chimed, followed by an announcement to notify them of the shifting gravity as they approached the atmosphere. "I don't know which is worse."

"They're both worse."

Maynard sighed and cast an eye at the octagonal observation window.

Children and the elderly huddled around it for the most unobstructed views. Maynard and Binh had done this enough times, yet the dancing maroons and pinks of the cloud layer always dazzled. Bolivar City yawned below them, expanded after New Lodestone earned recognition as a free Human planet, legally outside Collective jurisdiction and fully autonomous. Refugees from the conflict with Earthquake fled here as well as immigrants searching for a new life. The planet constituted a perfect new beginning, precisely what the Great Mystery religion preached. In the distance, past the forest thick with brickbark trees, their monastery poked through the canopy, the fingertips of the architectural design.

Maynard thought he caught a glimpse of a flashing light stab through the monastery, but at this distance, it could've been an optical illusion. Still, he fumbled for his omni-tablet—something wasn't right.

"Monks are allowed to have those?" Binh asked, eyeridge arched. "Are you checking the hive-ball scores?"

"It's never funny when you ask that." Maynard huffed as he turned it on, and the device booted.

"Which reminds me of how you're never funny in the first place."

"Wait, you turn it off, you monster? That's more upsetting than you having one."

Maynard sighed. "I won't use something I don't need in the moment. Doing so inflates the ego and deprives others."

"I bet the parties at the monastery are a blast. It's not like you're getting many notifications, anyway." Binh switched to a caricature of a Human-sounding accent. "Come quick, boss. We're still boring."

Maynard waved his free hand over his omni-tablet. "For your information, I received a ping." His eyes widened at the message, and his throat tightened. "We'll talk in the autocab. Something is wrong."

A trickle of passengers filed between them.

Binh's neck frills vibrated. "You're not messing with me?"

"Not about this."

———

Customs and decontamination behind them, Maynard and Binh finally settled inside an autocab on the surface. Brother Maynard punched in the monastery's coordinates, then opened another program on his omni-tablet and typed a series of commands.

To fit in the Human-sized space, Binh wrapped his tail and arms around his knees and arched his neck down. "What're you doing?"

Maynard raised a finger until he finished the program. A blinking white light inside the autocab near the roof darkened. All other functions resumed, and the cab sped toward their destination, winding through Bolivar City's streets.

Maynard stowed his omni-tablet. "After my brother's issue with being recorded and monitored, I've taken steps to make sure I can't be when I discuss Mui-xe."

Binh nodded—he'd spent a few hours with Ned before his untimely death at the paws of a mad scientist, eventually bringing Mui-xe into Maynard's care.

"The ping I got from the monastery..." Maynard pinched the bridge of his nose. "Mui-xe attacked and killed somebody. Then he *disappeared*. Nobody can find him."

"Attacked?" Binh asked.

"And killed. Could hyper-aggression be a result of puberty? Do Lo-sat adolescents get hostile?"

"Only around the right scent, and it's not like another one of my kin would've been hanging around to get those pheromones cooking."

Maynard inhaled as much calm as he could, resisting the image of Mui-xe attacking anyone, let alone killing. "You and Joka Bunear both said you encountered other hybrids in the scientist's lab. I know they were imperfect attempts to replicate him but," Maynard winced, "I haven't broached the topic with Mui-xe, but is it possible he might ... decompose into one?"

Binh pulled his limbs tighter to his torso. "Those husks were lifeless. Nothing to joke about with them. You know those harpoon cannons Earthquake uses to bust Collective armor? Barely tickled them. They were made with the same material as Mui-xe, but that scientist didn't get your brother's recipe quite right because those things were not as resilient as Mui-xe. Or he messed with it on purpose because he wanted something more expendable. Those other hybrids were made by fusing two living or already-dead people together, not from cellular fusion."

Maynard nodded, fighting a losing battle against anxiety. "So that won't happen to him?"

"The ones who knew carried that secret to the grave. But you didn't see their eyes."

"I suppose it's a relief, then, but that doesn't solve the accusations." Anger bubbled inside Maynard, threatening to break through the surface. "Some of our brothers in the monastery are less than tolerant of Mui-xe. Perhaps this was an elaborate setup." He winced. "Which would be quite the violation of our oaths."

Binh's neck frills extended. "Maybe one of your so-called brothers provoked him and had it coming."

"Mui-xe isn't a murderer," Maynard said with more ice in his voice than he intended.

"Maybe not." Binh shifted his body, released a spindly leg, and stretched it, rotating his foot at the ankle. "But he is a pubescent teenager. His hormones are outta control, maybe more than they would be for a Human or Lo-sat at his stage of development." He lowered his eyeridges and stared out the window. "Maybe the kid doesn't know his strength. And maybe the only people who really could know are dead."

The reminder of Maynard's late brother and sister-in-law stung but not as much as the truth. Much of Mui-xe's biology would remain a mystery.

Outside, Bolivar's buildings gave way to patches of blue-tinted grass and looming red brickbark trees.

"We need to investigate. Without knowing what happened, we'll never guess where he disappeared to. The way the ping described it sounds like he just blinked out of existence. That's ridiculous of course, but the fact that he got out unseen makes it a lot harder to find him."

Binh remained quiet for a pregnant moment. "Do you know that person Joka Bunear made me apologize to?"

"The archaeologist? Dr. Oze?"

"Yeah," Binh sighed. "She knew how to disappear. Then reappear somewhere else. What if she's not the only one who can?"

————

Aging Brother Talib opened the monastery door for them, bowing. Brother Maynard returned the gesture, stiffer and quicker than was exactly proper. Binh bowed without parody, which was new for him.

The halls teemed with too many monks. Brother Maynard's mind reeled from seeing so many at once outside of an official ritual. With so many volunteering the days away in Bolivar City, the exact number eluded him. A twinge of embarrassment poked at his neck; that was information he should've known off the top of his head. Yet he'd spent so many mental and emotional resources on Mui-xe, much of everything else fell through his mental cracks.

Yet here they were in this crowd of monks, many of whose gums flapped with rumors and accusations, none of which could be true, except one detail on everyone's lips: the art student. Maynard scrunched his brow at the mention. She wasn't supposed to arrive until tomorrow when he would've been there to oversee her visit and long after Binh departed. If that art student wasn't really a student, that might fill in the holes of this mystery.

He darted through the crowd, behavior unbecoming of an Abbot, but he didn't care. Binh followed, peppering him with questions, but Maynard's focus lay solely on arriving at the attack scene.

Approaching the dojo, the hanging open door greeted them.

Brother Rondo bowed. "Senior Brother Maynard, honored guest." He coughed, then tightened the scarf around his neck. The accessory was an accommodation Maynard allowed him to stay warm and fight his circulation issues—the only way Rondo stood out from the other monks.

Maynard accepted the greeting with a rushed bow. "Why aren't the authorities here?"

"Given the nature of Mui-xe's condition, I assumed you would want to handle things among ourselves. I went ahead and scheduled a hearing on your behalf." Rondo nodded. "Brother, are you sure our guest should be part of this investigation? Surely, we have some suitable accommodations where he could relax."

Binh snorted. "You're accusing the kid of murder, so I'll pass."

Brother Rondo fidgeted, appearing to suppress a scowl.

"Brother Rondo, has anyone else disturbed the area?" Maynard asked. "Anyone at all?"

"No. I was the first to arrive after I heard the junior monks shouting. Then I pinged you with the situation. The body is as it was when I found it."

"Thank you." Maynard turned to Binh. "Would you be able to smell a sign of struggle and decipher who was attacking?"

Binh nodded and entered the dojo, Maynard close behind. His eyes widened at the scene.

Webster—someone he trusted with his nephew's care—lay sprawled on the floor, lifeless. The self-defense instructor was among the few who treated Mui-xe as he was: one of their own.

Maynard clutched his erratic heart. He hadn't seen someone die in such a violent way since his childhood with Ned.

The sweatshop. The slavery. He blinked hard and remembered Symphora arriving that day all those years ago, guns blazing. She had enacted brutal justice. Maynard remembered cleaning their abuser's splattered blood off his shivering younger brother. He shook the memory away. He'd found peace with his past in the Great Mystery and triumphed over his trauma. Coming so close to a dead friend would not defeat him today.

Maynard stooped over what was once his friend, muttering the requisite prayers. Pain laced his words unlike all the times when he'd spoken them for aging monks or in the Bolivar City slums.

"May he find an answer to the Great Mystery in the next life. Rondo, we'll continue our investigation shortly. Please arrange for Brother Webster's cremation."

Rondo hesitated. "Shouldn't I watch the door?"

Binh sniffed hard and eyed him. "Is it part of your religion to talk back to your boss? Wish I would've known that years ago."

Maynard stiffened. "Binh, you must stop. Brother Rondo, do as you're told. We don't have time for arguments."

Rondo bowed and sidestepped from the doorway.

"Sorry," Binh whispered. "And I'm uh, I'm sorry about your friend."

Maynard forced himself to gaze at Webster's wound. Jagged claw marks sliced diagonally across his chest. Maynard grasped for the sense of calm he spent so long cultivating in meditation, but his pulse raced.

"If they were sparring, Mui-xe and Webster, it's inevitable that their scents would have rubbed off on each other, yes?"

"Yeah. And it wasn't just them in this room the last few hours. Scarf boy and a Human chick were in here, but not as long. Human chick had some exertion, but she could've been scared or something."

"Scarf boy?"

"Yeah, that other monk who was guarding the door. Wearing a scarf. None of your other bald clones wear one."

Maynard exhaled. "I appreciate your attempts at levity, Binh, but you need to take a break from them. Brother Rondo is sickly and gets cold. I've allowed him to break our uniform. But tell me more about the woman."

"She was sweating. And agitated. I've been around enough Humans to know she was not on the defensive based on this smell."

Maynard peered at the claw marks again—they looked so clean. "Can you tell where she went?"

"Nope. Everyone's saying she disappeared and dis-a-smelled."

"Dis-a-smelled?"

"Your language sucks, what do you want from me? Her scent is lingering here, but it's not *going* anywhere."

"That lends credence to the blinking out of existence statement." Maynard hunched over Brother Webster's corpse again. "Would the stench be overwhelming if you smelled the corpse directly?"

Binh gazed at the floor and cleared his throat. "Yeah, but I'll use this as an excuse for an inappropriate comment later. Is there something specific you want to know?"

"If his injuries have Mui-xe's scent."

Binh crouched over the corpse, and with more reverence than Maynard had come to expect, Binh peeled back the tattered robe and inhaled.

He cocked an eyeridge. "The wound doesn't have a special scent."

"Excuse me?"

"If Mui-xe had raked him, there would be traces of his skin or scales. Little bits of dirt or skin oils that would get stuck on stuff. There's nothing. This was done by some kind of metal alloy."

"So Mui-xe was framed, then? Someone knew how to make a cut to give the appearance of Mui-xe's hands."

"Claws."

"Ha—" Maynard inhaled. "Is there anything else peculiar?"

"Besides this entire situation? I'm getting plasma scorching—" He arched an eyeridge and his tail coiled. He stooped over Webster's arm. "He was shot. Right here." Binh pointed to a precise hole in Webster's sleeve. "Look at that hole. Someone had a plasma pistol."

"Mui-xe wouldn't use a gun."

"And I'm assuming you don't allow guns here?"

"No. A monk possessing or using one is a stretch. But a silenced pistol would explain why nobody heard a gunshot." A few monks were reformed members of Earthquake, but they'd sold any weapons for scrap and given the money to the refugees along with any other possessions. "It must've been that art student, whoever she was."

"She wasn't a Collective agent. They don't need to sneak around, and they wouldn't trust a dirty Human with teleportation tech." Binh stood. "Earthquake would pull this garbage, though. Infiltrate somewhere, feigning innocence. Stirring up some *nguc* and blaming it on another species."

"So Earthquake can teleport, then. Do you think they got that technique from Dr. Alize Oze?"

Binh shuddered. "That's worse than bad. They could be anywhere in the galaxy."

"So this woman killed Brother Webster, framed Mui-xe, and is hiding at an unknown location, search parameters being the entire galaxy?" Maynard exhaled. "Do you still have the ping address for Joka Bunear?"

Footsteps thundered from behind them. "There they are," Brother Rondo said.

A crowd of senior monks had formed around him, encircling Maynard and Binh.

"Brother Maynard, the rest of the leadership committee has learned about your cover-up of Mui-xe's connection to you." Rondo pointed an accusatory finger at Maynard.

An aging monk nodded gravely. "Brother Webster's death is on your hands. You knew full well how dangerous Mui-xe was."

Maynard straightened. "This is preposterous."

Binh's neck frills extended, and he whipped his tail behind him. "You've got a lot of nerve, Scarf Boy."

"Your hearing will be in the courtyard," Rondo said.

"No, it won't be." Dusting himself off, Maynard sighed. "Find a new Abbot. I'm finding my nephew."

TWELVE

(AMANDA)

In a government building, chased by official law enforcement because their priorities are in order

A BOLT OF plasma fire careened over Amanda's head, smacking the ceiling and burning a hole. Bits of plaster and metal shavings cascaded down in a smoky rain.

The two Symphora Squad members stepped in front of Amanda and Joka, rifles cocked. "You better hope that was a warning shot," the Lo-sat called.

"Stop!" cried an Arkouda. Amanda dimly recognized him as a representative.

The aggressor approached, and a compartment on the butt of his rifle unfolded, latching onto his arm. From there, the flexible gray material of military armor continued to unfold and spread over his body, going from civilian to soldier in seconds. "Quit running, Martinez."

Amanda eyed Joka. "Let's bolt."

"Hey Selbos," Joka whispered.

The Arkouda squad member peered down. "Yeah, boss?"

"Toss up an electrical shield. We're payin' a visit to Symphora and leaving. They won't shoot if she's with us."

Holding her ground, the Lo-sat grumbled. "You mean I can't shoot his dick off?"

"Calm down, Mel-za," Joka said. "And you owe the swear jar when we're safe."

Mel-za mumbled something in Lo-sat, too fast for Amanda to catch.

Joka smirked. "I know that phrase. Double donation."

Selbos tapped her armor, and a blue sphere of static ballooned out, covering the quartet. "Joka always hears the *ska*—doo-doo—you say." Her armor now fully protected them.

The representative at the other end of the hall shouted, "You can't initiate defensive procedures in a government building! It's against the law."

"So is shooting a representative!" Amanda called back, remembering how just a few years ago, they would've been well within their rights to shoot her. She nodded to Joka. "Let's go. Do you know how to find Symphora?"

"Mel-za can sniff her out," Joka replied.

As the group turned down the hall, Mel-za thumbed her snout. "Humans never think about smell.

We followed your trail. Be glad you were nervous the whole time. Mix that with your floral soap, and it was barely a search."

With Selbos and Mel-za jogging, Amanda and Joka ran to keep up. They passed a bunch of officials who dodged out of the way or else took aim—but upon seeing Symphora Squad members, they invariably lowered their weapons. Out of fear or respect, Amanda didn't know.

Gasping for breath, Amanda wondered if Earthquake could've ever achieved their status. They'd twisted enough times to land them in an office area she recognized again; Bugaro's blood stain was nearby. She couldn't bring herself to look. Amanda wondered how many other kind people with grand-cubs had been killed by Earthquake over the years. Maybe this attack really was her fault.

Selbos tapped her armor and deactivated her shield. "I need to save the charge on my armor. It'll shut off life support if I don't."

Mel-za tutted. "I'll turn mine on. It's not as strong as yours, but it'll last to the medbay."

"Don't," Amanda said. "There are injured people in the medbay; we can't risk rogue static from your shield frying some life support machines."

"Those are people who won't hesitate to arrest you," Joka said.

Amanda fought the urge to reply with how she might deserve arrest for the things she'd done with Earthquake or even the petty crimes so she could get food for her and her aunt as a kid. "Yeah. People with constituents who think like them. I'm going to change their minds."

They rounded a corner, facing the medbay, and five fully-armored Collective soldiers blocked the doorway.

Mel-za hissed. "Five against four. Not the worst odds."

Bugaro flashed in Amanda's mind. She wasn't about to fight anyone else today. She wedged between Mel-za and Selbos, eyeing the middle soldier sporting the additional rank stripe. "We're here to extract Symphora Ianna. This facility isn't safe for her."

Joka stepped forward. "I have a statement from her on my omni-tablet." She withdrew her device and scrolled to a message. A soldier squinted at it, shrugging at the commander.

The commander peered down at Amanda. "You're the woman I'm supposed to arrest."

Nervous sweat beaded on Amanda's neck, blending with the running sweat, and she hated how these other species could smell it on her. With a deep breath, she straightened her jaw and glared. "Then you're the guy who will have Symphora's death on his conscience." As Amanda's words reverberated in the cramped hallway, Selbos made an "oooh" noise and covered her muzzle. Normally, she would've spun around for a fist bump but instead pressed her verbal assault. "Do you want Symphora's death on your conscience? Or do you want to prove our *mutual* enemy correct that you think all Humans are terrorists?"

The commander peered at the two flanking soldiers, and Mel-za tightened her grip on her gun.

Joka tsked. "This is ridiculous." She leaned over, head facing the gap between the soldiers and shouted into the medbay. "Hey, Symphora! Wanna go home?"

A garbled growl responded from the other side.

Joka locked eyes with the commander but continued shouting. "Well, Lieutenant," her eyes strayed to the commander's insignia, "*Vara* is blocking our way. What's Vara short for? Naivara?"

Mel-za chuckled. "Symphora! It's Mel-za! Remember you said we could arm wrestle if I ever did you a favor?"

The muffled growl from inside the medbay grew louder.

Amanda folded her arms over her chest and stared the commander down. "I'm taking her, I'm bringing Earthquake down, and you'll be the guy who helped me or the obstacle. What'll it be?" Her fingers itched for a weapon, but she refused to repeat Rick's mistakes. "You smelled my pheromones and sweat coming down this hallway. You trained in interrogation and know how Humans smell when we're lying." She rubbed the back of her neck and waved her fingers in front of her face. "I know you have orders, and you'll get in trouble, but you have to understand that Earthquake will return and finish the job. This station is not safe as long as she's here. Am I lying?"

The commander's stare faltered. He blinked hard and averted his eyes. "Take her somewhere safe." He huffed and waved his comrades away. "Let them go."

"Thank you." Amanda exhaled her anxiety. "Got any cubs at home? We'll ask her to autograph a photo."

As Amanda and the others passed, the lieutenant whispered, "My daughter. Her name is Thorra. Thanks."

The crowd inside the medbay parted for Amanda's group like the sea in a prehistoric Earth story her aunt once told her.

Symphora struggled to sit upright on her cot, but seeing the approaching members of her eponymous squad brought a smile to her bedraggled face. "I don't suppose any of you scrubs brought momma a beer? Someone get my hairy ass onto a hover-gurney."

Watching the legend huff and puff as her squad shifted her to a gurney, Amanda's own smile faded. They'd get Symphora to Joka's ship, but then what? What if by removing her from a vulnerable position, they were also removing her from the medical care that she needed? Amanda shoved the thought aside. If Symphora stayed here, she was a sitting duck. At least on the move, she had a chance of survival. Maybe keeping Symphora alive would finally allow Amanda to earn that trust she definitely lacked.

THIRTEEN

(RICK)

**The remains of a fuel depot
in the Collective Fringe**

FIRE-EXTINGUISHING CHEMICAL STINK lingered in the stripped-bare fuel depot. Rick wondered what level of torture that stench must be for the Arkouda proprietor and if the solvents in the air would damage P'oki's ship if they stayed much longer. He hated making detours, but after a week in space, the two of them needed to refuel, and Rick wasn't about to let this old-timer do all the repairs by himself. There were too many broken lights for Rick's taste. He never would've let exposed wires fly back when he ran a barracks, and he wasn't about to let this man suffer.

From two meters below, the aging Arkouda called to Rick. "Just a little to your left. That ladder is replaceable."

With a grunt, Rick stuck a bent beam into place while P'oki braced the ladder. It wouldn't erase the destruction from the attack on this place, but this would restore enough power for the owner to resume business. Rick's image inducer was concealing his identity, casting an illusion of another face and an extra arm.

"You said we'd hurry," P'oki whispered from the bottom of the ladder. "Spirits around your liar device say it's losing charge."

"I did say that." Rick huffed. "We won't be long. Just enough that the old timer doesn't have to do it himself." He rubbed the repair nanites along the scorched side of the beam, getting into a crevice an Arkouda's paw could never reach. A hum cajoled the microscopic machines into action.

P'oki released one pincer from the ladder and pointed toward the exposed circuitry by the overhead light. "How many more stops will we make? Too many and our people die, Rix."

"Thanks, sonny," the owner called. "I never would've gotten in there myself."

"You're welcome." Rick popped his screwdriver into his mouth and descended the ladder, careful to move both shoulders to give the illusion of him using both arms, made more difficult by the Arkouda-sized spaces between the ladder rungs.

"You have undecided spirits," P'oki whispered. "I don't like that."

"Me, neither. But we might fail. I have to undo at least some of Earthquake's damage."

The depot owner, an aging Arkouda, limped beside them, supported by a cane. "Goddess bless you both. I don't know why they attacked me. I always gave a fair price to Humans."

At the bottom rung, Rick hopped off the ladder and grabbed his screwdriver. "Some people don't need a reason, I'm afraid." He arched an eyebrow. "Did you happen to turn on tracking software? In order to notify the fleet about the attack and where they went after?"

"Ha. The fleet wouldn't come out here. I stopped contracting with the military after they attacked Symphora two years ago."

P'oki skittered to the left, and a glint of the dim overhead lights reflected off her carapace. "Sym'fra live as refugee. Then she came out of hiding and works for government now."

The Arkouda leaned heavily on his cane. "You don't say? Well, I never was one for keeping up with current events." Old Timer shrugged. "Too much to monitor. I check the hiveball scores and not much else."

Rick grinned. "What's your favorite team?"

P'oki trilled disapproval at the question; Rick didn't need to see anything mystical to know she must have what she'd call "disapproving spirits."

"The Mazrah Royal Strikers," the Arkouda said with a smile that suggested he may have forgotten for a second that he was all alone in the galaxy. "As if there's any other team worth following."

"Respectable," Rick hedged. "My favorite's always been Ezlin Claws." Rick remembered a time when he could follow professional sports, before his quest for

Human independence blinded him to everything else. The last time he'd tried to watch a hiveball game was when he got that Earthquake tablet from Dion. Those messages it allowed him to intercept brought him here instead of the technically closer fuel spots they could have chosen.

"You must hate winning if you back the Claws." Old Timer released a paw from his cane and wagged it.

P'oki tapped her pincer on the floor and swiveled an eyestalk toward Rick's true wrist, reminding him of the illusion and his dwindling time before his face was revealed.

"I like an underdog." Rick eyed P'oki. "We really need to head out, though."

A weak grin creased Old Timer's muzzle. "You sure there's nothing I can do for you? Food or a place to rest?" His tone wilted. "The beds I have were my grandcubs', so you'd fit."

With more vigor, P'oki tapped both pincers against the floor, letting an echo bounce around the room. "Earth'quake stole two of our people. We are finding them to bring them home. We don't have resting time."

"Can you tell us anything about where Earthquake went or came from?" Rick asked. The repair nanites had skittered to the next piece of damaged metal behind him, squeaking as they plodded.

The Arkouda gripped his cane tight. "Please, I don't want to think about that day anymore."

P'oki averted all of her eyes, and Rick shook his head. "I understand. But anything you can tell us will help. Even a general direction would be useful for either coming or going. You don't have any security footage?"

The Arkouda huffed, surveying the few things Rick and P'oki repaired. It wouldn't recreate his financial independence immediately, and it definitely wouldn't resurrect the family and employees Earthquake stole from him, but it was an honest start.

After a thick exhale, he met Rick's gaze. Age slumped him enough that he barely looked down to him. "They stole every drop of fuel I had. Made me watch while they killed my sons and grandcubs. I don't have much in the way of security, but I can show you their landing and takeoff. Why would you want to go after them?"

"Earthquake took everything from her, too." Rick indicated P'oki. "And it's time I gave something back to them."

——————

Having disengaged his image inducer, Rick crouched in P'oki's scrapper ship. "I'm still surprised I can even fit in here."

P'oki swiveled an eyestalk back to him. "Makawe roll by shell sometimes. We need enough room to flip shells up. Too cramped with a low ceiling, and we might forget the sky-mother." Her inflection trembled on the last word. She swirled her eyestalk away. "Sorry."

He shut his eyes and pinched the bridge of his nose. "I never had children, so I can't imagine what you're going through. It makes sense that even saying the word 'mother' would be a challenge."

"Saying anything in Ar'kouday is challenge."

They shared an awkward chuckle as the scrapper lurched out of the fuel depot's air bubble.

P'oki shifted, and her carapace caught a glint of the overhead light. "I see empathy and confusion spirits around you. If you never had children, did you ever have a student, Rix?"

He pulled his gaze from the swirling space displayed on the viewscreen, cocking an eyebrow at her. "Not formally."

"But you taught people. In Earth'quake. One is missing, and you grieve, too."

Rick sighed. This woman was grieving her missing daughter and wanted to help Rick express his own emotions. "Thank you, I guess. Nobody went missing in the traditional sense."

"Spiritlost is worse than maplost." She was better than Rick's last therapist, for sure.

One image came to mind. A face he wished he could forget: Alejandro Moreno.

The young man Rick hand-picked as his second-in-command shortly after earning his own crew. So much potential was in Alejandro, but Tecton's rhetoric warped him. It became more about the violence and xenophobia than liberating Humankind. Years ago, he mutinied against Rick on Alize Oze's damn moon, forcing Rick to put a plasma bullet inside him. Some part of Rick wished the Unspeakable had gotten to Alejandro instead of him. It tore his heart out to kill him, and the scene made common resurgences in his nightmares.

"Rix?"

He exhaled with a shiver. "Spiritlost is a good word."

"Ar'koudar once tell me it not word."

"Because their language is deficient, and they're a proud species." Rick's expression softened, and he readied a finger to stretch his lip so he could say her daughter's name properly. "We're going to find He'nay. She's only 'maplost.' Whatever it takes, P'oki."

"Thank the spirits," P'oki trilled. "Get your pincer out of your mouth. You look like clown."

Rick stared at his companion, unsure if she meant for him to thank whatever she saw. He also wondered if they would find her daughter alive. Unless she had something valuable to offer, Earthquake wasn't known for feeding prisoners.

"Uncertainty spirits come back. You think He'nay is dead?" Her tone sounded threatening, tugging at memories fighting rebels.

"If she is, it's one more reason for me to take them down."

"Whatever it takes, Rix."

"Damn straight."

FOURTEEN

(AMANDA)

The Doh-riss Memorial Women's Shelter, Collective Fringe

OUTSIDE JOKA'S DOCKED ship, Amanda shimmied old military armor onto Symphora while Mel-za assisted. The armor's life support hummed after a few seconds, barely audible over the pollinator critters flitting about the aromatic garden. Amanda wondered who Joka named the place for but decided against asking.

Selbos waved goodbye to Joka's assistant manager at the women's shelter, and Joka transferred funds from her swear jar to the shelter's credit account.

Symphora breathed too heavily for Amanda's liking.

"Nobody has to know you're here," Amanda said. "The garden is tranquil... It's not the worst place to heal."

"You've seen how I attract attention. Nobody's safe if I'm around." Symphora sighed, gazing at the dome separating this asteroid from the void of space. "We need Bunear's camouflaged ship."

Mel-za smirked. "Then it's a good thing you're with us. I was going to apply for a strike team position after my tour of guard duty ended here. Since you've been working in the government and away from the Calamity station, the girls changed a few things. For one, Joka demanded that the second-toughest squad members patrol and keep everyone in the shelter safe. I disagree with that designation, but I'm honored to do my part."

Selbos and Joka paced the garden walkway between the shelter and the landing pad. Under the artificial dome, Amanda forgot this location was on an asteroid, sight distance from the government offices and a terrorist attack. This was supposed to be a safe place. Eyeing the quartet of Symphora Squad members guarding the shelter entrance, Amanda knew it was. Yet if Earthquake could teleport in here, it would only be a matter of time before they ambushed them. With Amanda and Rick out of the organization, they would definitely attack a women's shelter if they saw any value in doing so. Thank Earth this teeny asteroid didn't have anything else to offer.

Symphora coughed, then a cold grin ran up her snout. "I don't need anyone keeping me safe. There are plenty of ass—*butts*—I can kick before I go to the Goddess."

Joka scrunched her nose at Symphora. "You better not be thinking you're going into combat because I got you your backup gear. If there's any fighting, you're staying on the ship."

Symphora scowled. "My mom died when I was a cub, Bunear. I don't need another one now."

"And I don't need a death on my hands," Amanda said. "We're not fighting anyone. We're finding the Earthquake headquarters and calling the Collective Fleet." She almost believed herself. So much of her life had been spent cursing the Collective, the thought of relying on the Fleet almost made her laugh.

Selbos scratched the end of her muzzle while the entrance hatch to Joka's ship unfurled. "Do you know where to go?"

"I have some leads," Amanda said. "We'll meet some unsavory characters, though."

"Unsavory characters," Selbos mused. "So we'll ring up Mel-za's ex? They could give everyone in Earthquake enough venereal diseases to stop them in their tracks."

"Hilarious," the Lo-sat muttered.

With a stomp, Joka blocked the ship's entrance. "Not funny. Apologize right now. No bullying on my ship. Don't disrespect the Squad's sisterhood."

Amanda folded her arms, watching with a flicker of delight as the Arkouda hung her head but also wondering what caused Joka to react in such a way.

"Sorry," Selbos said. "Just trying to lighten the mood."

Joka pointed a stiff finger at Selbos, then stepped out of Amanda's way to allow her entry into the small civilian transport ship. The ship was perfect for getting a small group of people from one point to another but not so great at defending against a hostile terrorist group. It wouldn't do so hot against a rogue asteroid, either. Amanda was a bit too polite to describe aloud the pad of taped cushions in the pilot's seat as slipshod, but it suggested a "safety third" philosophy. At least, with Joka's camouflage features, it wouldn't be as easy to track as the ship they'd come here in.

Ships like these weren't meant for pan-galactic travel, even with some special camo tech. As the others spilled in behind her, Amanda eyed Joka. "Are you sure this is the best ship for us? Our destination isn't close."

Symphora heaved herself up the steps. "Careful. Bunear might think you're questioning her pilot—" She fell into a coughing fit. Amanda debated offering her some help but knew it would end poorly.

Mel-za followed her. "Yeah, she's more likely to forgive swearing."

Selbos and Joka entered next, and the ship's decontamination fumes hissed over them as the entrance hatch closed.

As Joka situated herself in the cockpit, she got a ping on her omni-tablet. She cast a grim scowl at Symphora. "Hey, do you remember me telling you about that..." her eyes flitted to Amanda, "kid I found in Diastrevlo's lab?" The way she said "kid" made Amanda wonder what she was hiding.

Symphora's ears flattened. "What happened?"

"Somebody else who knew about him pinged me. He's gone."

Amanda decided to let them have their secret for now.

————

Their day in hyperspace travel vacillated between Amanda garnering more details of Symphora's attacker and Mel-za asking them both how Earthquake fought and what she'd need to do to crack their skulls. They didn't leave the small table in the cramped habitation space except to get different games to pass the time while chatting. Amanda was too nervous to enjoy the Block Bash competitions or watch a hiveball match.

Amanda had thought her old quarters back in an Earthquake barracks had been jam-packed, but compared to this, it was a palace. Not that she'd wish to go back to those days.

Since Amanda didn't quite fit in with Mel-za and Symphora's activities, she checked on Selbos and Joka, who occupied themselves in the cockpit, spitballing ideas for Joka's next invention, which ranged from gravity harnesses for Lo-sats that could double as heat cells to a civilian version of her pressurized flight suit for Human pilots. That had sold well enough to fund her shelter; the Collective military purchased the official patent but only gave them to the few Human recruits joining the military—an uneasy concession made by mostly Symphora because of Amanda's insistence.

Over their morning meal of thick liquids, Amanda sipped her bowels-friendly protein drink meant for spacefarers. Amanda assumed it was primarily liquefied feet, but she added a pinch of powdered *bachar* spice, and it went down smooth enough.

Mel-za furrowed her eyeridge at it. "Wouldn't you rather eat a real thing?"

Amanda shrugged, placing her drink on the table. "Of course I would, but isn't this what you do on longer expeditions?"

A dreamy cloud bubbled in Mel-za's marbled bronze-yellow eyes. "I'd kill to go on a longer expedition—I'd just bring a terrarium. Since I've been guarding the shelter, I've eaten solids for my monthly meals."

Selbos gulped her own protein drink and wiped her muzzle with the back of her paw. "Don't act like you're getting real food. It's just synthetic meat." She wiggled an ear at Amanda. "It fills you up and has the right nutrients, but the taste is never quite right without a bone to crunch."

Without the predatory drive of an Arkouda or Lo-sat, Amanda could only imagine what they would think of her vegetarian diet.

Mel-za extended her neck frills halfway. "It's not synthetic! Joka would never give me the fake stuff. Joka—?"

Joka slurped her drink loud enough to muffle the question.

"Ha!" Symphora's burst of sound turned into a wheeze. "She's definitely giving you synthetic meat. My chef did the same on the Calamity. Saves tons of credits and nobody can tell. Plus there's a *skata*-load of extra vitamins and stuff in it so it's healthier. Quit whining and get with the times."

"You owe me a credit. And Symphora, I *know* you stash jerky in your armor." Joka shrugged. "Mel-za, someone suggested I put Human hot sauce on the synthetic meat to make it more appealing to Lo-sats. You sure liked it at the shelter."

Amanda peered at her, wondering where she'd heard that before.

Mel-za scoffed. "At least put synthetic bones inside so my teeth stay good. Hard bones."

"Hard pass." Joka returned to her breakfast drink.

Selbos sighed. "I'm done. I'll check the autopilot. Amanda, do they know we're coming?"

"Well…"

"Oh *ska*—poop sauce, you're kidding, right?" Symphora asked.

"Amanda," Joka intoned, "we're not showing up uninvited to *them,* are we?"

Mel-za stood, uncoiling her tail and tapping it on the floor. "We need to suit up and arm ourselves, right?"

Amanda set her breakfast beverage on the cramped table. "I was given an open invitation after I did them a big favor."

"When?" Symphora straightened in her cot.

Amanda counted the bubbles at the bottom of her glass, unwilling to make eye contact with anyone. "When I was with Earthquake," she muttered.

A buzz rang over the ship's small PA. "IMMINENT SHIP." Amanda hadn't heard an automated ship voice speak Human since her time with Earthquake. All eyes and heads lurched to the cockpit. The PA buzzed again. "TRACTION TECHNOLOGY DETECTED. REMAIN SEATED."

"You don't show up to Blekk pirates unannounced." Symphora's lip curled.

Amanda shook her head. "I helped take out a Drowned Star warlord a few years ago, so half the Blekk see me as a hero."

"No wonder the other government officials hate you," Selbos said.

Mel-za marched to the cockpit, the thud of her footsteps nearly shaking the ship. "I've never seen one of their cruisers up close." She tapped the command to display the viewscreen of the ship's outside.

Amanda hadn't seen a Blekk pirate cruiser since she brokered a deal on Rick Crith's behalf to defend New Lodestone after it was liberated. She and Rick used the unspeakable monstrosity on Dr. Oze's moon to take out the pirate king Sjorover. All his rivals lauded Rick and Amanda by extension, even if they remained hesitant about Earthquake as a whole.

They'd recognize her, which did not sit well, useful as it would be.

Yet all her old fears arose upon seeing the Blekk cruiser, a behemoth the shape of a jagged, hateful icicle, powerful enough to confront a Collective war-hive and threaten a space station.

"You never said these coordinates would lead to a pirate cruiser," Joka hissed. "Who are you trying to kill, Amanda? I ain't going. Someone has to stay and protect Symphora."

Amanda turned her back to the viewscreen displaying the approaching cruiser. "Look, I'll go alone. They don't need to know Symphora is aboard. I'll see if they have information on Earthquake."

"The Blekk who aren't outright pirates are traders." Selbos waved a paw. "You can't ask for something without anything to offer."

"I actually brought something to offer them," Amanda replied. Three sets of eyebrows and one pair of eyeridges raised. "They'll want some information I learned in the government archives. I have access to files on some of their captured leaders."

"Can you sign in Blekk?" Mel-za asked.

"Blekker," Selbos corrected.

Amanda nodded. "I have translation software."

"You do? Is that a government perk?" Joka asked.

Tapping her omni-tablet, Amanda prepared to tell them she'd paid for it herself after a bad experience with a free version, but the PA buzzed. "BOARDING DEVICE DETECTED. BRACE FOR—"

The public comm channel burst over the ship's system. An automated voice boomed in Arkouda, lacking the accent and inflection one would expect. "You trespass into Blekk space. Buy, sell, trade, leave, die. Pick your option."

Amanda marched over to the comm and placed her typed message into the messenger:

[This is Amanda Martinez, co-slayer of Sjorover. I was promised favors.]

Mel-za peered over Amanda's shoulder. "What kind of squiggles are those? Looks like somebody vomited noodles onto your tablet."

Joka scoffed. "I said no bullying on my ship. Don't talk like that about someone else's language."

"I think refusing an award given by nice members of your species is technically bullying." Mel-za cocked an eyeridge. "And not all Lo-sats are master linguists or care about that stuff."

Amanda tuned them out, staring at the message, expecting a reply. Gritting her teeth, she typed a new message.

[I also brought information to trade.]

The public comm buzzed. "Is a translator required?"

[No. I will enter alone, unarmed.]

She wondered how "unarmed" would render in a language for aliens with tentacles but trusted her software.

Symphora grumbled from the back. "Bunear, what's she typing?"

Joka slithered beside Amanda and scrunched her face. "I don't know what I was expecting to see." She glanced up at Amanda. "You're positive? No backup?"

"None. If you don't hear from me in more than thirty minutes, you bolt." Amanda let a tense silence hang in the air. "Blekk boarding tech doesn't do well with dry air. Superheat the seal, and it'll pop off. Initiate hyperspace as you're disengaging."

"The Symphora Squad doesn't leave a sister behind," Mel-za said.

"Quit tail-sniffing," Symphora groaned. "Martinez, I don't like you going alone."

"The Blekk will," Amanda snapped. "They need to feel like they're in control."

Selbos mumbled something, but Amanda ignored her and typed another message into the tablet.

[Boarding now.]

"Joka, where do you keep the breathers? Do you have the kind that'll wrap around my head?"

With a sigh, Joka tapped a compartment near the hatch, revealing a Human-sized mouthpiece.

Amanda affixed the device over her mouth and nose. The contraption unfolded, connecting to her decompression suit, and created a chilled plasma bubble around her. She changed the settings on her tablet to go into saltwater mode and tapped the hatch. If she could deal with government types, then trading with pirates would be like playing hiveball against a toddler. Or they'd strangle her immediately.

As it opened, Mel-za squirmed. "I'll be ready with my rifle if things go wrong."

Joka folded her arms over her chest. "Use those diplomacy skills."

"You better record this, Martinez," Symphora huffed. After a cough, she added, "Since my hairy ass will get grilled if you make some shady deal."

Amanda couldn't blame her. As ex-Earthquake, she was the most suspect person in the government, and this would look bad on paper. Exhaling, Amanda stepped out of the hatch into the Blekk boarding hall leading to the cruiser. When the hatch sealed behind her, a torrent of saltwater rushed at her, slapping the durasteel hull.

She bent her knees and braced herself against the rush. This was the unofficial endurance test before the negotiation. Gritting her teeth, she knew it wasn't enough to prove her resilience. Fighting the current, she pushed herself forward, advancing toward the Blekk cruiser. After a few labored steps, she pushed off the floor and swam.

Rick had prepared her for this, which made her skin crawl. The survival skills came from him, but the negotiation was all her aunt. She had taught Amanda how to negotiate with someone bigger than she was and had talked her way out of arrest several times. Amanda wished they'd had other options when she was little, but she appreciated those skills now.

Halfway to the cruiser hull, the docking bridge had filled with saltwater.

She swam as hard as she could, unwilling to let any onlooking Blekk see her as weak; she had to be the badass on her own.

Knowing the Blekk, they probably added some thrust to the onrush of saltwater to further complicate things, putting her at a disadvantage for negotiation. She pushed herself to the cruiser hull door and kicked it with her boot—the subsequent dull thud barely audible through her breather and oxygen bubble.

The hull glowed scarlet, then parted.

She swam through and the scarlet softened to magenta. A gentle tickle vibrated the outside of her suit, the Blekk version of decontamination. Any water backwashing behind her would get the same treatment. It wasn't the most efficient method, but it didn't leave the same scuzzy feeling decontamination spray always did, although the tangy salt odor would remain with her until she died.

Two Blekk floated in front of her, both of them boasting their coral-shaped waterproof scald rifles.

The multi-tentacled aliens' lithe bodies swayed gently in the pulsing water while lidless eyes appraised her.

Amanda pointed each limb of her body in a different direction, forming a sloppy version of the Blekker sign for their greeting phrase.

The two Blekk rotated, making a form of eye contact she couldn't comprehend. The one to her left pointed a tentacle at her omni-tablet, then swam backward to let her get a full view of them. They sprawled out their tentacles in an elaborate series of signs, building an entire sentence at once. Amanda strafed her omni-tablet's camera over their message.

The tablet offered a translation.

[State your business aboard the *Raitskip*].

TRANSLATION CONFIDENCE, 96%
Amanda clasped her hands together overhead, clicked her heels together, then waved her body in a gentle curve—her closest approximation for the Blekk affirmative.

The two greeters accepted the gesture, and Amanda typed the message.

[I want to know the whereabouts of Earthquake's headquarters. I will repay with information if it becomes useful.]

One Blekk shifted to read Amanda's message, then signed it to their companion.

The first made a sign Amanda recognized. "Follow."

Amanda complied, swimming deeper into the Blekk cruiser. Its cramped interior prevented standing, an almost welcome break from the cavernous arches in Arkouda architecture. This world wasn't designed for her, yet she could function more comfortably here than what she'd become accustomed to.

Twisting through snaking tubes, penetrating the heart of the cruiser, the cold cylinder indicated signs of kelp and small fish, either possible snacks for the crew or there to purify and beautify the place. It made her wonder how much of this would pass the Collective's safety and cleanliness protocols—if any of it needed to.

Amanda passed by an actual decoration against the wall. *Artwork on a pirate cruiser?* Rick never briefed her on their art, and she'd never read about it either. But the way the wispy kelp was arranged on the wall with bioluminescent coral fragments adorning it, there was no mistaking it. Amanda had no clue what it signified, but it was beautiful. Maybe the Arkouda had never seen this, either. Maybe they never bothered to find out that the Blekk had art. They just saw a species which they couldn't confine to their own standards and dismissed them as less-than, pushing them to piracy in the first place.

Maybe there was a place for them in the Collective, instead of beyond the pale of acceptable species. Amanda swam forward to keep pace with her guides, whom she realized were clearly lagging for her sake.

Some part of her old self screamed that this was all a trap. But they'd have killed her by now if they wanted to. A simple wrap of the tentacles around her neck, and she'd be done. They may actually recognize her and believe her. Or they wanted to extract something else of value.

They had honor, at least, and ridding the species of the pirate king Sjorover by way of a nightmare monster from the depths of a dead moon certainly helped.

The tunnel widened into a cavernous room, yawning into a bubble big enough to put Joka's ship and several others like it inside. Amanda smiled, observing the coral-crusted interior lining, flecked with gentle bioluminescent pieces. The mess was beautiful to the point where it wasn't a mess. It was merely beyond her capacity to comprehend.

Blekk smaller than Joka and bigger than Selbos swam in different directions above her while others remained stationary at floating computer stations, operating various controls for the ship. This ship was more of a city than a pirate cruiser.

Her guides drew her to the center where a Blekk, a measure larger than her guides, floated, unblinking eye transfixed on Amanda.

A rectangular screen floated beside him.

One guide spun around, signing a sentence. Before Amanda could strafe with her omni-tablet, the screen beside the larger Blekk displayed a message in Human script.

[Speak, Martinez-clutch Amanda. Your voice will be registered and translated for us.]

Amanda breathed deeply, then pulled her breather off her mouth. It suctioned beneath her chin, gently hissing moistened oxygen in front of her face. "Hello and thank you for the welcome. I come seeking information and will offer some in exchange. Whom do I have the honor of meeting?"

The larger Blekk remained more focused on Amanda than the screen transcribing her message into a flurry of Blekker characters. After she had finished speaking, the large Blekk waited a full five seconds before turning to the screen and signing a response.

[You have met Islk and Hmei. You stand in the presence of Cerad. You are the same Martinez-clutch Amanda who once served Crith-clutch Rodrick? Formerly with the Earthquake-pod?]

"Served is not how I would describe it but yes. I worked with him, and we left Earthquake … pod together. But we parted ways after."

Cerad repeated his long pause before checking the screen and responding.

[You aided in slaying Sjorover. Destroying his ship. Many Blekker died that day. Legend says it was a glorious fight. You know the truth of it?]

Amanda measured her response carefully, unsure of where this person's stance on Sjorover was. Four Blekk floated closer.

Well, she knew the truth, and it was what he'd requested.

Amanda closed her eyes and inhaled, hating the memory of the unspeakable monstrosity, growing to the size of a mountain as it batted away Blekk pirates like they were plasmasippers. "It's not an elegant story. One of Rick Crith-clutch's soldiers in Earthquake-pod murdered Sjorover's translator after Sjorover agreed to help Rick. The murderer acted without authorization." She paused to allow the translation software to keep up. "But Sjorover didn't know the murderer went rogue or didn't care. He arrived to kill Rick and the Earthquake-pod we had at our command."

Despite the puffing moist oxygen, her lips dried and her mouth tensed, her whole body unwilling to share what followed. "But something came out of that moon. There isn't a word for it in my language, so I'll try a few."

Flashes of the unspeakable creature streaked through Amanda's mind, and she struggled to keep focus. "Evil. Monster. Abomination. God. Demigod. Horrifying. Beast." She waited for the translation button to display her attempt at describing what was ineffable, to use words where none applied. The measured expression of Cerad bade her to continue. "It rose from the moon and grew. It went from bigger than an Arkouda to bigger than a ship. Then bigger than a mountain. Sjorover attacked it while Crith-clutch and I escaped." Her palms clammed up. "The monster pulled Sjorover's ship from the sky. It was bigger than this one, but it plucked it like picking fruit from a tree." Amanda let the words hang in the air while the translation finished. She hastily added, "I'm sorry. Picking fruit is a Human idiom."

Cerad waved a tentacle, a gesture she actually understood—she hoped. It felt neutrally dismissive, as if he were telling her not to worry about it.

Bolstered by the forgiveness of her poor choice of words, Amanda finished. "The creature snatched the ship out of the sky and slammed it into the lunar surface. The moon is unpopulated, but the death toll of the sailors in Sjorover's ship must've been catastrophic. Rick Crith-clutch let them die. He didn't include me in making the decision."

Cerad bobbed, appraising the message on the translation board.

[Did you contact Sjorover?]

"Personally, no. All his communication was through one of Sjorover's translators. We were not given the opportunity or invitation to come aboard any ships. He didn't honor us the way you have honored me."

[What was your opinion of Sjorover? Fair Blekk? Cruel?]

Amanda relaxed her shoulders, finally satisfied that her current translations surpassed the free beta version she'd used all those years ago. "He did what he said he'd do and refused to compromise. He protected his own and sent his crew down with him when the creature attacked. I don't think anyone survived." Cerad studied Amanda, and several bubbles escaped from between his tentacles. He signed his response.

[What happened after?]

Amanda's tension returned. "Rick and I brokered an agreement with Sjorover's rivals. They would help him if called, and they would operate with his squads to weaken the Collective."

By now, the other freely floating Blekk had congregated, creating an amphitheater of tentacles around them.

Cerad signed something directed at the crowd. Eventually, Amanda's tablet caught up.

[This one tells the truth. Martinez-clutch Amanda.]

"Did you already know those things?"

[Yes. Sjorover was my father and greatest rival. You honored me by ridding the galaxy of him and honored me by ensuring he had a notable death. Going down against a legendary beast from the depths suits a mollusk such as him.]

Amanda resisted a shiver. "So you'll tell me where Earthquake's base of operations is?"

The crowd of Blekk signed conversations with each other.

[You should know, Martinez-clutch. Not us. We haven't done dealings with Earthquake-pod since the days of Crith-clutch. We trusted him but not them. And you, I suppose. When he defected, Earthquake-pod told us our help was no longer needed.]

She should've known. Of course the xenophobic terrorists stopped working with other species without Rick demanding it.

"Can you tell me where that message came from? It would at least be a start."

[Make your offer.]

A smile creased Amanda's face, taking in the glowing art overhead. "What you've always wanted."

FIFTEEN

(ROSANNA)

Defying science with a flotilla at her back

TELEPORTING WITH AN entire ship should have changed the foul sensation of being stalked by that presence around Rosanna. It hadn't; probing eyes, clacking mandibles, and pervasive wrongness somehow bore into her psyche in the moment of transit. It must've been her imagination—the result of a brain which hadn't evolved to cope with instantly materializing in an opposite corner of the galaxy, although a tiny piece of her wished one of them would mention the judgmental presence she experienced.

She wasn't crazy.

Earthquake's harmless-looking ships blinked into space, allowing a pair of wide asteroids to conceal them from where the Collective fleet amassed to defend this area, which paired well with their scrambling and camouflage tech. Using the Chamayna chitin to teleport dozens of ships across the galaxy was only the beginning. Implementing Crith's own tactics in such a public way would draw the bastard out of hiding. The absence of Martinez and Symphora would guarantee conspiracy theorists would have a chance to spread rumors about her connection to the first attack. She really admired the Leader's genius.

Rosanna paced the disguised civilian cargo ship's interior, which had been retrofitted to look like a mineral hauler to any scanners. Cheap bio-bags filled rows of empty seats behind her—if any Collective scanners swiped the ship, they'd read it as full of civilians, harmless miners. Yet Rosanna stood alone. All the others she'd brought with her occupied the scrapper ships behind her, innocuous junk collectors with innocuous magnets for collecting scrap and harvesting ferrous asteroids for a quick credit.

The bastard Crith taught the galaxy to fear scrappers by putting them in New Lodestone's orbit, where the planet's powerful magnetosphere made their magnets strong enough to rip a warhive to shreds. He'd used them to commandeer ships. The fool wanted a navy, like he saw himself as some elegant admiral.

But Rosanna knew better. More powerful scrapper magnets helped replace them with real warships, sure. But their higher purpose would be realized today.

A ping came through from her contact.

[Confirmed Martinez is off base. Confirmed Symphora is also. They were last seen boarding a transport, designated *DR-1*.]

She tapped the port side of the hull, and the viewscreen coalesced, replacing the metal interior. Scrappers formed into position, concealed by the asteroids here. The same asteroids meant to protect this target would be its downfall. Large fighting ships couldn't get close, and they assumed that would protect them from the Blekk or any Earthquake attackers. They'd appreciate their folly once it became too late.

All Rosanna needed to do was keep focused and forget about that recurring sound when she'd teleported—that clacking.

Fate had demanded Rosanna be on the ground, rifle in hand, but instead, she gripped her comm, hating this command boveeshit. Her youth and ferocity meant she should be on the lines. But the Leader knew best, and this would lead her one step closer to revenge, so it was a necessary annoyance. "Scrapper pilots, find an asteroid and pull it in front of your ship. Team up on the bigger ones. This is a rehearsal for the ultimate targets."

A chorus of agreement rang through. By their tone, some of them sounded like they were sucking up. She'd strangle each one who tried. Not having someone else to do this garbage was regrettable. Why Crith craved it was beyond her. Her only solace was that this was a sign the Leader trusted her.

The ones who weren't kissing up had an air of passive indifference based on their blank expressions. It was just a job to them. Those were the heroes.

After they spread into position with ferrous asteroids in front of them, each scrapper scooted along to join Rosanna behind the largest asteroid.

Rosanna switched the comm to the public channel. "Human independence now!"

Rosanna knew the cry was now echoing in every warhive behind them and in the halls of every office building below—the Collective Fringe government offices. Every important person and agency who kept some semblance of law out here would all die today. Crith would've tried to negotiate or threaten—stupid asshole. Rosanna wouldn't bother—she had a schedule to keep.

At the command, the slow scrappers plodded beside her ship and launched their magnetic asteroids by reversing polarity.

No sounds carried in the vacuum of space, which was a shame because hearing screams or explosions would've been gratifying—each death in Earthquake's cause brought her a step closer to any of the people who could tell her the truth about her brother. Without that purpose, these asteroids smacking into the city seemed so random. Natural. Almost like an earthquake.

A meager series of turrets opened fire on the scrappers. It wasn't enough to end the assault. Scrappers had dense hulls for repelling asteroids, the same dense hulls cursing them with slow speed. The turret fire was intended for sleek fighters or kamikaze civilian ships, and the scrappers shrugged the fire off.

Within seconds, the asteroid holding the Fringe's government offices was eviscerated to metallic chunks floating in the field. Some piece of her wished Martinez and Symphora were still there, but the Leader assured her it was better this way. He had reminded her that it was necessary after her failure to kill Symphora.

Her scanner showed Collective warships closing on her, but the damage had been done, and not everyone in her crew needed to return to base.

Some part of Rosanna wanted to navigate her own ship through the wreckage and see if she found any familiar faces in the hovering frozen corpses, although with the utter destruction before her, any recognition would be impossible. While she had no love for Martinez, knowing bigoted assholes who would've gotten in her way floated among the dead brought some satisfaction. The Leader wouldn't be able to say Rosanna had failed this time. He'd tell her everything about her brother as promised.

But that was outside mission parameters, and she had to evac since this mission took a huge stockpile of chitin to complete. This wasn't the place to float around and wait for a flotilla of warhives.

She switched to the Earthquake channel and barked an order. "Grab some ferrous debris and get ready to launch it at the warhives, cruisers, and battle-darts. The Fleet is about to rain shit on us." She checked her list of names on her omni-tablet. "Therienne and Aureo, pull back beside my ship."

A chorus of obnoxious "yes ma'ams" replied, some higher pitched than others—scared asswipes. She just wished they'd do their stupid jobs instead of flapping their gums. The approaching Collective military ships took to firing upon the asteroids instead of navigating around them—not what Rosanna wanted but manageable nonetheless.

Pulverized asteroids floated apart, and the military fighters and command ships came into view, making Rosanna sweat. They were running out of time. She shouted the next order. "Fire!"

Magenta rays pulsed from the scrappers as they reversed polarity, collecting detritus from the destroyed government buildings and flinging it at the oncoming oppressors. After Crith's little stunts succeeded over New Lodestone, newer line military ships equipped themselves with magneto-baffling software, so the ships themselves couldn't become ammunition. No matter. The offices of their former representatives would suffice.

The first wave of battledarts fell, leaving the heavier cruisers and the two warhives. They needed more than detritus to take them down, and the big enough asteroids had been expended, were too far, or were obliterated already.

"Left flank, activate your teleporters. Right flank, grab the left flank and execute the slingshot maneuver."

Thwip.

The noise behind her made her wince, sending her back to the probing and judgmental eyes.

Rosanna glanced over her shoulder. The first scrapper pilot materialized in a seat behind her, displacing the bio-bag in one of the seats. "Activate the hyperdrive," Rosanna said. "We're leaving soon."

Thwipthwipthwipthwip

Rosanna grimaced at the unseen observer judging her and shook the noise from her head. This wasn't the time to get paranoid. Oze's warning about teleportation was an idle threat, nothing more. And the way the Leader was burning through their supply with these missions, it wasn't like she'd have to worry about it much longer.

The remaining pilots blinked into existence inside the ship accompanied by bits of destroyed chitin. Rosanna redirected her attention to the battle where the still-occupied scrappers launched the now-empty scrappers toward the larger fleet ships. One scrapper bored a hole through a heavy cruiser while others careened into the left warhive.

"Right flank, concentrate magnetized beams on the heavy cruiser before it breaks apart. Its shield will be down. Launch it at the right warhive. After it breaks, activate your teleporters."

She glanced at the first pilot to join her. The hyperdrive was almost ready. Thank Earth, because they didn't have much time before enemy reinforcements came.

The warhives unleashed plasma hellfire on the scrappers, destroying two immediately. The remaining ones launched the heavy cruiser as directed with enough force to snap the warhive in half.

In the last seconds before it happened, the warhives shot another round, catching the remaining scrappers.

A blue light above her changed to green: hyperdrive ready. Therienne and Aureo's ships were still beside her, awaiting an order which would never come. It had to be somebody, and the Leader said those two were expendable.

They never had enough teleporters on their ships to make the return jump. Rosanna stomped to the cockpit and ignited the hyperdrive, leaving two against a warhive. She didn't think they deserved it, but their deaths served a higher purpose.

Rosanna activated the piece of chitin attached to the ship, teleporting away with a crew half full of idiots, none of whom had anything to say about some invisible observer examining them. As she blinked out of existence, she wondered if she'd just been imagining things.

And the unseen presence returned to her, clacking insectoid mandibles together.

SIXTEEN

(MAYNARD)

On the Lo-sat homeworld of Vee, sweating and inviting plasmasippers

UNDER AN OCEAN-DENSE blanket of clouds that made a joke of the sun, Maynard dabbed at the sweat glazing his neck, gently shooing the bugs feasting there in the process.

"You can swat at them now, can't you, since you're no longer a Brother?" A smirk curled up Binh's snout. "So are you downgraded to a Step Brother? Ooh, what about Second Cousin? There's a Lo-sat word for a loser uncle who nobody likes but you still have to invite to parties—are you that?"

"Is that word 'Binh,' by any chance? An Abbot has never been expelled for having a secret nephew and then wanting to find him, so there's that."

Last week, Maynard knew who he was: running the monastery and caring for his nephew. But now that Rondo led the push to have Maynard ousted from the order after Webster's murder? Everything was in shambles. Maynard and Binh's journey through the stars had been blessedly uneventful, although he wished something would've happened to take his mind off the danger Mui-xe was in and Maynard's own uncertain future.

This morning, they'd reached the planet where Mui-xe's grandmother lived. Maynard never met his brother's mother-in-law, but from what he'd heard about the shaman Reck-xa, she was not one to be trifled with, despite how loving her letters were to Mui-xe. And that was why they needed her. Her chemical prowess would complement Binh's thieving skills and allow them to break Mui-xe out of whatever dungeon Earthquake had locked him in, not to mention her skills with medicine would help Mui-xe recover.

A nauseating buzz made Maynard glance up at the river of swarming insects under the flaxen atmosphere above them. Maynard shook his head. "They can strip me of my rank and title, but I still won't take a life, even of an insect attacking me. It just needs to feed." Even the insects were probably sweating under the muggy heat.

"And spread an incurable disease to you. The real Great Mystery is why you wouldn't take my bug spray."

Tar-mud swallowed Maynard's foot, which he wriggled free with some effort. Forsaking the Great Mystery monks' sandals for spacefaring gear was a blessing for how painful it was. But he wasn't a monk anymore. Rondo had made sure of that. "When my brother met Reck-xa for the first time, he said he was coated in insect repellent, and it offended her somehow."

Binh swatted at the muggy air in front of them, catching a plasmasipper between his claws and popping it in his mouth. "Of course it offended her. He refused a free snack." He licked his lips. "I gotta stop eating these. Don't want to spoil next week's meal."

Maynard ducked under a low-hanging branch that Binh pulled up for him. "How could Reck-xa live so far from civilization?" Maynard asked. "I'm surprised the whole planet isn't urbanized like some Arkouda worlds."

"We're not Arkoudae, genius." Binh's tone hinted he may have actually been offended, which Maynard didn't think was possible for him. "Wasn't our spaceport big enough for you? More people in that one city than on your beloved Planet Magnet Torture, and that wasn't even the capital."

"It was a big city, but I guess I expected more. My fault." He sighed, "And if Reck-xa is a spiritual seeker, I guess I should expect her to live in a remote location."

Binh's omni-tablet hummed. *"Nguc."*

"What?"

"I got a ping from Nut Puncher, and she only pings me for important stuff."

"Who?"

"The teeny Human chick who dropped Mui-xe off when he first came to you."

"Quit acting like a child and call her Joka."

"Fine. They haven't found Earthquake's headquarters yet, but the girly-girl with the curly-curl—"

The less civilized part of him wanted to demand Binh respect her. "Her name is Representative Martinez, and you'll call her that." Maynard had already violated his code over something more important, anyway.

Binh furrowed his eyeridges. "*She* talked to the calamari guys and knows where to head next. I was hoping they would've found it already."

Maynard sidestepped a spreading fungal patch. "By 'calamari guys,' do you mean the Blekk? How do you know so much about Human food?"

Binh cocked an eyeridge. "I wasn't kidding when I said I grew up on Earth."

"I thought you were being sarcastic. I'd assumed your time with Earthquake taught you the Human language."

"Nah. They taught me plenty of intolerance, though. The best thing about Earth was the hot sauce."

With a sigh, Maynard reluctantly pushed the plasmasipper off his neck, hoping to scare it off. "We've contributed more to the galaxy than hot sauce."

"Religious types. Always delusional." Binh's voice flattened. "We'll be at her place soon. No theological debates, alright?"

Maynard huffed as he pushed another insect off his neck. "I wouldn't dream of it."

"Also…" Binh sidestepped in front of Maynard, and his sarcastic tone disappeared. Neck frills extended slightly, he said, "Beyond the whole, 'all Humans look alike' thing… you smell like your brother. I know you can see the physical resemblance, but there's an olfactory one, too. I know that probably doesn't make sense to you, but I'm serious. Your presence will bring up some memories for her. You know that old stereotype about moms hating their sons-in-law by default. She might go *nguc* wild on you for no reason." He smirked and his usual tone returned. "You know, like all attractive women."

"That's somebody's grandmother..." Maynard shook his head, remembering he didn't really need his reflexive response of chastity anymore. If his late brother found a Lo-sat woman attractive, maybe there was something there Maynard could appreciate. "Perhaps you should drop the sarcasm, though? I scarcely think a shaman would want to be flirted with in this circumstance."

"Yeah." His neck frills collapsed. "You know my stance on religion, but some of the stuff shamans say, some of the *nguc* I've seen... Just proceed with caution."

As Maynard muttered an "of course," a hut not much beyond Binh's height materialized between wide fronds of leaves. Maynard could've sworn it wasn't there before, but this planet's dense humidity and the ounces of blood he'd sacrificed to the local insects possibly altered his perception.

The hut was fashioned from local vegetation with some bushes growing out of it. Maynard mistook it for a tree at first, but a gentle red light pulsed from inside, revealing the truth. Binh gestured for Maynard to follow, and they went up a small incline to reach the hut. A window no bigger than Maynard's head was cut into the side, and he caught the faint outline of a door beside it.

Before they could announce their arrival, the door jostled open from the inside.

An aging Lo-sat woman occupied the doorway. The sheen of her scales and length of her tail were the only signs marking her as Binh's species. Where Binh wore spacefaring gear, she wore a flowing robe, not wholly unlike Maynard's at the monastery. Warpaint of brilliant oranges and reds dotted the scales on her head. A bracelet of dulled bone knobs hugged the tip of her tail, and Maynard wondered if the bones came from a beast or another Lo-sat, but he was too afraid to ask.

She rolled marbled yellow eyes at Maynard. Even from this distance, he knew she was smelling him. Sensing him. Her teeth chattered, but Maynard didn't get the impression she was cold as much as she was subtly tasting the air around him.

Her eyeridges quivered for a flash, then her attention snapped to Binh.

While Maynard's Lo-sat vocabulary was limited, her words burst crisper than carved calligraphy. "You. This is not the visitor you promised."

Binh straightened and gave a tight nod, hiding his tail behind his back. "No, madam shaman. There was a…" The word that followed sounded like "development," but Maynard wasn't entirely positive.

She repeated the word. Her gaze shifted to Maynard. "Forgive my lack of greeting. Can you understand me?"

Maynard pursed his lips and folded his tongue for the best pronunciation he could manage. "Yebth."

"You are the brother of," her eyes fluttered and she winced, then changed her pronunciation and accent,

"Beh-neh-dict." Breathing hard, she gazed at him with softer eyes. "I can understand Human. The profane one will translate if needed."

Binh stared at his feet.

Maynard bowed. "Yes. Thank you for speaking my brother's true name. You may call him Ned if that's easier. I'm his older brother. Maynard." He debated whether to add "monk of the Great Mystery," but decided against it. She didn't need to know the shame incurred by abandoning the monastery to rescue his nephew. "I have unfortunate news about Mui-xe."

She bristled at the name of the child he was supposed to care for. This young man—kidnapped and alone.

"You lost him." Her tone mingled pain, accusation, and a matter-of-factness which baffled him. He wondered how much information he was leaking through his pheromones and sweat. "Who took him? Collective or rebels?"

"Earthquake." Maynard fought the urge to spit the word. A monk wouldn't speak with such hate, but maybe he could now.

Reck-xa shot a glare at Binh, who hissed something in Lo-sat back to her. It sounded like "Hu-man rebels. Previous leader killed Mui-xe's tormentor."

"So what do you think Earthquake intends to do with him?" Reck-xa asked Maynard.

"I think they want to finish experimenting on him and expand on what the scientist who kidnapped Ned and La-hok did to him." Maynard's throat dried. "They'll weaponize him."

"You came this far to deliver the news to me in person? What else do you want?"

Maynard nodded. "We need your help to find Mui-xe. You've told Binh you've wanted to spend time with Mui-xe. If we fail, that will never happen. If he's in a maximum security prison, we need someone with your skills."

She cocked her head to the left.

Maynard stared up at Binh. "Why is she giving me that look?"

"Ah…" The reformed thief traded glances between Maynard and the shaman. "Binh is an alias I give to Humans since most of you can't pronounce my real name." He hissed something quickly at Reck-xa.

She bristled. What Maynard caught was, "Each name is from gods… insult them." After uncoiling her tail, she turned to Maynard. "Do you know where he is?"

Maynard elbowed Binh. "Tell her about the lead."

After a long sigh, Binh wrung the tip of his tail. "Honored one, we heard reports of Lo-sat abductions throughout the Fringe. A contact of mine forwarded them. The Symphora Squad is checking into it."

The shaman nodded. "I've heard of Symphora. She could've done more good in her prime with an herbalist at her side. What's her squad found?"

"Binh received pings suggesting where they might be and places to check."

"Why are they abducting our kin?" Reck-xa asked.

Binh arched an eyeridge at Maynard.

A plasmasipper landed between Maynard's fingers. This incoming bite would be supremely uncomfortable in the coming days. He stared at the feasting insect. "Something Binh saw in the mad scientist's lair. He crafted soldiers: foul imitations of Mui-xe. Mindless. Unthinking husks. Each stitched from a Lo-sat and Human. If Earthquake is behind the abductions of Lo-sats, then they are being slaughtered to produce an unstoppable army."

Reck-xa stroked the end of her snout with her foreclaw. "You mean to use us as bait? Go to this place and wait for their violence?"

"Which makes you wonder about his sanity, too..." Binh intoned.

Ignoring Binh, Reck-xa pressed toward Maynard. "And after we're abducted, they will execute us."

"It will be dangerous if we fail. I will do everything in my power to prevent that." Maynard nodded. "I understand if you don't wish to join, but we need your expertise to help us break in and out to get Mui-xe out."

"But wherever they take us will be where my grandson is."

"Yes." Maynard dabbed sweat from his forehead and neck, shooing a plasmasipper away.

Reck-xa's gaze shifted to Binh, and she switched languages. "You approve?"

"Using myself as bait was my idea." Binh pointed at Maynard with his tail. "Also using you as bait was his."

"I have read about Lo-sat shamans. Your powers are great. I am sure we can find him together."

"Your compliment is not an empty one, May-nard," Reck-xa said, and Maynard noticed her turquoise talisman for the first time. She pushed on the chain holding it, making the tiny bone decorations on it shake. "I should also accompany you in case this mission claims my life. You will deliver my claws to Mui-xe if such comes to pass."

"And if such does come to pass, what should he make from your claws?"

Reck-xa placed her claws on her hips. "A potion. I've inscribed the recipe on the last supplies I sent him through the thief."

"Reformed thief," Binh muttered.

Maynard glared at Binh. "You smuggled things to him?"

"Of course," he grinned, "…buddy."

"Take whatever supplies you might need," Maynard said. "If we are correct, this will put us in the heart of Earthquake's operations. It will not be easy or safe. I can defend myself and the two of you if you are close to me. I will not take a life under any circumstances, though. Even if I sacrifice my own."

"Push you off a cliff?" Binh asked. "Got it."

Reck-xa waved her tail near Maynard's face, causing a flinch, and her trinkets clinked together. "I am unconcerned about the danger. My only worry is Mui-xe dying before me." Steel and stone coursed through her voice. "I've already lost my only child. Disease took my husband. If the gods decide to t-take—" A single tear escaped. She let it fall and straightened. "If the gods claim my grandson before me, I will be unworthy of the Peaceful Marshes. My claws will remain where they fall and return to dust in time. I will join those who remain in this mortal plane."

"I won't let that happen," Maynard said. A tree branch snapped in the distance, followed by some distant squawking.

Reck-xa's marbled eyes bore holes into Maynard. "I lack your qualms about killing. If Human rebels stand in my way, they will taste my poisons or my claws. I will bring my alchemy materials. We will board a transport to the abduction location. Tell your contact we are heading there. I can craft a salve to conceal our technology and materials from detection."

Before Maynard could respond, she grabbed his shoulders, her claws digging in just to the point of painfulness but not breaking the skin as she leaned down until they were nearly nose to nose. "Understand that if your nonviolence gets my grandson killed, you'll wish for the worst afterlife from *your* religion because I can guarantee it is nothing compared to what *my* gods have prepared for the wicked."

Maynard didn't have time to ponder where her gods fit into the Great Mystery. "I understand. We'll help you pack."

"First, May-nard, we have our own potion to make. A sample of my blood and yours. Together, our blood will mix into something powerful so we can find him better. Hold out your longest two claws."

Maynard offered her his index and middle fingers. "What'll become of this potion?"

"It will be how we'll know Mui-xe is close. Come inside."

"Take everything you need," Maynard said, dropping his hands and following her.

Binh nudged him to enter behind him. Her cramped hut should've felt spacious compared to his cell back at the monastery, but every inch of wall space alternated between talismans of bone and jewel hanging beside framed accomplishments of his sister-in-law's childhood triumphs and research accolades.

A framed image caught his eye—an Arkouda in police attire. He recognized Inspector Bikkolos, the detective who had visited New Lodestone to gather information about Ned a few years ago. He must have been in contact with Reck-xa about La-hok the entire time as well. He debated pointing out their mutual connection but didn't want to break any ritual taboo.

She approached a table which stood to his chin and their abdomens, crafted from a swamp-dwelling tree and stained with a lifetime's worth of work. She pulled vials off shelves, mixing them into a bowl. Glancing over her shoulder, she peered down at Maynard. "Come beside me. Watch what I do."

Rolling up her left sleeve, she held her scaly forearm over her mixing bowl. With her right hand, she dug a claw into her exposed flesh, plucking off a scale and letting it plink inside the pooled liquids and powders below.

Maynard watched with reverence and cold admiration. Participating in this ritual would never be acceptable to the Great Mystery. But since this was for Mui-xe, he had to believe that what he was doing was in the spirit of his vows of sacrifice and service, even if the methods were questionable. Despite his determination, he could never reach his arm over that bowl. It went past the top of his head.

Reck-xa hissed something to Binh, garnering a chuckle from him. Without warning, Binh hoisted Maynard up, high enough to repeat Reck-xa's gesture with his arm. He didn't need to brace himself for the pain. It was a simple extraction to help Mui-xe. While he would've preferred a stool to being held like a child, he didn't want to offend her or break her focus.

Her claw's point caressed the inside of his forearm, just over the radius. He closed his eyes and nodded, as if she needed or wanted his permission. The needle-point of her claw dug in, excavating a glob of flesh and blood, which spilled inside the bubbling bowl.

Binh set Maynard down, then hissed at Reck-xa.

With her tail, she pointed at another shelf on the other side of the hut. Binh marched over and found a bandage, then attended to Maynard's arm. The pain wasn't as concerning as the blood. While he didn't want to celebrate destruction of microscopic life, he was looking forward to the decontamination he'd receive once they returned to a spaceship.

"For the ritual to complete," Reck-xa said, "we must drink a mouthful; that unites the elixir with our souls. The rest will be used for my talisman."

Maynard's stomach contorted, dancing inside of him in a way that would've been frowned upon by his former order. His mouth dried at the prospect of the contents of this bowl. But for Mui-xe, anything was manageable. "I understand."

"Strong nerves," Reck-xa mused as she reached for a ladle and a Lo-sat drinking cup. These were in the shape of the thin flutes some Humans used for alcohol. Most people in Maynard's position would wish for a strong drink to chase whatever this concoction was, and maybe he could indulge in one himself now.

He accepted the potion, closed his eyes, and inhaled a mess of earthen odors and floral aromas which jolted his eyes back open. He imbibed, and the world around him darkened.

As he fell backward, he heard Binh mutter, "Are you sure I can't let him fall? It would be hilarious."

SEVENTEEN

(AMANDA)

Outer Lo-sat colonies, Collective Fringe

THE *DR-1* LURCHED from hyperspace, and the Fen-tal moon smacked into view, rolling in the orbit of a tangerine-tinted gas giant. Amanda's liquid meals threatened a resurgence, but she kept them down.

Selbos peered down at Amanda. "The Blekk gave you two locations to check. Why are we traveling to this one first? Were they more sure about Fen-tal than Za-thrin?"

Amanda nudged Joka, who remained focused on the piloting even though the ship's AI was in control. "I'm going to tell her, alright?"

"It's my contact but sure." Joka sighed.

Amanda held Joka's omni-tablet aloft. "One of Joka's friends—"

Joka cleared her throat as if she'd been stockpiling phlegm for this very occasion. "He's a fartsniffer, and I hate him."

"That's name-calling!" Symphora shouted. "Break her jar!" Symphora then devolved into a coughing fit.

"One of Joka's *acquaintances* is also on Earthquake's trail," Amanda corrected. "They told us they were checking out a planet, which happened to be the second option the Blekk gave us. If we split up and keep in contact, we can double our chances of finding the Earthquake base."

From the back, Symphora scoffed. "You're assuming it's all valid intelligence and not a trap."

Mel-za approached Symphora's cot and handed her a flagon of water. "If it's not, we'll go back to the Blekk and squeeze their tentacles until they blurt out the truth."

"So barbaric," Selbos muttered.

"I've updated the monk and the thief about our situation," Amanda said. "We'll meet up once we find the location of the abductions and the Bastion once we find it."

"What else have you been doing on my omni-tablet while I've been piloting?" Joka asked. "If you messed with my Block Bash high score, I swear…"

"I wouldn't swear around you. Besides, Block Bash scores are sacred." Amanda peered into the viewscreen, displaying the dirt-brown moon. "Is this the Fen-tal swamp moon? What kind of atmosphere are we dealing with?"

Selbos and Symphora groaned in unison. "A swamp?"

Mel-za bounded over to see the image on the viewscreen of the outside, displaying the muted colors of the local flora. "Finally!"

As they tapped the helm board controls, the ship hummed and an amber light glowed, signaling the gravity shift of descending into orbit.

The flight suit Amanda wore—Joka's patented design—contoured to her body, regulating her blood flow in time with the gravity shift. It wasn't as intense as she was used to from a lifetime of spacefaring. Joka was changing the future of Humans for the better with this invention, even allowing them to enlist in the Collective military for the first time—the first after the debacle with Crith all those years ago, of course.

"This suit is amazing, Joka." As the compliment left Amanda's lips, Joka winced but didn't respond.

"I can't go in a swamp," Selbos said, baring her teeth. "It'll mess with my allergies."

Peering over her shoulder, Joka addressed the whining Arkouda. "I've got some good news for you. You're staying on the ship."

Amanda gripped the edge of her seat, bracing for the storm. "So should you, Symphora."

"Like Nightmare I'm staying behind again," Symphora seethed. Eyes ablaze, Symphora struggled to sit upright in her cot and was gently pushed back down by Selbos.

Selbos cocked an ear in Symphora's direction. "Joka, I can understand Symphora staying behind—" her eyes swelled to the size of moons and focused on Symphora, "—o-o-only because you're injured, ma'am." Catching her breath, she addressed Joka. "But why me? So I can nurse her?"

Noticing Joka's scowl, Amanda placed a hand on her shoulder to placate her. "Earthquake is abducting Lo-sats on this settlement. Joka and I can mess with our hair to blend in—we'll style it to look like their cut. Mel-za won't stick out, either. Besides..." she plastered on the biggest smile she had, "they're afraid of Arkoudae. They won't crawl out of hiding if they see you. You're too tough."

Symphora exhaled and rolled over. "I accept that logic. Stop complaining, Selbos. Weren't you just bellyaching about your fake allergies, anyway?"

"Nice," Joka whispered to Amanda.

"Besides," Amanda added, "we need someone as smart as Selbos aboard to initiate Joka's tracking invention if we *do* scare the Earthquake losers off. And *I* believe you've got allergies, Selbos."

Selbos tucked her head down toward her chest and stared at the floor. "Thanks," she muttered.

"So I can't kill the Earthquake clowns?" Mel-za asked. "I was going to get creative with it—like Symphora would!"

Symphora grunted from the cot, kicking off her boots. "I'll tell you this much then. I never went out looking for a fight. Everyone I ever killed attacked me or my squad first or abused a vulnerable person. But be mindful of where you aim if you really want to give people nightmares. On Human males, their sphincters are parallel to—"

Amanda waved. "Nope. We're stopping there."

"Thanks for maintaining polite language on my ship," Joka said. "These brutes don't appreciate civil talk."

The ship touched down, pushing aside some low-rising vegetation. Amanda hated to consider how much fuel they burned by ignoring the space elevator, but they needed to stay away from any prying eyes. If Earthquake really was using Fen-tal as a base of operations, they would monitor traffic to and from the elevator. At least, it was what she and Rick would've ordered when they were in the organization, but who knew anymore?

Decontamination fumes hissed over everyone, and Amanda readied herself to leave with Joka and Mel-za. The two Humans affixed their breathers, and the Lo-sat affixed a grin while cracking her knuckles. The hatch door unlatched, allowing sunlight to enter the ship, accompanied by a noticeable wafting temperature change. Despite the moist air, Amanda's throat dried, hoping Mel-za's hunger for a fight would remain unsatisfied.

Selbos moaned. "The air even smells humid. Gross. Have fun choking on each breath."

"We will," Amanda called. "Keep an eye on each other for who owes the swear jar when we get back. Or get it out of your system while Joka's away."

"Both are acceptable," Joka said.

Joka and Amanda tended to each other's hair, using clips and barrettes to afford the illusion of compliance with Earthquake's lopsided hairstyle norms. Amanda momentarily wished for a disguise device that could just project a false haircut onto her, but then she remembered where she'd seen the device before and scowled. She was thinking of Rick Crith way more often than she wanted to these days.

Amanda didn't want to see herself in a mirror. Joka frowned as Amanda put the finishing touches on her hair.

"Yeah, it's an ugly cut, but you don't look that bad," Amanda said.

Joka's response came in a small voice. "No, that's not it."

"This is bringing up bad memories of Earthquake, isn't it?" Amanda said. For all the pain Earthquake had caused the galaxy, it felt realistic for Joka to have some pain attached to all its symbolism.

Joka shook her head. "Just memories of a friend. Last time I wore this ridiculous getup to blend in with Earthquake, it was with her. She, uh, she got me to try and talk nice. When she died, I made my swear jar out of her claws."

With a somber nod, Amanda placed a hand on her shoulder. "Thank you for telling me." Earthquake and the conflict around them had paved too much destruction and pain. Everyone had been affected, and it steeled Amanda's resolve. The Collective needed to accept Humans with full rights. Otherwise, they'd oust Earthquake only for a new group to surface. Maybe they'd call themselves Tsunami or Typhoon or something real creative like that. She'd take them down, too, which would prove to the Collective that Humans deserved Citizenship and prevent future insurgencies. Maybe even carve a real utopia. But nothing like that would ever come easy or without a fight, and she was ready for anything.

And none of that would change that she had let awful things happen when working for Earthquake.

Decontamination ended, and their grav harnesses adjusted to the lunar gravity and their breathers to the barometric pressure.

Mel-za stepped outside first, drinking in the luxurious humidity. Amanda wondered how much of it was genuine and how much was a gag to mess with Selbos. Selbos seemed like the type to hold a grudge.

The lush vegetation threatened to conceal their tracks as well as their ship, complicating their return. Verdant leaves wider than an Arkouda's leg choked the sunlight.

Glancing down at her omni-tablet, Amanda gauged she had enough of a charge in case they lost the trail.

"So if I were an Earthquake loser who wants to catch a Lo-sat…" Joka hummed.

"We need to attract them," Amanda said, wondering if "loser" violated the swear jar parameters.

Pulling back a loose branch, Mel-za winked. "Attracting people is not hard when you're as gorgeous as me."

"Tell me about it," Joka said. "There's a settlement nearby. It's pretty diverse based on the map data the Blekk gave Amanda. I saved it on my omni-tablet. We're close."

Under a mud-colored sky, traversing through ash-colored mud, Mel-za practically pranced like she was in paradise. Goosebumps rose on Amanda's skin as she realized why Earthquake would target her kind here. They loved the environment so much it put them off-guard. While the Lo-sats never complained about Arkouda dominance, they still felt the strain of living under the Collective with the standards always set to gravity and temperatures preferred by their still-larger rulers. Their status as full Citizens wouldn't make them any warmer. Really, Humans had an easier time in Arkouda habitats than the Lo-sats in this way. Humans were much more adaptable in general—an Arkouda could never tolerate this planet for long, but a Human could, even though it would be a difficult adjustment.

Amanda took a deep breath. Human laborers were at the bottom of the bottom. If they could find work here, away from Arkoudae but still under the protection of the Collective, it would be no small wonder they'd flock here, and Earthquake would attempt clandestine boveecrap.

Mel-za waved her tail in front of Amanda's face, breaking her reflection.

"What the—" Amanda flinched away from the scaly vine.

"Sorry." Mel-za brought her tail to her snout. "A plasmasipper was coming your way. I thought it was better for me to have a snack than for it to get a piece of you."

"Thanks," Amanda breathed.

Joka sneered. "You put sweetener in your protein drink, didn't you?"

"Yeah, I guess that was a rookie mistake." Amanda might as well have sent a written invitation to a plasmasipper nest.

The noxious swamp stench threatened light-headedness, and Amanda prayed they wouldn't have to run.

Squelching with each step, they trekked through the mud, Mel-za clearing out vegetation and helping them over rocks until they caught the din of a nearby settlement: metal scraping, Human voices mingling among Lo-sat hisses, and machinery moving large objects.

"It's a construction site," Joka whispered.

"Where accidents can happen any time," Amanda said. "Mel-za, how easy will it be for the three of us to blend in?"

"If nobody sees my gun? Very easy."

"You *had* to bring it, didn't you?" Joka asked. "That ruins the plan."

"Maybe not." Amanda toyed with the breather to help her think. "We can't go up to every Human here and ask if they're Earthquake. Someone might sell us out or figure out we're outsiders. Since Mel-za can't help but show off being a Symphora Squad member..." She grinned at the two of them. "Mel-za just caught us. She's been on the trail of Earthquake, and it brought her here. She needs to detain us while she continues her search."

Joka cocked an eyebrow. "I super hate this. How can we search if we're detained?"

"Because Earthquake sympathizers, if they're here, will break us out or a bunch of people will leave at once. Either way, we'll find our next piece of the puzzle."

Mel-za's tail tapped the rifle strapped to her back. "And after they tell you what you need to know, I strangle them with their own intestines. I like it, but how can you be positive?"

Amanda folded her arms over her chest and raised her eyebrows. "Hey, I found a mad scientist's laboratory on an unnamed asteroid. Also, Mel-za, when Symphora got creative with her kills, it only sounded cool when other people whispered about it in bars after the fact, and nobody was completely sure any of it was true. When you talk about wanting to do it, you sound a bit … unhinged. Like you need a therapist more than the rest of us."

Joka winced. "Yeah, I wasn't sure how to tell you. Plus, after we took on Earthquake last year, we're all Symphora now. It's not just her name—it's the Squad's name. Find your own way to carve out your unique identity."

"Without fantasizing about brutal murder," Amanda added.

"Fine," Mel-za huffed. "I guess you're both under arrest." Withdrawing her rifle, Mel-za ushered Amanda and Joka to march forward. Joka slapped some chalky mud on her suit to cover Symphora's symbol, and Amanda splayed some on her face to make her a bit more unrecognizable to a casual onlooker.

In Lo-sat, Mel-za shouted, "Got you, creeps!"

Joka shouted back in Human, "You'll never get me to talk!"

Words did not exist for how much she hated this farce. Wondering how many nearby Lo-sats understood Human, Amanda added in Arkouda, "Claws off me, slimeball." She hated the slur leaving her lips. One of the few things she probably still had in common with Rick—the man threatened to shoot a child but wouldn't use derogatory terms.

Hands at their wrists behind their backs, Joka and Amanda marched up the knoll, Mel-za holding a rifle behind them. A gaggle of Human construction workers and Lo-sat foremen and business types paused their work on what looked like a house.

Mel-za pulled out her collapsed helmet, letting it unfold and shine in the hazy sun. While it was fitted for a Lo-sat, the official helmet of the Symphora Squad showed her occupation. The stylized red mohawk cresting it to match their founder and namesake's haircut left no doubt. Amanda's Lo-sat was rusty, but what she caught of Mel-za's words were, "I found this pair … plotting … steal … our kin."

A chorus of murmurs from the Lo-sats thrummed, as many of them flared out their neck frills.

Amanda paid more attention to the Human reactions. Two head shakes. One grimace. Not enough to go off. One stepped backward, and Amanda caught the tip of a blue-green tattoo of Earth peeking out of his shirt sleeve, bright against skin that did not agree with Fen-tal's humidity. She didn't catch many features of this person but would recognize them again if they turned up.

Through the side of her mouth, marching at gunpoint, Amanda whispered, "Did you see that runner?"

"Yeah. We'll see if they spring us. Or murder us."

A Lo-sat dressed in business attire unsuited for a construction site slinked toward them. Her accent increased the difficulty of translation, but what Amanda caught from her was a greeting, a thank-you, and "I didn't know the Symphoras were here."

Mel-za reciprocated the greeting and accepted the thanks. "Yes... secret mission."

The businesswoman glared at Amanda and Joka before addressing them in Arkouda. "Enough of our kin have disappeared. We'll turn you over to the Fleet, and you'll rot in a cell forever."

Hating the performance, Amanda snarled. "You're just a puppet of the oppressors." Not quite a slur but another word she never wished to utter. Seeing Arkoudae only as oppressors was the Earthquake way. "Oppressors" was a buzzword which would act as a beacon. Knowing what to say twisted her gut.

Joka arched an eyebrow, then her eyes widened and faced the businesswoman with a gruff expression. "Once the Arkouda have no more use for you, they'll trample you underfoot without a second thought, just like they did to us."

"You're both full of *skata*," the Lo-sat hissed. Switching language, she eyed Mel-za. "I'm... you're taking them... your ship?"

Amanda's brain fried trying to listen, translate, and understand while still keeping her grimace.

"No," Mel-za replied. "Keep... days... continue... search. You... a place... I hold them?"

Smart. Amanda almost broke character to compliment her. This settlement wouldn't be large enough for a proper prison or detention facility. They were practically inviting a rescue if prisoners were held here.

The businesswoman led the trio toward a make-shift mobile office, the kind of prefabricated unit that could've stored a year's worth of jerky, a family's worth of furniture, or a cramped office depending on the need. Mel-za explained to the businesswoman how she didn't carry handcuffs since she wasn't expecting a surrender, only a fatal confrontation.

Thankfully, Mel-za's demeanor made that statement believable.

The businesswoman understood; the Symphora Squadron wasn't police, after all. What she ended up doing was having a foreman use zip-ties to restrain both their wrists to a chair sized for a Lo-sat, with a divot for a tail. The chair's divot strained Amanda's hips as she straddled it to avoid sinking in.

Amanda shot Joka an apologetic glance. She wasn't physically big enough to shuffle anywhere else on the seat the way she was restrained.

While Mel-za and the businesswoman hissed with each other, Joka whispered, "Don't look at me like that. I'm fine." Joka straightened with some effort. "A Lo-sat friend of mine always had perfect posture, so I'm trying to channel her."

Amanda nodded. She'd lost track of the Lo-sat conversation unfolding around them, but the foreman who had tied them up grunted about how the restraining ties he had wouldn't suffice to keep Amanda and Joka in place for long.

Mel-za cocked an eyeridge. "You have ... Humans here... their tools?"

The businesswoman folded thin arms over her chest. "You trust ... them?"

Mel-za waved her tail for emphasis as she spoke. "Humans in Symphora Squad... yes. Not all Humans bad."

The foreman and businesswoman exchanged glances while Amanda wondered if they were exchanging pheromones she couldn't detect as well, adding nuance to a silent discussion.

With a huff, the foreman departed. He returned shortly with a Human worker a bit older than Amanda, toolbox in hand.

The businesswoman leaned over him and whispered, "See what you can find out."

Amanda remained expressionless, unwilling to reveal she understood the simple phrase.

Mel-za stepped forward. "If that's your plan, we should give them space. Humans know it's easy for our kin to learn their language, so they might think this is a trap."

The Human worker dabbed some beaded sweat off his forehead with a rag that looked like it had been through a war or at least a few months of building homes too nice for him to ever own.

The businesswoman glared at Amanda and Joka, then hissed at Mel-za. "You ... listen from outside? You speak Human?"

After Mel-za agreed, the Lo-sats left. When the door closed, the Human worker lifted his eyes to them.

"Uh, hi." He had the raspy drawl of a lunar colonist like Amanda. "You, are you really with Earthquake?"

"Of course," Amanda said. "Pity I couldn't take that slimeball down with me."

Again, the slur. She wished she could use extra strength mouthwash to purge her lips. Or at least get hammered.

The Human recoiled at the word, but not like how she'd hoped. "You're just like these young bovees, out here trying to bring down a system bigger than you. Where are the abducted people?"

Amanda couldn't believe her stupidity and had to fight the urge to laugh. The exact type of person Humanity needed right now was the last person she wanted. "Show me your allegiance to true Humanity, and I'll talk to you. If you're with the Popsicles, do what you came here to do and get the hell out."

He pursed his lips, then withdrew some wire from his toolbox. As he placed a better restraint on their wrists, he sighed. "You give Humans a bad name. I'm embarrassed for our species because of people like you. I don't know who didn't love you enough as a kid, but you gotta grow up."

He left in a huff but had to place his toolbox on the floor to use both hands to reach up and heave open the door. He left with his toolbox, unable to close the door himself.

Joka glared at Amanda. "What the grimy gears was that for? Scaring him off like that?"

Amanda sighed. "He knows we're Earthquake now. He'll talk. We just have to trust the right person is listening and that Selbos and Symphora can use your ship's scanners to see if anyone hightails it out of here."

Shaking her head, Joka gazed out the window. "You're trying to kill me, right? But um… what's a popsicle?"

"You never had them on the *Calamity* in your Symphora days?"

"Clearly not."

Amanda blushed. "It's a frozen dessert on Earth"

"People on Earth can afford dessert?"

"It was a prehistoric thing, a recipe that survived the fall since it was easy and cheap. But, um, it's a slur used for Arkoudae."

"Because it's frozen?"

Amanda couldn't believe she was explaining this out loud. "Well, mostly because it's on a stick and where it goes... just add another credit to my swear jar tab."

"Done."

Mel-za entered, closing the door behind her with her tail. "Good performance," she whispered. "It sounds like they picked the right person to send inside, though." Her shoulders drooped. "I kinda wish I was wrong and all the Humans here were Earthquake supporters. It would've been helpful."

"Us, too," Joka said. "Hey, ping Selbos and tell her to watch the traffic for any ships leaving in the next few hours. Ask them if my contact updated them, too."

"You never know what kind of person you'll get in Earthquake," Amanda said. "Half of them would die for each other, itching to be martyrs for the cause. The other half are just desperate for safety and will leave the second things turn." She winced, realizing she'd spent time on both ends of that Earthquake spectrum. Every idea they purported depended on a foundation of xenophobia she wished she could've seen years ago, but some kind of willful ignorance kept her blind. But now she could do something about it.

Breathing deeply, Amanda met Mel-za's gaze. "You need to keep a safe distance from us. If you're guarding this office, you're in danger. I know you could hold your own in a fight, but Earthquake uses sneaky tactics to kill, like species-specific poison gasses. Plus, if you fight back and kill anyone who tries to rescue us, we've lost our lead and potentially useful information."

Tail stroking her holstered rifle, Mel-za winced. "Fine. I shouldn't be so trigger-happy, either. I just want to crack some skulls, Symphora-style, you know?"

"I know," Amanda said. "And I hope you never get the chance. We need to solve this with as little violence as possible. Nobody needs to die."

"I guess," Mel-za huffed. "I need to touch up your hair. The color is starting to fade." She reached into her belt pouch and grabbed some fungal spores, and then she rubbed them in Joka and Amanda's hair to tint the color, preserving their disguise.

Testing the resistance of their restraints, Joka sighed. "Somebody always dies. And it's usually the ones you're closest to."

Amanda didn't dare ask a follow up question and risk tugging at Joka's tapestry of pain; it wasn't sewn as tight as hers.

———

Over the ensuing hours, Amanda and Joka endured Mel-za visiting to sneak them food and make a farcical show of force while the businesswoman glared from the window. Construction around them continued.

The bustle resumed as if there weren't two self-proclaimed terrorists and serial abductors held hostage. The businesswoman pestered Mel-za to interrogate them more, but Mel-za used the intervening time to check on Selbos and Symphora. Amanda wanted to moan about the pain in her hips, but Joka's stoicism provided motivation enough to keep quiet.

As the sun set, the lunar atmosphere radiated a brown-turquoise hue, the host planet overtaking the star in the sky. Based on its size, night here lasted several days, making this place even less welcoming for the resident Humans. They couldn't get a fair shake anywhere in the galaxy. Amanda recognized enough Lo-sat phrases to catch a few slurs against the Human workforce through their open windows, which contrasted against the Humans mumbling about how they wished they could drain the swamp and make it easier to work.

Though at least enough Lo-sats patrolled that there weren't any plasmasippers to sneak inside and irritate Amanda and Joka.

Hours later, Mel-za returned, out of breath. "A ship full of Humans took off near the settlement. No clearance. It was a clunky one, too. Whoever left was in enough of a hurry to burn tons of fuel to get to escape velocity."

"That's our cue," Amanda said.

Joka's eyes widened. "Do you think Selbos got a tracer on them? Pre-hyperspace angular triangulations?"

Mel-za withdrew a knife and slashed their restraints. "I don't know what that means but probably."

Amanda slithered off the chair, stretching as sensation returned to her extremities. Joka appeared ragged from sitting in a divot, arching her back and massaging her lumbar.

"Ready to go?" Amanda asked.

Joka stretched, grabbing her toes. "Yeah. Mel-za, did you tell the businesswoman what was up?"

"Nah," Mel-za said. "I figured I'm the only one here with a gun. So if you run away and any of the Human workers here help you or obstruct my kin chasing you, we'll know if the Earthquake folks stayed or flew."

Amanda scoffed. "Sitting all stiff for hours and now you want us to run?"

"What?" Mel-za asked. "It's not like anything would happen."

Joka folded her arms over her chest. "And you're positive nobody else has a gun?"

"I mean, I didn't smell any..."

Joka pointed toward the door. "Let's get back to Symphora. Can I see your rifle?" Joka tapped her flight suit, and her grav harness floated off. Joka rose into the air for a half-second, then her suit adjusted, and she floated back to the floor. She affixed the harness to Mel-za's rifle, which hovered from the floor.

"Now the suspect is armed," Joka said. "Let's see how you like getting chased."

Mel-za smirked, then ran out screaming like she'd just seen a Galsan worm. "They've got a gun!"

Amanda and Joka sprinted out after her, Joka awkwardly bobbing the now-weightless weapon in front of her. Shooting anything now would be difficult if not impossible for them, but the locals wouldn't have that problem in standard gravity.

Mel-za sprinted, getting considerable distance in the construction site with her long legs. Joka cast a few deliberately wild shots which were much more precise than they appeared. Just away from Mel-za's appendages and close enough to further their illusion, making Amanda wonder if Joka had ever done this before.

Crossing the construction site at a sprint, Amanda's lungs burned.

Human voices shouted.

"Get those Earthquake chicks!"

"They're trying to kill a Symphora Squaddie!"

Amanda winced as she huffed. These were the good guys, and they wanted to kill her. She glanced over her shoulder and regretted it immediately.

The hubbub came from a crew of young Human construction workers, casting off protective gear as they gave chase, revealing muscles clearly honed from hard work.

Amanda and Joka couldn't outrun them.

Between heaves, Amanda called to Joka. "Any chance you can fire some warning shots safely at the guys behind us?"

Grunting, Joka checked over her shoulder. "Yeah. It won't buy us much time, though."

Amanda urged her legs to go faster. All her exercises in the previous years had been to stay healthy, not train for a sprint. "Anything helps."

Joka wheeled around, then fired at the mud in front of the workers, shouting, "Don't take this personally!" She fired another round just over their heads. "Third from the left, you can buy me a drink!" Mud and muck splashed onto them, but at least it wasn't plasma fire, thanks to Joka's careful aim.

Amanda smiled despite the sweat slithering down her back. "You should've told them you're ready to introduce them to your parents if you really wanted to repulse them." The men bounced away, staring at the plasma-scorched earth in front of them, the mud hyper-drying from the plasmafire.

"Funny, but I never knew my parents." Joka joined Amanda in their pursuit of Mel-za, who Amanda could tell was barely jogging now. They needed to fix this or somebody would catch on.

"Sorry, I—"

"Save it."

The brush was nearing, but the workers had already regained the ground they'd lost when they hesitated, possibly more from Joka's aggressive flirting than warning shots. A fresh sting hit Amanda as she realized the much faster Lo-sats had sent their slower Human workers to catch them, as if they couldn't be bothered to get their claws dirty.

The workers' boots splashed through the mud behind them. They'd be within tackling distance soon, not that Joka would mind, it seemed.

Straining to speak through gasps, Amanda said, "Change the gravity settings." After a gulp of air, she added, "Then toss them the rifle." The dense air made normal breathing a struggle.

With a huff, Joka rotated the oversized weapon, slapped the affixed grav harness, then spun around.

"Blue overalls, shave and call me." She heaved the weapon, floating at first, then careening as the gravity settings changed, hitting the biggest of them in the stomach, forcing him to the ground. Wheezing, Joka said, "On second thought, you were trying to arrest me, and that is a red flag."

The other workers stopped their sprint to hoist the weapon off their comrade.

Mel-za disappeared into the brush, Amanda and Joka following.

Once over the knoll and into the brush, Mel-za hissed at them. "Nice of you to throw my gun away without asking first."

Ready to spit out a lung, Joka glared at her. "Nice of you to arrange for the worst exit possible."

It wasn't exactly the swift and sudden exit they'd wanted.

"Give her ... a break..." Amanda wheezed, ready to choke on the air. "She was right. We know whoever left was the Earthquake crew or individual. These others were loyalists." Loyalist wasn't a slur, but she didn't like that word, either. It felt too much like her actual Earthquake days. Playing this character never worked for her before, and donning this persona made her want to vomit. Amanda and Joka limped after Mel-za, who cleared branches away for them.

Frowning, Joka grabbed a branch for walking support. "Where'd you come up with the gravity shift idea?"

What could Amanda tell her? That the man she hated the most and once considered a mentor fought a monster and mad scientist that way? She toyed with distraction by mentioning the image inducer she wished she had again. "I dunno. Where'd you come up with the desperate 'I want a boyfriend' shtick?"

Mel-za huffed. "Joka asked you about the gravity shift idea because she was trying to find a way to brag about how she killed a lab experiment by shooting at its grav harness."

Joka's face soured as if Mel-za's words brought some foul memory to the surface. "I actually don't want to talk about that day." After a sigh, she turned to Amanda. "Blue overalls wasn't that cute. It's been awhile since I've had a date. The Calamity station didn't make many port stops back in my days with Symphora. There aren't a ton of men visiting the shelter, so it's been awhile, alright?"

Joka's ship loomed ahead, onboard ramp open. Selbos waited in the hatch with her paws on her hips, elbows out. "Well it took you long enough. Joka's tracker is pinging us a location for that rogue ship but not for much longer. Let's roll."

EIGHTEEN

(ROSANNA)

Hunting prey in the Makawe Demilitarized Zone

NO CONGRATULATIONS CAME. She'd crippled the government in a third of all settled space.

The Bastion wasn't exactly a place Rosanna wanted to stick around. Tecton left her with a promise of telling her everything once she brought down Crith.

Rosanna took to the stars again, alone this time. A ping arrived on her omni-tablet after she cleared hyperspace and popped into an ocean world's orbit.

[Martinez is aboard a ship designated DR-1, approaching the settlement on Fen-tal moon.]

Rosanna glanced at the sender—one of the captains back at the Bastion. He didn't deserve her gratitude but needed acknowledgment since he did technically outrank her.

[Rosanna: Track her. Give me an update on the monk and the thief.]

Her ship's antigrav settings meshed with her own gravity harness to ease her body from hyperspace travel. Once steady, Rosanna finished the inventory of her teleportation chitin.

Just three of her own stash remained, which she kept separate from the pool at the base. These were a finite resource, and their Leader couldn't care less— she trusted he had a plan. With her thoughts drifting to the chitin, a chill rocked her spine.

The eyes of the judger, the force she couldn't name. Nobody else breathed a word about it. Rosanna shivered the thought away. She definitely needed an artificial means of teleportation, unattached to a dead species' body parts. Rosanna fumed, knowing Alize Oze might have some way to manufacture more if she would just open her mouth. She'd save that for another mission.

Yet once Rosanna wedged a knife wedged between Crith's ribs, none of it would matter anyway. She couldn't imagine much past the tip of that blade piercing his shriveled husk of a heart.

She knew Rick would see through the ruse of destroying the government offices. He wouldn't search there. But with the fake news going out about the impending attack on the Makawe rebels, he'd be too tempted to go anywhere else. He may know where the Bastion was, or he'd find some asshole way to discover it. With the image inducer he stole from the Human scientist two years ago, the bastard could slip by any Human without scanning tech. Knowing him, he probably relied on it as little as possible, which allowed a few camera traps to catch him. He relied on that compromised omni-tablet too much, and that would be his downfall.

So if Crith would find the Bastion's location, she needed to incapacitate him first. Or at least weaken him. He would gather allies, some pitiful lot that he'd just lead to die. His obsession with being a leader meant he would never do things alone. Always delegating, wasting time getting someone to cover his back instead of focusing ahead. He'd brought in the Drowned Star pirates—to the rest of Earthquake's collective disgust. Yet there was one group he'd always wanted but never managed to pull into the fold.

Makawe rebels—vicious fanatics whose hatred of the Collective and oppression as a Provincial species outclassed Humans who boasted the physical strength to snap a spine with their pincers. These sapients teetered on the brink of extinction, with many fighting like it. Others just accepted their fate, becoming subservient to the oppressors and going quietly into the night.

Rosanna approached the azure planet's cloudy orbit, shimmying around one of its two moons. In her periphery, a satellite blinked. A pre-recorded voice chirped in her comm, speaking in accented Arkouda.

"State business. Vessel for trading?"

Rosanna winced, hating how she was using the code words Crith learned. "Trade-trade. Buy salt, koknati nuts."

A crackle filled the otherwise long silence.

Glaring at the comm device, Rosanna willed a response to come through the other end.

Moments later, the response came in Ma'ak. Her omni-tablet provided a translation, utilizing free software. "You want the downfall?"

She didn't have time to play around with this software, so she spoke in Arkouda, the hateful language biting her tongue. "Yes. I want the downfall. Let me in and I'll talk. I'm unarmed."

"What is your Ma'ak speaking amount?"

"Only the code words."

A bulbous ship materialized through the planet's cloud cover, careening toward her. It was smaller than a battledart, sleek enough that a Human probably couldn't stand inside one. It definitely had some defensive weapons onboard—the thing couldn't take a hit, but it could snake through a blockade and cause some unexpected damage to a tender spot.

"We scan. Follow ship. Initiate communication, and we roast you from orbit."

Rosanna could respect that level of bluntness, at least, and she hoped her communiques to others came off as direct and threatening. Following through the atmosphere, she balked upon realizing this planet lacked a space elevator. She hated to waste so much fuel. These rebels could at least have a floating landing deck at escape velocity. She'd have to mess with her ship's antigrav manually to avoid burning too much of the ship's energy.

Following the ship's lead through the crystalline skies and low-hanging clouds, Rosanna's grav harness groaned, working overtime to adjust her field to the planet's oppressive gravity. No wonder Makawe were so low to the ground. Breathing was a labor like she hadn't known before. She approached the planet's lazily churning sea, struggling to produce waves in the gravity.

Her navigation software found a landing raft bobbing near a sandbar and vegetated rock island. Rosanna touched down, then affixed her breather before opening the cockpit. Makawe preferred alkaline atmospheres, even though they could breathe the same oxygen a Human or Arkouda could without issue. The air passing the filter gave an earthy must to the otherwise salty breeze. Two Makawe flanked her ship, rising from the ocean surface to appraise her.

She reminded herself that it wouldn't take much for one of them to crush her bones.

From the top, their chitinous red carapaces appeared identical, yet the one to her left had a wider belt, which indicated this was probably a male, if Rosanna's memory served. Upon closer inspection, he had black zigzags bisecting his carapace, obscuring his carved tattoos.

The wider-belted one propped himself on his pincer and rolled an eye stalk up at Rosanna. He spoke Arkouda; his accent was noticeable but unobtrusive. "You have the spirits of Earth'quake. A rebel. Why are you here?"

Rosanna had forgotten about the species' penchant to reference spirits. She thought it had something to do with their ability to see in the infra-red but didn't care enough to examine further. "You refused the last person to come here, didn't you? Rick Crith from Earthquake."

"No," the Makawe said, sounding irritated if she understood his inflection. "We refused Earth'quake. We liked him."

Rosanna grimaced, wondering if his so-called spirits would tell him how she imagined cutting out his beak and making his pincer into a lounging chair.

Before she could speak, the Makawe continued, "And your anger spirits tell me you don't."

"No," she huffed. Even though they didn't have advanced olfactories like an Arkouda or Lo-sat, these Makawe saw infrared and heat signatures, so hiding from them was impossible.

"I'm here to tell you the evils of the one who came here years ago. Rick Crith is a traitor, and he's on his way to kill you for refusing him."

"You cannot bully us into joining him now. We're not expectors."

She didn't want to suggest any weakness by asking him what he meant by "expector." "You'll get solitude when the Collective is destroyed. Join me and that *will* happen."

The Makawe stared at her, shifting his eyestalks while wavegulls cawed above. He was reading her infrared signature, and she hated it. "Earth'quake cannot destroy the Collective, though. Answer my question: why the anger spirits? Who do you hate?"

Rosanna fought the urge to lash out. Crith would be here soon, and she couldn't risk them helping him. "Since you refused Crith, do you know what has happened?" She let her hushed tone convey the impending doom for them.

A wave crashed ashore, falling hard on the rock.

The Makawe speaking to her scuttled around to the front, and the smaller retreated to the back of her ship. They hadn't even invited her down, but she wasn't a fool—they saw no reason to be polite to her. No wonder the Arkouda looked down on them.

The speaker stopped, eyestalks shaking. "I see a racist spirit on you. Just one. Black as my shell. Crush that spirit."

"You're perceptive," Rosanna said. "Listen, this Rick Crith has killed innocent people since he petitioned you. Prisoners. Women. Children. Families. He's threatened even more. The man is a monster. If he comes here, it's only a matter of time until he makes the ocean flow with blood."

The obstinate asshole straightened. "What spirits follow Crith?"

"Only hate, evil, and death." Rosanna assumed those were spirits, as if she could understand his nonsense. "He'll bring those spirits to you in revenge for not helping him before."

"You're so sure? I see a confident spirit around you."

Rosanna resisted the grin forming. "He's hunting you, and he isn't that far away. He blames you for his failures. He's coming here with intent to kill. Help me, and I'll make sure he doesn't damage a claw on anyone's shell. This is your last chance to get on

Earthquake's good side." She pointed to the weapons on her belt. "I suggest you take it. Joining Crith will mean declaring war on Earthquake. You're better off with me than against me."

NINETEEN

(RICK)

Desperate for allies in the Makawe DMZ

A NEWS HEADLINE burned Rick's eyes. "Frontier government offices destroyed in an ambush by Earthquake." Rick shook his omni-tablet as if his rage would make the reality disappear. Hopefully, Amanda was too valuable for Earthquake to slaughter. The attack stank like a hoofbeast carcass stuck in a trap, begging him to go investigate and expose himself. Whether Amanda escaped, was off-station, or died in the chaos didn't change his mission parameters.

But he wasn't about to endanger P'oki. He also had an idea of where to hunt for the new Earthquake base. But he needed allies first. P'oki, while capable, wasn't a fighter.

P'oki stomped on the floor, and the reverberation snapped his attention. "Rix, you are sure this idea is good?"

He huffed. "Why? Do you see some uncertainty spirits around me?"

"Yes. Sarcasm ones, too." A frustrated trill echoed in her beak.

Rick wished she'd let him speak to her in Ma'ak, despite how ridiculous he felt sticking a finger under his lip to form a beak shape. He knew her language well enough, but she didn't want him to embarrass himself, reducing her to broken Arkouda. She beat him in both language and compassion.

"I reached out to your kinfolk seven years ago but was stopped by my old leader. He didn't want to associate with Makawe." Rick peered down at her. "I could've had powerful allies. A real coalition, and I let someone else's xenophobia stop me. Everybody knew that I'd tried to do that, too. I'm surprised nobody else bothered."

P'oki swiveled an eyestalk at him. "Why you think Earth'quake coming here?"

The crushing pincers from his nightmares resurfaced. "I've been spying on their communications. They are coming here. I can use that to our advantage and recruit them."

"Use, you say." P'oki tutted. "You thinks my people tools? You are like Ar'koods."

The truth stung like a voracious plasmasipper. "Can you see honesty spirits around me? I don't think anyone who is sapient is a tool. I want to ask them for help."

P'oki trilled, but Rick couldn't parse the meaning this time. Maybe he was better off with her speaking in Arkouda.

"If my guess is right about where the Earthquake base is, we'll need all the help we can get. If we want any chance of saving He'nay, we need backup."

"Agreeing, Rix. You sure you can be around rebels without your trauma spirits rising up?"

"I wish I knew."

Their ship broke the atmosphere. A glistening ocean stretched in all directions, engulfing a pristine beach dotted by koknati trees flexing in the breeze, sagging with the weight of their head-sized nuts. The place was beautiful. A paradise. It should've been, at least. No place would truly be serene for the Makawe as long as they lived under the Collective boot heel.

They descended onto a landing pad in the water. P'oki scuttled to the viewscreen, examining the view with swiveling eyestalks. "Something is wrong, Rix."

"What do you see in the infrared?"

"Lingering spirits of a Hu'man."

Rick's heart tightened, hoping P'oki was delusional.

"Let's tread carefully, then. Shouldn't we expect a welcome committee?"

"Rix, none of my kin swim near here. Something is wrong. Makawe spirits of confusion and apprehension dance around the beach."

The landing pad taxied toward the beach, propelled by an unseen mechanism below, which was possibly automated. Water landings would allow for the tiniest fuel savings, which Rick appreciated. Economic efficiency was mandatory when fighting a revolution. Rick affixed a breather to his face as his grav harness adjusted to the gravity. He opened the cockpit, which, unlike ships he'd flown before, was a circular floor panel which lowered on a hydraulic for easier Makawe access, hissing decontamination spray on him as he descended.

He stepped onto the white sands with P'oki close by. Waves whispered against the shore, and wavegulls cawed in the distance. This was the kind of place he would come to when flashes of combat, both against soldiers and solid nightmares, sprang into his mind. Yet the silence and P'oki's body language gave him pause. This was no paradise.

"Steady, Rix."

"What?"

"One of my kin approaches with spirits concealed. That is never good."

Rick peered down at her. "You can conceal your-selves in the infrared?"

"You can hide from sight, can't you? You can be quiet to hide from sound, can't you? Humans strange with questions." P'oki scuttled forward and trilled a phrase in Ma'ak. Rick caught her name and not much else—her voice sounded so different, elegant.

Through the cover of the koknati trees, a scuttling figure emerged, close to the ground. Black zigzagged stripes streaked across a red tattooed carapace. Male, judging by the size of his pincers and the bluntness in his scuttling. For how little Rick knew of how Makawe aged, this could have been the same rebel who nearly snapped his spine over a decade ago. They never did take out that squad.

P'oki nudged herself in front of Rick, trilling again in Ma'ak. She didn't speak in simple enough vocabulary for Rick to follow, but her words gushed with a poetry he could never comprehend but could vaguely appreciate. The meter and intention made it feel criminal how Collective society forced her to speak a language requiring a tongue and muzzle. More inequality laid bare.

His responses, too, dripped in echoing syncopated poetry. No wonder their species made their mark on galactic society through music. All that was missing in their conversation was a set of Makawe knuckle drums. But the beauty of their conversation belied the sense of dread Rick intuited from it.

P'oki cast an eyestalk back at Rick. "He saying I can negotiate. He not trust you until talk to me alone. He saw a spirit of recognizing around you, so he figured out you understood some of our talking words."

Rick wasn't quite old enough to worry about losing bladder control, but the word "recognizing" tempted his regular body function. Tensing, Rick assured himself she meant recognizing some of their words and not recognizing his face, so he nodded, wondering how all that could possibly display in the infrared. Either way, he accepted the logic.

And arguing with her would be pointless. "Please tell him we only want to save your daughter and my, um... person. If they can turn in Earthquake members, there is a chance they'll receive clemency from the Collective. They won't have to live their lives fighting every day or hiding."

"I tell him, Rix. Careful, please. That spirit I saw of another softskin is close."

Goosebumps pricked on Rick's arms and neck as P'oki shuffled away, following this new Makawe. He wondered if P'oki could convince this guy. And what Rick could've done years ago if Tecton had just gotten out of his way and let him try to negotiate with the Makawe rebels. It was too late to know for certain now. It was too late for a lot of things.

He knew why he was on edge. This was a wasted venture. Earthquake wasn't here yet, and they had no reason to believe him. Rick was a shit leader, and that realization crushed more than any Makawe pincers ever could.

P'oki didn't deserve to be the next innocent person who died because of him.

As Rick marched forward to tell her to not bother, a gust collected the sweat on his neck. Wishing he could sniff like a Lo-sat, he spun around, and phantom pains tingled along with the urge to reach for a gun that no longer sat holstered on his hip.

"Who's there?" Rick hissed in Arkouda. "Show yourself." Darting his gaze in every direction, he relaxed. He was overreacting over a beach breeze.

A rustling koknati tree caught his attention above. "Rix!"

He darted toward the trees. "P'oki!" Damn distraction.

They'd walked into a trap. The clacking echoed in his mind.

The Unspeakable.

Mandibles. Mandibles.

Dripping. Dripping.

Makawe rebels, not too different from their greeter, pinching the life from him while he desperately called for air support that never came.

Shooting uselessly at regenerating abominations in Dr. Diastrevlo's lab of nightmares.

All of it.

P'oki's screams.

Rick pushed forward, sprinting but never fast enough.

In the mixture of sand and budding grass, P'oki laid, carapace half-submerged, spindly legs flailing. A thick metal crate pushed her carapace into the dirt and sand. Her eyestalks were submerged, and the bottom of her upside-down beak poked through. "Rix!"

A Human woman crouched atop the crate, brandishing a knife in one hand and a pistol in the other. She was clad in cobbled-together Collective armor, reforged and refitted to fit a Human, painted green and blue. She bore the tell-tale lopsided haircut of Earthquake and a giant tattoo of Earth with a diagonal line through it. The ink's colors on her bicep made her skin resemble polished rock more than muscle.

Most striking was the feminine version of a face he'd seen before, the face of a man he'd shot dead for mutinying, a face he'd seen years ago, when he lied to her and told her that her brother had died a hero fighting for Earthquake.

"Get off her," Rick hissed. As liberating as it was to speak in his true language, using it in this circumstance soured the experience. Her name tugged at his memory but not as much as those eyes.

The woman hopped off the crate. P'oki "oofed," but barely budged. "She'll be alright." Her gaze bored holes into Rick's psyche. This was the face of someone who intended to kill.

But she had the means to do it already, so she wanted something. "You know, I killed a Makawe a few months ago who had the same beak curve and shell pattern."

Rick's eyes widened, but no words came.

A hateful grimace stretched, revealing her teeth. "The Makawe I killed was a research assistant to Alize Oze. So you convinced a relative to help you find her? Smart move for a lying asshole like you."

Her last name came to Rick. "Say your piece, Moreno. Whatever your issues are with me, she's innocent. Makawe are the galaxy's downtrodden, even more than us. If you really believe in what your tattoos mean, you'll get that crate off her."

In his periphery, Rick noticed the male Makawe from before, cowering, pincers over a smaller Makawe woman.

"What did you do to them?" Rick asked. Her first name was coming. He'd had to memorize it before delivering the news of her brother's death to her family all those years ago.

"You don't get any questions." Pure hate dripped in each word.

He wondered what Tecton had told her. "I didn't want you to join the gang," Rick said. "I remember visiting you, Rosanna."

That struck a nerve. She lunged, slashing her knife, and Rick sidestepped out of the way. She was fast.

Anger would make her sloppy, he hoped. Knowing she wanted something would be what would keep Rick alive, unless she was the type who fought better when angry.

She didn't hesitate. "You remember, huh?" Another slash.

Rick sidestepped again, letting her go in front of him so he could kick from behind. But she was there with a gun in his chin.

Damn. She'd spun around by the time he raised his leg.

Rick fought to keep his voice even. "Yeah, I remember. Take the crate off my friend if you want to talk."

"She'll die. It'll be your fault."

"You said she'd be alright. What do you want?"

"Tell me how my brother died. Say his name."

He remembered training Alejandro. Grooming him. Wanting a second in command who was tougher, faster, stronger, and smarter than him: every teacher's dream. Alejandro Moreno had everything Rick wanted in a successor, but his ego got in the way. Alejandro eventually committed the green-eared mistake of thinking he was ready before his time, that he was out of lessons to learn when he was only getting started—a mistake Rick made repeatedly when he'd been in his twenties like Alejandro. That miscalculation cost him his life when he mutinied against Rick on the damned moon when the Unspeakable chased them. Rick hadn't hesitated to kill him.

"Alejandro Moreno." Saying the name hurt more than the gun pushing against his chin.

She grimaced, the name bringing new rage into her eyes. "You only fooled my parents." The gun beneath Rick's face quivered in Rosanna's grip.

Rick had told them that their son died in the service of Earthquake. How could he tell them about the Unspeakable? The clacking cockroach devil which grew as it was attacked and feasted on light and defied all technology and biology? How could he tell the Moreno family their son died a traitor to their already treasonous cause? He'd told them the most truth he could muster, and that had been enough for the parents. But Rosanna must have seen through Rick's incomplete story.

"What'd Tecton tell you?" Rick struggled to keep P'oki in his periphery, and he spied a grav harness sitting atop the crate, increasing the thing's mass. Her shell was hard, but not so much on her underbelly. She wouldn't have much time left before it would start to crack under the crate's weight.

Rosanna using grav harnesses in creative ways made him want to hurl; that was how he survived against the Unspeakable and how he killed Dr. Diastrevlo.

"Tecton told me enough to confirm what I knew as a kid. You're a liar." She pushed the gun up to his nose, forcing Rick to look at the sky.

"Don't ask me anything." Rick opened his mouth and bit on the pistol's barrel. Muffled, he said, "Go aheah and soot mee. You on't be-eive what I say."

She arched an eyebrow, and a quiver of hesitation stopped her trigger finger.

Rick pushed the barrel up, cutting his inner lip and forming his mouth into a beakish shape. He called out in his best Ma'ak, "She kill your friend. Check betray spirits."

The pair of Makawe onlookers trilled and charged. Rosanna pulled the gun from Rick's mouth and aimed at them, but Rick shoved her to the ground. He darted toward the crate, thumbing his grav harness. His insides lurched as he leapt, rising high enough to delicately land on the crate, hating to add even a kilogram to the force on P'oki.

He lifted the discarded grav harness from the crate, changed it to the lowest setting, then hopped off and shoved. It floated midair, hovering gently.

Safely aground, Rick switched his own setting back to standard for this rock's gravity.

The younger Moreno dove on him, pulling her knife again. The two Makawe assisted P'oki, and Rick grappled with his assailant. Trying to fling off the stronger woman, Rick summoned every bit of strength with one arm while phantom pains in his stump itched to help defend.

Shoom!

She fired her pistol, not to shoot Rick, but so the kickback would force her elbow down into his, bringing him down to a knee. As Rick gasped, she dug the butt of her gun between his neck and shoulder.

He howled and sank to his knees.

While he wouldn't be able to speak in full sentences through this pain, it might not be fatal. But he'd lose even more sensation in the left side of his body now.

Shuffling sand behind them signaled charging Makawe. Releasing Rosanna's arm, Rick summoned what strength he had left and leaned backward, causing his attacker to fall forward, the one move she never would've learned from studying him since Rick had always been the type to prefer death on his feet to living on his knees. She toppled, and Rick rammed his good shoulder into her abdomen before reaching for her gun. While he struggled to liberate it, she stabbed again, and this time the knife stuck in his cloak.

Heaving through the pain, he pulled hard on her gun wrist, jerking it while trying to shift his knees to stand. He should've used the image inducer, even though it wouldn't have fooled the Makawe's infrared sight.

The Makawe trio arrived, yanking her off him. As they did, she dropped her knife and rolled away, her lithe body slithering through their pincers. The two rebels had trained to fight Arkoudae, and this must've been P'oki's first fight.

Covered in sand, the attacker glared at Rick. "This isn't over." She pointed skyward with her gun. With her free hand, she reached into a pocket and withdrew a shiny black disk.

Rick had seen one before in the damn moon five years ago with the Unspeakable. That was chitin from a long-dead Chamayna corpse.

What was she—

Thwip.

"No!" Rick hadn't taken the bait and looked up when she'd pointed, but he did now. A sleek civilian cargo ship hovered overhead, modified for secret weapons, as was Earthquake's standard.

P'oki trilled. "Rix! She in that ship. Her spirits trail upward."

Teleportation. Her ship rose into the stratosphere. Rick huffed, feeling between rivulets of blood for his spinal injuries. "Ask your friends if they know first aid. We're following her. Will the spirits guide you in space?"

Delicately, P'oki placed a pincer over Rick's good shoulder. "Spirits show the way. Always."

Rick's vision blurred. He'd lost blood. Too much. Too damn much. No. He needed to chase her since she'd have information he needed.

P'oki trilled something to the other Makawe, and as Rick's eyelids betrayed him, he felt a lifting sensation, and the scuttle march back to their ship. There was medgel there. Maybe P'oki knew enough to catch the attacker's direction, the damn Moreno girl who grew into a hateful woman, all because of Rick's sins.

But if she was under Tecton's direct influence, there was only one place she could be going.

TWENTY

(AMANDA)

**Aboard the *DR-1*, tracking a
former ally through hyperspace**

STARS SWIRLED IN a kaleidoscope around them,
galactic nebulae twisting into oil spill paintings as
they zoomed in hyperspace. "You did amazing with
tracking those Earthquake runaways," Amanda said.
"I didn't think this was possible with how far ahead
of us they were. Do you think you'd accept a second
award for service to Humanity?"

Joka's tracker invention allowed the *DR-1*'s navigation to follow their quarry. Joka cast a weak glance
at Amanda. "I guess. Could you check my omni-
tablet again?"

This wasn't the first time Joka had deflected a compliment. Amanda wondered what happened to the
woman who stole a ship to answer a distress call—it

made her wonder if there was another reason Joka had shunned that award last year.

"No updates on your messenger," Amanda said. "Maynard and Binh haven't responded to our original message about the coordinates. Try not to worry about it. They'll be alright. If Binh could survive working with a bunch of murder-happy xenophobes, the business on that moon with Rick…" She shuddered, remembering the monstrosity. "Not to mention those hybrid monsters with you, he can survive anything." Amanda absorbed the display from the cockpit and grabbed the seat beside Joka. "You truly are an amazing inventor. Tracking without a physical beacon through hyperspace? I don't even know if Collective military tech has gotten that far."

"It hasn't," Selbos muttered from behind. "Whatever you two put in your hair to change the color stinks, by the way."

"Your attitude stinks, by the way," Joka replied. "It was dirt and pollen, so good for the environment and my wallet. If these guys we're tracking lead us to the Earthquake headquarters, we might be in for a nasty welcome if this camouflage doesn't hold."

"Maybe," Amanda mused. "If word gets out that some Earthquake abductors escaped a Lo-sat settlement *with* a Lo-sat, they might think we're with them if we arrive just behind the others."

"Let's hope." Joka glanced over her shoulder at Mel-za, pacing in front of Symphora. "Are you still mad about losing your gun?"

Mel-za glared. "I'd tell you how I really feel, but I'd rather not dump my paycheck into your swear jar."

That garnered a chuckle from Symphora. "Whoo, it's that bad, huh? At least you respect the captain."

Amanda faced the ailing legend. "How're you feeling?"

"The medgel is helping, but I'm old, and that Earthquake assassin did a number on me. Load me up with painkillers and beer, and I'll be walking around just fine. My aim will be off if we fight, though."

Mel-za bristled. "You better hope we don't, seeing as I was the only one who brought a gun with me."

"You still have your armor's shielding," Joka offered. "Even if it got weakened a bit."

"Symphora, we'll leave you with the ship again," Amanda said. "The Earthquake base won't be safe. We must get there and broadcast our signal so the Collective Fleet can find us."

Selbos tutted. "You reckon we can broadcast to the Fleet without also sending a beacon to Earthquake? Especially if we're outside their base? Joka, can you pull another invention out of your—uh, mind?"

Joka shook her head. "I'd need more supplies and time than what I got here."

Amanda sighed; they deserved the truth. "It wouldn't just be the Collective fleet joining us."

"You think a thief and an expelled monk count as reinforcements?" Joka asked.

"No."

Two Arkoudae and one Lo-sat sniffed the air. Amanda blushed, wondering what pheromones she'd released. "The Drowned Star. I told the Blekk where we were going. They agreed to help the military destroy Earthquake's HQ."

"Again with the Drowned Star?" Symphora groaned. "And you trust them?"

Amanda stood, straightening her spine. "It doesn't hurt that Tecton insulted them. And I think they're more than just pirates," Amanda said. "I've updated them on our location."

"Oh great, so they'll kidnap and ransom us or murder us outright." Selbos rolled her eyes.

"Then you'll get to say 'I told you so,'" Amanda said, brows furrowed. "But for now, we're going with my plan. The Blekk are more than people give them credit for. No disrespect to present company, but I think you can admit the Citizen species dismissed the Blekk since they can't conform to your Arkouda's expected norms like Humans and Makawe can."

Symphora growled. "You think I'm on the side of the historical government? I'm in this gig to change *skata* for the better. I know how bad Provincials have it. The only reason I don't know as well as you is because I'm not one myself." She huffed and addressed Joka. "And I know this is your ship, but if you bring up that swear jar right now, I'll mutiny."

Amanda waved a hand dismissively. "I'm not trying to start an argument with you. I know you're on the right side of this. We all are. But I think the right side includes the species the Collective won't even regard as sapient."

Selbos folded her arms over her chest. "Yeah, that's a load of it, for sure. They can officially deem the Blekk as pirate marauders and a galactic security threat but say they can't think. Total hypocrisy."

"And maybe they're reduced to piracy because they don't have many other options in society," Amanda added. "Let them show they care about civilization, and then they can join it. Not everyone needs to conform to Arkoudae's norms. Mel-za, can you really say you're not freezing in half the places you go?"

Mel-za coiled her tail around her seat, and her eyes dropped to the floor. "It would be nice if temperature and gravity settings were a bit more inclusive of others."

Symphora tutted. "I can't help standard ship and settlement settings, but the Calamity station was always inclusive. Wasn't it, Joka?"

Rising from her chair at the cockpit, Joka stood on the chair's seat to meet her former boss and mentor's gaze. "Half the reason I got into inventing was because I felt so useless *on your station*. My entire life was on the Calamity. Maybe that was my own issues peeking through the surface, but I wrestled with that—I was the smallest and weakest member of the smallest and weakest species aboard. I had to carry a collapsible stepstool around and even that wasn't enough half the time. I got called 'runt' more often than my own name some days."

Symphora stared at the floor. "I didn't know you had it that bad."

"You also never invited any Makawe aboard, even though we saved plenty. So don't act like you're perfect." Joka stared down the weakened legend, then added, "Ma'am."

Symphora trembled, and Selbos ran to put a blanket around her. The monitor by her cot flashed purple. "That's not good," she muttered.

Amanda stomped over. "What happened?"

Selbos grimaced at the monitor. "Her internal bleeding hasn't gotten better. We need to take her to a hospital."

"No," Mel-za said. "If we divert from that ship's path, we lose the trail."

Symphora spoke between wheezes. "I can … talk through it … so I'm … fine. I'll be real pissed if you stop this mission now."

Joka faced the cockpit again. "We've been in hyperspace too long, so the decision is made for us. Look what's coming up on the viewscreen."

Amanda's eyes widened. "You don't mean—"

The ship's overhead light shifted to green. Their grav harnesses and flight suits adjusted as the whirling panorama of color unwound to reveal the standard spread of space. Asteroids of various sizes abounded, colliding into each other like angleballs at a seedy bar. They were close enough to be suspicious, as if somebody had pulverized several large asteroids to create a semi barrier.

"I know where this is," Amanda muttered.

Behind her, Symphora retched, phlegm-colored vomit dripping to the floor and splashing.

"This is the Kuiper Belt," Amanda said, nudging Joka. "This is the same star system where Earth is." Goosebumps formed at the mention. This was the same asteroid belt which held a heretofore undiscovered Earthquake bunker, one she and Rick used years ago—the last place anyone would search for Rick. Plus, Tecton building something here was also a subliminal insult to Rick and maybe Amanda by extension.

It wasn't the worst idea. This asteroid was close to Earth for Human recruits with lots of varying-sized asteroids to hide behind. It was the small leadership position Rick and Amanda were given before their so-called success on that stupid moon, the success of getting functioning Collective armor and kidnapping Dr. Alize Oze. She'd ignored so many warning signs. But then they promoted him, and they built the homeless shelter on New Lodestone. At least there, she started doing actual good.

"Selbos," Amanda called. "Take off your armor and swap it for Symphora's. Her life support has been going too long without a proper charge, so yours will hold her over. If we take her to a hospital, we're the ones who will need life support from what she'll do to us."

"Damn straight." Symphora coughed with enough force to count as exercise. "Don't tell me how you know so much about Collective armor's life support."

Selbos stripped her armor off while Mel-za helped Symphora out of her medical robe.

Amanda peered at Joka and whispered in Human, "Will you leave me behind on this asteroid? Take Symphora somewhere she can get treatment? I think the Earthquake assassin poisoned her or did more damage internally than anyone realized."

Joka nodded. "Or she sabotaged the medbots who attended her back in the government offices."

If Symphora died in Amanda's care, that would rain down more hell on her. Symphora couldn't die on this rock.

Amanda tugged at one of her dangling curls. "If Mel-za joins me, I can at least front like I have an abducted Lo-sat. She's a fighter."

"I don't like leaving you alone." Concern rocked Joka's voice.

"I won't be." Amanda hoped she could suggest that same concern back to her. "And I don't like your women's shelter missing its director. I don't like Humans being without whatever your next awesome invention is. Binh and the monk will be here. Send them my coordinates, and I'll be fine."

Joka blinked hard. "If it does come down to fighting... you get behind Mel-za. She'll send them all straight to whatever heck they came from." Joka offered a hand.

"Whatever heck." Amanda clasped her hand.

Symphora stabilized and breathed deeply. "Good thinking, Martinez. Swapping armor is a bit of a taboo, but I think I'll be good for this mission."

Amanda addressed the Arkoudae and Lo-sat as the ship slowed to land on the asteroid. "I'm heading out there first with Mel-za. Joka will stay with the ship, and Selbos and Symphora, you two will cover our backs. Earthquake likes explosives, so we can't be too close if we're spotted. My alibi is abducting Mel-za. I can fake it enough to get inside. I'll leave a door open for you."

Symphora hefted herself off the table. "I don't like Selbos going in without armor. She'll stay here. Don't think I can't understand Human, by the way. I heard every word you two whispered. We're going out at the same time."

Amanda winced. "You have the most recognizable face in the galaxy. Everyone in that base who sees us will know it's you."

Symphora tapped a compartment on Selbos' armor, revealing a combat knife that would've been a sword in Amanda's hands. With her free paw, Symphora tugged on the end of her mohawk, then ran the knife through her hair, letting the iconic red dyed fur scatter to the ground. She shook her head, discarding more hair and appearing decades older. "I know Humans think Arkoudae all look alike. How do I look now?"

Amanda and the others stared slack-jawed.

"Sexy," Selbos whispered.

"But you're… you're Symphora," Mel-za said. "You can't just cut off your symbol."

"Look at your helmet, soldier," Symphora replied. "You're Symphora now." She glanced at Joka, wiggling her ears. "Broadcast the signal to the Blekk. Once you get confirmation from the fleet, leave and don't look back. We'll find a way home."

"Y-yes, ma'am," Joka stammered.

"I mean it." Symphora approached the hatch. "You put too much into that shelter to throw it away by sticking around here. If you follow us or linger a second longer than you gotta, Earthquake will be the least of your worries. Understand?"

Joka straightened. "It's been an honor, Symphora. And… thanks for rescuing me when I was a kid."

Amanda affixed her breather. "Let's go."

TWENTY-ONE

(MAYNARD)

**Local name: Za-thrin, Lu system,
approaching a settlement**

A WEEK AFTER departing planet Vee, Maynard, Binh, and Reck-xa trudged through a sun-bleached desert, the heat amplified by the pulverized diamonds that passed for sand here. They'd used most of their funds to acquire speedy transport, but they had to walk this last leg toward the city.

Without his years of ascetic training, he'd beg for water on this stifling rock. The bug bites from Vee made his skin crawl, and all his sweat negated Reck-xa's healing salve. She told him she'd made it in case his late brother ever visited her again.

Maynard pulled up his hood to protect himself from the harsh sunlight and the gust of sand kicking up behind them. Distant clamor from the city bolstered his spirits.

Reck-xa pushed her sleeves up. "Humans don't live like this, May-nard? My book about Earth says it has lovely deserts."

Binh flexed his tail to soak up more rays. "My parents were part of Earth's cleanup crew. Early entrepreneurs. Half the dustball was desert like this when they came, except fun and radioactive thanks to horrible mismanagement by its former tenants."

"Are you so intolerable because you overdosed on radiation?" Maynard pointed ahead at the city coming into view. "Is this where the town gossip said the abductions have happened?"

Reck-xa nodded. "Tongues loosen around shamans."

"Wait, did you use some inhibition-blocking drugs?" Binh asked with a tsk. "You have a truth potion?"

"Of course not. It's incense," Reck-xa corrected.

The marketplace boasted street vendors and open-air shops and stalls selling jewelry, tools, clothing, robot parts, and food. It reminded Maynard of Bolivar City ten years ago but with the differing Lo-sat clientele. There were far fewer street food vendors compared to jewelers and clothiers, although he whiffed charred rodent meat, which made his stomach turn. His eyes drifted from the bustling street activity when he caught stray Human words. Above, workers labored on rooftops, shaded by limp tarps as they erected new buildings.

"How old is this settlement?" Maynard asked.

"Maybe a year or two?" Binh replied.

Reck-xa's neck frills shook. "A wise place for abductions. The Collective hasn't fully established a presence here. There's no local law enforcement that anyone is afraid of."

Anywhere besides New Lodestone without the Arkouda felt implausible to Maynard. "None?"

"That's the funny thing about the scaly master race," Binh said. "We're dutiful and loving Citizens, unlike your one-hearted kind."

Reck-xa glared at Binh. "You were a thief. Cease your falsehoods."

Binh shrugged. "There's a few too many people here for anyone to notice if and when someone goes missing."

"Hence the abductions," Maynard mused. Knowing what Joka Bunear said the mad scientist had concocted in his attempts to recreate Mui-xe, Maynard shuddered. Any kidnapped Lo-sat and Human could be fused to make a mindless fighter, capable of immense destruction. And the people here were at risk of becoming the next cog in the machine of Earthquake's cruelty.

He wouldn't stand for it; he needed to do something for these people as much as his own nephew.

"Are you comfortable splitting up?" Maynard asked, turning away from the binary suns. "We can gather information and meet back up later tonight."

"No," Reck-xa hissed. "We remain together. Abducted Lo-sats, remember? We do not know Earth-quake's methods. Two of us are vulnerable, and a Human has limited access without a Lo-sat. We travel together."

Maynard accepted her logic, even if she didn't invite debate or discussion. "So should we start with the Humans?"

Binh flicked his tail, drawing a circle in the sand. "That's the only place we can start. Do you got any more of your truth smoke?"

"Incense," Reck-xa hissed. "You test my patience."

Maynard's stomach turned. "We shouldn't coerce people."

She moved in front of him and peered down to meet his gaze. "So it seems my love for my grandson outweighs your love for your nephew. I find that unsurprising. If you don't like it, I suggest you go home. I can continue this without you."

Binh scratched the back of his head. "Your fun little religious code is probably nice in your monastery, but this is the real world with real people in real trouble. You gotta get some dirt on your hands if you want to do anything close to the right thing."

Maynard's mouth dried but not from the climate. Several onlookers were casting glances their way. "Impure methods create impure results."

"And no results arise from your methods," Reck-xa snapped.

Closing his eyes, Maynard inhaled deeply. If they scavenged information in a slower way, it would prolong Mui-xe's suffering, which was worse than coercing another to speak the truth. "Fine," he said. "Let's do this as little as possible. Once we have our information, we turn and leave."

Reck-xa hissed a list of ingredients to Binh. "You obtain those," she said. "We'll be on the roof with those workers."

Binh's neck frills danced. "I thought you said you didn't want us to split up."

"You know these Earth-quake Humans better than me. You'll sense a trap. It also wouldn't bother me if you were abducted."

Binh honked a laugh, catching Maynard off-guard.

Reck-xa led Maynard into the building under construction. As Reck-xa parted the sand curtain to enter, a voice beckoned them.

"Come, come," an older male Lo-sat called. "We're open during construction."

Inside were racks of Lo-sat clothes, designed to protect eyes from sand but also drawing attention to themselves with layers of opalescent feathers. A shopkeeper hung a stretchy flexweave outfit over a Lo-sat mannequin.

He eyed Maynard. "I'm sorry, but I don't carry clothes for your kin. Try another shop."

"He's a worker," Reck-xa said.

"No toolbox?" The shopkeeper arched an eyeridge.

Maynard shrugged. "I don't have enough money to buy one." At least he could speak truthfully.

"Upstairs with you," the shopkeeper said and pointed to the back of the store with his tail.

Moments later, Reck-xa accompanied Maynard, and the shopkeeper blocked her. "Can I interest madam in some desert finery?"

"Can I interest you in stepping out of my way? I need to visit your workers on the roof." Reck-xa extended her neck frills, and Maynard's eyes bulged.

The shopkeeper held up a claw. "Not until you inspect my sales on the most—"

Faster than an aging person should've been able to move, Reck-xa dipped her claws into a concealed pocket in her cloak, then grazed the shopkeeper's snout.

He slumped to the floor.

"You poisoned him," Maynard whispered.

Reck-xa scowled. "And we're one step closer to saving Mui-xe." Her neck frills retracted. "He's sleeping. Come."

Maynard stepped around the shopkeeper, stooping to check for breathing.

"Now," Reck-xa hissed.

Muttering a prayer, Maynard followed her up the staircase—an exercise in flexibility. Living on New Lodestone had afforded him the luxury of Human architecture and functionality, but on a Lo-sat settlement, getting one foot to the next step proved a stretch. He wondered if Binh found Human steps dangerous being so much closer together, but the thief never complained about that, despite complaining about everything else.

At the top of the staircase, Maynard followed her into the sunlight. The Human crew prepared the next story for installation, setting support beams in the corners while muttering about which hiveball team was the most disappointing. Most of them wore bandanas and wide hats to stave off the sun and heat.

"Close the door, May-nard," Reck-xa hissed. "Use your martial arts to prevent anyone from leaving."

"It won't come to that. This also would not be an ideal place for a lopsided confrontation."

Reck-xa glared at him while the construction workers paused to watch their new interlopers. "Tell them what I am saying. Do not soften it."

"Fine." Maynard kept his bubbling anger in check. This emotion, like all things, would pass.

Reck-xa addressed the group, speaking in Lo-sat. "There have been abductions. We know Earth-quake is responsible."

Maynard translated, although most of the dozen Humans seemed to understand her.

"I am not with the Collective," Reck-xa continued. "But one of the abducted is important to me."

Maynard translated, noticing some of the workers passing worried glances to each other.

"Nobody leaves this roof until I am directed to where the abducted are taken. I am a shaman of the Lo-sat, and I can make this unpleasant."

Unsure how to translate her threat and keep his vow of nonviolence, after he relayed her message, he added, "But for me, I would rather us get the information without conflict, so please cooperate."

A worker stepped forward and addressed Reck-xa in choppy, accented Lo-sat. "Sha-man. We not part. Of peo-ple steal. We work. Feed fam-il-y. No more."

Reck-xa advanced on him, and Maynard's heart quickened. Some commotion transpired in the street below, like some kind of madness was spreading out down there, but he couldn't divert his attention from the roof to get a better idea.

The worker who spoke up waved his hands in a placating gesture. "Please. No Earth-quake us."

Other workers backed away, all of them with their hands raised. They didn't want to fight; some seemed malnourished, and their graying lips suggested they shouldn't be working up a sweat.

Maynard called out, "Surely, one of you knows something that could be useful."

"There's a bar nearby," another worker blurted. "Some of them hang out there."

"What bar?" Maynard asked.

Reck-xa flicked her tail. "What docking station do they use when they leave?"

The other workers paused, exchanging more frantic glances between each other.

After translating her question, Maynard pleaded, "Anything you can tell us." Before he could stutter another sentence, a *whoomp* from the door knocked him forward, sending him onto the rooftop floor.

Maynard collected himself and rose as stifled gasps chorused around him.

A group of Humans emerged from the door, all sporting the haircuts and tattoos of Earthquake.

A woman in the center flashed a homemade Human-sized pistol. "Someone said we've got a slime-ball bully up here."

Maynard surveyed the workers. A few pointed at Reck-xa while the others backed away, unwilling to engage.

Reck-xa slinked forward. "You're the Lo-sat abductors?"

The Earthquake woman scoffed and responded in Human. "You can learn my language, lady. We just appropriate justice where needed." She unholstered her pistol.

Maynard stepped between them. "She doesn't know Human. May I translate?"

"Not much point." Her four colleagues chuckled. "But go ahead."

Reck-xa dipped her tail into her cloak, rummaging. "Speak her words, May-nard."

"I don't think you want to know, but they haven't taken kindly to your handling of the situation. Can you let me handle things from here?" Without waiting for her to respond, Maynard addressed the Earthquake leader. "Ma'am, there have been cases of Lo-sats disappearing from this settlement."

"We don't need any self-righteous assholes coming around pointing fingers. We saw you from the street. Don't act like you're not here to stir trouble."

Inhaling deeply, Maynard measured the expressions of the interlopers; one shuffled backward, probably from recognizing Maynard's monk robes. "A tall, thin, Human boy was abducted. He has a genetic condition which makes him seem tangentially similar to a Lo-sat in certain lights. If Earthquake is behind the disappearances, you abducted an innocent Human." Throat dry, Maynard licked his lips and exhaled. "A child. My nephew."

The leader shook her head, and her lopsided hair flowed with her, elegant and intimidating. "Boveeshit."

She pointed her gun at Maynard. "You're an appeaser. Concocting some crap story as part of a police sting. You—"

Maynard noticed the twitch in her eye and finger. In the space she needed to finish her sentence, he ducked. A shot rang out, which otherwise would've killed him.

Shoom!

A sizzling plasma bullet sailed past where Maynard had been standing, instead finding the shoulder of a construction worker, who sank to a knee and screamed.

Reck-xa, either through reflexes or whiffing pheromones, sidestepped and withdrew a vial from her cloak.

Sweeping out his arm, Maynard smacked the gun from the leader's hand, grabbed it with his other as it bolted up, then threw it over the roof.

The other Earthquake gangsters spread apart, pulling out knives. The construction worker's scream melted to a howl.

In a flash, Reck-xa uncorked her vial, dumping saccharine liquid onto the nearest Earthquake member. The sizzle of flesh and hair would have caused most people to forfeit their lunch.

The leader pulled out a knife and lunged for Maynard, and he responded by sidestepping and deflecting.

"Reck-xa," Maynard called as he dodged another swipe. "Use some healing medicine on the wounded worker. I can incapacitate the others."

His eye drifted to the Earthquake member who Reck-xa dumped her acid on, writhing like a squashed insect in its last twitches. Maynard would have to utter the departing prayer for him, assuming he survived this fight.

The remaining Earthquake gangsters descended on him. One connected with a knife cut on his shoulder as he kicked another in the stomach to create space. All he wanted to do was incapacitate, but he couldn't kick as hard as possible since they were close to the roof's edge.

Wincing, he ducked the next blow and swept the attacker's legs. The leader thrust her knife, and he grabbed her wrist, twisting until she let go. He caught the falling knife and threw it over the roof, away from the street.

One attacker made to flee and the person who received Reck-xa's acid stopped twitching. The remaining two attackers with knives stabbed at him, and he stepped backward, grabbing one and jostling him to create distance between himself and the second fighter. He released for a half-second and struck the first attacker's wrist. When he reached for his dropped weapon, Maynard kneed him in the face.

The second attacker dropped his knife and ran.

Only the leader remained, and she was unarmed.

Maynard unclenched his fists. "I suppose you'll talk now. Where can we find my nephew?"

The leader grunted, then clambered to run back down the staircase.

Maynard bolted after her. He didn't want to hurt her, but as she ran down the steps, he jumped over the railing and smacked her into a wall. He didn't hit her at enough of an angle to knock her out, but she stumbled. He dragged her up by the collar, where Reck-xa awaited at the steps.

"The gunshot victim is tended to," she hissed. "Impressive fighting, May-nard."

"Violence is never impressive. Let's get her somewhere we can talk to her and get the information out."

A familiar voice emanated from the lower floor. "Hey, there they are." It was Binh, talking to the shopkeeper and helping him stand.

Binh cocked a grin and waved them over. "I told our friend here that there'd be some Earthquakers on the roof that he could turn in for some money. In exchange, he agreed there wasn't any need to report you or the one you're taking out."

Maynard scoffed. "Where have you been?"

"I found *them*." Binh waved his tail like a rattle. "I didn't smell the gun one of them brought, so sorry about that. I smelled the bullet wound and thought it might be you, Holy Roller. But I figured it was something you two could handle, so I nudged them your way. I have the ingredients we need for the compliance potion, by the way." He cocked his head, appraising the mumbling woman in Maynard's grasp. "So, this drugged-up lady is our guide?"

Reck-xa nodded. "She'll take us to the Earth-quake base in whatever ship they've been using." She glared at Maynard. "Whether she wants to or not. No exceptions. No excuses. Agreed?"

Maynard exhaled slowly. "I agree. We should not use unnecessary or excessive force, though. Agreed?"

Reck-xa peered at the shopkeeper. "We're taking her behind your store. Thank you for understanding our plight. Enjoy the reward for turning in the Earthquake people upstairs."

TWENTY-TWO

(ROSANNA)

Hyperspace lane, chased by the prey

MASSAGING HER BRUISED abdomen, Rosanna watched the colorful lightshow warping around her ship, displayed on the viewscreen. She had a chance to teleport and return to base faster, but her limited supply of chitin and the unnerving presence which haunted her stayed her hand. Besides, knowing Rick was giving chase made everything more exciting.

Her omni-tablet buzzed with a message from command.

[Ma'am, Martinez showed her face and tried to pull some sneaky crap on the Fen-tal moon. She ended up taking the bait and is en route to the Bastion per your orders.]

[Rosanna: Is Symphora still with her?]

[We watched the ship. She didn't disembark.]

Rosanna smirked. This almost compensated for losing her favorite knife while fighting Crith. She liked all the nicks and scratches the blade had earned over the years.

It would only be a matter of time before Symphora's death could be placed on Martinez's head. The thought made Rosanna grip her armrest until her knuckles whitened. Symphora's impending demise and Martinez's subsequent ruin didn't satisfy as much as it should have. Killing Symphora was more about proving herself than anything, and destroying Martinez's reputation was more of Tecton's goal, not Rosanna's; they were accolades she didn't need.

They were just a means to get to Crith. The bastard knew Rosanna wanted something out of him. She should've restrained him first.

But she'd beaten him.

Just like she'd beaten Symphora, even if it hadn't been fatal.

Two legends that she'd brought to their knees. Maybe it was for the best that they survived. Then they'd die knowing they'd lost.

And Rosanna was the new legend for surviving encounters with both without severe injury, a feat only a handful claimed. A gut bruise from Crith and a chunk of her ear from Symphora were the only hits they managed against her. Nobody in the galaxy could say that. The Makawe pincers caused more harm to her body than Crith's shoulder, anyway.

But those Makawe would never help Rick now. She'd demonstrated the price of assisting him. Rick would die alone once he'd confess the truth about Alejandro.

Her omni-tablet pinged again. A team on Za-thrin made contact with the freak hybrid boy's uncle, disgraced former Abbot of the monastery, according to her mole. He even collected the boy's grandmother, the Lo-sat shaman. Rick abandoning and insulting the mole last year was paying dividends for her. Having more familial samples to compare against the hybrid's DNA would increase and improve experimentation. No wonder the mad scientist kidnapped his parents if her intel was to be believed.

Earthquake's potential army of hybrid fighters obeying her every command was tempting, but she felt more alive fighting Rick just now than rescuing Tecton a year ago.

Her heart accelerated, wondering what she'd do after finally seeing Crith's eyes bulge in death. But that was a problem for another day. Her scanners chirped, demanding her attention. The slow speed paid off. A ship was tailing her—a Makawe scrapper.

It was Crith. Had to be. He'd get quite the welcome at the Bastion.

She checked the navigational charts. She'd gone slow on purpose to let him catch her, and they only had a few hours left in transit. Martinez's last location was near the Kuiper Belt as well. Rosanna would force Crith to watch Martinez die. Goosebumps rose on her skin. For a bastard with no family or other ties, that was the only fitting revenge Rosanna would achieve. Then she'd cut out his heart.

She debated taking manual control through hyperspace, just to send off a communication to Crith's ship, but she couldn't risk crashing into rogue debris when traveling faster than lightspeed.

But she knew what else she needed to do.

Rosanna had failed to break Dr. Oze before, and that would have to be rectified. All the archaeologist had to offer were ominous warnings of a force she wouldn't even name. Everything she said was a stupid ruse. If she wouldn't divulge any more secrets of the Chamayna chitin, Oze's only use was exhausted. Murdering someone important to her had already worked once, but the only person she still seemed to care about was that Io Kaluteros kid, and he was just that: a kid. Rosanna had been the same age when Crith had visited her family. Young, helpless. She couldn't bring herself to snatch him. Stealing a teenage monster was bad enough, yet she *had* done it on the Leader's orders.

But maybe there was someone else Oze would talk to. Someone who would be honest about what happened to Alejandro on that moon. Oze needed a visitor. Rick Crith.

He was on Rosanna's tail and would arrive at the Bastion shortly after her. He just needed some gentle guidance to get to the third sub-basement.

TWENTY-THREE

(AMANDA)

On a moon-sized asteroid in the Kuiper Belt

A TEAR STUNG Amanda's cheek, and the moisture dug into her skin like an icicle. Joka's flight suit protected her from the unpredictable temperatures in the lack of an atmosphere, but even it had its limits. The *DR-1* took off behind them, having sent the broadcasts.

Amanda regretted cursing the dank heat of the swamp moon a few days ago; it would've made for a nice reprieve from this frigid rock, made colder by the blue glow of nearby Neptune. Amanda patted the pouch on her suit that contained the false cuffs she'd placed on Symphora and Mel-za when they neared— she had real ones ready for Tecton as well.

Earthquake probably knew trespassers were here. For the level of technology they'd reached, the innovations they'd stolen from other species, they had to know.

Mel-za suggested shutting off their grav harnesses to leap to their destination faster, but Symphora advised against it.

"You gotta go in with a level head sometimes. Fighting pimps, enslavers, and drug lords, sure. Go in guns blazing as long as no innocents are around. Take trophies, set examples, and give the accomplices something to have nightmares about. These guys aren't them."

"Whoa." Amanda stopped in her tracks to gape at the towering structure before them while Mel-za and Symphora stared slack-jawed.

The Bastion was an oil-black spear puncturing a blue-black sky. Craggy plateaus and rocky peaks of the asteroid encircled it as if bowing prostrate to the nefarious pinnacle of Human architecture. It represented all of Monsieur Tecton's aspirations. Gaudy and threatening in equal measure, opulent and hateful.

Dr. Alize Oze was there, if she were still alive.

Rosanna Moreno lurked inside in all likelihood, stewing over her near-victory against Symphora. And according to the pings Joka got from Binh and Brother Maynard, so was Mui-xe, the hybrid miracle boy.

Most importantly, this would hold the throne room of Jacques Tecton, the man Amanda needed to bring to justice and expose the depths of his corruption.

They arrived at the edge of a plateau before a dip into a crater.

Amanda toed the edge. "Once we're inside, we need to find Dr. Oze. She'll know how to operate the

Chamayna teleportation. That is our only chance for success. After that, we have to find the hybrid boy. He has the ability to heal his own wounds as well as other people. He'll finish what the life support and medgel started. You'll be back to one hundred percent. Once they are both safe and we capture Tecton, we can tell the Fleet to blow this place to hell."

"If we can get that far," she huffed. "And I'll still be without a gun."

Mel-za pointed her tail at the Bastion. "How many of those armor-busting cannons do you think they have in there? I've seen the vids with those things. It's like an ancient fishing spear, except hateful and evil and kinda cool."

Flashes of Amanda's bodyguard dying to protect her raced through her mind. "I know. They have a lot. The only drawback is they are slow to fire and aim. Once you see one, move. Fast."

A ping notification made Amanda's omni-tablet buzz.

[Joka: [Fwd: [Scumbag: Hey Nut Puncher, tell the Girly-Girl with the Curly-Curl that I'm here with a Pacifist Primate and a Scary Potion Lady. We'll find some alternative entrances.]]]

Amanda cocked an eyebrow and fired a ping back.

[What the Earth?]

[Joka: Sorry. I'll translate it. Binh wanted me to tell you that he's here with Brother Maynard and a Lo-sat shaman. He used eight layers of unimaginative nick-names because he is a pathetic man-child. They're going to break and enter.]

Why Binh's nickname for Joka was "Nut Puncher" felt like a story for another day.
"So how do we sneak in?" Mel-za asked.
Amanda surveyed the landscape. Just under the size of a standard moon, the escape velocity difficulty for ships wasn't oppressive enough for a space elevator to be a worthy economic investment—easier to get to the stars the old-fashioned way. So that meant any supplies would be coming in from a nearby landing pad and a hover convoy.
Symphora and Mel-za agreed with her logic. Amanda pinged Joka.

[Amanda: Give Binh my direct ping address. Did you receive any word from the Fleet or the Blekk?]

[Joka: Done. And no. It's been like ten minutes. Chill.]

[Joka: ...]

[Joka: please don't die]

Amanda rubbed at one of the scratches on her omni-tablet, then holstered it. "We need to circle around this big tower wide enough so we won't be plainly visible. Wherever their landing zone is, we are on the wrong side of it."

"That's probably for the best." Symphora wheezed. "I need some time for the next round of painkillers to kick in."

"Bah." Mel-za scowled. "Let's get some action."

"You remind me of a younger me," Symphora said. Before Mel-za could express her gratitude, Symphora held up a paw and motioned for them to move. "That's not a good thing. I could've saved more people if I'd kept a low profile."

Mel-za tugged at the top of her mohawk-crest helmet. "I'll keep that in mind, ma'am."

"You better," Amanda said. "We want to avoid bloodshed. Earthquake is full of confused people who don't know how to channel their aggression at the society that left them behind. They don't have many other options beyond gang life, at least in their eyes."

The trio balanced on the side of the ridge, several hundred meters from the Bastion, the focal point for their journey.

Hiking through and around craters, Mel-za offered twice to carry Symphora, who insisted she was fine.

Mel-za spied a landing pad on the opposite side of the Bastion. A cargo ship docked on the cleared space sported yellow-brown dusting reminiscent of the swampy Fen-tal moon—the ship which disembarked once they made their faux capture known, which was visual proof of Joka's ingenuity yet again. No wonder her inventions had won awards.

The hangar gaped open with no sign of cargo unloading, displaying rows of stolen battledarts and modified civilian ships.

"It's a trap," Amanda said.

"No way," Mel-za hissed.

"It's definitely a trap," Symphora replied. "But they don't know the Fleet and Blekk are coming."

"We can't go with the ruse of Mel-za being my captured prisoner," Amanda replied. "We just have to get that guard to let us inside."

She fired off a ping to Binh.

[Amanda: Hey, it's Martinez. We've found an entry point where there are two ships docked. Find somewhere else in case we trigger a trap.]

"Maybe we *can* fake the prisoner thing," Mel-za hissed. "You already have the different hair color and those cuffs."

Amanda marched closely enough behind Mel-za that an onlooker from a camera wouldn't be able to tell she didn't have a real gun.

Symphora limped beside Mel-za, which would've provided enough distraction, anyway, especially with her haggard features. Watching a defeated and injured Arkouda march in front of anyone flying Earthquake colors was enough of a spectacle on its own. All they had were knives and claws, marching toward a base full of people with guns and no qualms against firing them.

A guard booth bulged from the hangar's left end. The trio veered toward the guard booth, and Amanda hated the script which formed in her mind. She angled her fake prisoners and herself so only part of her face was revealed, her dyed, straight hair obscuring her dirt-crusted face. Amanda summoned an Earther accent, speaking Human and hoping her friends wouldn't understand her. "Hail. I gotta slimeball ready. This Popsicle tried to stop me, but I kicked her ass and thought the boys might enjoy taking a go at her."

The attendant, an older man who bore the scars of years of fighting and scraping by, gave them a once-over. His gaze lingered on Symphora, taking some existential and vicarious satisfaction from seeing her in pain. For her part, Symphora winced on each breath, the only one not acting a role.

The attendant rasped in a drawling lunar accent. "How'd you beat her?"

"She was trying to start a business in the slimeball settlement. This was her business partner. They defended each other." Measuring the attendant's expression, she added, "The Popsicle wanted to protect her investment, you know. I kneecapped her, then got a knife in her gut. My gun was fried, and I didn't want to leave a body."

"Ah, right." The attendant smirked at Amanda's false prisoners, then tapped something into an omni-tablet.

The hangar door creaked open, and Amanda dared to make eye contact. "This is my first successful hunt. Where can I take them?"

Before responding, the attendant squinted at his omni-tablet. "There's a cargo elevator. You want sub-basement three."

"Earthquake moves the galaxy." The hated phrase crossed Amanda's lips, sapping most of her remaining composure.

"Hmpf. Damn right."

Amanda's heart quickened—that guard didn't ask for any identification or where they'd landed. Either negligence ran rampant or someone was privy to their arrival and wanted them inside. Her breath hitched at the thought.

Good thing she had some surprises of her own.

TWENTY-FOUR

(ROSANNA)

**The Bastion, toying with the prey,
stalled by inferior hunters**

CRITH'S PISSY MAKAWE scrapper ship descended from orbit, approaching the more fortified hangar. Rosanna disabled half the autoturrets while the other half were ripped out by the defector's magnets as they fired at him. It was an impressive show of Crith's strategies for civilian ships utilized in combat.

Rosanna could've activated the cannons and ended it, but then she'd never get her answers. The scrapper absorbed enough fire before it ripped open the hangar door so Crith would find his entry deserving. Perfect. She needed him to think he'd earned his way inside.

Rosanna glared at the squad leaders and security chiefs gathered in Monsieur Tecton's office.

Neptune's light glowed through the window, casting a barely noticeable aquamarine tint over the room. Something in the cosmic light reminded her of the in-between space when teleporting, the place where the watcher lurked.

"Word arrived that Martinez is here," Rosanna said.

Displaying her omni-tablet with the most recent pings, she paced the room while the security chiefs remained seated. "The bastard defector Rick Crith is here as well. They are both inside the complex. You all followed the plan so far, now make sure your cadets and recruits do so as well."

Glares, cocked eyebrows, and flared nostrils flew around the long conference table. Tecton measured the audience with beaded eyes. Calculating.

Not that Rosanna cared. She had her own agenda. "Nobody interrupts them. Nobody takes a shot. We need Martinez and Crith alive, understood?"

No response followed.

"Understood?" Rosanna hated many things. Repeating herself was near the top of her list. A few nods and a "yes, ma'am" followed, which was not what she'd hoped, but ranked better than the silence. Knowing the Leader had her back solidified her confidence.

"Martinez is traveling with an unidentified weakened Arkouda and a Lo-sat from the Symphora Squad."

One of the security officers paled. "She brought one of the Symphoras?"

"Calm down." Another one scoffed. "They're not as tough now that Symphora herself went into politics."

From the other side of the table, a younger officer pointed a finger. "Don't talk bad about them. I was saved by Symphora as a kid. Lots of our crew was."

"Enough," Rosanna hissed. "It's nothing we can't handle. But if either one dies, we can't get what we need out of Martinez."

"What about Crith?" the younger officer pressed.

"And what about him?" Rosanna asked. "He was shuffling around space with a Makawe but appears alone. The security footage we have shows him checking his omni-tablet, so he must be in communication with somebody. Be alert. He's traitor-shit, but he's crafty."

Tecton folded his arms. "Crith could be loaded with explosives. He doesn't have anything left to live for."

Rosanna turned on him, softening her glare. "I don't think so, sir. He wants to save Alize Oze." Rosanna's words were met with more scoffs and indignant whispers. "We have escape pods and the hybrids to deal with any other surprises, which is part of the reason we're keeping the floors clear."

An older officer raised a finger, and Rosanna scowled at him. He'd been in Earthquake years before Rosanna, long enough to maybe know Alejandro. "We're wasting a lot of time on not killing two people," he said.

Before he could blink, Rosanna unholstered her pistol and shoved the barrel against his forehead, making him whimper. "We need to extract information from both of them. They're useful alive. One more comment out of any of you, and I won't be able to say the same."

"Back off," Tecton said. "You made your point. I have a list of who you can threaten, and he isn't on it right now."

The officer's eyes widened, and a bead of sweat trickled down his forehead, wetting her gun.

Rosanna holstered her weapon and cooled her tone. The Leader was right, after all. "We let them roam until we get what we need. We're monitoring the situation closely."

In her periphery, Rosanna watched Tecton tap a button on the side of his chair, and a corresponding small green light glowed in the far corner of the room. His private hatch. The bastard had his escape pod ready to go. He didn't believe in her plan.

Through a grimace, Rosanna added, "If we just kill them outright, they're martyrs. If we get the information we need first, and record it and broadcast it, we've destroyed the Loyalist cause forever. We won't be seen as radicals but as saviors. That's what we all want, right? Now go back to your stations and monitor carefully, keeping your squads at bay. We'll need them soon."

TWENTY-FIVE

(RICK)

The Kuiper Belt, hiding under Neptune's shadow, approaching the Bastion

RICK HAD BEEN in enough traps to know he'd stepped inside one, and that was why he had to bid P'oki farewell. The resistance was too flimsy. Some autoturret 'bots. All it took was a hard enough yank from P'oki's scrapper magnet, and they were out of commission.

When her magnet lifted the hangar door, all doubt had been removed. That damn thing wasn't even guarded. Putting up a token resistance was amateurish and sloppy—they made him sweat for his entry, but they should've made him bleed if they wanted to sell it. Earthquake wanted him inside. These sons of Galsan worms thought they could toy with him. It was their funeral. If Earthquake had teleportation capabilities and Oze was here, all he'd need to do would be find and free her, then she could escape herself with He'nay, assuming they were still alive. Who knew if Rosanna could be trusted?

Strapping on his barely functioning combat gear, Rick handed P'oki the omni-tablet that he'd pilfered from Dion last year. "If you get the signal from me, destroy this place. Don't worry about anyone inside. I don't know if killing Tecton or destroying this tower will stop Earthquake forever, but it will confuse and bankrupt them, which is good enough for now."

"I should come with you, Rix," P'oki said, voice wavering. "I can help."

"I know." Rick checked his pistol's ammo. "I'm not a good leader. Most of my ground assaults have resulted in casualties. You deserve better. If I can't avenge He'nay, you will with our backup plan."

"She is alive, Rix."

"You see her spirits?" Rick asked, trying to hide his disbelief. "You can sense them?"

"There are too many spirits on this rock. Not know perfectly."

He didn't want to point out that her hope came from ignorance. "I will find her if she's here. Whatever it takes."

P'oki opened the hatch for him. "Whatever it takes."

Rick left, and P'oki's scrapper hovered out of the hangar. He watched her fly away from the asteroid, taking cover for when things went down. After glancing in each direction for onlookers and security cameras, he fired up his image inducer, which allowed him to have the appearance of somebody else, an

Earthquake recruit. He wished he knew enough about the image inducer to have coated P'oki's whole ship with it for a stealthier entry, but if he could slip in like this while everyone was searching for him, he might have a chance to penetrate deeper inside.

And if everything went to shit, he could fight his way out. If he couldn't… saving He'nay and freeing Oze wouldn't be the worst final mission for the spotted career of Rick Crith. Nobody would remember him as a hero, which was fine. He'd settle for being remembered as a troubled asshole who tried his best, but being forgotten might be the greatest victory of all. He'd done enough awful shit to deserve nothing more.

The Bastion's interior design matched Tecton's taste and ambition. Unnecessary displays of wealth and power. For the Earthquake recruits who grew up in poverty, this must have seemed luxurious. Paintings and finery across the halls, shimmering their mineral reflections in the light. For the money spent on lavish decorations, Tecton's sycophants could've had better equipment, higher quality living quarters, or more personnel.

Battledarts and modified weaponized civilian ships to defend the Bastion occupied the hangar, but Rick found no trace of Moreno's ship. Perhaps there was another landing bay since he couldn't have beaten her here. Even with the Makawe speed scrapper design, a scrapper couldn't outrun a ship intended for long distance travel. All the more reason to believe this was a trap.

Rick grabbed Rosanna Moreno's knife, and his scowl melted to a wince, knowing if he had been a better leader, the brother may never have defected. Finding the hangar door to the base proper, he opened it.

At least Earthquake deserved credit for appropriately-sized doors, which was a small consolation. Too bad Rick would bring this whole damn tower down today.

A ping notification on his omni-tablet snapped him from his griping.

[P'oki: Rodrick. Have you located He'nay?]

[Rick: No. Get in position. What's your mineral scan saying?]

[P'oki: The scan let me see into the other hangar. A group of people were inside but left and went past where I could scan. They only had a little bit of metal.]

Rick's heart leapt into hyperspace, leaving rational thoughts behind.

[Rick: Who?]

[P'oki: There's a curious mix of women. A Human, a Lo-sat, and a limping Arkouda, which almost sounds like the setup to a joke. Lots of spirits bounced around them. It's hard to tell what they're here for.]

Rick checked where he was walking as he typed.

[Rick: Were the Lo-sat and Arkouda her prisoners? Was the Human with Earthquake?]

[P'oki: She has some of the spirits you do. Her hair is styled in their fashion. If one of the Earthquake people injured an Arkouda, isn't that something they'd want to parade around the headquarters? It's strange she isn't trying to draw attention to herself.]

[Rick: Fair point. Are they inside?]

[P'oki: Yes, and they displayed nervous spirits as they entered.]

[Rick: Damn. Wait for my signal for the distraction.]

Rick sighed and stowed his omni-tablet. He had one trick they wouldn't see coming. All thanks to P'oki.

The Bastion displayed the triumph of Human architecture, Tecton's grand middle finger to the Collective. While the thought made Rick want to hurl or punch something, it allowed solace in the fact that he could intuit the layout. Tecton had waxed for years about building this stupid thing, so when Rick found the service elevator, he tried the bastard's birthday.

Input rejected.

Rick arched an eyebrow. Tecton may have been an Earther, but he didn't love the planet or her people as much as himself. Yet he did love people thinking he loved the planet, so Rick tried another code: Earth's coordinates. Another show of false patriotism.

Wherever Oze and He'nay were kept, it would be in the lower levels. The question was if they would be placed where any moron could find them. Rick stared down at the illusion coating his body, giving the appearance of an Earthquake grunt. His illusory false hand moved with mental coaxing.

As long as they hadn't already developed counter-measures for the image inducer, he would remain safe for the moment.

Examining the elevator's access panel, he spied a real keyhole. Damn. A low-tech security measure was not on the list of things he'd expected and prepared for. Sometimes those were more effective than the expensive ones that over-relied on technology. That key must allow access to the sublevels for prisoners, especially the prisoners Tecton would want to hide from the general population. How many floors did the Bastion boast? At least Rick knew where Tecton's office would be, which would simplify the surprise P'oki had for Tecton if all else failed.

Rick shut the elevator doors, then crouched to examine the keyhole below the floor buttons. Rick dug out Moreno's knife, probing the keyhole's edge. The blade slipped out the first time, and Rick adjusted his grip. On the second try, he came in at a bad angle and nearly chipped the blade. A phantom pain tingled, and he wished he could try with a different hand. He rotated his hold and attempted a new angle.

Snap.

He removed the access panel by jiggling the keyhole itself loose. Old tech wasn't so useful against old solutions. Inside the tangle of wires, the red release latch beckoned. Scowling, he prepared for the drop to whatever floor called itself the sub-basement. If he ran into fatal trouble, his vital signs would drop and his omni-tablet was set to alert P'oki, and she'd enact their final gambit.

TWENTY-SIX

(AMANDA)

Inside her worst nightmare, walls pressing in

ZIGZAGGING THROUGH THE Bastion, fake prisoners in tow, Amanda's stomach turned at the sight of the interior decor, especially considering how Symphora and Mel-za could barely stand straight in the Human-sized hallways. The Bastion was a literal tower of darkness from the outside with its sheer black color scheme and jagged needle design, yet the interior resembled a gaudy royal mansion from Earth's prehistory.

Monsieur Tecton wanted to display his ill-gotten wealth through ornate floral arrangements, gold-plated mirrors, and holographic paintings depicting long-forgotten scenes from prehistoric Earth's literature and maybe even mythology. She doubted Tecton himself could recognize any of these for what they were, letting their supposed abstract grandeur speak for themselves, though with all the mismatched components, they created a cacophony instead of an honest conversation about art. She wondered how the Lo-sat abductees must've felt coming through here.

Probably unintimidated.

Symphora scoffed at the display. "Typical crime boss flex."

Mel-za raised an eyeridge. "You've been here before?"

Wincing, Symphora shook her head. "Seen one, seen 'em all. Arkouda, Lo-sat, Human... drug pusher, enslaver, or brothel owner, it's always the same. They wrap themselves in some sort of culture to give themselves an air of legitimacy and class, but really it's for making themselves forget about how they've gotten this money by hurting others. Makes me want to rip out a throat."

Amanda stopped herself from explaining she had a different proposal for the Bastion's interior design half a decade ago. She would've commissioned art students to help them gain experience and paid them a fair wage to do so, but it would be art for art's sake, not whatever these gaudy monstrosities were intended to be.

She much preferred the Blekk's coral and seaweed art—at least that felt real.

This whole structure needed to come down. But they couldn't be sure who was in the complex. It seemed deserted except for the attendant, although Amanda couldn't shake the feeling they were being watched.

With all the mirrors and decorations, twisting hallways and sharp corners, they could easily be under surveillance. "Watch out," Amanda said. "Earthquake had technology in development to fool your heightened senses."

"And what became of it?" Mel-za asked.

"I don't know. I've been out for years. Just be mindful, alright?"

Mel-za sniffed the air again. "There's an elevator ahead."

"You can smell an elevator?" Amanda asked.

Mel-za tapped the floor with her tail. "Just like you can see one. I receive information and my brain processes it. I don't know what else you want me to say."

"Fair enough," Amanda said. "The elevator on the left looks occupied."

The two non-Humans exchanged a glance while Amanda summoned the elevator on the right. "We have the code to get where the prisoners are held. We need to find Oze first." She didn't add that she'd ask the archaeologist to teleport Mel-za and Symphora somewhere far away to safety. She had no clue how the teleportation functioned, but the thought of more people caught in the crossfire was unacceptable.

The elevator arrived and the trio entered, Mel-za and Symphora grunting as they hunkered down to fit. Symphora's girth and Mel-za's tail cramped the space, and Amanda wondered what the weight rating was on these.

Sub-basement three. Amanda input the code, and the trio descended.

"We could still be walking into a trap," Symphora muttered.

"Good," Mel-za hissed. "I'm tired of sneaking around in this shiny glimmering palace."

"Remember, you're still my prisoners. Hopefully, there will be someone to guide us down there."

The elevator reached the bottom, and the trio nudged out amid oofs and grunts. Amanda's elbow thunked against Symphora's injured side, which Amanda hoped she wouldn't feel through her armor's hip pad.

Ammonia-scented fog pooled around the floor, concealing their feet, which was an interesting trick to disorient any potential escapees. The walls here had a shiny gloss to them, making the fog appear thicker. With it came a chill as if they were inside a refrigerator.

Amanda's breath caught in her throat. "This doesn't make sense. Earthquake thinks Arkoudae are the enemy, but these temperatures are suited for them."

"They probably execute my kind immediately," Symphora said. "Safer for them."

Mel-za rubbed her arm scales together. "This was meant for a Lo-sat. If I were stuck down here, this would chip away at me, forcing me to shiver and survive instead of slowly freezing to death."

Amanda wanted to say that was cold-hearted but decided against it, realizing Earthquake must've had something else planned for their Lo-sat prisoners instead of simple execution. She shuddered, more from the possibilities than the temperature. "Mel-za," she whispered, "can you smell any other Humans down here besides me?"

"I think a f-few." Mel-za shivered. "But the ammonia is too strong."

Symphora sniffed the air and winced. "I can't smell for *skata*."

"Are we talking more than five?"

"Somebody went through h-here recently. Dripping in pheromones." Mel-za sniffed again. "Male."

"No," Symphora tutted. "Female. Definitely a female." She glanced at Amanda and added, "Not you, though."

Amanda pinched the bridge of her nose. "Is the ammonia getting you high, or are you smelling different people?"

"M-maybe." Mel-za pulled her tail close.

"I'm gonna puke if I have to take a deep breath again, Martinez."

Amanda huffed, examining the different passage-ways yawning before them. "Can we just start walking down one? We can turn around if any of the scents weaken or cut off. Where is the male scent weaker?"

"On the right," Mel-za said.

Symphora sniffed hard. "But the female one is stronger down there. I can sense what you were getting before. Definitely two people."

"Was the female stationary or walking? If she is almost stationary, that might be Alize."

After some sniffs, Symphora sighed. "I'm getting a few different feminine scents. Sorry, it's hard to smell past you. No offense."

"None taken," Amanda said. "You should meet the Lo-sat Joka's been pinging. He never shuts up about how Humans smell."

"Real mature," Mel-za said. "But also understandable."

They turned another two corners, both in dead ends, until they reached an opening in the walls. Empty cells big enough for a Lo-sat greeted them.

Mel-za shuddered. "I don't like this place."

"At least they're empty," Symphora offered. The fog swirled thicker here, up to Amanda's chest, Mel-Za's thighs, and Symphora's hips.

More empty cells should have been a relief, but questions flooded Amanda's mind about why they were needed in the first place.

"That's not necessarily a good sign," Amanda said. "How's the female scent?"

"Hey!" someone called out. "Who are you?"

Amanda froze. She recognized that lunar accent. It belonged to a woman Amanda admired and had once held prisoner.

Dr. Alize Oze.

TWENTY-SEVEN

(ROSANNA)

**Sub-basement three of the Bastion,
stalking the prey from the rafters**

ROSANNA THUMBED THE pheromone-neutralizing pill before chomping down, wincing at the chalky taste. Her mouth dried, lips puckering in revulsion. An itch scurried across her body as her pores vacuum-sealed shut, heating her up in defiance of the sub-basement's chill, even though she was near the ceiling, away from the frigid mist.

While the lower temperature should have been enough to confound advanced alien olfactories, she insisted on the pore-sealing pill; anything to further throw off the Lo-sat and Arkouda trailing Martinez. For how Crith praised Martinez, one would expect greater intelligence—but overconfidence would be her downfall, just like him.

From the rafters, Rosanna took stock of the poorly disguised Martinez and her two companions, a Lo-sat and a limping Arkouda. Rosanna had fought enough armored Arkoudae to know their body language when their armor's life support was desperately working to keep them alive.

From her vantage point, she found two quarries diverging with Martinez approaching the cell block.

Rick Crith bumbled about on her left, retracing his steps in the maze.

But Martinez neared Oze's cell, and Rosanna's mouth watered over what the conversation might reveal.

Boots tied together and balanced over her shoulder, Rosanna crept along the basement's rafters. She couldn't risk a single echo clueing the Arkouda to her surveillance. All the scent-concealing supplements in the galaxy wouldn't muffle a boot on metal.

With her folded sniper rifle ready to go in her pocket, it would've been child's play to off Martinez and her companions, then drag her corpse in front of Crith and watch him break before she completed her revenge. While satisfying, the defeat still would not offer information about Alejandro since she still needed answers from Oze. She needed to know what happened on that moon.

Rosanna came within earshot of them and perched.

"Amanda," Oze said, voice heavy, "it's been awhile. I was about to congratulate you on leaving Earthquake and winning that award last year, but I guess I heard wrong."

"It's a disguise so I could sneak in and find you," Martinez replied. "They aren't really my prisoners." Her tone softened. "Are you alright? I'm so sorry about everything that happened all those years ago. I wish I had an excuse, but I don't. We are here to rescue you, though."

Oze exhaled and folded her arms. "I guess I'm not in a position to turn down a rescue, and to say you owe me is an understatement." She uncrossed her arms and tapped on her prosthetic leg.

"Agreed. I hate to ask, but did you know Earthquake figured out Chamayna teleportation?"

"Yes." Oze sighed. "It's my fault. A few months ago, they came for me in the museum. I had a research assistant. They took her, too. They interrogated her, then murdered her in front of my eyes." Oze stared at her feet.

"They coerced you into telling them how it worked?" Martinez asked.

Oze stiffened. "I didn't tell them everything, though. Before you ask, I'm not so sure I can trust *you* with any information, either."

Rosanna leaned closer. The Arkouda with them huffed as if she had somewhere better to be. Something about her felt familiar, but she couldn't put a finger on it.

Martinez nodded. "I understand. We were hoping to give you whatever you need and teleport us all out of here. You can leave me behind if that makes you feel better."

Oze examined the two aliens and shuddered. "The secret I found, the reason why I couldn't go public with the teleportation is that the technique is sacred."

The drop in Oze's voice made goosebumps rise on Rosanna's arms, despite her sealed pores, making her itch all over.

"I appreciate other cultures as much as the next reformed terrorist, but we're in a bind here," Martinez said.

"You don't understand," Oze said, rubbing her temples. "It's sacred like—" Her voice hitched and she stared at her feet. "It's sacred in that it's meant to be off-limits. The Chamayna were capable of impossible feats by carving glyphs, but they only did so in the rarest of circumstances because they were tempting … it. The Unspeakable."

Memories snapped to Rosanna's mind. The presence. The observer. The judgment. The feeling she couldn't name. Those wretched clacking mandibles.

Martinez adjusted her stance. She stiffened. "The … thing from the moon?"

Every hair on Rosanna's arms stood at attention. Could Alejandro have been there when that thing came out of hiding?

"Yes. It was the source of the Chamayna's power. They exploited it until it grew too powerful and destroyed them. I'm going to let it do the same to Earthquake."

"The teleportation jumps are helping it grow more powerful." Oze's voice darkened. "Once you let me out, I can bring it here."

Something about the way Oze said "bring" made Rosanna shudder.

The clacking mandible sound reverberated in Rosanna's mind, and she didn't even have an urge to teleport. She must have inhaled too much of the fog on the floor earlier. She wasn't crazy.

Martinez addressed her companions in Arkouda. "This moon where Alize and I met, in my time with Earthquake, they unearthed something primal. It slaughtered dozens of Earthquake's people. It ripped a Blekk pirate cruiser from the atmosphere..."

Rosanna had believed Crith murdered her brother, but it was some dormant creature?

No wonder Crith didn't want to tell her or her parents the false-sounding truth—Rosanna barely wanted to believe it herself. Yet it made some level of sense. Alejandro was a good soldier. He probably died saving some of the Earthquake members who escaped. He must have died fighting it. Heroic. But Alejandro might have died saving Rick. This should have made Rosanna feel something. Anything.

The knowledge, the realization, the truth of what happened to her brother... nothing happened. She'd spent years seeking the truth, and she felt as empty as ever. Alejandro was still dead. Her once-stiff arm hairs fell, along with any sense of her purpose.

Rosanna's trigger finger itched to fire her sniper rifle and kill one of the four people, but that might tip off Crith. He might not have murdered Alejandro, but it was still his fault for dragging Alejandro to that moon and letting him die there. He needed to answer for his crime.

Talking about some monster, Oze must have snapped. And even if she possessed the capacity to summon some cosmic demon here, Rosanna had a way off this rock.

Oze was useless otherwise—she had no more information. That meant it was finally time.

This pitiful group would be no match for her hybrids. She pulled out her omni-tablet and initiated the command.

Lambda: Activate.

Sigma: Activate.

Displayed on her tablet was a message notification she'd ignored in favor of eavesdropping.

Intruder alert.

Those security chiefs were such garbage.

She dismissed the message and stowed her omni-tablet. Watching the triumph of Human ingenuity defeat an Arkouda up close again would be satisfying. Taking out a Symphora Squaddie would be impressive. And taking out Martinez would prove Earthquake was the dominant force in Human ideology.

But none of that mattered until Rosanna got payback for the brother Crith stole from her. She needed the full story, every detail, before she stabbed him in his shriveled heart.

TWENTY-EIGHT

(MAYNARD)

**Somewhere in the Kuiper Belt,
painfully close to Humanity's home**

BROTHER MAYNARD STARED at the sun-scarred nape of the pale woman's neck in front of him. Coerced by Reck-xa's poisonous fumes to do her bidding, she'd brought them to Earthquake's head-quarters, now looming in front of them, washed in Neptune's light. Three of the blue sphere's moons obstructed the view of the planet; Maynard lamented not knowing their names, but it was a poor distraction from their prisoner.

His heart ripped asunder at what they were doing to this poor woman. Rationalizing, moralizing—it defied his training. Yet the monks rejected him, and he'd already started on this path. If the actions here increased the number of lifetimes he would need to endure before finally joining in the Great Mystery, before finding the Answer Almighty, so be it. He would help Mui-xe now. Any way possible. This was his only choice, yet it hurt to make.

Maynard peered through the viewscreen, displaying an image of the outside. This rust-brown rock sported a tower, a jagged palatial estate rivaling a space elevator, soaring high above the asteroid's surface. It boasted anti-asteroid defense guns at the top. How many of these magnetized asteroids could be scrapped and recycled, creating funds to give to the poor?

For as much as Earthquake claimed to want what was best for Humans, feeding and providing shelter seemed low on their list, especially when stacked against pointless fighting. He handed the buzzing omni-tablet to Binh. "You've received another ping."

"Thanks, Zany Mayn-y," Binh replied. "It's Her Majesty's team. They beat us there. We're definitely going to the right place, which is nice."

"Of course we are," Reck-xa hissed. "This one is under my spell." She stretched spacefaring gear and breathers over her shamanic robes, protecting herself as much as possible from the impending environment.

"It's not magic," Maynard mumbled in Human. "It's hallucinogenic chemicals that will produce long-term brain damage." Beyond not wanting Reck-xa to hear him, he had no clue how to say hallucinogenic in any language besides his own. "How will we enter their base?"

"A shaman has ways of entry," Reck-xa replied. "No buildings made by Humans can withstand the will of the gods."

Binh wiggled his eyeridges. "Explosives?"

"Nothing of the sort," she replied. "May-nard, in my satchel, find the vials labeled with the Lo-sat Zodiac. We'll produce a salve which will render us invisible to security devices while we're outside."

The ship dipped toward the landing pad. A single cargo ship sat there, sporting the stains of moisture and fungal spore-dusting that would come from time outside on a swamp or jungle world. Perhaps that was Amanda Martinez's ship.

Maynard found Reck-xa's requested materials, fighting his disbelief in her alchemical prowess.

Reck-xa wrapped her tail around the coerced Human's neck. Once the ship touched down, Reck-xa placed a claw on the woman's nose, then cut an incision in the septum.

"What are you doing?" Maynard shouted. He clenched his fists and stomped over.

Binh waved a claw to keep Maynard away. "Not what you think. She's putting her to sleep. She'll be fine. Or not, what do I know? She was sniffing that 'agreeable powder' so long she might be brain dead."

"Enough complaining," Reck-xa hissed. "We have some balms to apply for everyone's safety. Unless you want the chill of space to stop your heart."

———

Outside, Maynard winced at the salve around his cheeks threatening to dribble into his mouth—a concoction meant for ridged scales, not smooth flesh. The scent stung his eyes.

The unsophisticated bubble over his head intensified the pungent odor. The shaman made Binh chew on a root with her.

"Sun root," she called it. "It fortifies our blood against the chill in the lack of atmosphere."

"It tastes like feet," Binh muttered.

"I see you struggling with this disguise, May-nard," Reck-xa intoned. "Even a Makawe in their connection to the spirit world would fail to see you. This won't come off in decontamination sprays, either."

"Right," Binh said. "Their imaginary friends won't help them."

"I thought they could see…" Maynard struggled over the Lo-sat word for infrared, so settled on "heat signatures."

"Perhaps that is your rationalization." Reck-xa directed them to follow her, slinking toward the Bastion at an angle. "A rationalization inherited from Arkoudae in their quest to belittle other species."

Binh jabbed his tail at the Bastion. "Heads up, Potion Lady and Your Holiness, we're close enough now that anybody checking a window could spot us. Use the comm if you want to keep chatting."

"May-nard." Reck-xa's voice bubbled in his ear through their local comm. "No matter what your code is, no matter the oath, you must use your skills to protect, even if it means harming another. I respect your values, but there is no place for hesitation."

"And there is no place for murder. We've added enough—"

"Oh shut up," Binh whined. "Let's get the kid and go home. You both have different philosophies and religions. We get it. The monk will use self-defense for others-offense but won't kill. The scary shaman who's chomped on a few too many mystical mushrooms will not use excessive force. Let's just get inside."

Sticking close to the asteroid's surface and slinking against obfuscating crater walls where possible, they neared the Bastion. Where the Great Mystery monastery resembled praying hands, this structure resembled a cruder gesture, metaphorically directed at the rest of the galaxy, Arkoudae in particular. He didn't know what horrors awaited inside but resolved to do anything to protect Mui-xe. He'd come this far and broken enough vows. Perhaps the shaman had a point.

Instead of approaching a door, they met a wall.

"Can you smell a trap door or secret entrance?" Maynard asked.

"Secrets don't carry scents." Reck-xa set down her satchel and several ingredients and jars pushed at the top, bobbing upward in the asteroid's lack of gravity. She caught a few floating jars in her claws, pushing the rest back inside before resealing her satchel and pulling out a crisp mushroom the size of Maynard's nose.

She crushed the cap, then stamped her open palms against the wall, leaving a chalky handprint. Using the powder on the wall, she traced an oval from the ground to her head level, then slapped her palms against the wall again, creating another two outlines on either side of the original.

The shaman opened a compartment on her breather mask to expose her snout. She readied the next ingredient contained in a vial. It glooped around its container, slow but viscous in the low gravity. In a swift motion, she uncorked the bottle with her tail and shoved the open bottle into her mouth. Eyes watering, she drained the liquid without swallowing, then stuck out her tongue and licked the wall, smearing it with her purple-stained saliva. It reacted with the powder, hissing and bubbling.

Reck-xa stepped away and affixed her breather to cover her snout again. She exhaled, and a purple cloud of breath fogged the bottom of her breather. Her next ingredient was in a stone jar, floating less deftly than the previous two components. This contained a salve, similar in texture to what she'd rubbed on their bodies for camouflage. She coated her claws and palms in it, then touched the hissing oil and powder mixture on the wall. After spreading the bubbling acid around the traced oval, she stepped back. The concoction had calcified around her palms.

It sizzled, crackled, then roared, eating away at the wall.

Within seconds, the Bastion had an opening big enough for a Lo-sat.

"Will all the oxygen drain from the inside?" Maynard asked. "Did we just kill Mui-xe?"

Binh shook his head and whispered, "You don't get out much. This is just the outer layer. We'll go through airless maintenance vents until we find an airlock."

Relief flooded all of his embarrassment over his lack of knowledge.

Reck-xa entered the hole first while bits of the Bastion's building material flaked off and floated away.

Binh measured Maynard's expression. "Don't worry. This ain't enough of a hole to cause real structural damage. Contained demolition and whatnot, like a doctor opening a wound for surgery. And I kinda like vandalizing Earthquake's property."

"So we have to crawl around and find an airlock, right?" Maynard asked. "We'll still have to enter by a door."

"Thief, grab my satchel," Reck-xa said, her voice coming out thick.

"Man, I love doing other people's bidding." Binh winked at Maynard. "Just follow Potion Lady. Remember, she's got that freaky blood talisman to tell us where Mui-xe is."

Maynard eyed the partially healed wound where she drew blood from him barely two weeks ago, but it felt like a lifetime with the galactic crisscross they'd done. He just wanted his nephew back at the monastery where he could be safe. It didn't matter if Maynard were reinstated as Abbot or even as a junior monk. Anything would be an improvement to get Mui-xe away from Earthquake and the Collective. Maynard winced, realizing how foolish it was to consider the place Mui-xe was kidnapped from "safe."

Their boots echoed through the service corridor. If this had been a building in the Collective, cleaner and repair 'bots would already be on the case, investigating and patching the hole Reck-xa made with her alchemy. The fact that no alarms blared was unsettling, although by now he trusted the salve obscuring them from security technology.

As Maynard snaked through the building's outer layer, knowing Mui-xe was just on the other side of these reinforced walls twisted nausea into gut. How could he be so close and yet feel even farther away than he had on the desert world rooftop?

They pressed forward until finding a wall.

"Found an airlock," Binh muttered. "Now would be the time for more door-melting drugs."

Maynard pushed ahead of the Lo-sats. "Wait." He approached the wall and grabbed hold of a latch. "That door handle is small enough for a Human to use, so Earthquake must have Human repair techs going through these walls periodically."

Binh fiddled with the lock. "I bet they call that 'economic stimulus.'"

Reck-xa's neck frills shrank into her neck, and she loomed over Maynard. "Hu-mans are unable to afford 'bots?" Her tone suggested her agitation wasn't directed at him.

Maynard nodded. "It's cheaper to hire a Human than to program and maintain a 'bot in the short-term. It's impossible to make big investments when you're experiencing poverty."

"Pff." Binh draped his tail around Maynard's shoulder. "That's why I choose crime."

Maynard shook his head and unlatched the door. The monastery had been specifically designed for Humans, just like this place. It was nice not to struggle through opening a door, but the symmetry between the monastery and this place made him shudder.

The airlock's quarters forced Reck-xa and Binh to duck their long necks. Maynard sealed the door behind them, and the airlock hissed closed.

Their grav harnesses adjusted. Maynard's was able to shut off since the Bastion was set to Human standard while Binh and Reck-xa huffed at the change. Segmented hydraulic arms with hoses descended from the ceiling. Purple decontamination spray followed, ending with a release of oxygen, and the concealment salve they'd used gooped off like oil in the rain.

Reck-xa cocked an eyeridge. "They would know this protocol initiated because the seal was opened and closed, yes?"

"Yes," Maynard replied, "and I don't think this decontamination spray would—"

"It did," Binh hissed. "All the stuff we smeared on ourselves washed off. This is the cheap spray that eats at clothes!"

"Sabotage!" Reck-xa's neck frills flared, and she wheeled on Maynard.

Maynard held up his hands. "I wasn't thinking about blowing our cover, and I didn't know they'd use the cheap decontamination spray. I was thinking about getting us inside without sucking all the air out of the facility, which would also kill Mui-xe."

Reck-xa pushed her tongue between her teeth, letting the three-forked whip jiggle while murder danced in her marbled eyes.

Binh stepped between them. "Look, the ex-monk has a point. Although suffocating all the Earthquake geniuses would be a nice way to simplify this rescue."

"Don't joke about killing people," Maynard said.

Reck-xa pointed her tail at the panel beside the interior door. "May-nard, open this. You've taken this mission out of my claws. We are exposed. It is now on you to keep us hidden."

"Yeah," Binh said as Maynard approached the command board. "Pray until we disappear. See how it works."

Maynard found the option for entry. It asked for a fingerprint and retinal scan. "I find myself praying you'll disappear sometimes."

As Maynard submitted himself for inspection, Binh flared out his neck frills. "What the *nguc* are you doing?"

The door into the Bastion unlatched and screeched open. "It just wanted to prove I was a Human." Maynard smiled at his companions. "I don't know much about programming, but I can tell you my genetics are not in their system."

"Don't be too sure about that," Binh muttered. "You saying that reminded me that Ricky Rickster tried sending a mole into your monastery. Who knows what intel they have on you."

"You… you never brought that up before?" Maynard stared at Binh. This hurt differently than the faux betrayal on the desert world. A mantra rose in his mind to soothe his bubbling anger.

Binh's neck frills retracted, and he switched to speaking Human. "Lots of bad memories around that guy. I've been trying to forget them. And that particular morsel never felt important. I don't know if the mole ever infiltrated or not. I know Lefty gave the order, but I abandoned him the first opportunity I got.

I figured the mole probably bounced once Slick Rick surrendered. Either way, if there were a mole, you're probably right that he didn't snag your biometrics."

Reck-xa exited the airlock first and sniffed the air. "Mui-xe was not brought here. We need to check elsewhere." Her gaze dropped to the mixed-blood talisman around her neck. "May-nard. Left or right?"

Joining her inside the Bastion, Maynard's first reaction was revulsion at the potted plants whose dead branches were topiaried into meaninglessness. The entire wall was a mural, covered in stylized images of generic Earthquake goons charging over corpses of Arkoudae. The halls stretched far, even though they lacked rooms. This complex was big for bigness' sake.

Maynard shook off the distraction. "There must be a sign or a map close by if we'd found an airlock... there!" Maynard pointed above, finding a painted sign on the wall.

"You can read that?" Binh asked. "Is that some prehistoric Human dialect?"

"Technically, yes," Maynard replied. "It's called cursive. It's more of a style of writing. It phased out before Earth collapsed, but it was preserved in a few books. It's mostly used to look fancy, but I guess it has an added advantage of confusing other species." He eyed his Lo-sat companions. "Not that I'm happy Earthquake is taking any advantages. Come on, the elevators are close."

The shaman and reformed thief followed him to the left and grumbled as they entered the elevator which was too small for them. Examining the elevator panel, Maynard glanced at Reck-xa. "Can anything in your satchel fry circuitry? There's a passkey required, and I don't think my thumbprint will suffice to get us to any secure levels."

"I can always vandalize something," Binh muttered.

Reck-xa peered at the control board, a disdainful eyeridge lowered. "Get the elevator to go down. I'll put it in free fall."

As the elevator descended, she withdrew a red powder in a vial, larger than the one she had earlier. Maynard snuck a glance in her satchel—she didn't have many ingredients left. The red powder slithered about as she rotated the vial, shaking it. Sniffing near the control panel, she uncorked it and dumped it over the buttons. Then she withdrew a stone and a metal knife. With the caution of an herbalist, she laid the stone on the control panel. With the savagery of a desperate parent protecting a child, she struck the stone with her knife, creating a spark. The spark landed on the powder, sending the control board aflame.

"What in the *nguc* are you doing?" Binh hissed.

Calmer than one should be near an electrical fire, Reck-xa re-affixed her breather and suggested by gesture the men do the same. Pointing to her gravity harness, she demonstrated turning the gravity to the highest setting, increasing her mass as much as possible. Maynard followed suit, and his stomach plummeted. With the increased mass and the smoking control board, the elevator dropped.

Satisfied the elevator would continue its descent without their added mass, Maynard switched his grav harness to the lowest setting, bypassing the building's artificial gravity and letting the asteroid's natural gravity elevate him. He refused to vomit in his breather mask, but every acidic juice in his body cascaded into his mouth. Eyes watering, Maynard swallowed it, seeing Binh and Reck-xa experience similar troubles. The lowered gravity allowed the trio to bounce off the elevator floor when it finally crashed, the elevator doors folded open in the burning shaft.

Binh hissed. "Granny Shamanny, you don't want that rock back, do you?"

"You're wearing gloves," Reck-xa replied. "You retrieve it."

Binh grumbled as he snatched it, swearing at the flames on his sleeves as he patted them out.

They stepped into the bottom sublevel of the Bastion. A chill rocked Maynard's spine.

Binh and Reck-xa sniffed the air. "Humans are nearby," Reck-xa said. Maynard stole a glance at her talisman, glowing a lighter hue than before.

The room was refrigerated, yet Maynard sensed his shivers weren't only from the temperature. Something wasn't right. Fog pooled around their ankles, the likely source of the temperature. Maynard couldn't see his own feet after entering mere seconds ago. The mist cloyed around him as if it were sapient, examining him.

Binh arched his head. "Good to stand straight again. Don't know how these hairballs can stand being so short. Sometimes I'd put things in Baldy's monastery on high shelves just to mess with the short ones. Well, the shorter of the—" His sarcasm dropped. "There are familiar scents here."

"Mui-xe?" The name of Maynard's nephew caught in his throat.

Binh shrugged. "There's a couple. The coolants are complicating things for me, but there are some Humans I—"

"Who?"

Binh's eyes and neck frills widened in tandem. "We need to leave."

Maynard glanced at the three elevators. The one they used was burned, one was clearly broken, and the third seemed fine, but Maynard wasn't too confident about it. "What do you smell?"

Reck-xa sniffed sharply. "There is something non-Human lurking, but it's not Mui-xe."

Maynard strained his ears, and thought he heard a *thud-slap* along with a faint moaning, somewhere distant in the jagged corridor. The Lo-sats didn't seem to notice.

"Do you recognize the scent?" Reck-xa asked.

Binh stiffened. "We need to get to that elevator and leave this place. Forever."

Reck-xa snarled and her tail whipped up to snatch his wrist. "Coward. We're not leaving until we find Mui-xe. Tell us who you smell."

The *thud-slap* and moaning echoed louder.

Binh spun in the direction of the third elevator, bringing Reck-xa and Maynard's attention along with him.

A hulking mass shuffled forward, taller than Maynard and stockier than Binh. *Thud-slap. Thud-slap.*

Moaning.

Obfuscated by the shadows and mist, it bore the silhouette of a mangled Lo-sat, limping like an agonized Human.

"We're too late," Binh muttered.

With another thud-slap, the intruder came into view.

Red, marbled eyes: Mui-xe's color and pattern.

Maynard's heart raced.

"No," Reck-xa hissed. "That is not my grandson."

"It's not," Maynard said. "Whoever they are…"

Binh slithered out of Reck-xa's grip. "Just run for *nguc's* sake!"

As the last word escaped, the shambling interloper raised an arm, displaying mottled Human skin and Lo-sat scales with an outstretched hand and a mismatched set of fingers and claws, all bending in impossible angles.

The hand began to glow.

Maynard followed Binh, grabbing Reck-xa by her wrist and dragging her along.

The Lo-sats outran Maynard within seconds. Binh peered back at him over his shoulder, huffed, and stopped. When Maynard caught up, Binh grumbled and fumbled with Maynard's grav harness until he changed it to the lowest setting. As Maynard protested, Binh pulled him onto his back, then ran again.

"Human backpack," Binh said. "A technique I've seen done once before."

"Thank you," Maynard said.

"I hate this and you stink."

TWENTY-NINE

(AMANDA)

Struggling with a prison cell block

AS MEL-ZA AND Amanda puzzled over Alize's cell, the floor shook, and a thin fissure spidered through it as if an earthquake threatened the asteroid. Accompanying the shake was a metallic *boom-slam* that threatened her ear drums. Symphora howled and covered her ears as she fell from the sound's impact.

Amanda and Alize both stumbled, but Mel-za braced herself with her tail, balanced between two sides of the new floor crack that could've swallowed Amanda.

Eyes wide, Mel-za helped Symphora stand. "Do you smell something burning?" Mel-za asked.

Symphora nodded. "Something on fire just crashed into the floor."

Amanda pushed off the floor on shaky arms. "That's ten kinds of bad, right?"

"Unless that means you brought some careless reinforcements from the Symphora Squad." Alize should've been on her feet first with the help of her cybernetic leg, but however long she'd been imprisoned had taken a toll.

"About those reinforcements—" Amanda stopped speaking to cough against the freshly kicked-up dust. "It's someone you know. The thief Binh Ten-trom. He's on his way here to help us rescue you and someone else." She tried to take her mind off Alize's prosthetic. Amanda had been the one to order it for her in the aftermath of the debacle on that moon five years ago. The evidence of Amanda's past wrongdoing stared her in the face.

Alize sighed. "Binh? Is he still unbearable? I don't know who I screwed over more when I ditched him with you—him or Earthquake."

"Both." Amanda managed a smile. "I also asked the Drowned Star to come. And the Collective Fleet. We just need to survive long enough for them to get here."

Thud-slap.

Symphora's ears pricked, and she darted her head around. "Someone else heard that, right?"

Thud-slap.

Amanda opened her mouth, but Symphora shushed her with a stare that would've made a statue crack.

With a sharp sniff, Mel-za turned to the group. "Something is coming."

"Yeah," Symphora said. "But what?"

Thud-slap.

"Nothing good," Amanda said.

"What's happening?" Alize asked.

Thud-slap. Thud-slap.

Amanda whirled around. "It's coming from behind us."

Symphora sniffed, then cast a dark gaze at Amanda. "I think I know what it is but not from my own experience. Joka told me about something in Dr. Diastrevlo's lab. A hybrid monster. A mix of Human and Lo-sat."

"Rick wouldn't tell me much, but he called it an 'abomination.'" Amanda's heart sank, remembering the look in his eyes when he'd used the word.

Alize pounded on her cell wall. "Look, if something dangerous is coming, you better escape. I'll be safe here, unfortunately."

"No way," Amanda said. "We're getting you out."

Thud-slap.

Mel-za faced the approaching sound. "Are these things sapient?"

"Not according to what Joka told me," Symphora replied.

Amanda squinted at the lock. She lacked the programming knowledge to hack anything. She only opened the elevator because somebody had handed her a key.

Somebody handed her a key.

Thud-slap.

They wanted her down here.

Thud-slap.

They meant this for *her,* and she was the idiot who'd brought them all down here. "Symphora, did

Joka tell you how she beat them? Rick said he had to shoot out its grav harness."

Thud-slap. The creature came into view, obscured by shadows and chilled fog. It bore the features of a Lo-sat mashed into a Human or maybe vice versa. It was impossible to tell.

Thud-slap. The moaning crescendoed as Amanda caught the source's crimson eyes.

Once, Joka described the hybrid boy as having the marbled eye pattern of a Lo-sat yet a red color neither species would ever have. This thing couldn't be that hybrid boy.

Amanda shuddered at the bestial display, hoping Joka and Rick were right that these things couldn't think or feel.

"Mel-za," Amanda said. "Try calling out to it in Lo-sat. Symphora, after she does, try in Arkouda. Then I will in Human."

"You can't be serious," Symphora growled.

After a stuttering hesitation, Mel-za hissed at the hybrid. From what Amanda knew of her language, it sounded like a greeting with a question of identity.

The hybrid continued its moan.

"Are you a prisoner here? Do you need help?" Symphora asked.

Amanda repeated the question in Human. Nothing. They may as well have shouted at a wall.

The hybrid raised a hand, mismatched Human fingers and Lo-sat claws on display. As it slumped forward, Amanda noticed a malformed Human breast on the left side of its chest. This wasn't someone raised from childhood. It was surgically altered and fused corpses. Its uneven gait was the result of mismatched legs and an uneven spine. If it had even dim awareness, this thing must be in sheer agony.

The outstretched hand glowed an iridescent orange, and the ambient temperature around them raised.

"Dodge!" Amanda shouted.

Mel-za and Symphora parted, and Amanda took cover behind Symphora. As the three hugged the wall, a pillar of flame shot between them.

"*Skata,*" Symphora cursed.

"They can regenerate body parts and heal each other if in pairs," Amanda said. As she looked at the destroyed wall beside her, an idea formed.

Mel-za forced a laugh. "You said we can pull out a grav harness to kill it?"

"Not until it frees Alize for us," Amanda said.

The hybrid's moan devolved to a howl, and it spread both hands, each glowing white-hot.

Amanda ducked and circled around Symphora, approaching the hybrid. "I'll pull on its tail! You two, grab its wrists and aim them at Alize's cell. We'll cook the lock and free her that way."

As Amanda neared it, the next volley of fire erupted, singeing Amanda's suit. It knocked her off its tail, and she thudded against the wall. The hybrid trained on Symphora.

Mel-za whipped her tail at the hybrid, grabbing a wrist as Symphora charged.

They were both too slow.

Fire erupted, and the stench of singed fur attacked Amanda's nostrils. Symphora howled and cursed, but Amanda didn't have time to look back.

Sweating from her proximity to the fire, Amanda scrambled toward the creature and pulled on the tail, more of a malformed club than the lithe appendage of a Lo-sat. Her pulling straightened the hybrid's spine. This forced both arms up enough to redirect them at the ceiling.

"*Skata*," Symphora said through a heave. "Just missed my face." After a grunt, she latched onto the other wrist.

Tail coiled, Mel-za groaned. "The smell is too strong. I'm going to throw up if we don't do something."

"Mel-za, aim at Alize's lock. Symphora—" Amanda winced through the words. "Aim at its collarbone."

Howling, the hybrid stomped and squirmed, sending Amanda off her feet but not breaking her grip. With the natural longer muscles of a Lo-sat alongside agony, rage, and adrenaline super-powering its movements, the hybrid could've snapped Amanda's spine. As it lifted her off her feet, Amanda kicked out her legs to brace against the wall. The heat from the erupting flames made sweat sting Amanda's eyes.

Circuitry fried and sizzled.

Mel-za shouted over the fire. "The lock is busted. Time for this to die."

"It's not enough to get the grav harness inside its flesh," Amanda called. "It can still flame us as it rises."

"Right." Symphora released one paw from the hybrid's wrist and slashed at its forearm, sawing it off until a limp hand squelched to the floor. Mel-za followed suit and chomped on the other forearm, her serrated teeth digging into it like a ravenous predator.

The hybrid's shouts hammered into Amanda's eardrum. With another stomp and shake, it shook Amanda off, throwing her into the wall.

As cyan-red speckled blood splattered to the floor, the fallen hands shriveled and blackened, unable to heal themselves of their own flames' damage. Gushing blood flowed out, yet a gurgling sound emanated from its severed forearms.

"It's already healing!" Amanda shouted. "Get the grav harness out."

With a heave and a trickle of blood dripping from her nose, Symphora slammed the hybrid to the floor, the chilled fog rippling around it.

Amanda's eyes widened. It was cold-blooded or at least partially. The refrigerants would slow down its healing.

"Dig at the collarbone," Symphora wheezed, revealing the burnt sections of her fur beneath her melted armor. Whatever life support the armor had been providing would begin to fail within moments if it hadn't already. Any healing of Symphora's injuries would be negated by this fight.

Mel-za and Symphora slashed at their downed foe while Amanda grabbed the charred hands.

Prying out the claws, she used them to wedge into Alize's burnt lock.

With crackles and sparks, she pried off the mechanism, and Alize stepped out of her cell, whispering a "thank you," inaudible over the hybrid's agonized moans and Symphora and Mel-za's savagery.

"Got it!" Mel-za pulled the weightless abomination to its mismatched feet, then shoved it upward to speed its ascent into the basement ceiling.

They'd slowed it down enough for the lowered gravity to take care of the rest.

Alize bowed. "Thank you all. Symphora, my best friend idolized you. She had an action figure of you in her locker at work."

Amanda averted her gaze, remembering hearing about Alize's friend. An Arkouda woman, ex-military. Killed defending Alize. Her name was Kaluteros or something. Rick's debriefing snapped into Amanda's mind. Alize's best friend was killed by Alejandro Moreno, who resembled Symphora's attacker.

That was why Amanda recognized her.

"Alize," Amanda whispered, "did a woman from Earthquake interrogate you about someone from Rick's old crew? A guy who mutinied?"

The archaeologist cocked an eyebrow. "She never said anything about mutiny, but yeah. Rosanna Moreno. Said her brother served under you and Rick."

Amanda's heart dropped into her stomach. "She wanted us to stop here and get burned alive by that thing. Unless she's watching us right now, she assumes we're dead. If we can't use that to our advantage, we're in big trouble. We have one more prisoner to save and a trove of Chamayna chitin to get you."

Another moaning echoed. Symphora perked up. "There's another one."

Mel-za sniffed. "And more Lo-sats." Sniff. "One Human. And another hybrid."

Amanda's heart raced. "I need to send a ping."

THIRTY

(ROSANNA)

Pouncing on the prey

ROSANNA DIDN'T KNOW what caused the crash which threatened her balance, but at least it snapped Crith's attention to the direction she needed him to face. Her omni-tablet buzzed with another notification, but it didn't matter. Martinez and her fake captives would be dead within seconds once the two hybrids cornered them.

Knife handle clutched between her teeth, she lowered the setting on her grav harness and jumped from her position in the rafters, descending toward the unsuspecting Crith.

With her personal gravity lowered, she landed gracefully despite the height and distributed her weight enough to conceal herself in the fog rolling around the floor. Her body wanted to shudder as she returned her gravity setting to Human standard, and her insides churned at the change. She pulled the knife from her teeth.

He'd bruised her last time.

Her hit to his abs meant he was already weakened. It wouldn't be the dreamed-of fight, but she wouldn't allow for any regrets like those with Symphora, and she'd make sure he survived long enough to know he'd been defeated. Once she'd thoroughly trounced him, she'd drag his defeated ass to Monsieur Tecton, and they'd get the recording they needed for whatever propaganda the Leader had in mind.

Then she'd force the rest of the truth out of him. Blood and adrenaline surged through her veins as she charged the unsuspecting Crith. So close—

The veteran spun around with a roundhouse kick, connecting to her chin.

She fell to her knees, but he didn't hit hard enough to dislodge anything.

Weakling.

"Sneaking up on your elder?" Rick asked upon recognizing her. "Too cowardly to fight honorably?"

Rosanna spat on the floor. "You always fought with deception. Don't pretend like you have any moral high ground."

"I'm an old man and no threat to you," Rick grumbled. "Shouldn't you be attending to that crash? Don't you smell the fire?"

Smoke tickled her nose, but she didn't care. That was someone else's problem.

"This place is chilled for a reason. I don't give a bovee's ass about your age." She lunged at him, slashing with her knife. He spun out of the way, but Rosanna was faster. She swept with her foot, catching his ankle and tripping him. "Tell me about the monster that killed my brother."

Rick pushed himself up on his arm, then rotated his hips to get up to a single knee. "Alejandro. I wanted him to replace me."

Rick saying his name sent goosebumps through Rosanna's body. It didn't belong on his tongue.

"Don't you dare act like that—" Rosanna stabbed again, this time connecting to his shoulder as he rolled away and stood.

Grimacing, Rick pulled back for a punch. He had a solid ten centimeters on her, and his reach proved it. He connected with her nose.

No stars, only some blood. A mere step back and she recovered.

Pulling his punches? Rosanna's nostrils flared. He didn't see her as worth full force. Rage bubbling, she lunged, preparing a strike, daring him to dodge. The second his weight shifted to the side, she changed directions and stuffed her knife into his tricep. The squelch and blood spray should've been invigorating, but it didn't close the chasm in her heart.

He howled.

In the distance, she heard some moaning. Must be the hybrids closing in. Crith's yelp melded with the hybrid's agonized calls. Lambda and Sigma must be doing their work.

Rosanna yanked on the knife, pulling Crith with her like he was a puppet.

"Any last requests?" Rosanna asked.

"Yeah," Rick breathed, "can I send a ping?"

Rosanna slammed him into the floor and booted him in the stomach.

THIRTY-ONE

(RICK)

Opening eyes on the real enemy

THE AMMONIA TANG of smelling salts forced Rick's eyes open. If it weren't for that stench, he would've sworn he were in the burning afterlife promised by the Abrahamist religion. Because he stared into the face of Jacques Tecton. Smiling.

Always goddamn smiling.

Blinking hard, Rick absorbed the rest of the surroundings. He was propped upright by the Moreno girl, holding him by the collar so he could kneel in the middle of the room, facing Tecton's dictatorial desk. The twinkling lights of the cosmos provided the room's main source of light, aided by gentle decorative lamps along the floor.

Tecton's office boasted opulence and darkness, for however that was possible. A wide window gazed upon the asteroid's surface and the vista of the Kuiper Belt with Neptune and its moons on display. Neptune's azure light blanketed a long conference table where a bunch of bobbleheads could agree to whatever Tecton or his favorite lackey of the moment would say. The office nearly matched Tecton's ego.

Disgusting.

Instinct and pride demanded Rick stand and take some action, but he was bound at the ankles, and his wrist was tied behind his back to his belt.

Words formed on his lips, but Tecton cut him off. "I did good work getting you here." He leaned over Rick, probably enjoying being bigger than him for once. "I got lots of good pictures of you while you were unconscious. You're perfect proof of what happens to traitors." He reared back and smiled to himself. "I truly am amazing."

Moreno's grip on Rick's collar tightened, providing its own salty burn into one of Rick's exposed cuts.

Tecton ran his left hand through his quaffed hair. Always reminding Rick of what he didn't have. Smug as hell. Phantom pains tingled in Rick's missing arm, begging him to strangle the asshole.

"You're a slippery guy, Rick," the man Rick once called Leader said. "I took you in when the Collective spat you out—"

Lie. Rick defected.

Tecton's face puckered. "—I treated you like a son—"

Lie. Rick was his tool.

"—I made you famous—"

Lie. His reputation preceded him. Infamous, maybe.

"—and you managed some great things under my command—"

Lie. Rick's accomplishments were in spite of Tecton. Getting Collective armor. Developing advanced scrapper magnets. Developing the Equalizer. Capturing Collective warhives. Bringing Dr. Diastrevlo to justice after he reanimated those hybrid corpses. But as the bastard's list of falsehoods continued, a pinch twisted in Rick's heart. All of Rick's so-called accomplishments only increased the pain and suffering in this galaxy. Except killing Dr. Diastrevlo. Rick would do that again.

"Was this why you wanted him… sir?" Moreno adjusted her grip, voice racked with frustration. "So you could taunt him?"

Rick straightened. "What were the lies you told her about her brother?" He turned his head as much as he could in her direction. "I bet he never gave you the full truth of anything." Her grip faltered a fraction. "Any question you had about Alejandro, he gave you a sliver or a half-truth. Whatever it is you think he knows, he'll never—"

Tecton interrupted with a slap to the face.

The force from Tecton's pampered hand was enough to turn Rick's head a centimeter. It wouldn't leave a bruise or a mark. Tecton's other hand stayed behind his back.

Rick laughed. "I've got an itch on my shoulder if you want to hit that next."

Moreno's grip loosened again. Any more and he'd have an opening for an attack.

"I'm sorry about your brother, Rosanna. It tore my heart out to kill him… It pained me to see him corrupted by Tecton's rhetoric." She released him, giving him a chance to stand. "I intercepted a message from him—"

A flash of light came, more hellish than Neptune's storms.

Jacques Tecton had pulled a gun and sent a plasma bullet right in Rick's face.

The instant stretched to eternity, allowing him precious time to reflect in these last few moments. Rick had only wanted to be the hero. He would've settled for being one person's hero. He couldn't even get the plaque from the museum back to Oze.

But dreams were just dreams, and Rick was a failure.

As his face burned, incinerated by a plasma bullet, his personal omni-tablet reading his vital signs buzzed a gentle reminder to drink more water since he may have been dehydrated. Then it chimed, denoting that its final program to send off two messages had succeeded: Rick's final act of defiance.

He didn't get He'nay or Alize freed.

But this place *would* be crushed by P'oki.

He crumpled to the floor, and Neptune's blue light washed over his corpse.

Interlude:

```
Message 1 of 2:
Sender: Crith, Rodrick
Recipient: P'oki KaWhetuMa
Subject: I failed
```

P'oki, this was the message programmed to auto-send if my vitals went too low. You're getting this because I'm about to die or already have. I'm sorry. I hope you still have a chance to grieve in peace if you survive my damn crusade. But I'm sure as you're reading this, you're rolling your eyestalks at me and hoping to find He'nay.

P'oki, weaponize your scrapper magnet. Throw something at this damn Bastion. Tecton and his main lieutenants will be on the top floor, no exceptions.

If Earthquake survives today, you need to get to the other side of the galaxy and fast. Change your name and sell your ship. Go halfway across the galaxy. Then change your name again and go across the galaxy in a different direction. Some recruits are ruthless hunters and have too much pride and arrogance for their own good. They won't be able to stand the insult of you surviving.

You mentioned once in flight that your daughter asked Dr. Oze to help her carve a tattoo into her carapace, a Chamayna glyph. If you can ever find Dr. Oze, ask her for an explanation.

The Chamayna words carried power with them. I don't know how, but maybe you can figure it out by listening to your spirits.

P'oki, you've given me more compassion and patience than I deserve. Rip open this damn tower and find He'nay. Whatever it takes.

Thank you.
Onward,
RC

THIRTY-TWO

(AMANDA)

In a refrigerated, melting prison

DESPITE MEL-ZA'S PROTESTS, Amanda and her companions agreed their next search item would be remaining Chamayna chitin. Amanda wanted to find their whole supply, but Alize insisted she only needed the tiniest shard of it.

Alize explained what Binh had told her about the Chamayna chitin's scent from when she discovered it with him six years ago. It didn't seem to land, so she listed off chemicals found in their carapaces, which earned a nod from Mel-za. As she described the color and texture, an incoming message stole Amanda's attention.

From Rick Crith.

Amanda scowled but knew she needed to open it. She angled her shoulders to conceal the message from the others.

She fought the urge to imagine his voice.

```
Message 2 of 2
Sender: Crith, Rodrick
Recipient: Martinez, Amanda
Subject: I'm sorry


Amanda. I've programmed my omni-tablet
to send off two messages if I die in
this tower. You always said I should
install a fitness and vital signs
tracker in this damn thing.

The other message is going to a Makawe
named P'oki KaWhetuMa—you can recog-
nize her from other Makawe because she
has a Chamayna glyph hiding among her
shell carvings. She came with me here.
Earthquake abducted her daughter in
connection with Oze.

Whatever you do, stay away from the
Bastion. I have a plan to bring the
whole thing down. Use the ping tracker
to show the government where it is, if
anything remains.

You were the person I wished I could be.
```

I should have listened to you and put more focus on feeding the homeless than developing weapons. I know you once believed in my ideals about freedom by force before I went too far, and I'm glad knowing you abandoned them. I'm sorry I took you down with me.

I know you'll always try to do the right thing. You're the best of us.

I'm guilty of awful things. I refuse to march into my last battle without admitting you were the bright spot in my years of darkness.

I don't know if you can remember our mission on that damn moon, but you intercepted a message from a mutineer, Alejandro Moreno. He sent a whiny note to Tecton, pissing about us. Since you never delete anything, you might still have access to it. If you can, forward that along to his sister, Rosanna Moreno. That might save you some pain later.

No matter what, I have to say thank you. Whatever you do and however you do it, you'll make Humanity proud.

You'll move the damn galaxy, not
Earthquake. Amanda Martinez, I salute
you. And stay away from the Bastion.
It's getting obliterated one way
or another.

                              Onward,
                              RC

A pit wormed through Amanda's stomach. She'd joined Earthquake because she wanted to send money to her aunt and because she hated the government system that forced them into poverty. And here she was ten years later, still that same punk kid in over her head.

While the logical part of her brain hated him, the emotional part of her remembered the man who was once heroic, a man she had conversations with about buying refrigerators and watching his blood pressure. The person who revolted her was also proud of her.

But she didn't have time to decide if she was sad or relieved. "Alize, I hate to ask, but was there another prisoner with you? A Makawe?"

Alize nodded, slowly reaching behind her back into her tattered clothing. "Her name was He'nay." Alize produced a brittle fragment of a Makawe shell with a carved tattoo. "This is all that's left of her."

With a shaky finger, Amanda pointed at her omni-tablet. "This message I got says her mother is looking for her."

Some moisture budded around Alize's eyes, and Amanda looked away.

Her eyes drifted to Rick's warning to stay away from the Bastion. She definitely remembered that note from all those years ago. If getting Alejandro Moreno's whiny note in the psycho assassin's hands meant less bloodshed, it would be worth it.

Goosebumps pricked Amanda's skin. "Ladies, we need to find this chitin or some other way out and fast. This place is rigged to explode."

Symphora scowled. "And how do you know that?"

"Because Rick Crith messaged me. Could you figure out the Chamayna scent from what Alize said?"

Symphora and Mel-za traded a glance.

"And Alize, you'll know the chitin if you see it?"

The archaeologist closed her eyes slowly as if she lacked Amanda's enthusiasm for escaping.

"This place is huge," Alize said, mulling it over. "We can't hope to luck onto it. I have one thing I'm going to try. There is one theory I kept back from Rosanna and the Earthquake interrogators."

Amanda waved her hands. "Is there a quick version of this?" This analytical slowpoke would get them killed. Alize narrowed her eyebrows and glared at Amanda, triggering Amanda to remember what she'd done to Alize under Rick's command.

Thud-slap. It broke Amanda's concentration for a second, but she dismissed it as an echo.

Alize reached for the severed hybrid bone on the floor, uncharred from the assault. The last bits of flesh flaked off in her grasp. "The Chamayna's abilities were borrowed from the Unspeakable. Each time they used its power, they also made it stronger. Earthquake has been strengthening it whenever they teleport. I don't need Chamayna chitin. I just need to carve with something organic."

Thud-slap.

Amanda's eyes bored holes into Alize. "What are you going to do?"

All emotion drained from her voice. "Invite it."

Thud-slap.

Symphora seethed. "We need to do something right now."

Alize scraped a line into the floor, the squeak of bone against metal as grating as her plan. It left a little line of ground bone in the floor like chalk. "You came here to save me." She glanced up with a weak smile. "Mission accomplished. Earthquake thinks the only way to use the power is with the Chamayna chitin, so you'll need to destroy it. Do you have an extra breather?"

"What aren't you telling me?" Hands shaking, Amanda offered her spare breather.

Thud-slap. Moans followed.

"I won't be coming back alone."

Thwip.

Alize blinked from existence, the bone she used to carve disappearing with her.

The chalky bone bits remained on the floor, but whatever glyph she'd carved vanished.

Mel-za sniffed the air. "I'm high, right?"

"Careful what you wish for," Symphora muttered. "Martinez, she ditched us. I don't know if she's coming back, but we need to escape. I'm not fighting another one of those things after its freaky twin nearly roasted me alive."

"She could come back," Amanda said, steel in her voice. "We still need to find the hybrid boy."

Remembering traditional Human architectural layout was more complicated than she expected. So long accustomed to the Arkouda way of doing things, she had to comb her memory for what should've been natural.

"The elevators were close to the center of a wall. We need to find an opposite end. We'll barrel through these walls until we can find them. We'll use your senses to make sure we don't bump into any hybrids."

Amanda took off running in the opposite direction from the shambling abomination heading their way.

Symphora and Mel-za flanked her, but this time, it was the Arkouda who couldn't run as fast as the others. Her injuries were taking too much of a toll, and she was fading fast.

Mel-za sniffed the air and called for a halt. "We have a visitor."

A buttery voice Amanda hadn't heard in years called back. "What you have is a problem with having two mammalian companions."

Binh Ten-trom stepped in front of them, an aging Lo-sat to his left. Human hands wrapped around Binh's shoulders from behind. He rotated, revealing a middle-aged Human riding piggy-back like a child.

Seeing Amanda, a grin curled up Binh's snout. "Well if it isn't Madam Political Title in a bad disguise. Guess who almost died?"

THIRTY-THREE

(ROSANNA)

Finding new prey

ROSANNA STARED AT the corpse which belonged to the man who dominated her thoughts over the better part of a decade. The person she hated most, who stole everything from her.

Or so she'd thought.

She was supposed to feel satisfied but felt as disgusting as an octopede.

"You can't believe a word out of his liar mouth," Tecton tutted. His pistol went back into the holster under his suit jacket. "He lived like a dog." He shot Rosanna a smirk. "Died like one, too."

Rosanna's hollowness wormed inside her. Even though she'd defeated him twice, the kill wasn't hers.

Killing Rick was the one thing Tecton had promised she could do. And he stole it from her, right when

Rick was about to say what she'd needed to hear. She couldn't have been wrong about the Leader being the right man for Humanity. Alejandro had spoken so highly of him. Alejandro wasn't some idiot.

And Rosanna wasn't crazy.

For how close the three of them were grouped when Tecton pulled the trigger, he could've taken her arm off, not that he seemed to care. But he'd said he'd take care of her. She'd saved his life, for Earth's sake.

Rosanna exhaled and reached for her omni-tablet. "Word came from the scouts. You were right about the Collective Fleet coming here. They're only a few minutes away. They apparently aren't too happy about the fringe government's destruction."

"Is there an 'and' or a 'but' coming?"

Rosanna stowed her omni-tablet to look him in the eye, but he'd already returned to his desk, summoning a cleaner 'bot to attend to Crith's corpse.

Rosanna stepped over the body, letting her boot drag across the chest. It didn't make her feel better. "There's an 'and.' The Blekk are en route."

"Drowned Star?"

"Not just them. A few pirate factions. All inbound."

Tecton spun around in his chair. "Why? We left those tentacle freaks alone."

She strutted beside his desk, closer than she'd ever come before, close enough to strangle him before he could grab the gun if she chose to. But he probably had a good reason for his actions, even if they did infuriate her.

Rosanna couldn't just attack him. She wasn't crazy. "I don't know why, but they're coming."

The wrinkled leader of Earthquake glared back. "Then what good are you?"

She still had value. He couldn't treat her this way, even if he was the best of Humanity. Rosanna pointed at Tecton's holster. "Sir, if I may, when you executed Crith, you didn't hold your gun properly. If worst comes to worst and you have to use it to defend yourself, your grip might get you killed. May I?"

Tecton rolled his chair back to allow her to get close. "Fine, make it quick." He undid his holster, heavy with the gun, removed the ammo, and handed it to her.

Why would he remove the ammo? She wasn't crazy.

"See, you took it out with your wrist overextended." She adjusted the strap and put it on with her right hand, letting her left hand ready a piece of Chamayna chitin. Once she got the holster on her, she pulled out the gun. "See how I got that faster?"

"Looked the same to me. Quit wasting my time and give it back."

"Why did you kill Crith? What was he about to tell me?"

"Hell if I know. Give me my gun back. You're acting crazy."

Rosanna rotated her grip on the gun and smacked him across the face with it. While his head was turned, she dropped the shard of chitin in his shirt pocket. "You stole my kill. I'm going to prepare defenses for whatever assault is coming our way and send a request to the Blekk to fight the Collective instead of us when they arrive." She exhaled and forced a smile. "In the meantime, I suggest you figure out some deal you can make with them that's better than what they have with the Collective. We can't take them all. Sir."

Tecton cradled his bloodied face, wailing into his hands. She knew he'd have some foul nickname for her, but she couldn't care anymore.

He'd be fine.

As Rosanna strutted away, she realized that *she* wouldn't be fine, though. She'd insulted him, and he likely had more defensive weapons in here.

Rosanna darted toward the elevator.

Maybe she could sell herself out to the Collective. They'd have to want mercenaries or bounty hunters. But they'd never let her walk with what she'd done. Her only chance of survival was staying with Earthquake and fighting like hell to stay alive and out of a cell.

THIRTY-FOUR

(MAYNARD)

Among strangers, fellow Bastion intruders

MAYNARD CLUTCHED BINH'S shoulders while keeping an eye on Reck-xa.

A tremor ran through Binh as he spoke, jostling Maynard. "Did you find... Alize?"

Maynard craned his neck, scanning the three women: Human in a poor Earthquake disguise, Lo-sat, and an Arkouda who felt vaguely familiar.

The Arkouda folded her arms, wincing and heaving. She straightened, still putting up an intimidating posture. "Are you the ones Martinez has been pinging?"

Maynard stiffened. He'd heard that voice before. He let go of Binh, sliding down his back in a likely undignified fashion and stared up at her. "Y-you're Symphora." He wondered if she'd cut her mohawk recently but feared asking.

Reck-xa stepped in front of him. "Where is the boy?"

The Human in the group bridged the distance between them. "Binh, I'd say it's good to see you, but we never see each other in good circumstances." She addressed the others. "You must be shaman Reck-xa and Brother Maynard. This is Mel-za, and yes, that's Symphora, but we need to keep that quiet. My name is Amanda Martinez. We found Alize, but she disappeared."

"Disappeared?" Maynard didn't see the need to remind Ms. Martinez that he remembered her from New Lodestone. People called him and his Brothers saints and holy, yet she was still a reformed and remorseful ex-Earthquake member trying her best. He had been careful to remind refugees of that, lest they get overly attached and dependent. She was an excellent choice for Human representation in the Collective government.

Snapping Maynard back into the moment, Binh tsked, and his demeanor restored. "Typical. How many times did you insult Alize to get her to do that? I had to go at her for days before she gave me the slip."

Ms. Martinez glared at him. "You know what she did. She teleported without having any Chamayna chitin. I barely know how Earthquake can disappear with it." Her eyes darkened. "We have a bigger problem, though. Something is going to happen to this building, and it won't be pretty. We have to rescue the boy. We don't need to escape the asteroid, just get outside before the Fleet arrives."

Teleportation? It was like something out of fiction. But Maynard reminded himself that people could say the same of Mui-xe.

Maynard turned to Reck-xa but spoke in Arkouda for the benefit of the rest. "We can trust them. They're good people."

Reck-xa tugged on her talisman, stepping toward the others. "We follow this. No time for questions."

The Lo-sat, Mel-za, inclined her head and shielded her eyes with the tip of her tail, which was proper reverence around a shaman and a talisman.

"Fine," Amanda said. "Can you describe the boy's scent for my companions?"

Reck-xa eyed Mel-za, hissing in their shared language. The poetry and chemical terms ran faster than Maynard could translate. When she finished, Binh shrugged and addressed Symphora, pointing at Amanda and Maynard. "Human body odor without the awful hair stench. Think of Baldy's scent and mix it with a Lo-sat with a scale condition."

"Let's go." Symphora limped yet strode forward in the cause of helping a boy she never met. This was the Symphora people whispered about, why tales of her exploits, even the crass and gross ones, inspired courage and fantasy. She experienced agony yet did not suffer. This was the essence of the Great Mystery. Overcome suffering. Overcome ignorance and falsehood.

He missed the red mohawk, though.

Thud-slap.

Thud-slap.

Goosebumps danced across Maynard's skin.

"Can we run away from this one?" Maynard asked.

Ms. Martinez nodded.

Reck-xa snarled at the question. "If it's in our way, we fight it." Tugging on her talisman, she pointed toward the shambling sound. "We have to face it."

Binh tsked. "It's guarding the kid, you think?"

"We can take it," Mel-za said, cracking her knuckles. "We already downed one."

The group of six advanced. Maynard braced himself for conflict. A mindless minion, tortured into agony.

Thud-slap.

They turned down three more halls, pushing toward the maze's center. Delving deeper and keeping speed meant the space narrowed, and there wasn't time or room for discussion. Symphora barely had room to walk, and her panting was growing more intense. Reck-xa's talisman glowed brighter in each passage and hummed.

Each new twist in this hallway felt like excavating his own consciousness, witnessing all these people working together for Mui-xe. The Great Mystery brought them together, and they would succeed.

For the boy. For the galaxy.

Wherever Mui-xe was, Earthquake would be there, wanting to kill any would-be rescuers.

Thud-slap. Louder this time.

Binh sniffed the air and whispered to Maynard, "You smell scared. Worried it's a trap? That thing isn't as close as it sounds."

"Earthquake could have hidden gunmen," Maynard whispered back. "They may have concocted a method to hide their scent from Lo-sats and Arkoudae."

"Hmpf. We're making enough noise for them to hear us coming, that's for sure. And the good news for you is you'd be the last one on their list to kill. All they have in their files about you is how you pissed off Lefty when you wouldn't teach him your martial arts a few years ago."

"Imagine if I had," Maynard replied. "Perhaps the discipline involved would have reformed him."

"Unless you had a technique for pulling the stick out of his ass, I doubt it."

Reck-xa hissed at them. "Be quiet."

Thud-slap.

A moaning echoed down the corridor, and at the next turn, a shambling hybrid appeared.

"*Nguc!*" Binh shrieked.

"Outta my way." Mel-za sprinted to the front.

The moaning tortured creature extended a hand.

"No more flames." Reck-xa rotated her hips and grabbed the hybrid's wrist with her tail. Mel-za extended her own tail and reached for the opposite hand. Both women struggled against it.

"Don't kill it!" Amanda shouted. "We can use its fire to free the kid."

As the hybrid roared, Binh wheeled on her. "Have you lost your nuts?"

"Shut up and help her!" Maynard shouted. He ran toward Reck-xa's tail and clamped on the beast's wrist as hard as possible. Binh grunted and did the same on the opposite wrist.

Reck-xa strained against the mutant's resistance. "Wherever they're keeping him captive—*hrrk*—must be something fireproof."

Symphora limped forward, ready to slash. "Grandma's right, Martinez."

The hybrid stiffened, then jerked enough to throw off Reck-xa, who clattered to the floor. Mel-za faltered but kept her tail grip.

Maynard rushed to cradle the shaman.

"It's too strong," she hissed.

Mel-za shrieked as she leapt away from a pillar of flame. Binh and Symphora moved to restrain the beast while Amanda dove between its legs and grabbed its club of a tail.

"Anything remaining is to destroy Mui-xe's cell. I can't use any more reagents or elixirs." Reck-xa's talisman thrummed.

The hybrid's moans rose to a howl and its malformed snout glowed in the same way its hands had to shoot fire. Maynard's eyes widened, and he lay Reck-xa down.

"Get away from its mouth," Amanda shouted. "It's going to breathe fire!"

"*Nguc!*" Binh cursed and leapt behind it.

Symphora sank her shoulder and rammed it into the creature's neck, startling it into jerking its head upward. Crimson fire erupted from its mouth, illuminating the dark basement, and signaling like a beacon to any members of Earthquake precisely where they were.

Maynard had never considered what a burnt tongue would smell like, and he wished he hadn't learned. The stench of burnt scaly lips and a tongue too deformed for words attacked Maynard's nostrils.

Binh and Mel-za's snouts puffed, but Reck-xa snorted and struggled to her feet.

Amanda used the moment of confusion to yank on the creature's nub of a tail, pulling the spine into an arc.

Symphora retched and stumbled backward, round ears folding limp. Her fur was singed in a few places from contact with the creature.

"Go find Mui-xe," Maynard said to Reck-xa. "We'll catch up."

Reck-xa slithered past the struggling science experiment, and Maynard charged it.

He remembered what Binh had told him about the hybrid Joka Bunear defeated in Dr. Diastrevlo's laboratory: grav harness surgically embedded inside its body. Collarbone.

Maynard summoned as much calm as possible, shut off his own gravity, and leapt.

At the top of his jump, he forced his grav harness to the maximum setting and descended on the writhing creature as his own mass increased.

The impact knocked it down, allowing the others to scatter.

He knew what he had to do.

With each hand in the viper fang position, he struck at the creature, excavating an entire bone. His increased mass allowed his fingers to puncture the skin and muscle. Struggling to maintain calm, he ripped out both clavicles. His arms burned as his own bones struggled to keep pace with his increased mass.

"If there is any consciousness within you," Maynard muttered, fighting to breathe with the new pressure on his lungs, "know this brings me no pleasure."

He threw the bones aside, jostling them to yank them free of tendons and snaking tissue, already regenerating.

Exposed yellow flesh and stringy muscle squelched together over purpling blood. Maynard struck again, hitting the limp grav harness inside. He tore it out, then rolled off the creature.

Desperate to find the strength to move his hand to his own neck, he thumbed his gravity harness and returned it to its normal state, stomach heaving with the gravity change.

The hybrid rose, belly first toward the ceiling. Its club of a tail whished and its arms flailed, glowing in bursts.

Mel-za grunted and hoisted the creature over her head, throwing it into the air. Bubbling blood gushed from its wounds as the creature ascended.

"That was disgusting," Amanda said. "But thank you." She sank to her knees and tended to Symphora.

"By 'disgusting,' I think she means awesome." Binh approached Maynard and slapped his back. "Aim for *not me* when you puke next time."

Maynard stared at his hands. His index and middle fingers carried the not-red-enough-for-Human and not-cyan-enough-for-Lo-sat blood stains. Bits of the hybrid's flesh and scale mesh were stuck under his fingernails.

If that thing wasn't truly alive as the others claimed, then it wasn't murder. But it didn't feel like an act of compassion. Yet saving his companions' lives was.

Wincing as his gravity returned to a standard state and his insides rioted against him, he collected himself, watching Mel-za assist Symphora beside Amanda. The legend's tongue lolled out of her muzzle, a desperate attempt to cool down. She shouldn't have been over-heating here when everyone else was shivering.

"We'll lower your gravity again," Mel-za suggested. "Carry you."

"If I get nauseous and puke," Symphora replied, "I'll lose too many fluids." She winced and coughed. Each breath must've been agony. "Leave me here. Go catch up to that grandma."

Amanda took Symphora's paw in both hands. "We'll come back for you."

Mel-za's neck frills flared. "You would dare leave her?"

Breathing deeply, Maynard came between them. "We are close to Mui-xe. If Amanda, Binh, and I pursue Reck-xa and she finds him, we'll be able to find you by your scent. Symphora needs to rest. You could per-haps remain here and guard her."

Mel-za glared at him before craning her neck to Amanda. "I don't remember anyone putting him in charge."

"We didn't," she replied, "but he's right."

Binh swooshed his tail near Mel-za's snout. "Trust me, I'm not keen on the unfortunate ratio of stinkies to the master race that's happening around me, but we gotta save this kid. If we survive, I'll give you my ping address. We'll have a great time together, and I'll even let you pay."

Mel-za hissed something in Lo-sat too fast and harsh for Maynard to understand.

Binh chuckled and started down the path Reck-xa took. "Easiest way to get a lady to leave me alone is to ask her on a date."

Amanda bade her two companions a farewell, and Maynard bowed to them, especially deep for Symphora, then they ran to catch Binh.

Maynard owed his life to Symphora, and abandoning her made him feel sick, yet morality demanded it. All his life, he'd tried to do whatever was right yet never settled with any real decision of what that was. Letting Ned pursue his passion for science and encouraging him to marry the love of his life seemed right, yet it led to his death. Accepting his nephew into the monastery resulted in Mui-xe's kidnapping and a fellow monk's death. Perhaps leaving Symphora behind would condemn the galactic savior of the downtrodden to her death, too.

Maynard summoned energy from his burning chest to keep pace with the much faster Binh as he followed Reck-xa's trail.

They turned a sharp corner and were met with a hissing wail.

Reck-xa.

Binh put an arm out in front of Maynard and Amanda, who both stopped. "She's not alone."

Four gun-wielding Humans surrounded the shaman.

"Leave her alone," Amanda shouted in a fake accent. "She's supposed to go upstairs to the boss."

A muscled man stood like a boulder, moving his aim from Reck-xa to Amanda. "That's enough outta you, Martinez. Nobody is fooled by that disguise. Your ass is trapped. Surrender before I start shooting."

Maynard charged in with a jumping kick against the nearest gang member. When the attention turned to him, Reck-xa flared her neck frills and tripped another gangster with her tail. Maynard's foot connected with a chest, hitting armor. His attack wouldn't do any damage, but it knocked something loose.

Binh grabbed a third gangster and spun them around, using them as a shield. "That's somebody's hot grandma, you *ke-noks*." The gangster stomped on Binh's foot and elbowed him in the jaw. Maynard dashed over and kicked him onto the floor.

Recovering from the attack, Maynard peeked at Reck-xa's buzzing talisman, illuminating a brighter hue. Whipping his head around, he caught a break in the wall a few meters ahead. Unable to reach it, he leapt onto the chest of the downed Earthquake recruit, snatched their dropped gun, and aimed it at them. He hated himself for holding it, for even initiating the attack—the low gravity offered to release it from his grip. But they would not listen to reason, and there was no time.

From above, a thud rocked the Bastion's foundation, and all the Humans stumbled. It was as if something had hit the tower hard enough to unseat it from the asteroid.

Reck-xa used the opportunity to bite into the exposed neck of the person she'd ensnared. She ripped into the carotid artery, and blood splurted, rising to the ceiling as the rafters collected the blood. Maynard's training made him want to scream to keep pressure on it, but the armored man stumbled backward and fell over.

Dead.

By a shaman's bite.

Unwilling to process that act, Maynard readied another leaping kick to the leader, but Amanda approached the tower of muscle.

"I don't know what shook the foundation, but you're under attack," she said. "The Collective and the Drowned Star are both coming. You can fight us and lose, or you can get the hell out of here and live to see tomorrow."

"Fat chance," he barked.

Shaking, Maynard raised his pilfered weapon. "Do as she says," Maynard said. "After you release the hybrid boy."

"The freak?"

Binh raked his claws against the leader, digging ribbons out of his cheeks. "Say that again and your tongue is next."

Maynard repeated the command. "Release the hybrid boy. My companions are less generous than I am, so I suggest you cooperate."

As the leader of the group sidestepped toward an intersecting corridor, Maynard eyed the gangster Reck-xa killed as he passed the corpse. "May you find the Answer in your next life," he muttered.

Binh rotated between the other two recruits, pointing the stolen gun at them.

Amanda stepped beside Maynard. "Not bad for a negotiation. I don't want any deaths, either."

"I always admired you. Your work for the people of New Lodestone eased the suffering of many people. It's an honor to stand beside you now."

"Whatever that thud was upstairs, I don't know how much longer we have to stand. I hope it was the Fleet, but if so, they might blow this place to hell."

With the leader busy, Binh motioned to his two captives. "The scary sexy shaman behind me will eat you if you stick around and not in the fun way. Drop the itty bitty knives your commander makes you hide in your boots. Then how about you scamper off?"

Exchanging a hurried glance, the two gang members on the floor unsheathed concealed knives in their boots—which floated away in the absence of gravity—then scrambled to their knees and bolted away with a stumble. That wasn't a good sign. The building must be losing power if its artificial gravity was failing like this. Even Binh and Reck-xa's tails floated above the floor, despite their grav harnesses.

Binh turned the gun over in his claws and offered it to Amanda. "I'm a bad shot. I couldn't hit an Arkouda's ass in a lunch line. It would be cool if you didn't turn around and shoot me with it."

Sighing, Amanda accepted it. "I never took it personally when you betrayed Earthquake."

Binh harrumphed. "Well your one-armed former employer more or less enslaved me with his ridiculous debt—"

Amanda raised a hand. "—I am not on Rick's side at all, but the debt he put you in was because Tecton wanted him to execute you when your debt was paid.

Rick adding to that debt saved your life. Show some respect, asshole."

The two continued talking, but Maynard didn't wish to invade their privacy. Besides, he needed to see his nephew.

With ginger steps, he approached Reck-xa and the gang leader near the break in the wall. As Maynard neared, it revealed another corridor, narrower than the others, with the room's ubiquitous mist sitting half a meter higher than the rest of the basement complex, rising from the failing gravity. Reck-xa's talisman glowed brighter.

The object's luminance exploded into shades of red, cyan, and a painful white. The radiance rivaled a star.

Alchemy.

Maynard's stomach churned. It shouldn't be possible. What chemicals and ingredients she must have mixed together must be beyond Maynard's comprehension.

The gang leader had a different reaction. Through stutters, he cursed at Maynard. "W-what'll she do to me?"

"Let you survive, if you take us to the boy. That I can guarantee. You will regret acting otherwise. It's not like you have any other options."

Reck-xa leaned close, and her talisman nudged itself left as if pointing toward a row of cells in the narrower hallway.

"Tell her he's in the third cell. It's unlocked."

Maynard stood his ground. "You're coming with us to verify."

The gang leader entered the hallway, Reck-xa ducking to fit behind him.

On either side of the corridor, narrow prison cells lined the wall. The first two Maynard passed showed the impact of the hit to the Bastion's foundation earlier: empty with exposed wires and hoses left dangling. As were the second two. The third on his right was no different, then Reck-xa gasped.

Maynard turned to the third cell on the left, a small room partitioned off by dura-glass.

Mui-xe.

Unconscious.

Breathing.

Tears flowed from Maynard, and he forgot how to breathe.

Reck-xa's neck frills flared like she was pouncing on prey. Tears clouded her marbled eyes as she glared at the Earthquake member. In Arkouda, she hissed, "Release him." After a hard three blinks, she attempted a croaking Human command. "Out. Let-him."

"You heard her." Maynard's voice trembled.

The gangster tapped commands into the control panel. Maynard examined the remaining cells nearby. All sat empty, and the corridor stretched on for what seemed like an eternity or at least the circumference of the asteroid. Whatever else they held here or were prepared to hold, this compound could contain an army. And this was only the basement. He shuddered to imagine how many Earthquake mercenaries and recruits lodged above.

Mui-xe's cell glowed blue, and a hiss of mist swirled inside.

His translucent eyelids retracted, revealing red marbled eyes. A breathing mask fell from his snoutish mouth and nose. Maynard's heart raced. He'd crossed the galaxy for his nephew, forsaken his morals and home, and Maynard had to hold himself back—his reunion wasn't as important as the other family connection here.

The boy gazed upon his grandmother for the first time. His mouth fell open; a pointed asymmetric fang protruded from his lips.

Maynard nudged in beside her. "Mui-xe, it's good to see you. This is your grandmother." He hadn't considered the resemblance between her and his mother before. Lo-sat aging was generally mysterious to him, so in Maynard's eyes, they appeared identical, switching La-hok's lab coat for Reck-xa's shamanic garb. This must have felt like something out of a dream for the boy.

Reck-xa crouched down, meeting his eye level. "Granny is here. All will be well." She wrapped her tail around his shoulders and pulled him in for a hug.

Mui-xe croaked back in Lo-sat, "You're … Granny? Have I been drugged again?"

Grandmother and grandson embraced, and guilt squeezed Maynard's stomach. He should have found a way to let them see each other months ago.

Steeling himself, Maynard faced the Earthquake member. "I'm not here to judge. What have you done to the boy?"

The gangster stepped back, hands in the air. "N-n-othing."

"Not you." Maynard stiffened. "What happened to him while he was here?"

"T-tests."

"Try again."

"They experimented on him. I don't know. I'm not one of the science guys."

Mui-xe croaked in Human, "He wasn't one of them, Uncle Maynard."

Maynard met his nephew's gaze. "Are you strong enough to walk? I know this is a lot to ask, but there's someone who needs your help. We're going to leave this place."

As the boy nodded, the gangster scampered away. Reck-xa motioned to pursue, but Maynard halted her. As he did, the basement lights turned red, staining the swirling mist around their legs a sickly pink.

An alarm blared with an automated Human voice: "Intruder alert. Collective inbound. Intruder alert."

THIRTY-FIVE

(AMANDA)

Shouting over a blaring alarm

SEEING THE HYBRID boy Mui-xe with his uncle and grandmother offered a measure of relief to Amanda, but the repeating alarm warning of an intruder made her tense. Rick's detonation plan hadn't triggered yet, or maybe the explosion before they found the boy was it, and the upstairs would be in ruins.

They all ran off.

The reality of Mui-xe being a scared teen who needed his family made Amanda's stomach turn, not because of his appearance, but because of what was done to him. The abominations that attacked them weren't adult versions of Mui-xe. Those hulking husks were surgically augmented corpses with the Lo-sat trait of regenerating tissue placed into overdrive.

Mui-xe's gait wasn't so mismatched, and his append-ages had their normal function.

Amanda hoped Mui-xe wasn't planning to ditch them like Alize had: each passing second assured Amanda that Alize had lied about returning. Amanda couldn't blame her.

With the Collective fleet inbound, they didn't have much time.

"We're almost to Symphora," Amanda shouted, timing her words to fit in between the blaring siren's warnings.

Binh pointed down a hallway at an intersection, and they all rounded the corner.

Mel-za lay slumped over Symphora's heaving body. Three male Human corpses in Earthquake gear littered the ground.

A singed hole had punctured Mel-za's neck frills, and Symphora had one through her exposed paw. The group slid to a stop, nearly slipping in the blood puddle. The stench of plasma-singed fur stung Amanda's nose and eyes, so she could only imagine what the Lo-sats were experiencing.

Brother Maynard faced Mui-xe. "Can you heal them?"

"If you do, they'll defend us while we escape," Amanda said. "They helped us get here."

Mui-xe approached Symphora as if she might explode or swipe at him.

Maynard came beside him. "This is the woman who saved me and your dad when we were kids. Did he ever tell you?"

Mui-xe crouched in front of her. "That's Symphora?" The boy's croak made it sound like each word hurt his uvula which wasn't quite made for Human or Lo-sat speech. "Where's her mohawk?"

In another situation, Amanda would've chuckled, wondering what stories this kid's dad must've told him. But this wasn't the time for frivolity with everyone's icon on her last legs. Again. "She cut it for this mission."

Binh crouched before Mel-za and lifted her off Symphora. "This one's still breathing. Hey Scary Granny? Mind offering a claw?" Binh pressed his scales against Mel-za's, which looked grayer than the metal surrounding them. Heat transfer was more useful for Lo-sats than a blood transfusion for Humans. "She's really cold!"

Reck-xa knelt beside him, coiling her tail around Mel-za's.

Mui-xe sat with a straight posture only the Great Mystery monks could have taught somebody, and Amanda's jaw dropped. Mui-xe's hands glowed. Not the hateful red-orange of their previous attackers but a soft and milky pearl caught by light, radiating warmth.

"I've never healed an Arkouda before," Mui-xe said. "I'll do my best."

Symphora's groan drowned out the alarm. Maybe Mui-xe couldn't heal an Arkouda and was increasing her agony. Or maybe he was giving her some form of surgery without any painkillers.

Curses both horrifying and unrepeatable spilled from her muzzle, and Amanda grabbed Maynard's shoulder. "What's he doing to her?"

"The same thing he has to do to himself every time somebody without a conscience abuses him for science."

Mui-xe's hands glowed brighter, and Symphora's eyes shot open. The plasma hole on her paw closed. Flesh and fur across her body merged and squelched back into place, and the smoldering fur stench evaporated, the smoke lost to mingle with the mist around their feet.

Amanda peered at the corpses on the floor. She didn't recognize them, but she deduced from their skin tone they were Earthers. A certain rugged stubbornness grew from staying where Humans could only rebuild with alien support. The corpse nearest Amanda clutched a pistol and a knife. Amanda grabbed both weapons; they might need to defend themselves, and Symphora and Mel-za were both unarmed. The pistol could potentially fit in Mel-za's grip, though it would be tiny in her claws.

Amanda read the name on the soldier's armor, wondering what kind of life this person lived; had Earthquake been his boyhood dream, or something a series of misfortunes led him toward?

Symphora spluttered, hocked phlegm, and coughed. Breathing heavily, she growled in Mui-xe's face. "You rearranged my organs."

Mui-xe stood, offering his hand to her, which she accepted, though her weight pulled him down. The boy stared up at the legend and replied in Arkouda, "My dad said you were tough enough to withstand anything. I didn't think you'd react like that."

Binh chortled. "He just sassed Symphora!"

"Hey!" Amanda called. "What about Mel-za? Can you heal her?"

"Mui-xe needs to eat first," Maynard said. "Healing another or himself drains too much energy. He'll pass out."

"I can do it, Uncle Maynard," Mui-xe croaked.

"Symphora," Amanda said, "I know you have jerky hiding in that armor. Give it to the kid."

Symphora mumbled about how she'd show them how tough she was and tapped a plate on her armor which unfolded a compartment near her abdomen to reveal dried meat sticks along with some *bachar* candy. Good thing about the Symphora Squadron was how they didn't have the same regulations as military. It was one of Earthquake's benefits, too, but Amanda pushed the thought aside.

The boy accepted the offering and turned his attention to the downed Lo-sat.

As Mui-xe chewed the jerky and set to work on Mel-za, her tail coiled and uncoiled. Scales rearranged and reformed, and Mel-za hissed as the bullet hole sealed. Her eyes bulged like she'd seen a ghost.

Symphora stretched, cracked her neck, and punched the air. "I know we gotta get the Nightmare out of here, but *skata* I feel good. Haven't felt this good sober since before that Earthquake teleporter shanked me."

Mui-xe glanced over his shoulder at her as Mel-za writhed beneath his hands.

Maynard cocked his head at Binh. "That must be the teleporter Joka Bunear told us about."

Amanda nodded. "Rosanna Moreno. She ambushed the fringe government offices and attempted to assassinate Symphora and derailed the session that would have otherwise heard my bill for Human equality."

Binh released Mel-za from his embrace, gently placing her on the floor. "Not a surprise. They don't want equality in the Collective. They are pissed and want to fight. What are the odds it was the same teleporter who attacked the monastery? The scent I found was the kind of woman who would lick a knife after stabbing someone."

"All that from a scent?" Amanda asked.

Symphora belly laughed, which turned into a hacking cough. "Ugh. I hope she didn't lick her knife after stabbing me."

The shaman, Reck-xa, uncoiled her tail from Mel-za. "Cease this talk around my grandson."

"I'm not a little kid, Granny," Mui-xe said. "She's ready, by the way." He stepped away from Mel-za.

Mel-za coughed, then rose to her feet, plasma wound sloughing off as a scab. "Thanks, little man."

Mui-xe sighed weakly, shuddering. Reck-xa ran to him and held him tight. "You forced him to overexert himself. You're no better than the scientists who've ruined his life."

Joining Reck-xa in steadying Mui-xe, Maynard hushed her. "Healing her was an act of compassion—"

"Stop it, all of you," Amanda said. "We need to leave. Mui-xe, if you are too drained to walk, Symphora is the strongest among us, and she will happily repay the favor."

"You could've asked first," Symphora mumbled.

"I-I'm f-fine," Mui-xe muttered, stumbling forward. Symphora caught him.

The sight made Amanda do a double-take. While a teen, Mui-xe was taller than most adult Humans Amanda had ever met, so seeing him in Symphora's arms was almost comical. "Did either of you get any useful information from those Earthquake recruits before killing them?" Amanda asked.

"Between the racist slurs, not much," Mel-za said. "Although they were out of breath and didn't smell like the basement."

Mumbling in Symphora's arms, Mui-xe stirred. "I think I recognize those guys. They came from upstairs. I think there's another way up besides the elevators. I can't detect a scent trail, but do you think you could find the stairs?"

"Nightmare, yeah," Symphora said. She adjusted her grip on Mui-xe and gently placed him on her shoulder. "Let's go."

Mel-za and Symphora led Amanda and the others through the complex until they reached a wall with a staircase. The snaking mist had risen to Amanda's chest by then.

Amanda stepped in front and faced the group. "These stairs were meant for Human legs and feet. Treat it like a jagged ramp and watch your footing."

"Bossy Curls isn't kidding," Binh said.

Amanda glared at him. "It's Ms. Martinez to you."

"I thought you forgot about that," Binh hissed.

"And I thought you grew up. Let's go." Amanda and Maynard bounded up the stairs while the larger species climbed sideways.

The stairwell gave them reprieve from the alarm, muffling the warning. It had been chiming for long enough that it would ring in her ears for years at night whenever she'd want to sleep.

Intruder alert. Collective inbound. Intruder alert. The announcement repeated like a song she wished would end, hating its unforgettable melody.

Hustling upward, renewed energy surged, despite her reluctance to return to the first floor. The steps wound up again, and the Lo-sats took to skipping three steps at a time, and Symphora walked up sideways, bracing herself by placing her open paw on the bottom of the next level. They were doing it. Escaping.

The blaring alarm paused for an announcement in the voice of Jacques Tecton. "Rosanna Moreno is a traitor! She led the Collective here. Kill on sight."

The others glanced at each other, but Amanda knew what this meant. She'd heard a similar communication about herself and Rick. Something was transpiring above that would further complicate their escape. Shouts echoed in the distance from above.

Amanda found the first floor, noting the same gilded frames and manicured potted plants. How many people experiencing homelessness could have been fed with the money it took to show off here? Binh muttered something about stealing stuff, but Amanda hushed him once she heard footsteps nearby. After those footsteps passed, they continued.

A few steps into the hallway, now lit by emergency lights, and another announcement interrupted the alarm: "Anyone who can't get to a fighter ship, suit up and get outside to fight the oppressors. No mercy and no prisoners!" A cough. "Fight like hell! Moreno turned on me and assaulted me, but it made me stronger. Stick it to the Popsicles and make them regret tangling with us."

A stampede of footsteps shook the ceiling, but they ran in the opposite direction to what Amanda expected. The Bastion must have another hangar, better concealed from their original outside vantage point.

Yet the moment Amanda accepted this, a cluster of Earthquake recruits stopped dead in front of the door. "It's Martinez!" one called.

Guns clicked as a semicircle of gangsters formed around the stairwell entrance.

THIRTY-SIX

(ROSANNA)

**Ten minutes ago: Approaching an elevator
in the predator's throne room**

ROSANNA KNEW AN old maxim from Earth: never meet your heroes. She wondered what that bit of wisdom would say about pistol-whipping them.

But if the Collective Fleet destroyed this place and took the Leader prisoner, she had a way to get to him again because of the Chamayna chitin that she planted on him.

He was swearing up a storm as Rosanna walked into the elevator, and she turned around, watching this man sob. He didn't seem so much like the invincible and infallible Leader she'd idolized.

When the elevator dinged and began to close, a ship bubbled into view from the grand window, making Rosanna pause.

A Makawe scrapper, one she'd seen before, the ship Crith had been using. Bobbing in front of the scrapper was a chunk of asteroid, held by a magnetic field. Rosanna's breath caught in her throat. If she had just murdered Tecton outright instead of wasting time with a creative revenge, she'd already be in the elevator shaft. This was about to be the least safe place in the Bastion: the scrapper's magnetized asteroid chunk reared back, then launched toward the building.

The foundation shook, and the floor slanted upward. Tecton leapt from his desk with the speed of a lecherous old man finding a lawyer. The grand window overlooking the Kuiper Belt and Neptune imploded, raining shards of glass across Tecton as shrapnel from the ceiling fell. The cleaner 'bots that had been attending to Crith's corpse scattered.

So Crith had an accomplice and a plan for revenge.

A rafter plummeted onto Tecton's back, pinning him to his desk. "Help me!" The desperation in Tecton's eyes was pathetic.

Without that rafter, the ceiling buckled, cracking down the middle like a lightning bolt. The ceiling caved in. Rosanna had seconds before the last gasps of air left this room.

Rosanna sucked in as much air as possible and shook her head. There was no way this buffoon would reach his escape pod. She left the elevator shaft and ran toward the stairwell.

Behind her, the stairwell door vacuum sealed shut.

Jacques Tecton would die in there, and it did nothing to quench Rosanna's fury. Perhaps Crith orchestrated the attack and extracted final vengeance, but Rosanna chose to let Tecton die. It almost made up for Tecton stealing her kill.

But now *she* needed a way to escape, and that would only be possible by finding Martinez. The Fleet wouldn't kill a government agent, and Rosanna could trade her for amnesty. She opened her omni-tablet and punched in new orders.

[Rosanna: Apprehend Amanda Martinez and any of her followers. The station is on full alarm. We're under attack. This is not a drill or a ruse.]

The security chief pinged her back, requesting confirmation. Bolting down the crumbling steps, she fired a reply back.

[Rosanna: The asteroid impact killed Tecton. I'm in charge now. Check the vitals on his omni-tablet.]

No response came, but the tower's alarm system began. The feeling of ultimate authority bolstered her until the alarm clarified: "Intruder alert. Collective inbound. Intruder alert."

Sweat from exertion and nerves mingled on Rosanna's skin. The Collective fleet was coming for them.

Dodging crumbling debris, she opened the door to her target floor, the eighth. The defense hangar, not the pitiful decoy Martinez entered earlier. This one boasted their modified civilian ships and pilfered battledarts. Crith had installed algorithms inside some of them to fling themselves at larger ships to destroy them. According to the explanation he gave, it was something inspired by Human prehistory called kamikaze. Considering the Collective would rain down more than enough firepower to level them, it was appropriate.

Rosanna fired up her omni-tablet's control panel and input the command for five ships to disembark, ready to strike at the Collective. She eyed a transport for herself, just in case. She didn't have any teleportation chitin squirreled away on a safe base anymore. Some part of her knew this would be the final confrontation, but the stupid fleet wasn't supposed to show up. It was supposed to be an execution and nothing else. She was down to one piece of chitin, her second-last in the now-dead Tecton's shirt pocket.

As the programmed ships rose from the floor, her omni-tablet buzzed with a ping from her security chief.

[Dumbass 4: Negative. The Leader is alive. We have him in recovery.]

Her eyes widened and she cursed her naivete. Surviving that collapsing room would've been impossible. The roof fell on top of him for Earth's sake.

[Rosanna: Until he's healthy, I'm in charge.]

[Dumbass 4: He's coherent and he didn't say that.]

Goosebumps pricked on her arms, temporary stains she couldn't remove. He must've snuck out between debris, no small feat for a man as out of shape as him. Unless he had access to something Rosanna didn't know about. He had a gun ready to defend himself. Maybe he wore some armor as well. Maybe he'd injected himself with some of the hybrid DNA to give him more regenerative abilities. That would explain him slithering out like the Galsan worm he was.

Rosanna stormed toward the transporter she had her eye on. If Tecton were here, she needed to run to the other side of the galaxy like a damn coward. She'd—

The transporter rose but not from pre-flight ignition. It sat on a hydraulic lift, rising to a higher floor. Somebody above her had programmed it as an escape ship.

She slammed on her omni-tablet.

Hangar: override. Alarm: terminate. Alarm: disengage. Hangar: open. Display: escape_pods=available.

Nothing happened.

Earthquake recruits filed in to man the fighters and weaponized civilian ships, a mix of the brave and foolish who chose to defy the unstoppable Collective Fleet. But she wouldn't die among them.

The blaring alarm paused for an announcement in the voice of Jacques Tecton. "Rosanna Moreno is a traitor! She led the Collective here. Kill on sight."

Rosanna sneered and glanced around the hangar. Fifteen ships remained, and all of them had someone piling inside.

Knuckles white, she sprinted toward the stairwell.

Another announcement echoed through the stairwell: "Anyone who can't get to a fighter ship, suit up and get outside to fight the oppressors. No mercy and no prisoners!" He coughed, but the jackass continued.

"Fight like hell! Moreno turned on me and assaulted me, but it made me stronger. Stick it to the Popsicles and make them regret tangling with us."

In front of the stairwell, a recruit, a younger man, stared wide-eyed at Rosanna. He stuttered something, but she didn't listen once she noticed his handgun.

She darted left, rose right, and kneed him in the chest, forcing him to stumble backward, dropping his weapon. In her next breath, she adjusted her grip on his gun and fired. This goon was one less person to get in her way, this dumb kid following bad orders. But he'd stood between the predator and her prey.

Point blank plasmafire singed the outside of her clothes, exposing her armor underneath, giving her a radiation burn that would require a scrub later.

As she flew down the stairs again, some tiny part of her wondered if he had a younger sister who was now without an icon and role model.

She blinked hard. He couldn't have been much of a role model if he listened to Jacques Tecton.

The building had sloughed off a chunk.

She dove into the stairwell and cascaded down like a flood. Nobody was getting her transport. Sprinting, jumping over the railings at each landing, she wondered if Martinez had escaped her certain death like the slime Tecton had. For all the abominations Rosanna unleashed, they should've overtaken her.

Her expression soured and her lungs burned. If Tecton had wrested control over them, they would be heading outside as well to deal with the oncoming Fleet and Blekker pirates.

That would be a sight—onrushing Collective foot soldiers getting baked alive by the hybrids' flames. Most importantly, it would provide distraction for her to escape as fast as possible without the burden of people watching her retreat. Simple survival.

No holding back—

Two more recruits piled into the stairwell from below. Just when she was getting close to the entrance level, she halted and readied her gun.

After some splurts and stutters, they told her to stop where she was. Poor saps. Rosanna unleashed a round and jumped back for cover. The first recruit, a young woman, fell as the odor of plasma-singed flesh filled the stairwell.

Rosanna left cover and fired three rounds, then pulled back. When she heard a scream and a thunk, she left again to see her victims. These were two women who looked almost identical, twins, maybe. A sick memory rose of her own brother.

If she hadn't hero worshipped her brother, would she have ever joined Earthquake?

Nearing the first floor, the thought of her inability to kill her main targets loomed large in her stomach. Symphora, who survived because Martinez had surprised her. Rick Crith, just enough to let him fight another day the first time and just enough to let Tecton steal the kill. No wonder she felt like such a failure. No wonder she'd picked a failing organization like Earthquake to support.

She'd been such an idiot. But if she could just escape, she could start over somewhere across the galaxy where nobody would know her name. No other avenue of escape presented itself besides holding Martinez hostage. And for all Rosanna knew, maybe Martinez was one of the few surviving people who could honestly give her answers about Alejandro.

The truth had probably died with Crith. Tecton was so far removed from his soldiers and sycophants that he wouldn't know the truth or care to find out. He wanted to have a sliver to taunt Rosanna with. But no more. She cursed her stupidity.

She descended the last stairwell, and voices echoed as she neared the landing. The door was open on the first floor. Lots of commotion, which made sense given the context of what was happening. But then she stopped dead in her tracks: below her were an Arkouda carrying a thin body on her shoulders and three Lo-sats, one dressed like a medicine woman. Two Humans followed, one dressed in the monastic robes she'd seen on New Lodestone and the other in spacefaring gear.

Rosanna gulped. *Martinez.*

As Rosanna readied her weapon, she took a closer look at the body slumped over the Arkouda's shoulder.

It was the hybrid boy. One of the Lo-sats, a male, glanced up and noticed Rosanna. "See? I told you someone else was coming down."

Rosanna held a finger over her lips and exposed her other palm to show she wouldn't kill him.

Below, Martinez addressed someone on the other side of the doorway—getting out with them was her only chance.

Rosanna eyed the Lo-sat. "You won't get through that way. I know another way out. Tell them to run up to this floor and follow me."

THIRTY-SEVEN

(ALIZE)

A moon which should never have been disturbed

THWIP.

Dr. Alize Oze collapsed onto the lunar landscape on all fours, struggling against the vertigo that accompanied teleportation. Planet Dusoi's gaseous light commingled with the Xechas star, giving the green-tinted lunar rocks an effulgent glow. The thin atmosphere chilled her, but it didn't bother or excite her like the first time.

A few years that could've been a lifetime ago, she was here with her best friend.

Now, all she had was a breather, her resolve, and the intervening years of research. Her heart ached for He'nay—she would've loved to take pictures of this place to show her mother. But Earthquake had killed her, just like it stole everything else from Alize.

The breather sat tight against her face, and the seal helped her restrain the nausea which threatened from her jump.

Two broken statues interrupted the moon's plateaus and jagged peaks. These once depicted the original inhabitants of this moon and a few other distant planets: the Chamayna, an extinct insectoid species who left behind more questions than answers and their exoskeletons which never rotted or decayed. Their chitinous carapaces had so many more applications than she'd divulged to Earthquake and probably even more that she could've discovered with more years of uninterrupted research. Their power didn't derive from their own biology, but their willingness to utilize a force of nature which they couldn't understand and shouldn't have disturbed.

The Unspeakable.

The moon trembled beneath her. Teleporting here had broadcast to the creature where she was, had been, and would be.

She'd once escaped this moon using its power, leaving behind Rick Crith, Binh, and Amanda Martinez.

Tremble.

Alize had mixed feelings about abandoning and endangering Amanda and Binh, but Rick Crith? She relished abandoning him. He may have lacked Earthquake's xenophobia, but he'd chosen the darker path for Humanity. The sad part was how he convinced himself he was in the right.

Tremble.

Yet the person she regretted leaving the most was the one whose final resting place was on this moon. Good friends will make drunken claims about how they would take a plasma bullet for each other. Filenada, Alize's Fil, her best friend—she proved it.

Fil's passing spurred Alize to improve working conditions at the museum and in academia and use her discoveries for the good of civilization. Alize once dreamt of using inspiration from the Chamayna to craft a real teleportation device, one that would allow instantaneous travel without strengthening the Unspeakable.

Earthquake destroyed that possibility.

Alize's heart raced as her enlightened rage coursed through her body. Rage at Earthquake. Fury at the Collective for creating a system in which Earthquake felt like a reasonable choice for people. Her justified anger radiated, pushing goosebumps across her skin and letting a hated thought come to mind.

Violence.

She imagined a Chamayna weapon returning to her hands. The grip, the heft. The blade.

Tremble.

Closing her eyes, she watched herself take that weapon to Alejandro Moreno, the one who killed Fil. And again to Rick Crith for following her to the moon. Even that idiot who informed Earthquake about Alize's theories in the first place. And to Alize's former boss, mostly because she sucked. And every single member of Earthquake who had pointed a gun at her and Fil.

The moon rattled and shook as if seismic activity threatened to rupture the surface.

Alize glanced at the abyssal heavens and watched the light from the gas giant and star fade.

The planets weren't disappearing, only dimming—but not from any ecological or solar disasters. The astral light above her dimmed because of what approached. The trembling grew to such intensity her knees buckled.

But she didn't give in.

She welcomed what arrived: an unholy goliath. Its appendages resembled tree trunks mixed with a dinosaur. Peeking between sagging cloth wraps which could have clothed a whole city was its oval-shaped carapace, a union of an Earth cockroach and a jagged ribcage.

Four arms protruded, one holding a mace, the same one which flattened a spaceship. Mandibles on its head clacked together, loud enough to defy space's vacuum, and its compound eyes broadcast a jagged series of lines and curves—Chamayna glyphs.

The Unspeakable towered, rivaling the mountains.

Knowing it had the capacity to reason and understand, Alize was not about to waste the creature's time.

Sweating despite the lunar chill, she jumped in place, letting her grav harness do the work to keep her from floating away. She hopped forward a half meter, then again to the side. She repeated this, zigzag hopping and dragging one foot along where appropriate: a nonsensical pattern to some.

But not to the Unspeakable. Alize's pattern formed Chamayna glyphs.

The Unspeakable lowered its head, mandibles clacking in a rhythm, some other layer of communication that flew above her comprehension.

She stared into its compound eyes, and jagged lines appeared in them, conveying a simple message.

Destroy.

It could have squashed her in an instant. It didn't need to give her the dignity of an attempt at communication, but perhaps it understood that Alize warned Earthquake about abusing its power. Whether the Unspeakable was an elder god from an era when the universe hadn't formed fully or a species unto itself that nobody could begin to understand, it didn't matter. It knew the Chamayna and they knew it.

And Alize was the galaxy's expert on the forgotten civilization. She pointed at her glyph pattern, stamped out from lunar dust.

Revenge.

The Unspeakable extended an unfolding platform that might be called a hand, wider than a house. This appendage could squash her with a snap. Emboldened, Alize jumped onto it; the palm felt sturdier than the moon itself.

It rose to its full height, the same height which had been sufficient to rip a Blekk pirate cruiser from the atmosphere, and brought Alize directly in front of its eye.

The jagged lines in the eye faded, then changed color and returned in a different pattern.

She had theories about the color of Chamayna glyphs but hadn't proved them and lacked the means to test them. Yet the color change was significant somehow. Perhaps just a final warning.

The new glyph in its eye took the slant of a question, what she called the interrogative angle in her notes.

Them?

Alize opened her mouth, but no words followed.

Its power, although passive, was too intense. She couldn't form any words. She couldn't speak in its direct presence. Its full attention was more intense than the still-dimming star and gas giant above her. The galaxy itself enveloped into darkness in its might.

She moved her forearm and thumb to form half a glyph shape, then repositioned for the other half of the shape.

Yes.

Clack-clack-clackaclack

It knew.

Clackclackclackclackclack

It hungered.

Whatever palette and appetite the Unspeakable had was vengeful hunger. Earthquake had been using and exploiting the Unspeakable's power, and it was time for a reckoning.

The lines forming the glyph for "them?" in its eye faded and changed color again.

A slash of new marks replaced it.

We join minds.

Alize's eyes widened. No. Absolutely not. That wasn't part of the—

Hrrk!

Sensation and awareness melted into each other, becoming a swirling black madness.

Lines in impossible directions. Perfection, destruction. Everything burning—rocks, time, and hate. Bubbling. Chamayna buzzing around the Unspeakable in prostrate worship, wings chittering in anticipation of their dark deity's grandeur.

Pathetic weaklings.

Teleporting around the galaxy as if there were no consequence. Creating the tomb as a desperate defiance. The Unspeakable claimed them all and laid them to rest, aware of its own destructive capabilities, disinterested in fostering more chaos, yet needing an outlet for the growing rage and power of each subsequent insult.

As the madness offered direction, Alize struggled to find her own psyche and center. The Unspeakable didn't need her mind to find Earthquake's location. It needed Alize to understand what she and Earthquake had disrupted all those years ago.

Furious melancholy the size of an eon ripped through her chest. She'd disturbed its slumber.

It didn't want revenge.

She understood now.

Transmit.

Transmit.

Thwip

Alize's insides settled. The green lunar rocks had vanished, replaced by the gray-brown of a Kuiper Belt asteroid.

THIRTY-EIGHT

(AMANDA)

**Sprinting upstairs toward a hangar
while Mel-za wrestles racists.**

AN OLD PHRASE from prehistoric Earth rang in Amanda's mind: "stuck between a rock and a hard place." Below, Mel-za traded fire with Earthquake goons. Above lay the unknown. She had to help Mel-za. They had no clue if escape lay upstairs or not; upstairs just had fewer guns.

After she descended the first step, a scaly tail tip wrapped around Amanda's wrist and yanked her backward. Amanda glared at Binh. "What was that for?"

"Let the fighter save us while we head up to the next floor. Somebody's up there. Smells helpful—somebody defecting from Earthquake. This person got the drop on me and would've killed me if they wanted to. That nervous sweat has to be from someone trying to escape."

At the landing to the ground floor, Mel-za tapped her armor, and an electro-static shield bubbled out in a blue pulse. "What the *nguc*? You want to fight?" Mel-za made a one-woman barrier between Amanda and the Earthquake goons. Reck-xa, Maynard, and Symphora were close behind, with Mui-xe across Symphora's shoulders.

Symphora snarled over the barrage of plasma fire peppering Mel-za's shield. "I can't smell for *skata*." She faced Reck-xa. "Take the boy. I'm helping her."

Mui-xe limply slid off Symphora's shoulder. "I can walk," he croaked.

When Symphora ducked under the door frame and got beside Mel-za's shield, Amanda stomped up the steps. "Did any of you see this person Binh found?"

"I was watching the door, but I heard movement up there," Maynard offered.

"Not so helpful," Amanda muttered. She spied the second floor door above them closing, angry she didn't catch this person's face. She hated leaving Mel-za and Symphora below them, but the exchange of plasmafire below told her to keep moving, and Amanda could definitely empathize with anyone who wanted to defect from Earthquake.

"It's pronounced 'thank-you,'" Binh said. "Come on. Anyone in Earthquake who saw us and didn't open fire must be a defector. It's simple traitor's arithmetic—I should know."

"Fine." Amanda cast a glance at the lower doorway, just seeing the tip of Mel-za's bubble shield. She and

Symphora wouldn't have much time left before that protection dropped. But if anybody could handle a few Earthquake goons, it was those two. Amanda followed Binh, hating herself for choosing the unknown above instead of the danger below.

"Have your breathers ready," Maynard said from behind her. "In case more of the building breaks apart and we're exposed."

"You wish I was exposed," Binh tutted.

They entered the doorway to the next floor. Binh opened the door to let Amanda enter first.

On her first step inside, a gun barrel nudged her temple. "Martinez."

Amanda faced her assailant, letting the gun tap the bridge of her nose. "Rosanna Moreno." She recognized her from the assault on the government offices. The near-killer of Symphora. "I have a file about your brother you'll be interested to read if you put that gun down."

"You're coming with me." Rosanna's tone was flat, but Amanda could tell she'd been through hell in the last few minutes. She was dripping in sweat and stank of a plasma burn.

Binh lunged inside, but Rosanna was too fast.

She sidestepped away from Amanda, pointing the gun at Binh. "Stop. Walk." At gunpoint, Amanda and Binh left the doorway.

Behind her, Reck-xa, Mui-xe, and Maynard came through. Amanda caught a line of offices down the hall, all spitting dimmed light. A whiff of smoke tickled her nose. The building was falling apart, and something nearby was aflame—a great place to talk.

Binh's neck frills extended. "You're the chick who kidnapped Mui-xe."

"And you're the idiot who worked for Crith." Upon noticing the boy, Rosanna's eyes widened.

"Put the gun down, Rosanna," Amanda said. "I have something you want."

"What I want," Rosanna seethed, "is to get off this Earth-forsaken asteroid. Tecton betrayed me and killed Rick Crith. He stole the thing I wanted more than anything else. Worthless jackass."

Hearing that confession aloud tugged at her heart. Irredeemable asshole murderer or not, she and Rick were friends once, even if her opinion on him had soured. She'd known it from that message, but hearing it out loud was another story. And then knowing Rosanna was betrayed by Tecton made Amanda pity her, even though it didn't excuse her actions.

"P-put the gun down," Amanda said. "None of us are safe if what you're saying is true. But I know you want information about your brother. Get us on a ship out of here, and I'll share it with you." Amanda fixated on Rosanna's gun.

Mui-xe's breathing increased. "Don't trust her."

Amanda hated putting her life in Rosanna's bloody hands, but they were surrounded and in a crumbling building. This woman had nearly killed Symphora and was letting Amanda live. "You're hoping for a pardon, aren't you?"

A chunk of debris fell from the ceiling at the offices' far end.

Rosanna scowled at the group of them, but her expression cooled upon landing on Mui-xe. She blinked hard. "I … was following orders. But I'll get us out."

Mui-xe's hands balled into fists, giving a slight glow. "Point a weapon at any of us again, and you'll regret it."

Binh and Reck-xa sniffed like they were searching for something. "She's being honest," Binh said. "And stinks like ass."

"If we survive this tower, you and I will have words," Reck-xa said, glaring at her. She exhaled and faced Amanda and Mui-xe. "But the crass one is right. She does not have the liar's pheromone."

Brother Maynard pulled Mui-xe close to him. "You'll forgive my hesitation. Put your gun down."

Rosanna slowly holstered the weapon. An audible grinding crack snapped everyone's attention to the back of the hallway as a lightning bolt fissure formed in the windows.

A matching crack streaked across the ceiling, the floor above them buckling.

"Come on." Rosanna led them down a snaking path through the offices, nowhere close to a wall that would have an elevator or stairwell. They dodged falling chunks of the roof which fell in powder, pellets, and shards. Creaking furniture above poked through the ceiling cracks.

A black flash sped by a window, but it moved too fast and Amanda was too pressed for time to stop and investigate.

She pushed herself to sprint and match pace with Rosanna.

Rosanna called for a halt once the others caught up. "We're directly over the exit hatch downstairs. If we increase our mass by more than seventy-five percent with our grav harnesses, we'll be close enough to the exit that we won't have to fight our way through."

Amanda bit back the name of Symphora. "We have friends down there. They covered our exit while we followed you."

"They're probably dead," Binh muttered.

She glared at him, hating the possibility. If they were still fighting down there, they may be drawing enough attention to clear their escape. With Rosanna and Mui-xe, they could help Symphora and Mel-za. "Fine. We increase our mass. I know a surrender code we can transmit to the Collective Fleet that will give us safe passage."

Reck-xa flared her neck frills and got in between Rosanna and Amanda. "If you think for one second my grandson is going on a government vessel, you—"

"We don't have time for debate," Mui-xe said.

Amanda thumbed her grav harness and raised the setting to its maximum. "I'll keep him safe." She winced as her insides plummeted.

The others followed suit. Maynard muttered something in Human that sounded like a prayer. As the floor creaked under the six of them, Amanda noticed Mui-xe croaking the same words.

Rosanna groaned. "Once the floor breaks, flip the settings in the other direction so you don't break half your body."

The floor wasn't breaking fast enough. Grimacing, Amanda summoned all her strength and jumped, bones creaking and tendons straining. With her increased mass, it was barely a hop. It wouldn't be enough.

Breathing deep, she reset her grav harness and floated into the air. Her eyes watered and cheeks puffed, fighting all kinds of nausea. Bobbing toward the ceiling, Amanda reset her grav harness and dropped into the buckling floor, letting them tumble backward to the story below.

As they descended, Amanda reset her grav harness and lifted up her breather to allow a quick spit.

Among the debris and rubble, they were back in the hangar they entered through, where more piles of garbage and broken pipes and support beams collected from the collapsing higher floors. Amanda helped Reck-xa stand while Binh did the same for Mui-xe and Maynard. Rosanna got up on her own, dry heaving from the gravity change.

This wasn't good. They all needed water with that gravity shifting. Amanda didn't know if Mui-xe could heal dehydration, and she wasn't keen to find out.

No ships sat in this hangar. A few Earthquake goons darted past them, not noticing or caring enough to stop. Apart from their thudding sprints, the only sounds were their cursing.

"Let's get outside," Amanda said. "And hope there's a ship left."

"Hope is all we have," Maynard added.

They sprinted through the hangar, avoiding falling chunks of the ceiling. Binh cursed as some fell onto his eyeridge.

With breathers fastened, spacefaring gear ready, and the Lo-sats' heating cells thrumming, they left the gaping hangar. Amanda's insides twisted, thinking of the doomed Symphora and Mel-za.

She couldn't leave them behind. Stopping in her tracks, she pulled out her omni-tablet. She forwarded the old message from Rosanna's older brother to Binh, then activated the homing feature for government workers.

The others halted to stare at her.

"What the Earth are you doing, Martinez?" Rosanna snapped.

Amanda handed her omni-tablet to Maynard. "There's a message on here for her to read when things calm down. I sent a copy to Binh in case. You all find a safe spot, and the Collective fleet will get you. I'm going back for the others."

Maynard accepted with a bow. "You're certain? They could have died."

"They'd do it for me. I can blend in somewhat with all the chaos if anyone's left." She shifted to Mui-xe. "Don't let anyone order you around, got that?"

Mui-xe cocked an eyebrow. "That sounded like an order."

Amanda caught Rosanna's next scowl approaching, so she cut her off. "And you—you don't have to live your life chasing whatever you're pissed off at. Try protecting someone and see how that feels."

"Quit acting like a politician," Rosanna said. "Save your speeches for your voters."

"Go. All of you." Amanda headed back inside the crumbling Bastion.

THIRTY-NINE

(ROSANNA)

Among former prey on an Earth-forsaken rock

ROSANNA BREATHED AS much sweet oxygen as possible, not that her apparatus allowed much. She gripped the omni-tablet while her eyes danced across the screen. A message from Alejandro taunted her. He'd sent it to Tecton all those years ago, detailing a plan to mutiny against Crith.

```
Exalted Leader,

Let's begin with acknowledging that
I shouldn't have access to your mes-
saging account. I took it from my
supervisor, Commander Crith. I under-
stand that is grounds for reprimand.
```

> I will accept that when the time is
> appropriate.

Rosanna blinked hard. She'd called Tecton "Exalted" before, yet the idea of Alejandro saying it twisted her stomach. What did he mean by "accepting reprimand"? Her brother wasn't some sniveling clown. This was the guy who knocked a bully's teeth in for her when she was a little kid. She skipped over the next bit detailing Crith's dalliances with the Drowned Star Blekk pirates and Makawe rebels.

> Crith doesn't believe in Earthquake's
> values. He's attempted diplomatic nego-
> tiations with aliens. He's preached
> empathy for the Arkouda and repri-
> mands degrading talk about the enemy.
> I have recordings of him saying not to
> kill a Collective soldier in battle if
> possible, which would deny our squad
> members a bounty.

"Earthquake's values" felt hollow. They had destroyed the Collective's government in the Fringe. Destroying it in the Galactic Center would've been next, and they could've done it if Tecton hadn't been so preoccupied with trifling matters. Maybe the only things people in Earthquake wanted were bits of information or attention from Tecton, and the only definitive pieces of truth she'd gotten had been from Crith and this stupid letter.

Commander Crith is unfit to lead in your organization. His symbolic value served its purpose.

I've spoken to the other members of our squad. They're willing to follow my lead instead of Crith's. The only member I didn't approach is Commander Crith's staff manager. She's too close to him, and rumors abound of an inappropriate relationship between them.

Martinez. A crew had mutinied under Alejandro while they were on that moon. No wonder Crith killed him. Realizing Alejandro probably shot at him first made her blood boil.

I know what's at stake in this mission. I'll find the weapon of unspeakable power. It'll become a tool for Earthquake. If Crith gets it, he's liable to destroy it. Or he might even try and use it against you in a bid to replace you and steer Earthquake down a dangerous path. With your blessing, I'll lead this squad unflinchingly. I know Commander Crith argues against your decisions. It's disgusting.

Disgusting to argue against an idiot? Alejandro wasn't some pitiful bastard. A thought had trickled in that this might be some stupid forgery, but something about "unflinchingly" made her pause. When they'd wrestle and play-fight, his rule was whoever flinched would lose. Even if she'd made him bleed, he would never flinch, and he'd call her a flincher.

```
Until now, I've been biding my time,
waiting for a promotion the standard
way, but that relic won't retire any
time soon. I can't prove it, but I
think he even has active Arkouda con-
tacts, and he's not using them for
Earthquake's greater good. My rec-
ommendation is a demotion from you.
Barring that, I'll lead a bloodless
mutiny against him. He's too proud to
expect it.

Rodrick Crith is a threat to Earthquake
and Human supremacy. He must be stopped.

Earthquake moves the galaxy.

                    -Alejandro Moreno.


          <end of message>
```

"Are you alright?" the monk asked, sounding genuine.

Rosanna stared at the others, who had been watching her read with one exception.

Martinez was running off to be a hero, saving some Arkouda and Lo-sat while Rosanna stewed about how her big brother had devolved into an ass-kisser to a lecherous worm of a man. Maybe the person she'd idolized wasn't perfect; maybe he'd crossed into bad territory and wasn't worth emulating. She wished she'd stopped after reading the first line. Hero worshiping her brother had ruined her life.

She wouldn't settle for that boveeshit. She'd tortured, murdered, and left squadmates to die in her crusade for knowledge. And one of those people she'd traumatized stood in front of her, watching her like a thrown grenade.

This didn't sit right.

Fighting a scowl, Rosanna addressed the group. The building trembled and shifted again, exposing new cracks in the floor and ceiling. "Look, I know you hate me, but I'm your best shot of escaping alive. I know where the escape pods are. Stay close to me. Any goon who comes close to us is dead. Once the Collective shows up to grab you, I'll leave."

"Liking kidnappers *is* difficult," Binh said. "Astute observation."

"Forgive us if we're reluctant to trust you," the monk added.

Unblinking, Mui-xe glared at Rosanna. "I pity you."

"We're not joining you," Reck-xa hissed. The grandmother wiggled her neck frills enough to let Rosanna know she was on thin ice.

Mui-xe shook his head. "This place is a maze, Granny. We'll get squished if we don't join her."

A new fissure opened in the wall and ceiling as they raced forward, breathers fixed over their mouths. Reck-xa sidled beside Rosanna mid-step. "You'll prefer your Hell to what I will do to you."

Outside, swarms of Blekker and Collective fighters traded fire with Earthquake civilian ships, all modified to have unconventional weapons. Most were sturdy scrapper ships, absorbing fire and tossing the other ships at each other with their magnets meant for ferrous asteroids. On the ground, a horde of hybrids, the entire manufactured force, marched forward, away from the crumbling Bastion toward another... tower?

They burst through a ruptured hangar door, and Rosanna blinked hard at the sight.

It wasn't a tower. It wasn't a mountain, either. It was the watcher. The observer. The judge. The presence she'd felt each time she teleported. She'd tried to name it, but all words drained from her the longer she beheld the abomination. The cosmic monstrosity. Stars around it felt dimmer. Even Neptune's cascading azure glow faded in its presence, and one of its moons dimmed into a black sphere.

"No," Binh said. "It can't be..."

Reck-xa and Maynard stopped in their tracks, muttering a prayer in their native languages. Mui-xe gasped.

Rosanna's heart rate quickened. "What is it?"

"I c-can't..." Binh stuttered.

So it wasn't just her. "Where'd you see it?"

Binh lowered his eyeridges. "On the same moon where I met Rick Crith. The same moon where I betrayed Dr. Alize Oze. The same moon where I watched your brother die." He shook his head and cocked a grin. "Assuming your brother was the guy who smelled like you, ate steroids for breakfast, and thought guns were a fashion accessory."

Rosanna clenched her fists at the insult and her trigger finger itched. He'd pay for that comment later. "You … don't match the files." She *had* looked for this bastard, but all records of him had evaporated. "You don't look like the—"

"I healed him," Mui-xe said.

Binh flicked his tail. "What did your files say, Stabby? That my scale condition made me look freaky? No more gray. So anyway, back to the nightmare demon from everybody's hell… We're gonna die."

Rosanna glared at the marching hybrids, shuffling toward the hulking death's feet. Ships from both sides swarmed its head, and it swatted them down.

The unspeakable creature stomped toward the Bastion, forcing tremors into the asteroid's surface like a terrestrial earthquake. Battledarts and Blekk drones opened fire, but the colossus ignored them like a tank driving through raindrops.

Rosanna scanned the area. There should've been ships docked in this auxiliary landing pad—the staging area for her grand ruse which became a magnificent failure. The ship she'd promised them was gone.

Tremble.

Reverberations beneath their feet warned that this thing was coming straight for them. It might've sensed Rosanna, ready to exact payment for all the times she'd used its power, if Oze were to be believed.

A sizable chunk of the Bastion crumbled off onto the surface, bits falling upward in the low gravity—a corner of an office. The rest of the building had slanted in the opposite direction, so they'd be safe taking cover there, assuming they weren't stomped by the encroaching deity.

"Head there," Rosanna shouted.

The others tore their eyes from the thing that should not be, and a Collective warhive descended, turrets illuminated.

This wasn't one of the battleships Crith commandeered in his last months with Earthquake but the newer model, a floating city carrying its own flotilla of battledarts and enough of an onboard arsenal to obliterate any who dared attack five times over.

The oppressors had learned their lesson after Crith embarrassed them a few years ago—the whole thing was demagnetized. Half the Earthquake scrappers exploded after one salvo of fire from the warhive.

And this one lowered to match the walking nightmare's eye level. The eyes—if they could be called that—looked like two segmented and paneled crimson domes with markings down the sides which didn't seem natural. Not that anything on this thing did. Its facial structure bore a vague resemblance to prehistoric Earth insects, although the resemblance lay more in how it unnerved her than any physical appearance. Mandibles sprang from what might've been a mouth.

These mandibles clacked together, echoing in her ears despite the void of space. They slammed into each other like demonic percussion, and the warhive fired all its turrets and cannons against the creature, enveloping it in a brilliant chartreuse light which blinked into a sage color and disappeared.

The beast seemed larger than when they'd first stepped outside. It reached out and grasped with two appendages on either side of the warhive's nose while its other two arms batted down smaller ships.

From the rear, the warhive's engines glowed saffron, preparing to disengage. As the thrusters intensified, the unspeakable abomination's arms resisted. The creature moved a half-step back, then yanked the warhive, pulling it down and grabbing it with its other clawed hands.

The asteroid trembled under the creature's planted feet.

With a roar that Rosanna heard more in her heart than ears, the beast drove the warhive into the asteroid's surface with enough force to send a fissure cracking the rock apart. It repeated the action as chunks of the warhive floated off in all directions. It slammed the ship so hard into the asteroid that a hunk of the rock floated away into the asteroid belt.

Neptune darkened. Even the too-distant sun blinked out of view.

The hybrids had reached the giant and comparatively tiny pillars of flame shot from their hands around where it stood.

The disgusting abominations were nothing to it.

Yet somebody nearby must be controlling them. Rosanna scanned the area, straining to see anything above the asteroid's surface in the dimming light. Enough Earthquake ships remained in the sky that a security officer could be sending the hybrids orders.

Not that there was any reason. This place was lost. Rosanna's nostrils flared. She couldn't find the transporter ship with Tecton aboard anywhere in the atmosphere. But she didn't have to see it. She had one more kill that she wanted to make.

She'd failed against Symphora, Martinez, and Crith, but there was one more person she could murder. Martinez told her to be a protector, and this would definitely protect the galaxy.

Safely in the debris patch, Rosanna addressed the group. "You stay here and use Martinez's little beacon to get picked up. I've got something to do." She cast another glance at Mui-xe. An apology formed, but she gritted her teeth and sprinted toward the hybrids.

"Ditching us already, Stabby?" Binh shouted.

She didn't dignify it with a response. She was ending this conflict permanently. Jacques Tecton was about to escape, alive. No matter how many times that sonofabitch was defeated and proved himself a disaster, disaffected people flocked to him like a folk hero. She had to end it here and now.

Her mind drifted to the last piece of Chamayna chitin in her pocket. If she teleported up there, they could have other armed thugs ready to defend their pathetic leader. But there was one thing that would not be defeated so easily by plasmafire.

Pressing forward, she closed on the hulking monstrosity and the legion of shambling corpses besieging it. She eyed the atmosphere and found one small cargo ship hovering midair, avoiding the firefight against the Collective.

That must be the control ship—separate from Tecton's escape ship. Rosanna slowed to a jog so she could type a message on her omni-tablet. Switching to the public system as an administrator would hide that it came from her specifically.

[To anyone controlling the freaks: order them to melt the rock around the feet instead of attacking the feet directly. They'll turn into goop after too long, but we don't have a choice.]

The hybrids all formed a moat of death around the behemoth. Maybe the commander got the order and considered it. For now, what she needed was for them to remain focused on the larger target.

Looking up, she stared into the thing's eye which was bigger than her childhood home. Somehow, it perceived her. Goosebumps rose on her flesh. This thing wanted to stomp her.

Fine.

She needed to make one delivery first. Closing in on the crowd of hybrids, their moans made her ears throb. Despite dying before their fusing operations, those creatures still knew agony. She'd abducted some of the sacrificed Lo-sats personally—she recognized one with a bent tail. Some of the Human hosts were former Loyalists whom she had murdered.

Too many.

It was time to right the only wrong she could. She prepared her piece of Chamayna chitin. She'd come close enough to the hybrids to see details of their scabbed-over surgical scars.

Only one chance.

It hummed, glowing brighter in the presence of the demon, and she dove on the back of a hybrid.

Thwip.

Knowing what judged her in transport failed to assuage the horrid sickness. Eyes. So many eyes. All appraising her and finding her inadequate. Worthless. A source of darkness in the galaxy. Just like it was.

In the instant of transmission, the hybrid spun around, face frozen in a howl.

Thwip.

Rosanna rolled away, hitting a cold metal floor and a tattered suit jacket. Inside a cargo ship.

Jacques Tecton lay on a naval cot, hooked up to wires and tubes. Two of his lackeys hunched over him.

And the hybrid moaned beside her.

The lackeys' jaws dropped upon beholding the freak: the perfect soldier, too far from its controller.

The cockpit lay open, a hapless pilot inside, too slow to react in the split second of their arrival.

Rosanna rose from the shredded clothes and darted to the cockpit while the hybrid continued spewing flames, aimed at two gun-wielding chiefs past their prime who were huddling around a shell of a man. But Tecton was lucid enough to look Rosanna in the eye and know he was about to die.

She couldn't relish in the *whoosh* of fire surging behind her.

No time to watch as the screams of three men filled her ears. Tecton's howl did give her some satisfaction, though.

This cargo was meant to haul minerals, so it had a cockpit seal. Stepping inside, she slammed the button, sealing off the hybrid from the charred corpses.

The pilot stared at her.

"You're going to open the cargo hatch and dump the contents."

His eyes widened. Sweat formed on his brow as the color drained from his face.

"I'm not repeating myself. After you do that, take us back to the Bastion."

FORTY

(P'OKI)

In a place only grief knows

A MAKAWE COULD survive a crumbling building. They didn't require air like the other fleshy sapients populating the galaxy.

But could a mother survive a broken heart? P'oki banked her scrapper around the collapsing tower. Spirits bubbled, tugging her toward the wreckage in progress, ignoring the unfolding battle.

There weren't any Makawe spirits on this asteroid, none living at least. Makawe spirits hummed and glowed unlike the furry or scaled sapient species. She'd hoped the lack of spirits was from the tower concealing them, but P'oki couldn't ignore the truth any longer.

He'nay might be in the wreckage, but there weren't any spirits around to suggest this.

She wasn't below the surface level, either.

All of the spirits she could detect were directed toward the battle, and the panic in them buzzed loud enough to shake her carapace. Something more horrific clouded the Humans fleeing the tower and befuddled the spirits.

Her scanners couldn't pick it up, but she saw it through her dimming viewscreen.

A stalking leviathan of death. Like an ancestor-spirit from her own mythology, the kind a grand spirit would have sealed away beneath an ocean or exiled to a forgotten moon.

Some bits of mythology were born of deep history, especially those shared throughout cultures. Makawe and Blekk alike agreed a star had been drowned to seal away cosmic evil. Blekk used incorrect names and places, of course, but the central story held.

The ancestor-spirit outside was a glorified representation of creatures with exoskeletons. No wonder the other species of the Collective despised the Makawe so. This was their pinnacle, terrible as it was.

P'oki swiveled an eyestalk to behold the ancestor-spirit.

Spirits scattered from her vision, reducing her to body-sight. Something about this creature bent the light around it, making it impossible for her to truly see it. Light itself feared this monstrosity.

This ancestor-spirit should never have been released. However, it was providing distraction from the crumbling building, which fell slower than it would have if not for the asteroid's low gravity. She could search the wreckage and rubble.

Maybe someone helpful like another prisoner would notice the glyph tattoo on P'oki's shell and recognize He'nay's matching one. Then they'd be reunited, and Rodrick Crith's final mission would not have been so much of a disaster. Her daughter was either in that falling tower or dead. Crith's dying message urged her to leave. Panicked spirits arose, buzzing at her to flee with her life.

But neither Crith nor the spirits around her were mothers—they couldn't have understood.

She banked her scrapper hard, careening toward the surface. As chunks of the building fell, she grabbed them with her scrapper magnet and scattered them in all directions.

One collided with a Collective battledart, just like the chunk of the asteroid she'd removed earlier collided with the Bastion. Someone would arrest her for that if she survived, but she'd like to see anyone try. Not when she had to get to He'nay or whatever was left of her.

A Blekker pirate flew too close, and she flung another falling bit of the building at it. The Drowned Star would call that a blood debt, but she'd chop off their tentacles with her own pincers if they got in her way.

She lobbed a third chunk of the building at one of those Earthquake monsters, and she didn't care. They could come for her, but fighting the unnamable ancestor-spirit would occupy too much of their attention for them to divert any to P'oki and her scrapper. For all they knew, she was a wildcat miner looking for easy scrap during a battle.

Spirits suggested a safe spot to land, a flatter spot which wasn't threatened by the fissures in the ground. For extra precaution, she turned her magnet to reverse polarity, just in case any hunks of the tower decided to descend nearby.

Decontamination couldn't go fast enough. She didn't care what bacteria and parasites she brought to this unspirited rock. The atmosphere didn't have any sulfur, so she was fine without a breather. The surface would mineralize her blood as she walked, anyway. Buildings climate controlled for Humans were bearable, and she wouldn't be inside long.

The hangar gaped open.

She was close enough now and far enough from the creature which darkened the skies that her spirits whispered properly in her midst, buzzing which direction to go.

By their reverberations in her shell, they told her the same thing. Spirits of Earthquake members were easy to ignore since they bounced like Humans and were darkened by racism. Besides those, only three souls remained inside the dying Bastion: a Human, Lo-sat, and Arkouda.

Maybe one of them was Dr. Oze. If she could save her, the mission might not be a total loss. Maybe she could tell P'oki more about He'nay's last days, or perhaps in finding Dr. Oze, she could sense He'nay's spirits. If nothing else, she wanted to thank her again. He'nay getting excited about Chamayna civilization and culture was so inspiring, especially because Dr. Oze defied social norms by hiring a Makawe research assistant.

Nobody had ever done that before. It was such a big step and a glorious day for Makawe everywhere and a nice excuse for matching mother-daughter tattoos. He'nay had said the Chamayna glyph meant "power," but P'oki went along with it because it was a nice reminder of her pride and joy. While this path led to He'nay's death, it also led her to great happiness, and Dr. Oze deserved gratitude for that. He'nay had even mentioned Dr. Oze having an adventure with a Lo-sat and an Arkouda, so maybe that's who was inside with the Human. Stranger things had happened already, so why not? He'nay was always saying things like that.

Bolstered by the low gravity, P'oki scuttled toward the collapsing building.

FORTY-ONE

(AMANDA)

Running back inside a collapsing building like a genius

AMANDA'S SAVING GRACE was the asteroid's low gravity. The antigrav inside the Bastion was failing with each crumbling chunk—not that it changed the amount of industrial crap cascading before her, thankfully slower in the low gravity. Dodging as the falling plaster and metal came down, she cleared the hangar, running into the opulent hallway, lit brown by failing lights. At the other end, she'd find Symphora and Mel-za alive or dead.

A beam above her head cracked, and she looked up only to see ceiling tiles racing toward her head. She ducked, covering her head with her arms as dust and debris exploded into a grayish cloud. A whoosh raced by her head, and she could make out a tangled lighting fixture swinging before her, nearly removing her head. She swallowed.

As more chunks fell, the mess of what transpired outside sped the collapse. Enough walls had collapsed to expose the outside. Trembles in the floor suggested the monstrosity nobody could name was a stampede of one, snuffing out any life below. Gentler crashes suggested falling ships crashing from the atmosphere.

Just like the first time Blekk pirates had tried to attack that thing.

Maybe Amanda was safer inside the Bastion.

As she pushed forward past cracked mirrors, ripped canvasses, and fallen vases, she strained to hear anything other than the last gasps of the building. She'd see open air above her soon. Or death. Both felt likely as she jumped over a fallen bathroom sink. As she landed, a faint murmur made her pause.

Somebody was swearing between labored breaths.

Eyes wide, Amanda pressed forward, preparing to leap over a fallen toilet from the cracked-open locker room on the above floor.

Something squelched underfoot and Amanda halted. She'd stepped on a corpse. This body once belonged to someone in Earthquake whose pelvis and stomach had been crushed by a falling toilet. She felt sorry for whoever this was, but this might've been preferable to dying at Symphora's paws or against whatever nightmares lay outside. She gingerly removed her foot, sidestepped, and ran again.

More swearing.

"Symphora!" Desperation rose. "You there? Mel-za?"

"M-m-artinnnnezz?"

"Are you stuck?" Amanda asked.

"Why the Nightmare else would I be sitting here?"

Amanda rounded the corner toward the stairwell. A pile of dead Humans surrounded Symphora.

Another ceiling tile cracked off and landed behind Amanda. Smoke tendrils curled around the remaining support beams, and sprinkler systems sputtered in the inconsistent gravity.

"Where's Mel-za?"

Heaving, Symphora bent to pull up a collapsed chunk of steel, tossing it aside.

Symphora checked over her shoulder at Amanda, eyes full of regret. "I'm looking for her."

Amanda's heart stopped. "Is she alive?"

"She's mumbled a few times, and I can hear her breathing. I think her heat cell got damaged. I told her if she died I'd kick her ass."

"Where is she?"

Symphora indicated the accumulated debris pile. "At the bottom."

The two colleagues shared a glance, and an entire conversation passed unspoken. They both believed the other should leave yet knew they couldn't convince the other to do so.

Amanda approached the debris pile and rolled off a pipe. "Mel-za? Can you hear us?"

"Of course she can." Heaving, Symphora shoved off another metal beam.

While Amanda moved a ceiling tile, she spied blood splatters on Symphora's fur. Mostly red but a few spots of Arkouda indigo and one splotch of Lo-sat cyan.

A series of rhythmic taps echoed from behind her.

Squatting, she lifted and pulled off a chunk of collapsed ceiling, which scraped against an overstuffed toilet. Amanda sidestepped to avoid the glooping liquid inside as it spilled out, and she appreciated her breather's ability to block scents.

"Nightmare that reeks," Symphora tutted. "That stench probably knocked her out more than the debris."

The six-rhythm of taps repeated, closer this time. Amanda fought the urge to peer over her shoulder as she hefted a broken sink that had been spit in a few too many times. Accidentally digging her foot onto a trash pile, she grunted to get it back on the solid floor. "I don't want to step on her. Can you smell if we're close to her?"

"She's breathing, Martinez. I'm surprised you can't hear it."

Another voice. "You save friend in pile?"

That accent belonged to a Makawe struggling with speaking Arkouda. Amanda whipped around to see a Makawe woman, shell covered in tattoos, a bicolor stripe criss-crossing her carapace. Her eyestalks showed signs of age and weariness.

"Yes," Amanda said. "Can you help us?" Symphora glared at her, but Amanda shrugged. "What? You think she's with Earthquake?"

The Makawe woman scuttled over. "Spirits show me your friend. Not much breathing. Fast work."

The trio set to work with renewed vigor, rummaging through chunks of the fallen locker room, yet the Makawe interloper kept an eyestalk trained on Amanda.

"I help get friend yours," the Makawe said. "Have you seen Makawe woman younger than me?"

Symphora grunted as she threw a folded scrap of steel that was once a locker over her shoulder. "Huh?"

Amanda pulled out a loose pipe. "She'll help us dig out Mel-za but wants to know if we've seen another Makawe." She addressed their new companion. "I'm sorry, but you're the only Makawe any of us have seen."

The Makawe dug her smaller pincer into the bottom of the pile. She latched onto something, then motioned with her eyestalks to Amanda and Symphora. "This spot."

After a quick mutual glance, Amanda and Symphora complied, focusing on the spot over her pincer. After removing a few chunks of debris, Amanda's eyes widened, finding a spot of green.

Mel-za's snout, embraced by the tip of the Makawe's pincer.

"Gentle I pull her. Some breathing spirits."

Symphora gasped. "Th-thank you..."

"P'oki, me," the Makawe trilled.

"It's nice to meet you, P'oki." Amanda pulled away more garbage, revealing Mel-za's shut eyes. "I'm Amanda." She eyed her companion. "And this is Symphora." She winced at the idea of moving an injured person, but it was move her now or waste time clearing out the area around her which could lead to Mel-za's heat-death.

"Sym'fra?" P'oki wiggled Mel-za by the snout, untangling her from wiring, and inching her out of the pile. "Where is your tall hair?"

Coughing below made the trio look down. Mel-za's head popped out of the detritus, and she gasped for air between coughs.

Symphora hoisted her up from the pile, which collapsed on itself. "I got you."

Amanda knelt to meet P'oki's eyes. "Thank you. Can we answer your questions while we escape? This place isn't safe." Furniture from the second floor collapsed nearby.

"P'oki have question first." She tapped her pincer against the floor; Amanda knew it was some Makawe body language, but its meaning was lost on her.

Symphora slung Mel-za over her shoulder. "Fine. Just, quickly, alright?"

"A'lize O'ze. Doctor. She is here?"

Amanda's breath caught in her throat. "How do you know that name?"

"She is here?" P'oki trilled inside her beak, and it felt hostile.

Symphora stomped over and yanked Amanda by the shoulder to bring her to a standing position. "The archaeologist? She was. She also carved some kooky *skata* and teleported away."

P'oki scuttled an inch to her left as loose chalky debris billowed from the ceiling. "Alone or with Makawe friend?"

Inhaling deep, Amanda fought to speak calmly. "She told us that she had a Makawe companion. I'm sorry to tell you this, but Earthquake killed her companion. Alize kept a piece of her carapace, but she disappeared with it."

P'oki's eyestalks rubbed together, and the wet friction between them made Amanda's stomach turn. A noise approximating a sigh echoed in her beak. The spiny legs supporting her carapace buckled. "Earth'quake dies today. We're leaving. I have ship."

"Finally," Symphora huffed.

P'oki scuttled beside Amanda. "Your Earth'quake disguise fail. Spirits show truth. Did A'lize speak of my daughter's last moments?"

Amanda wanted to ask if her spirits could show them a faster way out. She stopped in her tracks and met the Makawe's gaze. "No. Alize said she'd come back to us. We'll get your reunion with her and some answers."

FORTY-TWO

(ROSANNA)

Standing victorious over fallen prey.

THE STUTTERING PILOT failed to hold eye contact. "I-i-it's done." He indicated the dashboard display. Between blinking lights and switches, a screen displayed the cargo hold. Empty. Jacques Tecton, his last two lieutenants, and the hybrid abomination who killed them, were all emptied into the vacuum of space outside. Their floating corpses would already be ice.

"Turn on the viewscreen," Rosanna commanded. Three frozen corpses and the hybrid drifted in the vacuum of space. These deaths also failed to bring Alejandro back. It failed to close the rift in her heart, and she knew it wouldn't even be enough to stop his movement completely. Maybe Crith had gotten to her, after all.

Rosanna clenched her fists. Tecton's death was supposed to make her feel better. "Now return us to the Bastion." Watching the hybrid, she remembered the kid. He wasn't brainless like this thing. He was her age when Crith visited her family to lie about Alejandro's death. She didn't want him to turn out like her.

"You saw th-th-that thing, didn't you? We can't go back there."

Rosanna shoved her pistol between his eyes. "I know how to fly this ship. You're alive right now because I don't want plasma ash on my clothes."

His bottom lip quivered.

"I'm sure there's some cleaner in the back, so I can really handle this myself if you won't cooperate."

He gulped and entered the course reversal command.

"Now, when we arrive, I'm going to kill that monster." Rosanna flashed a sarcastic smile. "You get to help. Fun, right?"

Rosanna had read the secret files. Rick's own reports. They'd thrown everything at the beast. Guns, blades, cannons, entire ships, and nothing worked. Rosanna had even read Oze's journal notes. The creature awakened at violence. It grew stronger around it.

Oze thought it was some metaphysical, mystical boveeshit. At first, it sounded to Rosanna like something a college student would conjure after a few too many experiments with ravedust. But seeing it for herself... it didn't behave like any sapient species she'd seen before, and she'd crisscrossed the galaxy rising through Earthquake's ranks.

Crith and Oze agreed this thing could not be stopped by conventional violence.

Rosanna boasted expertise in unconventional violence. This thing must have a weakness, and she would exploit it.

And if not, she'd get the whole Collective to implode trying to fight it, which was an even better option since they were the ones who would want to bring her to justice for the lives she'd taken.

She winced hard. She was a murderer in service of a liar, seeking answers but refusing to ask the right questions.

Alejandro wasn't the hero she'd imagined but a flawed man who believed in the wrong guy and grew too stubborn or jaded to see the truth.

The cargo ship returned to the asteroid's proximity, and the dogfight unfurled before her.

Collective military ships buzzed around the thing Oze called Unspeakable in her notes. Blekk pirate ships avoided it, focusing fire on Earthquake's armada of stolen Collective fighters and modified civilian ships. Roving dots on the ground ignited red and orange— the hybrids attempting to attack the Unspeakable. How they could ignite flames in the absence of an atmosphere gave her pause. Perhaps their flames weren't truly fire, and Rosanna hadn't paid close enough attention to the research notes.

Rosanna initiated her omni-tablet.

[Monsieur Tecton has died from injuries sustained in the crumbling Bastion. Continue the assault on the creature's feet with the hybrids.]

She glared at her pilot. "There's a debris pile beside the Bastion with survivors. That's where we're going." The kid and his group deserved a chance to get off that rock.

Not her.

FORTY-THREE

(MAYNARD)

**Huddling together as the galaxy
crumbles around them**

SURPRISING MAYNARD, MUI-XE pulled him back, avoiding a ripping fissure in the asteroid. Binh and Reck-xa jumped to either side.

"We can't sit around here, Uncle Maynard," Mui-xe shouted over the cracking rock.

Binh turned his attention to the beast he called Unspeakable. "That thing is coming our way, so it won't matter. It'll stomp us flat."

The Unspeakable ripped a Collective battledart from orbit and crushed it in its hands. Each movement shook their foundation. At its base, the hybrids born from suffering and evil groaned at their helplessness. Their attack seemed more focused on the rock than at the creature. The behemoth was so large and close

that he couldn't see the horns on its head without craning his neck.

Maynard glared at Amanda Martinez's omni-tablet. With his limited technical experience, the device felt like a labyrinth, but he saw the homing function. If any Collective troops were searching for government operatives, they would find them.

The Unspeakable's proportions and features made it more reminiscent of a walking collection of symbols from mythology than an actual sapient being. As fighter ships rammed into it and fired enough plasma into it to decimate a building, it trudged forward, shaking the surface with each step—approaching their group, threatening the asteroid's stability.

Reck-xa clicked her tongue. "I don't know of any spell or potion to contain this beast. And if I did, my reagents are all spent."

"If we can stop this beast, will the two sides stop fighting?" Maynard asked.

"That's funny," Binh said. "Ever try stand-up?"

Reck-xa glared at him. "You should try silence if you don't have anything to contribute."

"Maybe standing up is the answer," Maynard intoned. "We could get to a higher vantage point and be more visible to any rescuers in the Collective."

"While also making an easier target for Earthquake," Binh shot back. "Not to mention that... that thing."

Mui-xe stepped toward the hulking creature. "I don't think I can be killed." His voice carried too many grim notes for one so young, as if all the counseling they'd done in the monastery had evaporated. "For everything Dr. Diastrevlo did to me or maybe from whatever my parents put in me, I don't know. I've stepped away from plasmafire, knives, gasses, and snapped bones. I'll go up to it."

Hearing the litany of injustices ripped Maynard's heart. Monastic tendencies or not, he would make that so-called "Brother" Rondo pay.

In rapid Lo-sat, Reck-xa unleashed a verbal barrage too fast for Maynard's ears.

"Go up and what?" Binh asked. "What'll you do? It's not like you can talk to it."

A *whooshing* gust from a descending cargo ship muffled Maynard's response.

A small cargo ship hovered above, brandishing Earthquake's symbol. Maynard stood in front of his nephew. Even though the boy was taller and more powerful than him, he'd stand against any foe to protect him. A prehistoric religion, a forerunner to the Great Mystery, once taught that each life force had a sacred duty. While it predated the religious syncretization into the Great Mystery, Maynard understood that he'd found his: protect the boy.

He sank into a combat stance. Whoever this was deserved to know what they faced. He would break his vows.

The ship's cargo hold folded open. Rosanna Moreno occupied the open cargo bay, and the ship lowered to ground level. A cold grimace had replaced her boiling scowl.

"This rock is about to get real unsafe. Get in," she said.

FORTY-FOUR

(AMANDA)

Aboard a Makawe scrapper

AMANDA PUSHED MEL-ZA'S tail around the one warm pillar in P'oki's cramped scrapper, desperate to give her some heat and distance herself from P'oki's gentle sobs. The pillar had an exhaust vent from the engine; it only puffed out hot air, but Amanda didn't know enough about Makawe design practices or biology to understand why. Symphora stripped her armor so Mel-za could get some of her fur heat as well; she resembled a weeping mother, holding the limp Lo-sat's neck and head in her lap and between her arm and ribs.

"She'll survive," Amanda said.

"Don't even finish that thought," Symphora growled.

P'oki trilled from the front. "Problem, Marti'nez."

Amanda sat down beside her in the cockpit, remembering how her aunt used to ask questions to take her mind off things when she was a kid. "What is it?"

"Spirits of your other friends." P'oki's eyestalk gestured to the viewscreen. A cargo ship with Earthquake symbols hovered over where Maynard's group was supposed to be. "They in that ship unless you know another group of Hu'mans and Lo-sats traveling together."

"Damn." Amanda spun around. "Hey Symphora, I'm pinging your omni-tablet."

"Damn," P'oki repeated, her voice steadying. "Hu'man word. My old friend like it."

Amanda grabbed Symphora's omni-tablet from beside her discarded armor and fired off a ping to herself, knowing Maynard would receive it since she'd left it with him.

[It's Amanda. You OK?]

[Yes. Symphora is alive? What about Mel-za?]

Getting the ping back from Maynard was a relief.

[Yes.]

"P'oki, can you see any of your spirits around the Unspeakable?" Amanda asked.

"The what?" Symphora asked.

P'oki's voice lowered. "Spirits avoid it."

A ping came back from Maynard.

[Rosanna wishes to destroy the monster.]

[How?]

Amanda had a hard time imagining the conversation Maynard and Rosanna must be having.

Trilling, P'oki snapped Amanda's attention back to her and banked the ship hard. "One spirit I see. Faint."

"Any clue how to destroy it?"

"Spirit I see is not from the creature. From the rider. It feels familiar."

"*Rider?*" Symphora grunted. "How good is your Arkouda?"

"Rider is on the creature," P'oki insisted. "A Hu'man."

"Someone from Earthquake?" Amanda whispered. She measured the distance between themselves and the Unspeakable and Rosanna's transport ship. If they'd figured out how to teleport, controlling that creature wasn't a far stretch. They needed to stop that thing before it ripped the galaxy apart. Amanda pinged Maynard.

[You go to the monster. I have a plan.]

Amanda's fingers twitched as she typed "monster." Forming any words about this thing took a toll on her, even in print. She puffed out an exhale and continued typing.

[We have a scrapper magnet. It's not as powerful as the Earthquake ones, but we can grab an asteroid and pelt anyone who gets too close if needed.]

[...]

While Amanda was typing "I know it's crazy, but," a response came.

[...Rosanna agreed, but threatened to hit me if I didn't say that you aren't in charge. If the ship is destroyed, the person I came here to rescue may survive. Please save him. My shaman companion wishes to let you know she will become a ghost and haunt you if this fails.]

Amanda remembered the Lo-sat woman and shuddered at the prospect of a haunting from her if Mui-xe were to suffer more. Mui-xe might be able to survive anything if he survived whatever freakish experiments Earthquake tried to do to him, even though Amanda could only guess at what they were. Not to mention whatever the mad scientist concocted before Rick got him.

Rosanna's ship zoomed forward, and Amanda wondered if she'd just sent them to die, as if that was the cost of leadership. That felt like something Rick would say and it turned her stomach; she couldn't claim to be *that* different from him.

"Their ship will get the rider off the Unspeakable," Amanda said. "We'll follow them and protect them from any incoming ships. Is your magnet strong enough to fling anybody close enough to get caught in Neptune's gravity?"

"Nep'tune?"

"What in the Nightmare is a Nepatune?" Symphora grumbled.

"Sorry," Amanda said. "That's the Human name for that blue planet up there."

P'oki banked the ship and zoomed toward Rosanna's cargo. "Pretty name. He'nay would have liked it."

"I think it was a prehistoric name from an Earth culture's mythology," Amanda said. "An ocean god or something."

P'oki shook a pincer at the dimming blue planet. "Ocean god? Cosmic spirits have a humor sense. The Blekk are not the only drowned star today."

"Maybe," Amanda intoned. Outside, the hybrids swarming the Unspeakable were being crushed underfoot yet also writhing around it. As they sped closer, Amanda's heart leapt to her throat. "Something about that rider doesn't make sense."

"Nothing about that thing makes sense." Symphora caressed Mel-za's limp neck frills.

Amanda said. "Fly us closer. Avoid it as much as possible. Don't throw anything at it."

Wordless, P'oki maneuvered the ship forward.

The small dot upon the Unspeakable's head solidified as they approached.

Amanda's eyes widened. "I need to ping Rosanna's ship. Alize Oze is sitting on top of the creature." As they neared the beast, Alize became less of a dot and more of an outline. They were too far away for Amanda to see her as clear as she was: they could see her outline because the light around Alize was bending somehow as if the woman was absorbing it into herself.

"Alize did say she would come back. I'm not sure how I feel about her keeping true to her word."

FORTY-FIVE

(ROSANNA)

Above crumbling hunting grounds

ROSANNA PRESSED HER pistol into the nape of the pilot's neck but turned her attention to Reck-xa. "Lady, do you mind taking a turn to threaten this guy?"

The pilot kept course and his focus. "It's really not—"

"Shut up."

The Lo-sat shaman complied, measuring Rosanna through slanted eyeridges and taking a few too many sniffs. "Don't mistake survival for forgiveness. You will answer for what you've done to my grandson."

Rosanna huffed but had no rebuttal. "Pilot, when we get on top of the monster, open the cargo hold and make an oxygen bubble again. This thing won't attack us if we don't attack it." She had read Crith and Oze's notes enough times to know this thing's rules, but she wasn't about to let this thing kill everything in sight.

Binh put an arm around Mui-xe. "There's a lesson here, kid. Don't fight the thing that wants to kill you. Just run up to it and give it a nice back rub. And make sure you don't listen to the handsome rogue who watched it kill people."

"Please don't touch me," Mui-xe muttered. "Are you positive this won't attack? How do we know you're not just trying to kill us?"

Noticing the kid wouldn't make eye contact with her, Rosanna let out a tight sigh. "If I wanted to kill us, I'd have killed the pilot and plowed into a rock. I'm done with Earthquake."

"I understand." The monk's tone felt honest. Nonjudgmental. New. "Are you positive this … thing won't retaliate as we approach it?"

Maybe this guy had forgiven her. Religious nut. She didn't deserve it and damn sure hadn't earned it. "It's focused on the attackers below." The word "hybrid" almost escaped her lips. "If Oze is really on it, we might have a chance of getting her off. Definitely avoid the horns around its face and mandibles."

Reck-xa peered out the viewscreen, keeping her tail coiled around the pilot's shoulders. "This is the Oze woman? That dot on the creature?"

Binh entered the cockpit and scoffed. "Yeah, that's her alright. Man, will she be happy to see me."

A warning chimed from the ceiling and a recording of a Human voice intoned, "COLLISION IMMINENT."

Rosanna snapped her attention to the viewscreen. A Blekk pirate skirmisher flew forward toward them. As its guns lit up and aimed at their ship, a mauve ray of light washed over it. The ship stalled, and then rocketed upward, pulled by a scrapper magnet.

Rosanna found the source—the Makawe scrapper that Martinez was aboard. Amanda Martinez could have let her die. Nobody would have been the wiser. She could have escaped.

Rosanna breathed deep, accepting that Martinez was saving all of her friends aboard, not her. "Open the hatch. We're close enough."

The pilot nodded. A thin quartz-colored bubble descended, providing a semipermeable barrier. Once it covered the hatch, the cargo bay door opened, unfolding into the atmosphere above the asteroid. In the distance, battledarts and pirate ships clashed against the crumbling Earthquake fleet.

People she knew and tolerated were in those ships. People with little sisters. People who didn't deserve to die at the claws of a monster.

Below her, barely two meters away, Dr. Alize Oze sat between the base of protruding horns on the Unspeakable's head. Rosanna recognized the position from her brief foray inside the Great Mystery monastery.

"Alize," Rosanna called. Pulling her head back, she barked at the pilot, "Get closer!" She hated how stupid this felt. The archaeologist would hate Rosanna and sooner spit on her than get in a ship with her.

The transporter shimmied closer, nearly grazing a downturned horn which was bigger than the ship.

"Alize." Rosanna was close enough to see her breather and dyed pink hair. A black silhouette encased her body, as if somehow light funneled into her.

The archaeologist turned her head toward Rosanna, eyes shut as if this were a relaxing afternoon for her.

Her eyelids flung open, and what was behind them was not Human. Compound eyes like those on insects stared back at her. Jagged lines ran through them.

While Rosanna stared slack-jawed, the woman she thought was Alize Oze stood—and approached.

FORTY-SIX

(VESSEL)

Ascended

WITH MY BORROWED sight, the Vessel observed the interloper shouting from a miniscule ship.

Behold, a Bringer has arrived. This one was not so different from the old worshippers. This new interloper would make prostrations in my honor. What a fool. *Go to the Bringer.*

The Vessel advanced at my behest.

The Bringer shouted from her pod of metal, which floated above as if it placed her on the cosmic level. Pitiful. More lessers abounded, smacking into this form as if it would do anything. They were all unwilling to learn. That will consume them before the cosmos does.

The Bringer shies away from the Vessel. Unacceptable. The Vessel resists, as if she ever had a choice. The results of her hubris created its chains to me. I give the Vessel speed to jump aboard the metal pod. She complies, unable to express how I desire the Bringer. So much chaos in that one. Potential. Much like the earlier Bringer.

In the pod, the Bringer shouts. Vessel wishes to respond but may not. Any response would come in a form the Bringer could not comprehend. This one only knows my word for teleportation.

Inside the metal pod, the Vessel is surrounded by other pitiful life forms.

A devotee to a falsehood swirls around the Vessel, chanting. She draws circles with her tail. That won't work on me—not here. The devotee's poetry fails. I find her heresy pathetic, and I will crush her for it.

In the metal pod's front, a denier shrinks into panic, coaxing the pod to spin away from me. A bother. It delays the inevitable.

A different devotee meets the Vessel's gaze unblinking. He speaks a different meaningless chant, but it resonates with the Vessel. The Vessel's emotions stir, but they are void inside my control. I can feel the Vessel's resolve falter. Each passing second makes her more my puppet as I dissolve her memories and individuality.

A second denier kneels beside Vessel and speaks again in a language this denier should not know. It resonates stronger with Vessel. The Vessel's urge to respond is powerful, but a powerful grain of sand against me remains a grain of sand.

One more life form is in this pod, and the Vessel does not know it. This one is not a denier or a devotee and certainly not a Bringer. It is not natural.

It—

The Vessel twitches, which I did not will.

Stop.

This other. It should not be. It is not of the cosmos.

The Vessel squirms. That was not permitted. I force Vessel to the floor, hard enough to crack bone.

Stop.

Stop stop

The other summons warmth. No. I will make the Vessel colder than stone to defy it. The Vessel blinks.

The Vessel screams. *No.*

Stopstopstop

The other—

It is not from a tree dweller, an insect, an ice digger, a sun-baker, a swimming one, or a shelled crawler. I gaze upon it through the Vessel's eyes and draw my full attention on the metal pod.

I step forward, shaking off the things that swarm around me. I will rip that metal pod from the sky and crush it. The other's warmth, whatever it is, cannot withstand me. The Vessel must leave this life form's presence.

Vessel. Vessel. *Vessel.*

Hrrk—

———

Alize vomited onto the ship's metal floor, despite the soothing warmth coursing in her body.

A teenage boy massaged her shoulders. His touch was warmer than it should've been. He spoke, his voice more of a croak than an accent. "You're safe now."

Alize blinked hard at the speaker.

He mixed the features of a Lo-sat and a Human but not like the hybrids she'd seen trudging about the Bastion's prison—he was sapient. Kind. Emotive. While his marbled red eyes and malformed appendages matched those monsters, he was something they could not be. He was the experiment Earthquake couldn't recreate. She rubbed her eyes, coming away with an inky coating on her hands. The Unspeakable couldn't comprehend this boy. He freed her from its influence.

"You with us, Alize?" Binh asked.

"I think so," she replied after a painful inhale. Binh was one of the last people in the galaxy she wanted to see.

Rosanna Moreno, her former captor and the actual last person in the galaxy she wanted to see, shuddered.

A Great Mystery monk and a Lo-sat shaman stood above her on either side of the hybrid teen.

"Binh," Alize said, "where the Earth am I?" The ship lurched forward. "Besides getting away from the Unspeakable?"

Rosanna knocked Binh out of the way and grabbed Alize's shoulders. "What the Earth happened to you?"

Alize wiped the bile from her lip and clenched her fist. "Don't you dare speak to me." She turned her attention to the others. "The Unspeakable and I merged consciousnesses. I'm not sure why."

Binh's eyeridges raised. "What was that like?"

Alize winced and shook her head, then turned to the hybrid boy. "I don't know what you did, but thank you."

Breathing heavily, the hybrid nodded and indicated the Great Mystery monk. "My name is Mui-xe, and this is my Uncle Maynard." He winced as if he was fighting to stay standing. "I saw you were hurting, so I healed you."

"My grandson is quite gifted." The Lo-sat shaman sniffed around Alize. "You'll need more thorough treatment soon for whatever happened to you. And I am Reck-xa, shaman of the Lo-sat."

Alize slowly absorbed the madness and decided not to ask about the family dynamics.

Binh flicked his tail in her direction. "They're more trustworthy than me. Also, I'll give you a more formal and intentional apology for my ... Binhiness after we escape."

"So it won't come is what you're saying." Alize cracked a smile. "The Unspeakable is conflicted. It needs a new tomb. It's grown too powerful for me to reason with it. I shouldn't have tried. Bringing it here was a mistake."

Rosanna offered Alize a hand to join her. "Is there another tomb?"

"No." Alize slapped her hand away and stood on her own, assisted by the cybernetics in her prosthetic leg. "It was destroyed by the Drowned Star pirates a few years ago. Much like this asteroid is about to be."

On shaky legs, Mui-xe stepped forward, breathing hard. "What can I do? I can make things really hot."

"You need a break." Alize shook her head. "Whatever healing you did for me sufficed to chase it out of my head. But there are other hybrids, not like you, who are down there, and their heat isn't doing anything to the Unspeakable."

"They aren't like him," Rosanna clarified, breathing heavy. "They're dead bodies sewn together and revived with spliced DNA. They also decay as they use their powers. They are going to turn into goop soon." She smacked her lips as if her mouth was drying.

Alize wondered what was happening to Rosanna. She looked like she needed some water or something, but Rosanna could suffer some discomfort after all she'd done. "We need to build a tomb for it."

"The one you found the first time was ornate and huge," Binh said. "We don't exactly have time for all that carving."

"I don't think it needs to be anything fancy," Alize said. "Just an enclosed space where it can be left alone." She shot a glare at Rosanna and added, "Without anyone using its power, either."

Sweat glistened across Rosanna's forehead. "Well, I'm out of chitin. I used my last bit to get on this ship and kill Tecton. But we are in an asteroid belt with ferrous asteroids, and we have some scrappers left."

Alize stared into the viewscreen. Despite distancing themselves from the Unspeakable, it didn't seem smaller. Hunks of asteroid floated away from the center. It wasn't moving as fast as it should have, as if something were gumming up its footsteps. "Is there any way we can get Earthquake and the fleet to stop fighting each other and the Unspeakable for a few minutes?"

Rosanna held up an omni-tablet, shaking slightly. "The Collective doesn't know Tecton is dead yet. I can ask for a cease fire." She pointed at the monk. "And Maynard over here has a politician's omni-tablet. We can do this. Are you good at negotiating?"

The monk nodded. "I had to moderate conflict in the monastery. I simply think of what Binh would say and do the opposite."

Alize placed her hand against the viewscreen, covering one of the Unspeakable's horns. "Time to rest."

FORTY-SEVEN

(AMANDA)

**Fleeing a crumbling asteroid because
this is why she got into politics**

P'OKI'S SCRAPPER BANKED hard to the left, catapulting Amanda into Symphora's lap on top of Mel-za.

Mel-za huffed. "Get your own girlfriend."

"You both wish," Symphora groaned as she moved Amanda off her.

"What's happening?" Amanda called to P'oki.

"More spirits inside the other ship." P'oki looked back over her shell at Amanda. "A'lize is safe but not us."

More asteroid chunks broke apart as the Unspeakable threw them into the surface. None of the three amassed forces would retreat. All wanted the glory of destroying the others and the monster, which was running out of room to stand as the asteroid broke up. The Blekk were probably staying to avenge Sjorover or prove Cerad's dominance over him.

Symphora's omni-tablet chimed with a message from Maynard.

[While impersonating you, we're going to tell the Collective to cease fire. You have Jacques Tecton in custody if anyone asks.]

[And what the Earth are you going to do?] Amanda fired back.

[Rosanna will tell Earthquake to enclose the Unspeakable in the magnetic asteroids. Then we're going to fling it into Neptune.]

[My words won't carry enough weight.]

Amanda scrunched her brow, pissed at the world for her lower status. She wasn't important enough as a politician to call for a cease fire. She dug her fingers into the too-big tablet.

Too big because it belonged to Symphora.

She had Symphora's omni-tablet.

"Do you trust me?" Amanda asked Symphora as she opened the government channel.

"Do what you gotta do," she said, cradling Mel-za.

Amanda prompted the command to broadcast. Inhaling deep, she let her fingers fly.

[Hey maggots, it's your girl Symphora. I got that Tecton *skata* stain in custody. Quit firing on Earthquake and pull back. Earthquake will surrender after we lock up the creature.]

A message came from the remaining warhive in orbit above the planet.

[Hail, Symphora, this is the *Kalayne*. We have this thing where we want it. If we destroy its footing, we can let it float in space.]

P'oki piloted the ship in a sharp downturn, avoiding a rogue wing which had snapped off another ship.

[Negative, stupid jackass. It's surviving in open space just fine. We need to lock it up. Tell the Blekk to stop firing, too.]

Amanda switched over to the conversation with Maynard.

[Did you get the Earthquake pilots to listen?]

[There aren't enough asteroids and scrappers to do it.] Maynard replied.

"Damn," Amanda muttered. "Hey P'oki, how much of the Bastion is magnetized metal?"
"Scanners said most of it."
Amanda steeled herself and fired off another message to Maynard.

[Tell Earthquake to get behind our ship. We're going to push this asteroid into Neptune.]

Without waiting for a response, she came to the front of the ship and sat beside P'oki. The Bastion's ruins came into view, a rubble pile. So much had broken apart it might not push into one discernible entity for the magnetic beams to repel.

A cracked-off rock careened toward the viewscreen, narrowly missing them. The ship lurched forward, banking around the bottom of the asteroid. The scrapper magnet's mauve beam ignited, and a cone of light washed over the destroyed skyscraper.

P'oki initiated the polarity reversal, commencing the magnetic thrust away from her tiny ship, inching toward Neptune, the nearest gravity well nearby. It wouldn't be enough.

Amanda stared at the one mismatched tattoo on P'oki's carapace: a Chamayna glyph. Her heart raced. If the glyphs on Chamayna chitin had distinct properties, perhaps…

"What does your Chamayna glyph tattoo mean?"

"A'lize said it means power. Feminine energy. He'nay got one to match."

"Do you mind if I take a picture of it and send it to them?"

"You have good spirits, A'man'da. I trust you."

She opened the camera on Symphora's omni-tablet and sent it to Maynard.

[Show this to Alize. Ask her what it can do.]

"The magnet can not move it." P'oki grunted against the controls. "It's not enough."

Amanda glared at Neptune above and the crumbling asteroid ahead of them. To their left, an Earthquake scrapper aligned with them, adding its repulsion beam to P'oki's as Maynard's response came.

[Alize asked if the Makawe you're with is named P'oki.]

Amanda's breath caught in her throat.

[That's who I'm with.]

[Alize said to ask her if you can cut off part of her shell and put the chipped tattoo on the scrapper magnet's engine. It needs to be on organic material or it won't work.]

Amanda stared at the struggling Makawe. "Dr. Oze has a plan. She says the Chamayna glyph tattoo on your shell could be useful if we cut off that part of your shell. I don't want to hurt you, but I trust her, and we are running out of options."

"My last connection to He'nay?" P'oki huffed, banking the ship hard. "We had no time to look for her remains, and you ask me to remove it?"

"He'nay sounds like an amazing person." Amanda breathed deeply. "What would your daughter do if she were here?"

After a long trill echoed in her beak, P'oki slapped the floor with her pincer. "Do it. Dying hurts more."

"Symphora," Amanda called, "is an Arkouda's bite stronger than a Makawe's carapace?"

"Nightmare…" She removed Mel-za from her lap with an oomph and trudged over. "Why?"

"P'oki, Symphora will remove part of your glyph. The Chamayna language can … do things. Your tattoo might enhance your ship enough to send this asteroid into the planet. I know each of your tattoos are meaningful, but Alize says it's worth a try."

"He'nay trust A'lize." She shifted her focus to Symphora. "I say this to your species, not you Sym'fra, but bite me." She breathed hard, at least that's what Amanda thought was happening by the hollow sound coming from her beak.

"Eh, we deserve it." Symphora cringed. "I'll be fast. I've done a lot of crazy *skata* but nothing like this."

"Just do it," P'oki said through a shudder. "It's what He'nay would want."

Amanda's throat dried. P'oki could get seriously injured, Symphora could choke, and their ship could get swatted by a monster, all of which would be her fault. All she was doing was barking orders while others paid the price.

"You can do this," Amanda told them, as if it would do anything. She pointed to the tattooed glyph on the outer edge of P'oki's carapace, and Symphora bit down.

"Your mouth is going to get scratched-up. That'll take months to heal," Mel-za tutted.

Symphora reached into her drooling muzzle and pulled out a jagged piece of shell with indigo blood dripping from the sides. P'oki's bone-rattling ululation made Amanda flinch.

P'oki's eyestalks jiggled, blurring at the edges with moisture. "Last piece of He'nay that was. Be careful, Sym'fra."

Amanda struggled to watch the bloody display. It may have been Alize's idea, but Amanda had agreed to it. She could've demanded a different plan. "Was the glyph damaged?"

Symphora pointed to her muzzle and shook her head, then showed the shell chunk to P'oki.

"No damage," P'oki said.

"And will you be alright?" Amanda asked.

"Shells regrow," P'oki replied. "Not daughters."

"What about you, Symphora?" Mel-za croaked.

Symphora spit out blood and nodded.

Outside, a jagged chunk of the asteroid collapsed. The once rocky ball was becoming more of a cylinder. If the Unspeakable shook it much more, it would break free.

Another Earthquake scrapper aligned to the right of their ship, adding a repulsor ray. Yet bigger chunks of the Bastion's debris flew off the asteroid from the scattering pressure, reducing their ability to nudge the asteroid toward Neptune.

"We've got the shell piece with the freaky tattoo. Now what?" Mel-za asked.

Amanda took the wet shell, still dripping with Symphora's saliva and mouth blood. She read her newest ping to them. "Alize will take her tattoo piece and do something to it. Once she does, this one will start vibrating, and it will empower whatever it touches. I need to have this against the magnet by then."

Symphora sank to her knees and stroked P'oki's shell, holding her while she cried.

Mel-za slithered closer to Amanda. "What'll happen to whoever is holding it or close by?"

"Alize isn't sure," Amanda said, watching green-black blood bubbling from P'oki's damaged shell. "Maybe nothing. But I'm going."

"No you won't," Mel-za huffed from the back.

"I'm the smallest," Amanda said. "It has to be me."

"Small, but you can't condense your ribcage or flatten out those mammal hips of yours." Mel-za flared her neck frills and pushed herself off the floor. She stomped over to Amanda, grabbed her wrist with her tail, then pulled the shell out of Amanda's hand. "P'oki has to fly this thing, and you and Symphora are politicians. I'm the least important person in here. P'oki, the access hatch is what I was coiled around, yes?"

"Yes," P'oki said, standing in drips of her own blood. "Don't ruin my ship."

"No!" Amanda ran toward the access hatch, and Mel-za tripped her with her tail.

"My ancestors slithered, Martinez. I can slide in places you can't." Mel-za's eyeridges quivered. "I'll slide out, too." She spun around, lithe body wrapping around the engine exhaust access hatch.

Symphora lumbered over and helped Amanda on her feet, just in time to watch Mel-za slither inside, tail vibrating as she descended. The woman must be in agony after what had happened, but the warmth from Symphora heated her blood enough to give her a chance at speed. Beneath them, a clank echoed from the floor.

In front of them, the repulsion beam intensified, illuminating from its mauve color into an amethyst tone. Symphora and P'oki balked as the asteroid containing the scraps of the Bastion and the Unspeakable careened away from them, hurtling toward Neptune.

Heat from the exhaust vent hit the back of their neck so hard, Amanda had to step out of the way of the onrushing air.

A rattling hiss followed, but it wasn't from a piece of the engine overheating. It was Mel-za.

The floor itself grew hot, and P'oki trilled something. "Makawe shell make good conduits. It will regrow in time. I can get a new tattoo."

"Thank you," Amanda whispered.

The asteroid flew away from them. In the distance, two other Earthquake scrapper ships flung smaller asteroids out of the Unspeakable's path.

"It won't be enough," Amanda said. "It's already slowing down."

"Gun it!" Symphora barked.

P'oki sped the ship forward, chasing the asteroid they'd just thrown. The ship lurched, knocking Amanda and Symphora off-balance. P'oki engaged the repulsor again. This time, the asteroid rotated. The Unspeakable corrected itself, straightening the asteroid's path. The monstrosity folded in a sit up, bringing clacking mandibles to bear. Somehow, Amanda felt their rhythmic slapping in her bones, even through space's vacuum. The beast was unmistakably larger than it had been minutes ago.

Heat beneath them intensified, followed by another hiss, this one more of a shriek and yelp than anything else. "Mel-za," Symphora whispered.

P'oki swiveled an eye stalk behind her. "Ping A'lize's ship. We can bring oxygen bubbles together. We dive on their ship. Get safe. Autopilot AI will be more aggressive than P'oki."

The odor of charred scales wafted from the exhaust vents. Symphora's nostrils went wide. "Mel-za's been infinerawed." Her words came out mushy as blood spilled from her muzzle with saliva.

Amanda slumped to the floor. That should've been her.

A metallic *thunk* echoed from the access hatch, still hanging open. A green-tinted shadow poked through. "Like *nguc* I was."

Amanda's stomach flipped into knots, staring at the claw marks made on the exhaust shaft and then back up to Mel-za. She ran over and pulled her out. "How did you survive?"

Symphora spat out another line of blood and helped.

"That piece of P'oki's shell," Mel-za muttered, "it protected me. Some weird glow."

"Thank He'nay," P'oki said.

Once Mel-za got back on the floor, she plucked off blackened bits of her scales and shivered. Half her tail was gone, and one of her legs was flattened and limp. Symphora tended to her, and Amanda pinged their plan to Maynard. She hated it, but this thing was too powerful, and it was time to trust P'oki.

Maynard's response came quickly.

[We'll get you. Is everyone's breather ready?]

A Makawe scrapper ship was faster and sleeker than the other species' designs, but it was still a slow vehicle. Rosanna's transport broke in between the line of scrappers within seconds. A flaxen aura around it suggested they had used the power glyph somehow as well.

P'oki ignited the oxygen bubble, smacked something into the autopilot AI, then scuttled toward the hatch. She pinched Amanda's ankle. "Husband built this ship. He'nay took first steps where you stand. I'm giving everything for plan."

Amanda nodded slowly, eyeing the bite mark on her shell. "I understand. Thank you."

When the hatch opened, they found the transport bobbing beside them, cruising ahead in space, speeding in a losing race toward the azure planet. Brother Maynard and Binh occupied the entrance, ready to catch them. Alize and Reck-xa had their backs to the door. Behind them, Mui-xe knelt over Rosanna, who was clad in a spacewalk suit and writhing on the floor.

Double-checking her breather, Amanda ran through the oxygen bubble. It's gelatinous texture glomped onto her before letting her ooze out into the cold of space. The tips of her hair froze instantly, and Binh's tail reached out to grab her. P'oki jumped, which for a Makawe meant spinning like a disc, and more of her dark blood splattered as she did. Brother Maynard reached out for her pincer and dragged her back in.

Symphora threw Mel-za through, and she zipped like a harpoon inside. Bracing herself, Symphora barreled behind them, jumping forward, but she didn't have a spotter like Amanda and P'oki. But she'd be fine. She was Symphora, for Earth's sake.

Getting her footing, Amanda spun around to see Symphora, flailing in zero gravity, untethered in space. The beginnings of ice crystals formed on the tips of her fur.

Both ships were passing without her, the galaxy's hero.

FORTY-EIGHT

(ROSANNA)

Awakened

CLUTCHING THE BURNING piece of Makawe shell flaking away in her hand, Rosanna realized Mui-xe was kneeling over her; he must have nudged her back to consciousness after she took Martinez and Oze's suggestion to cradle that shard from Oze's friend. Rosanna wondered if Oze had kept that secret and had a plan to use it against Rosanna in some revenge plot.

Her vision had blurred, but she heard Martinez, a Lo-sat in Symphora Squad gear and a trilling Makawe discussing Symphora in frantic tones.

Rosanna pushed the kid away, harder than intended. Her vision clarified, yet a sharp black tinge coated her eyesight. She gazed upon her throbbing hands while the shaman and the monk stared at her.

Something enveloped Rosanna. Whatever they'd done to enhance the scrapper's repulsion magnet had also increased the Unspeakable's power.

Rosanna stared at the ship's still-open oxygen bubble into the black cosmic vacuum. Symphora was flailing in space, ice crystals forming on her fur. A half-second window remained before she'd die. Symphora was supposed to meet her end from one of Rosanna's bullets or blades, not the bleakness of space. And she would have to regrow that mohawk, too.

This would hurt.

Rosanna sprinted forward, passing through the oxygen bubble, sped by an energy she didn't understand. But understanding and harnessing were different. She burst into the small frame of open space between the two speeding ships as the cold of space enveloped her body, despite the protective space gear. She grabbed hold of the woman she had wanted to murder, spun her to face the transport ship, then shoved her inside.

Once she saw Symphora's chest expand with an inhale, Rosanna shouted into her space gear, not knowing if the message would be heard on their ship's comm. "Get out of here!"

The ship sped away. They were probably glad to be rid of her.

Steadying herself, Rosanna thought the black tinge intensified, and she realized it wasn't her eyesight, but something around her, protecting her from space's chill and oxygen vacuum. With the onrush of energy, she willed herself to catch the speeding scrapper with her hands.

Pain rattled Rosanna's arms as her bones shook with the vibrations of the scrapper, which struggled to push the Unspeakable into Neptune's gravity.

The magnet alone wouldn't be enough. The creature had almost shaken free of its molten rock foothold, the source of the ferrous material the scrapper needed to repulse.

Unsure how beyond her sheer will, Rosanna propelled through space, closing on the ship. The ebony energy swirled around her.

The Unspeakable's judgmental gaze settled upon her again. She knew what it was this time, and she didn't have the energy for fear. "Watch me throw you into a planet."

A word formed in her mind and the creature grew, its torso elongating and its head pulling away from her.

Bringer.

Whatever it was didn't matter. The only thing Rosanna was bringing was an ass-whooping.

Eyes widening, she realized the Unspeakable had changed its trajectory. It careened toward one of Neptune's moons and would get caught by its gravity instead of the planet's. The moon itself was barely visible around the creature's body.

Boosted by an unknown speed, Rosanna reached the scrapper ship, itself consumed by a pulsing black glow. Its magnetic beam cast the mauve light of repulsion, now flecked with a glimmering ebony aura. Rosanna grabbed a jutting edge of the ship, then used it to propel herself, ascending the hull like a rock wall. Pain rocked through her forearms and rattled her spine, but she pressed forward. When she reached the edge, she smacked the side of the beam emitter. The new angle wouldn't be precise, but it was enough to let them avoid the approaching moon. The planetary gravity would ensnare them soon.

She jumped in front of the repulsor beam, which catapulted her onto the crumbling asteroid. Rocks dug into her space suit, which she realized had already been tattered. Whatever this dark aura was, it was shielding her from the void.

The Unspeakable had folded itself around the asteroid and hammered at the rock's sides, making more fragments fly off to rejoin the Kuiper Belt. One of Neptune's moons absorbed a few chunks, adding to its craterous landscape.

Rosanna had wasted so much of her life on fury at herself. Failing to kill Symphora, Martinez, and Crith had deepened her rage. Indirectly killing Tecton only showed her what an empty shell she'd become. But something else guided her now.

With black wisps encircling her, Rosanna steadied herself on the asteroid, and flecks of grit flew off the rock.

Vacuum-sucked hybrids had melted and splattered onto the Unspeakable's legs from their assault, trying to regenerate from bubbling stains. So many lives taken and wasted. The mess of exploded organs and splashed blood made for a gruesome tattoo on its legs. Rosanna ran around the edge of the asteroid, smaller now than it had been with the Bastion. What was once the size of a dwarf moon had been reduced to a city's size.

The Unspeakable ceased its hammering onto the rock, shifting its focus to her. Six pounding limbs became an obstacle course, striking at her like she was a troublesome insect.

Solidified shadow sped her, but the toll on her body was becoming more apparent. Her lungs ached, and her heartbeat melted into something spongy.

Maybe Mui-xe did something to her. Maybe it was the carapace. But watching the creature's movements, observing the darkness around her, the more logical explanation was that this power came from *it.*

Not that it mattered.

Rosanna propelled herself up its leg, and it smacked down on its own knee just above where she was, hard enough to snap its exoskeleton.

One leg remained soldered to the asteroid so the rest of its body flailed without half its support. The hybrids had come through for her, melting the rock with their fire and adhering to the creature once they'd become goopy messes.

The Unspeakable came down on its other knee and snapped itself off from the asteroid, but the rock was already descending toward the planet. Rosanna leapt off it, zooming toward the flailing monstrosity.

Bringer. The word echoed in her head, but it was not her own thought.

She shoved the word from her mind and focused on the descent to Neptune: blue and beautiful. Intense winds blurred her vision, and a low, throbbing hum muffled out any other sound, but on some primordial level beyond base sensation, she felt the Unspeakable.

She reached the severed stump of a leg. This thing was missing an appendage—not too different from Crith and Oze now.

Bringer.

Rosanna grabbed hold of a shattered piece of the exoskeleton and pushed herself toward the creature's midsection. The ebony tendrils of energy slathered onto the Unspeakable, as if the power wished to return home.

Rosanna didn't know if it had a heart or blood or lungs, not that breathing was possible with Neptune's hypersonic winds.

They had already ignited in their descent, buffeted by the wind. The flames were a welcoming tickle before the ammonia ocean swallowed them, pulling them toward the planet's core.

The remnants of the asteroid crumbled around them, entombing her with the beast. Rosanna's heartbeat slowed to nothingness, ending her hunt with another predator.

FORTY-NINE

(MAYNARD)

**A galaxy away from the monastery
and surrounded by compassion**

STARING OUT THE viewscreen aboard the Earthquake transporter, Maynard pulled Mui-xe close.

A beast or demigod they couldn't name descended to Neptune's gaseous surface. The titan shrank to a mere dot, engulfed in flame like a falling meteor. After it disappeared from view, the dimmed planet felt brighter. Even the ship's interior lights seemed back to normal.

"Is it dead?" Mui-xe croaked.

Reck-xa wrapped her tail around Mui-xe's arm. "That is not something which can die, methinks."

"She's right," Alize said, tracing a circle around Neptune on the viewscreen. "But it can be laid to rest."

"If it's not dead, it's not a threat at least," Maynard said. "There's nothing solid to colonize on Neptune."

Mui-xe stared at Maynard, red marbled eyes twitching. "But what about *her*?"

"Nobody survives a fall like that," Binh said. "She's gone."

The Makawe woman sank low and inhaled deeply. "I could follow her spirits. They are gone. Even from this distance, I can tell. The cosmic one has stopped buzzing."

From the back of the ship, Mel-za coughed. "I got a surge of power from the glyph. It let me survive the inside of an engine, but I don't think I could've survived falling into a gas planet." Mel-za knelt beside the heaving Symphora, stroking the fur by her muzzle.

Alize tore her gaze from the viewscreen. "Thank you for doing that, by the way. I know it wasn't fair to ask you to do that." She crouched beside the Makawe and placed a hand on her pincer. "It's good to see you again. Thank you for sacrificing your shell."

P'oki sighed, but if it was sadness, relief, or acceptance, Maynard couldn't tell.

"P'oki really did save the day." Amanda pushed off from the ship's wall. "Tecton is gone, too, along with other big players. Pilots, foot soldiers, and the odd mechanic are all that's left." Amanda leaned toward their own pilot. "Right?"

Their pilot shook his head. "I d-don't know, Ms. Martinez."

Amanda's eyes narrowed. "That's Symphora back there."

The pilot stiffened. "Well, there were some other people off-base."

Binh chuckled. "Well, we know where Brave Boy's loyalties are. Were you saluting your representative in the Collective two hours ago when Tecton was in here?"

The pilot stared at the command board in silence.

"Then who is left?" Amanda said. "Where are they?"

A rush of adrenaline hit Maynard. "I know one. There's another high-powered agent on New Lodestone. The person who infiltrated the Monks of the Great Mystery. The one who allowed Rosanna into our temple in the first place which led to Mui-xe's kidnapping. There's somebody still there."

Binh folded his arms. "Can't be anyone too high up."

"It's still something we need to resolve." Maynard faced his nephew along with the truth. "And it's why New Lodestone isn't safe for you anymore."

Mui-xe hugged Maynard, catching him by surprise. "I know, Uncle Maynard. I'll go to Vee and learn about being a shaman from Granny." He pulled away from the hug and offered a weak smile. "I'm half Human and half Lo-sat, so it makes sense if I combine both religions, too, right?"

"Two sets of imaginary friends," Binh said.

"Why does everyone let this offensive man say what he wants all the time? Isn't anyone ever offended?" Reck-xa leaned toward him, neck frills extended.

Binh shrugged. "I'm offended by how turned on I am by somebody's grandmother, if we're being honest."

Symphora huffed from the back. "That was sexist. Are you trying to say older women can't be attractive?

How about I snap your spine?" Her voice sounded hoarse and muffled.

"I'll do it for you," Mel-za said.

Binh waved his hands furiously and backed away from Symphora.

Reck-xa stepped between them. "Instead of killing him, might I ask a favor? Perhaps you could arrange for my and my grandson's passage to Vee?"

"Of course," Symphora said. "I might punch him in the face for fun, though."

As Binh backed into the wall, Maynard's gaze drifted across the others in the ship. His nephew needed to go with his maternal grandmother. They both deserved that much.

Amanda and Symphora needed to restructure the government.

This mole business belonged to Maynard and nobody else. "Madam Martinez, could you arrange my transport to New Lodestone? I'll go alone."

Binh scoffed. "What? Too good for me now?"

"I didn't want to speak for you." A smile parted his lips. "I'd welcome a quiet, well-behaved companion."

"Well, it seems like the shaman isn't into me, so..."

Amanda tsked. "I'll get you two on a ship first so I don't have to hear you speak again."

Maynard approached Symphora but feared placing a consoling hand on her broad shoulder. "You saved my brother and me years ago. You helped save me again. There are no words in any language for how grateful I am. Thank you."

Symphora spoke slowly. "Your brother didn't make it, huh? That's why you're taking care of the kid?"

"My brother was the one saved by Joka Bunear."

Symphora's eyes widened. "Then I think I owe *him* some thanks, too. Joka came back from that mission changed, and she set me straight."

————

In a cold government transport ship, Maynard pulled the too-big blanket around his shoulders tight and counted his blessings. His injuries had been mild compared to the others. He could sit on this bench, for one.

The room guard, a youngish Arkouda, eyed him and dropped to a knee, meeting Maynard's eyeline. "Are you alright?" His concern was genuine, either from compassion or fear, considering Symphora's orders were to muzzle-punch anyone who entered the room with an intention to touch Mui-xe. Her threat was also clear—he could expect a muzzle-punching if he failed.

Symphora's near-death recovery was the buzz around the medical ship the last few days in space. Sitting on the bench, staring out the viewscreen, sipping on de-stimmed stimbrew, the memory swelled of his first time on a Collective government ship. After Symphora saved him and his brother as kids, they were granted passage to New Lodestone, a planet deemed unfit for Arkoudae and Lo-sat colonization for its intense magnetosphere. Ned felt cramped there, and even though he couldn't get a proper education, he read every book he could find and got a research assistant job. People even treated him like a real scientist.

For Maynard, New Lodestone brought the promise of redemption through the Great Mystery. The religion showed him how his life had meaning, along with every blade of grass and single-celled organism in the entire cosmos. But taking care of Mui-xe brought him a level of purpose he hadn't dreamed before. Caring about another individual on a familial level felt like a higher calling than anything he'd ever read or prayed about behind the monastery's walls. Being an uncle made sense, and his attachment to the Great Mystery had felt forced. He'd find a new way forward.

He didn't want to bid Mui-xe farewell and wasn't sure where either of them stood with the Great Mystery anymore, but he maintained the principle of non-attachment as a function of love and compassion. Maynard couldn't stifle the boy under rigid monasticism anymore. Mui-xe deserved to spend time elsewhere to become the adult he wanted to be. And Maynard would go elsewhere, too.

He placed the de-stimmed stimbrew down beside him on the bench. The cup which he needed two hands for was an Arkouda shot glass, and he smirked thinking about his old master at the monastery admonishing him for use of intoxicants and a younger version of Maynard desperately explaining it wasn't how it seemed. He rose from the bench and approached Reck-xa seated on the floor in a meditation style not too different from his own. Mui-xe sat beside her in the same fashion, although he couldn't drape his tail over his shoulders in a scarf the way she could. Communicating with their gods, ancestors, or each other, he couldn't tell.

Reck-xa opened a single eye. "We smelled you coming, May-nard." Although seated, they were nearly eye level. "You were also just talking to a guard. Loudly. So we heard you, too."

"Sorry, I didn't mean to interrupt." Experiencing the world through scent—something the monks could never teach Mui-xe. This reassured him. "We'll reach the departure point soon, and I wanted to bid you both goodbye before we're rushed."

Mui-xe exhaled, let his posture slouch, then gazed at Maynard, head tilted up slightly. "Granny said I shouldn't forget anything you taught me. I promise I'll keep studying the Great Mystery while I'm with her."

Maynard offered a hand to help him stand. "If that's what you really want to do, go ahead. If it helps you find happiness and to help other people in your own way, go ahead. Promise me you'll continue studying self-defense in case anyone else tries to kidnap you. You understand your abilities enough to help other people. It's more important to me that you learn everything possible from your grandmother. You only have so much time with her."

Reck-xa rose and smirked. "May-nard, I'll outlive *you* unless the gods call for me. Perhaps you should engage in sensitivity training at the monastery. Do you know how long a Lo-sat's life is?"

Maynard's eyes widened, and he cleared his throat. "In Human culture, it's rude to ask someone their age. I assumed it crossed cultures, and I'm sorry."

She cocked an eyeridge. "The crass one was right." After a polite elbow nudge to Mui-xe, she added, "It *is* fun to make your father's people uncomfortable."

Maynard opened his arms to embrace them. "We'll stay in touch. I love you, Mui-xe. You're the future. Your parents would be so proud of you. I know I am."

———

Days later, the space elevator descended from orbit, embracing a rush of maroon sky under thick clouds.

Maynard peered into the distance and spied the Great Mystery monastery's iconic praying hands shadow. Upon witnessing it, he shut his eyes tight then turned to Binh. "I appreciate you joining me, especially with how this planet's magnetosphere bothers you."

Binh shook his head, then pointed to a small necklace hanging limp over his chest. "Potion Lady gave me this. She said it was magic and would stop my headaches on this planet. I think there's just some low-grade chemicals I can't smell rubbed on it."

Maynard examined the craftsmanship. An object similar to Reck-xa's talisman, crafted from bone, sat on the end of the necklace. Intricate lines draped across its small surface. "Maybe there's no difference between magic and chemistry for her."

Binh shrugged. "She denied the chemistry I had with her. Oh well. There will be other hot grandmas."

Maynard cast a timid eye at the reformed thief. "How ... old are you?"

"Old enough to be offended by your question. Don't worry about it, Baldy."

"Were you really offended?"

"Are you really OK with your haircut?"

Maynard rubbed his dome and made a squeak noise. "So when we get to the monastery, you promise you won't insult anybody, right? We need to find this mole and hand him over to the authorities."

"That son of a Galsan worm almost got the kid killed. I'm not taking any chances on catching this jerk."

Maynard pulled his hood up. "It's been almost a week since the surrender and news of Tecton's death."

"Think the mole dug his way out?"

"He might have. If he's left the planet, we need to find him." The elevator car had descended enough to pass the higher buildings of Bolivar City. Odd how similar it seemed. Although maybe the only thing that had changed in this car was the two of them. "He might know where the other officials in Earthquake are hiding. We can't reach true peace until he's apprehended."

"Only apprehended?" Binh asked.

"Earthquake's ideals poisoned Humanity," Maynard replied. "Strong poison needs strong medicine. We'll root it out and do what we can peacefully."

The car reached the bottom level, and the ammonia stench of decontamination spray flooded the space.

"What if the monks want you back? Apologize and whatnot," Binh asked.

"We'll explain the situation and begin our investigation, with or without their help. They can restore my title if it eases their hearts, but we're only going there to get clues. We're starting with Brother Rondo. He might not like my more fluid understanding of my vows." The car's doors opened into Bolivar city, letting the last decontamination fumes spill out with the passengers. "We'll find this mole and his last few contacts. For Madam Martinez and Mui-xe."

FIFTY

(ALIZE)

Ka'in'ga, Makawe Demilitarized Zone

GENTLE WAVES LAPPED at Alize's bare foot and prosthetic leg. The cybernetics gave an irritated click, shifting to saltwater mode a minute later than they should have; Alize would need to get them serviced soon. Sunset painted a tableau across the crystalline sky—too pretty for a funeral. But maybe that softened today's sting. Alize wished to reach for somebody's hand like when she'd grabbed the paw of her best friend's mother at the last funeral she'd attended. But Alize wasn't close to Joka, she didn't know Amanda like that, and Symphora was not the kind of person Alize would touch without written and notarized permission.

Instead she clasped her own hands together, but not in the prayer style she'd seen Pops do a few times.

This was her first Makawe funeral, but she kept her anthropological brain in check and ignored any desire to culturally analyze the beautiful dance before her. She'd ask P'oki for a book about it later, though.

P'oki scuttled in a semicircle around an effigy of He'nay. The effigy of koknati bark and seaweed bore more symbolic resemblance than physical one. More attention was paid to recreating the tattoos carved into her carapace than getting her facial features or proportions right.

It captured her essence—jolly spirit, ready to analyze Chamayna glyphs with Alize in the museum, and the kind defiance which pushed her to lead tours around the exhibits to patrons who looked down on her in more than literal ways. She'd reminded Alize of herself.

A glint in the effigy's center caught Alize's eye—the one shrapnel of carapace she'd kept. Alize wanted to save it for this precise purpose. A ritual she didn't understand.

Two dozen Makawe lined the beach, individually joining P'oki in her scuttle dance, following a rhythm Alize couldn't guess at.

She measured the same stunned and respectful silence from the other non-Makawe gathered. The inaudible song concluded, and the pod of Makawe gripped the effigy and slowly scuttled toward the water's edge. P'oki broke off and approached their group.

"A'lize," she trilled. "Help push." The echo in her beak reminded Alize of He'nay. "You were friends. This is part of grief."

Alize slowly rotated her wrists the way He'nay would with her pincers when she'd offer thanks. At the effigy, Alize grabbed a tip of the bark pincer and walked beside the other scuttling Makawe to the water. Four funeral attendees followed behind, carrying large stones in their pincers.

When they'd reached knee-level, the Makawe shoved the effigy, and Alize released. The four stone-bearers lobbed their rocks into the water, landing atop the effigy, which sank immediately.

Alize knelt to meet P'oki's eyeline. "Thank you for letting me grieve with you. I can't imagine how you're feeling."

P'oki's eyestalks angled toward her, and she extended her knees so her beak left the water. "Cry until low tide. Then we move forward."

Alize marched beside P'oki as she left the water.

Memorializing Filenada had stung, but Alize used that pain to push herself forward. She'd missed Pops' death and unceremonious cremation, but when she stuck his plaque on that museum bench, it brought some piece of him back.

Both deaths were ones she'd blamed on herself for years, defying logic.

But seeing P'oki's refusal to blame Alize, she knew there was no reason to anymore. Feeding the fish at the bottom of an ocean was the proper Makawe send off. P'oki didn't blame Alize. It was a relief, but it didn't give her guidance on what to do next.

———

Alize summoned her best Makawe pronunciation to thank their waiter, who bowed. Amanda pulled out her credit chit and left a big tip since they cut their food into Human portions and stacked three tables atop each other for them.

Joka passed their plates, stone disks with delicate carvings like Makawe tattoos. "What'd you get us?"

"Fish for you two," Alize replied. "I think. I didn't think you'd only want seaweed."

Amanda sniffed the bite-sized chunks of salt-crusted seaweed. "Yeah, there's fish under that."

"And they de-boned it?" Joka asked.

Alize picked at hers to make sure she interpreted the menu correctly. "Yeah. I guess I picked up more phrases than I realized."

"Why haven't Symphora or Mel-za joined us?" Amanda asked. "You invited them, right?"

Joka nodded. "They're en route to the Calamity. The new line of helmets for the elite squad members will sport a design mirroring Mel-za's claw marks since she can't fight anymore."

Alize sipped from her glass, gulping triple-filtered water. The Makawe beak shape and size allowed for both species to drink from similarly-sized vessels, although she was thankful for a straw, knowing how they'd clasp the glasses with their whole beaks.

"How sad was that funeral, huh?" Joka asked.

"I thought it was beautiful," Amanda replied. "But yeah, total downer."

"I could go without any more funerals for a long time," Alize said.

"I'll drink to that," Joka said.

Amanda cast a downward glance at her food, letting the silence pass.

Biting down on her salt-seaweed wrap, Alize let the aroma fill her mouth—same recipe He'nay made once. And it was perfect.

After savoring it, Alize swallowed hard. "So, uh, about two years ago, Joka, do you remember coming to my museum and offering me a job?"

Joka twirled her fork. "How could I forget? Nobody turns down an offer from Symphora."

Eyes wide, Amanda gasped. "Symphora mentioned wanting you for the job but never said she'd offered. I'm sure you had your reasons, but I wish you would've taken it, although in hindsight I'm glad you didn't. The person Symphora got instead to help me with educational affairs—" Her expression fell. "She died in the Earthquake attack on the government offices."

Alize stared at the carvings in their plates, remembering He'nay's tattoos. "I can't think of a polite way to ask if that position is still open."

Chewing with her mouth open, Joka winked. "I think you just did."

Amanda gave a mirthless smile. "It is, but that wasn't exactly why I agreed to this lunch."

"As if my company isn't enough," Alize replied with a forced scoff.

Amanda fumbled with her fork, failing to twirl it like Joka had. "I wanted to offer both of you jobs." She exhaled like she'd been holding something painful. "Joka, I know you love running the women's shelter, but I'd love to have you on my team."

Joka wiped the fish sauce from her chin with her sleeve. "Whoa. That's uh—no. I-I'm gonna pass. I'm not done at the shelter. Seeing exploited people on our little mission showed me I'm where I'm supposed to be. I want to focus on individuals, not big galactic problems." She scratched the back of her head. "...Sorry."

"Don't be," Amanda said. "I'll keep a swear jar on my desk and funnel donations to yours. A reason to keep in touch."

"You better." Joka made faux stabbing motions with her fork, pointing at Amanda.

Amanda turned to Alize. "So Alize, I actually don't think you're right for the education minister job that Symphora offered to you."

Alize slouched. "Oh..."

"N-no! I have something else in mind. Big legislation. Part of that includes opening a ministry of antiquities and cultural preservation. The Collective never had one, and you're the most qualified person in the galaxy to head it."

Nearly choking on her water, Alize nodded. She knew she needed to play it cool and negotiate before accepting. "I can start today."

Amanda smiled and gently fist-pumped the air.

"I've got one condition, though," Alize said. "When funds are available... my old museum was destroyed. There aren't any museums in that sector of space now. Build a new one. And no matter how much money anybody donates, I'm naming it. The galaxy deserves to know about the amazing research He'nay did. She was the one who cracked the 'power' glyph in the first place."

"I'll drink to that," Amanda said.

Alize clinked glasses with them while other Makawe patrons swiveled judgmentally angled eyestalks at them, but she didn't care. She was among friends.

FIFTY-ONE

(AMANDA)

**Kayraytha City, Arko,
Galactic Center, one year later**

AMANDA PULLED HER coat tight around her shoulders and stifled the urge to shiver. A Lo-sat representative trudged by her, wearing so many lagomorph furs she almost resembled a dirty Arkouda, and the radiation from her heat cells warmed Amanda's face. The representative living on Arko would be miserable all the time, just like another species living under New Lodestone's intense magnetosphere. Most species weren't designed to live like Arkoudae.

Symphora broke her concentration. "Nervous, Martinez?"

Amanda shook her head and pressed forward down the hall. Her footsteps echoed in the ribcage-shaped halls of the government legislative building. "Should

I be?" She forced a mirthless chuckle. "Last time I walked beside an Arkouda to introduce some legislation, events went … poorly."

"Heh. Fair. But hey, you weren't with me. Are you still keeping in touch with his family?"

"His grandcub got promoted in her dance troupe. And you wouldn't have been much help that day, considering you were hungover and napping in your office."

Symphora shrugged. "Wouldn't have been a fair fight with Rosanna otherwise."

"Do you think the legislative body will go for it?"

"What? Your bill?" Symphora waved at the grand architecture, gesturing toward the murals of hunting scenes from prehistoric Arko. "My people always believed they were on top. Even though the Lo-sats are legally our equals, we have never treated them that way."

"I don't think I need to remind you of my resumé. I'm fully aware of how Arkoudae see themselves, which caused more than a few problems. My aunt wouldn't have been forced to raise me, and we wouldn't have had to resort to petty crime to eat if the system had been fair from the get-go."

"You're bringing them a hard truth, and a lot won't want to listen."

Amanda examined the mural as they passed. Quadrupedal Arkoudae, wearing armor carved from bone, encircled a mammoth lagomorph; she'd had to learn when in history Arkoudae started walking upright, but it never felt important enough to remember. "So, does it have a chance?"

"I'll get Lo-sat support, for sure."

"They'll jump outta their scales."

An Arkouda representative approached them, stars in her eyes and goofy grin on her muzzle, clutching an omni-tablet tight to her chest. "E-excuse me, but can I get a picture?"

Symphora sighed. "Yeah, hold on—"

The representative made a nervous chuckle and shied away. "Actually, I wanted one from her." She knelt, meeting Amanda's eye level. "Ms. Martinez, Earthquake killed my brother. When news broke last year that you led the coalition to destroy their HQ, my family felt like we could breathe again. I told my mom you'd be here today, and it would mean the galaxy to her if she had a picture of you."

Blinking fast and straightening, Amanda nodded. "Sure. Um, I can send your mom a video, too."

The representative gasped. "Seriously? You're not too busy? Goddess, she'll be so happy. Her name is Babush." Her eyes went back to Symphora, and she held out her omni-tablet. "Would you mind?"

Symphora cleared her throat. "Of course." She accepted the omni-tablet, and the representative draped a heavy arm over Amanda's shoulders.

Amanda waved at the omni-tablet. "Hi, Babush. Thank you for the support! Your daughter is really awesome." She hoped she wasn't too awkward. Her training was for press conferences, not "hi to mom."

The representative retrieved her tablet from Symphora. "Thank you so much." Her tone steadied. "For years after my brother died, my mom was so anti-Human. But then she heard about how you defected and joined the Collective—she'd never heard of a respectable Human before. No offense."

Amanda waved her off, stifling a sigh. "You know what? I used to have problematic ideas about Arkoudae, so I understand."

The representative smiled. "I told her about how you've been trying to make a difference and then how you brought Earthquake to surrender. She hired a Human to work in her shop." She averted her gaze to the floor. "He was an intern who used to work for me. I fired him because I thought he was stealing. After hearing about you, I decided to verify and realized he hadn't done anything wrong."

Symphora folded her arms over her chest. "You compensated him and your mom is paying a fair wage, right?"

The representative wiggled her ears and scowled. "Not that it's any of your business but yes." Returning to Amanda, her tone warmed. "We'd heard about a Human archaeologist, but my mom thought she was just an anomaly, too. But following your career, she really abandoned her old way of thinking. And I did, too. I know you're busy. I just—thank you so much for your time."

"Yeah," Amanda said, trying to regulate her breathing without looking like she was trying to regulate her breathing. "Nice to meet you!"

The representative walked off backward, waving again.

Symphora sighed. "Do I need my mohawk to be recognizable?"

"Maybe," Amanda chuckled.

"Hmpf. Honestly, I didn't hate that. It was nice not being the center of attention."

"I'm happy for you. I almost puked."

"You better get used to it."

They approached the double doors of the legislative hall. Armed and armored soldiers welcomed them.

The hall resembled a grand honeycomb which spiraled down to the center at a more gentle angle than the one in the old Fringe offices. As they entered the outer hexagon, a legion of Arkoudae and a tenth as many Lo-sats all watched them.

From an overhead PA, a speaker announced, "The Collective welcomes Representatives Symphora Ianna and Amanda Martinez."

Amid the applause and shouts, Amanda realized the speaker had used the Human pronunciation for her name.

A young Arkouda who wore a page's garb ushered them to the center hexagon, where they were shown to their seats and podiums. One was sized for her. No stepladder for the podium or cushion for the chair but something intentional.

An aging Arkouda approached the floor and introduced herself; her suit's decorations suggested a long career in government and military. Amanda recognized her name from an old Earthquake hit list. "I'd like to introduce Madam Martinez." The crowd of legislators hushed. "Per custom, I'll summarize her bill, and she can argue the finer points. Her bill, if accepted, will allow full Citizenship for all sapients, erasing the status of Provincial for Human and Makawe and legally recognizing Blekk's culture. Any future sapient species discovered will also be granted Citizenship if desired."

Amanda thought her "art, agriculture, arithmetic" line was catchier, but she nodded along anyway.

Symphora leaned over to Amanda and whispered, "She's an old veteran. Getting her was a huge coup. Nicely done."

Amanda didn't want to tell her why she already knew who this person was.

"Further," the decorated woman said, "membership will not be forced on any planet or population center. It will be up to the residents to decide." She turned to Amanda. "Do you find the summary sufficient?"

"Yes." Amanda probably should have leaned into the microphone to respond.

She stepped up to the podium, ready to move the galaxy.

While the Earthquake War may have ended,
there's a big galaxy out there, and nobody ever
caught Rondo. Look out for AFTERSHOCKS!

BOOK CLUB QUESTIONS:

1. There are several themes in *Besieged Bastion* such as prejudice, loss, inadequacy, impostor syndrome, regret, and redemption. Which were you most drawn to and why?

2. Both Amanda and Rosanna have a past relationship that defines their worldview. Where do you see the similarities and differences between their responses?

3. What's your theory on why Earthquake couldn't truly replicate hybrids like Mui-xe?

4. Share your theory about how Mui-xe managed to exorcise the Unspeakable from Alize.

5. Rosanna thought she was redeeming herself by attacking the Unspeakable, but do you think she earned it? Explain.

6. Share your theories about Earthquake's survivors and what they'll do in the next series.

7. Of all the different alien cultures, which one was your favorite and why?

8. Share your theories about how well Amanda's legislation will fare in terms of changing social dynamics in the Collective.

9. Which character do you think changed the most from their introduction to the end of the series? Explain.

10. How do you think Rick will be remembered in history?

AUTHOR BIO

PC IS A science fiction and fantasy author from the Great Lakes region of the USA. Sci fi has been a deep love for PC, growing up on Star Wars movies and reading the Animorphs series. The Star Wars novels along with classic sci fi greats like Asimov and Le Guin are constant sources of inspiration and wonder. PC loves taking his daughters to the zoo and the occasional sushi or taco date with his wife. With the help of friendly scientists and science documentaries, PC tries to blend what is just on the technological horizon with the impossible in his stories. Be sure to follow PC on Twitter for updates. @nottingham_pc or Instagram @pc_nottingham

Visit PC's website at authorpcnottingham.com and sign up for the newsletter for updates and exclusive content!

Discover more at
4HorsemenPublications.com

10% off using HORSEMEN10